BARSK
THE ELEPHANTS' GRAVEYARD

BARSK

THE ELEPHANTS' GRAVEYARD

LAWRENCE M. SCHOEN

A TOM DOHERTY ASSOCIATES BOOK
NEW YORK

BARSK: THE ELEPHANTS' GRAVEYARD

Copyright © 2015 by Lawrence M. Schoen

A Tor Book
Published by Tom Doherty Associates, LLC
175 Fifth Avenue
New York, NY 10010

www.tor-forge.com

Tor® is a registered trademark of Tom Doherty Associates, LLC.

Library of Congress Cataloging-in-Publication Data

Schoen, Lawrence M.
    Barsk : the elephants' graveyard : an anthropomorphic novel /
by Lawrence M. Schoen.
        pages cm
    ISBN 978-0-7653-7702-9 (hardcover)
    ISBN 978-1-4668-5339-3 (e-book)
    1. Imaginary wars and battles—Fiction.   2. Space warfare—Fiction.
I. Title.
PS3619.C44927B38 2015
813'.6—dc23

                                                    2015023323

Our books may be purchased in bulk for promotional, educational, or business use. Please contact your local bookseller or the Macmillan Corporate and Premium Sales Department at (800) 221-7945, extension 5442, or by e-mail at MacmillanSpecialMarkets@macmillan.com.

First Edition: December 2015

Printed in the United States of America

0   9   8   7   6   5   4   3   2   1

For Sol, Neal, and Ghang,
you gave me no choice but to invent nefshons

ACKNOWLEDGMENTS

The creation of any book takes significant time, but the origin of *Barsk* goes back almost thirty years. This pretty much guarantees that I will forget to express my appreciation to one or more people who helped to make this book possible, so the first acknowledgment has to be both generic and anonymous. I know you remember who you are and what you did and why I am grateful, and I trust you will vigorously remind me of this when next we meet.

All of this began with a random comment made to a student at New College during the fall semester of 1987, my first term as a college professor. The ink was still wet on my doctorate, and I was living on campus in the dorms. The student, Watts Martin, was editor of *Mythagoras,* a magazine of anthropomorphic fiction and artwork. I wrote two chapters for him, and the rainy world of the Fant was born. Thanks, Watts.

I wasn't a good enough writer to actually craft the book that I wanted to write (though I tried). Eventually, I set it a drawer pending the day when I had the necessary skills. Years passed, and in 2010 I climbed the mountain and attended Walter Jon Williams's Taos Toolbox, where he and Nancy Kress generously showed me many things I didn't know that I didn't know. Anything compelling in this novel's plotting or clever in its clarity of language stems from their instruction. I am forever in their debt.

When the book sold (on the strength of an outline and sample chapters), I went in search of an agent, which led me to John Silbersack, whose experience and vision will surely be shaping my career for years to come. Thank you, John.

At that point I had to finish the book. I brought in a group of friends and colleagues who helped me to "break" the novel. This involved the death of some characters, the creation of new characters, wild changes to arcs and subplots, and all five of Kübler-Ross's stages of grief. It was both intense and essential, and Tim W. Burke, Oz Drummond, Greg Frost, Catherine M. Petrini, and Fran Wilde have my infinite appreciation for their generosity of time, spirit, and insight. Oz and Fran, it should be noted, showed up in custom-made T-shirts proclaiming "WTF Otters?," a truly perplexing display of love that I will never forget.

I also benefited from the patient critique of my long-suffering workshop, the Eastern Court of NobleFusion: Tim Burke, Arthur (Buck) Dorrance, Barbara Hill, and Catherine M. Petrini. And when all their work was done, Laurel Amberdine and Paula Billig stepped up as beta readers to catch the majority of particularly stupid errors before I sent the finished manuscript to my editor.

Speaking of whom, the only reason you're seeing this book is because of Marco Palmieri. He pursued the idea of this novel, saw in it the promise that had burned in me for more than two decades. He encouraged me to write it, deftly worked around my massive ego to address issues that needed attention, championed its nicheless nature, and never ceased encouraging and supporting the story. *Barsk* has no greater friend, and I cannot imagine having a better editor for this book. Thank you, Marco, you are a mensch!

A lot of this novel is about the past, as the dedication hints at. But my present and my future belong to my wife, Valerie. A word like "acknowledgment" doesn't begin to cover how she inspires me to create worlds and characters and stories for her entertainment, just so I can see that look in her eyes. What greater reward could any author ask for?

These limits only I place upon you,

    that never shall a Speaker summon a Speaker,

    that never shall a Speaker summon the living,

    that never shall a Speaker summon herself.

By these laws abide.

As for the rest, may your conscience be your guide.

          —Margda, "The Speakers' Edict"

BARSK
THE ELEPHANTS' GRAVEYARD

ONE

A DEATH DETOURED

RÜSUL traveled to meet his death. The current had carried him away from his home island as if it understood his purpose. He lost sight of the archipelago before dusk, as much a function of the falling rain as the southerly wind that pushed him onward. In the days since, the sun had risen and set unseen, a slightly brighter spot that eased itself across the overcast sky. Nor had it cleared at night to permit a glimpse of the heavens. The clouds changed color as the rain ebbed and flowed, and the wind drove him across the water of its own accord toward an unvisited destination. Rüsul didn't care. He had no need to hurry. He could feel the increasing proximity in his bones and that was enough. More than enough. An aged Fant on a raft alone and at sea, the wind filling his makeshift sail and carrying him toward the last bit of land he would ever stand upon. His father and mother had each left in the same manner, and their parents before them. That's how it had been, going back generation upon generation to the very founding of Barsk.

He'd felt it coming on all season. His every perception called out to him, less clairaudience than common sense. It was part of the way of things. One felt the change in pressure that signaled the nearness of a lull in a storm. One smelled the sweetness of tevketl long before the berries actually ripened so as not to miss their brief span for picking. And one knew when it was time to die. Rüsul could no more fail to recognize his coming death than he could be surprised by a pause in the rain or sour berries.

The certainty came to him one morning. He'd never been the type to awaken easily, always struggling to cross that daily border between slumber and the responsibilities of the wide awake world. But that day he had opened his eyes and known. Death had announced itself, named a time and place, and left him instantly alert. Rüsul had risen and gone about his day with a wistful smile, a bit sad that his time was ending but also relieved to know for sure. That knowledge signaled the start of the final rite of passage for every Fant.

His assistant had seen the change in him at the workshop that day, acknowledging it with a simple question. "You know?"

Rüsul had smiled. "I do. The last lesson I need to learn. No sadness from you, Yeft. It's long overdue. Besides, I know you've wanted my tools since the day you ended your apprenticeship."

The younger Fant ignored the barb and instead asked, "Is there anything I can do to help? Do you have enough time for everything?"

Rüsul had been thinking it through since breakfast. Time enough to complete the game board and pieces he'd promised to his elder daughter's husband after drinking too much beer on the night of their Bonding. Time enough to finish the lintel for the great window in his son's new home. And time also to build a stout raft and gather together the supplies he would need for the voyage. He had no goodbyes to say. Yeft had seen the knowledge on his face as much because they'd worked side by side for thirty years as because it had been so fresh. The rest of his loved ones would realize what had happened after he'd left. None would come seeking him. Until the day they each woke to their own invitations, they wouldn't even know where to look.

~~~~

HE'D been on the open water for five days, seated comfortably enough at the front third of a raft, his back against the short mast that held the only sail. A tarpaulin covered a jumbled pile that occupied most of the other two-thirds. Beneath it lay jugs of fresh water and beer to quench his thirst, assorted fresh fruit to enjoy before it spoiled, and dried fruit for after if the wind died or the current slowed and delayed his journey. There was grain and salt for making cold porridge, and an assortment of succulent leaves as much for dessert as for late night snacking. Rüsul had also packed a scattering of various soft woods and, despite his promise, held onto his favorite knife. At the last moment he'd been unable to part with it, though of course he wouldn't need it when he reached his death.

For the last five mornings he'd eased leisurely from sleep as usual. His daily ritual consisted of breaking his fast and then tending to his ablutions over the back end of his raft. He'd raise the sail and often as not tack in the direction that felt right. That done, he would take a chock of wood and his knife from under the tarpaulin and settle in with his back once more against the mast and spend the day carving. His hands and trunk did the work with the familiarity of experience, freeing his mind to wander at will through a lifetime of pleasant memories. When he grew thirsty he'd stop for some midday beer, and when hungry for an early supper. By dusk he'd set aside his knife and furl the raft's sail. As the last of the day's light fled, Rüsul would examine the statuette he'd made, the face of some old friend or relative gazing up from the wood as clearly as it had from his memory. His talent at carving had brought him a modicum of fame and security. His work had become quite collectible, but these pieces would never be admired by anyone else. Before laying himself down for sleep, he made a point of saying farewell to the day's effort and pitching it over the side for the ocean to claim.

This sixth day had gone much like the others. Rüsul's left hand had all day long guided the knife slowly back and forth across the chock in his right. The constant rain created the illusion that the outer layers of wood were being washed away to reveal the figurine beneath. Later, as the sky began to lose its glow and he sat finishing his porridge and fruit, the rain faded entirely. For the briefest of moments the heavy clouds parted and Rüsul enjoyed the unfamiliar sight of sunset and felt the red light of Ekkja on his skin. Defter than the touch of a loved one's nubs, warmth flooded through the folds and wrinkles of his naked body, relieving all weariness while reminding him of just how weary he'd been. Then it passed. The clouds closed again and the rain resumed. He took down the sail.

Rüsul finished his dinner and leaned over the edge of his raft to rinse his bowl and spoon before tucking them away under the tarp along with his carving knife. With his trunk he cradled the day's work, a perfect rendering of Margda, Barsk's long-dead Matriarch. Her face looked back at him with complexity. There was pain and certainty, confidence and confusion, as if she'd just been thrust deep in the throes of one of her prophetic seizures. It was possibly his best work ever.

He had muttered a farewell to the carving and raised his trunk high, preparing to fling the figure into the sea, when the ocean dropped away.

The raft, which had risen and fallen with the sea's mood, froze stiller than calm water. The sudden stability caused Rüsul to tumble over backwards. The tiny rendering of Margda slipped from his nubs as he landed on his backside. He rolled onto his knees, one hand moving back and behind the bottom of his left ear to rub at a sudden stitch in his side. His other hand braced against the raft until his balance returned and allowed him to crawl to the edge.

Peering over the side he saw an expanse of grayness below the raft. It sloped down in all directions too far to measure in the rain. Beyond that lay water. The ocean had not so much dropped from beneath him as something else had surged up from below it, lifting him and the raft.

"There! At the far end. Take him, now. And quickly!"

Rüsul turned. From beyond the other side of his raft, a gate of some sort had opened in the gray below. A tall, bizarre-looking person stood next to the opening and three more poured from it. All four had been wrapped in fire-bright plastic, more plastic than he'd seen in his entire life. The legs of their slacks thickened to form heavy boots. The sleeves of their shirts flowed into gloves and the collars rose up into hoods that hid their heads. Following their instructions, three of them advanced upon Rüsul. Translucent gray masks covered their faces. Two had hold of his arms in an instant and hauled him upright like a wet sack of leaves.

It all happened so fast, so unexpectedly. He was on his way to die. The sameness of the past days had helped him to distance himself from the world and his past life. None of this should be happening. His brain wanted to deny it, disbelieve and make it go away. The hands gripping him made that impossible. As his feet scrabbled beneath him, the greatest piece of strangeness came clear to Rüsul and he struggled to pull free. No trunks. From even a short distance, their plastic hoods and masks rendered his assailants anonymous. But this close he saw the truth. Tiny pointy ears set well back. Long snouty faces with little black, slick noses. And all younger and stronger than him. His pitiful attempts to break away from the two holding him ended as the third wrapped more red plastic around each of Rüsul's wrists and pulled them behind his back. The three pulled him from his raft and began marching him over the grayness toward their gate, past the fourth figure.

"You're Dogs. Cans, aren't you? I've seen pictures. But you can't be here. You're not supposed to . . ." He passed within the grayness and stopped speaking, his eyes trying and failing to make sense of the featureless surface surrounding him on all sides. He knew he moved because his feet stumbled and scraped as his captors dragged him along. His stomach flipped and for a moment the possibility of his evening meal coming back up distracted him. They seemed to move in a broad arc and the grayness gave way to painfully bright light that defined a corridor. The three Cans stopped. Rüsul steadied himself against them, squinting down the walls that somehow existed where nothing belonged but the open sea.

Another person came toward him, taller and leaner than the others and clad in blue plastic that lacked hood or mask. She advanced on him with a liquid gait. A Cheetah with a significantly flatter face, a smallish nose, and even beadier, black eyes than the Dogs regarded him and drew back her lips to reveal gleaming teeth.

"I am Nonyx-Captain Selishta," said the Cheetah. "Do you have a name?"

Rüsul blinked. The light hurt his eyes but the questions racing through his mind hurt more. Why were there Dogs on Barsk? Why a Cheetah? Why were they speaking to him when he'd left all conversation behind. Why would anyone ask the name of a dead man? Could any adult be so ignorant and stupid?

"I'm on my way to finish dying," he said.

The Cheetah sneered at him. "Of course you are. You all are. And of course that's why you're naked as well? How foolish of me to think otherwise. Well, old man, your demise is going to have to wait a while. My people have many, many questions to ask you, and I need you alive for that."

The Fant shook his head. "It doesn't work like that, I . . ."

A cold plastic hand slapped Rüsul across the face. And then again.

"*My* name is Selishta. This ship and these men obey my will. I'm the only one who gets to say how things work here." She pulled her hand back, staring a moment at the glove as if her fingers had touched something disgusting, then stepped back. She directed her attention to the Cans.

"Maybe this one will know something useful about whatever shrubs and leaves the drug comes from. Hold him here a moment while the rest of the crew secures his flotsam, and then put him below in one of the vacant isolation cells."

"Shrubs?" said Rüsul, more to himself than the others. "I was a wood carver, but that's past. I've died."

The Cheetah stepped back, waving one gloved hand in front of her stupid-looking nose. "If you had, I've no doubt you'd smell better than you do."

Rüsul's eyes widened and he studied his surroundings for the first time. As the Dogs had hauled him in he'd acknowledged only the formless gray of the place, but now the clear outlines of plastic wall panels, metal floor tilings, and piercing artificial light removed all doubt that he was inside an artificial structure. He gazed longingly back at the open gate they'd brought him through, where Nonyx-Captain Selishta stood silhouetted against the darkening sky. Rüsul watched as other Dogs in their red plastic suits hurried past the Cheetah, carrying away his supplies in the tarp that had previously covered them. Other Dogs had dragged the mast and sail in and down another corridor. Moments later, more of Selishta's crew entered with the disassembled pieces of his raft. And then he saw the Cheetah stoop to pick up something else. As she straightened up and regarded the object in her hand, Rüsul saw that Selishta had found his carving of Margda.

The Nonyx waved the carving in a gesture encompassing everything that moments ago had made up Rüsul's raft. "You won't need any of that where we're going." She paused and regarded the image in his hand. "This is one of your women? Unbelievable. And I thought the males were the ugly ones." She tossed it away.

The Cheetah dismissed Rüsul with a wave and the pair of Dogs took him away, deeper into the "ship" as the captain had named it. But it wasn't like any vessel of good wood that he had heard of, open to rain and sky. The world seemed to close in around him, and at first Rüsul imagined that he had actually died. But he knew it wasn't time yet. Time, in fact, seemed to have stopped. A claustrophobia that he'd never known before squeezed at his heart.

To the chagrin of the Cans leading him, Rüsul's body went limp. Head and trunk down, he began to wail, as mournful a sound as any living being could manage. The Dogs dropped him.

They clutched at their heads and kicked him until pain silenced him.

"Why do they all do that?" said one of the Cans, over the sound of the Fant's moans. "I think my ears are bleeding."

"Shut up and grab an end," said another. "I just want to get him into a cell before he catches his breath and starts in again."

"Why do I get the smelly end?"

"The whole thing stinks. All the more reason to hurry up and dump his ass where he won't be polluting our air."

One took Rüsul's arms, the other his legs. Neither Dog came anywhere near touching his trunk or ears.

"How can something that's been sitting out in the rain for days smell this bad?"

"Yeah, every time we grab another one, I worry the ship's recycler is going to break down and then we're all screwed."

They hauled him ever further away from his death.

TWO

POSSIBILITIES AND MYTHS

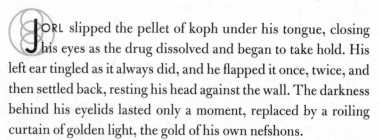

JORL slipped the pellet of koph under his tongue, closing his eyes as the drug dissolved and began to take hold. His left ear tingled as it always did, and he flapped it once, twice, and then settled back, resting his head against the wall. The darkness behind his eyelids lasted only a moment, replaced by a roiling curtain of golden light, the gold of his own nefshons.

The first perception granted by the drug induced panic for many novice Speakers. One moment you were alone in the darkness of your own head, and in the next you saw yourself swaddled by shimmering subatomic particles of memory. Those layers of golden fabric could suffocate a beginner. A successful Speaker imprinted on it, learned to identify the unique tang that permeated every gleaming particle. Then it only required an act of will for the Speaker to blind herself to it and move on.

Jorl had been Speaking less than a year, but he had disciplined his mind in academia. At the first glimpse of his own nefshons he banished them from his perception.

He filled the resulting darkness with images from his own

memory, imagining a familiar room in a house on the island of Keslo. The dimensions and materials, the colors and textures and scents formed around him. That easily, he sat in a small alcove that lay just off of the kitchen of the home maintained by his friend's widow. The walls were beech, yellow, bright in their own right and polished to a high sheen. A hand-braided rug covered the floor from the kitchen's threshold to the hidden door in the back wall that provided a less obvious entrance to the house. A tapestry woven of wild flowers hung on that wall, filling the air with light, sweet fragrance. Two comfortably curved benches faced one another, set far back against opposite sides such that their occupants would be unseen by anyone passing the opening. Jorl saw it all in his mind, just as he had seen it before taking the koph and settling into that very spot after dinner.

While his best friend's widow busied herself with after-dinner tasks, he muttered a name aloud, "Arlo," and began summoning particles, luring them with memories: sitting in a classroom in his grandmother's hall learning to cipher . . . sampling their first efforts at distillation . . . introducing him to Tolta, the daughter of a friend of his mother . . . laughing in the rain as they took a raft to Gerd for the first time . . . embracing him, trunks wrapped around one another's ears, the day he left Barsk . . .

When he had a sufficient number, he willed the particles to coalesce into his friend's form, occupying the bench opposite him, visible to anyone who possessed the Speaker's gift.

"Your wife made the most amazing dinner tonight," said Jorl, the mental construct of himself smacking his lips with satisfaction while in the real world his head pressed back against the wall, his trunk draping languidly down his chest, a trickle of drool starting at the corner of his flaccid mouth.

Arlo smiled. It started at his eyes and spread with exaggerated slowness across his face, until his ears gave a little flap of merriment. "Did she? You say that like you're surprised. Tolta's always been a great cook. You know that."

"Of regional dishes, sure. The safe and same traditional meals that everyone's aunt knows how to make. I'm talking about recipes from other worlds, places where no Fant has been in centuries."

"Now you're just being foolish. No one is going to bother venturing into space just for dinner. Not even you."

"I didn't say we left Barsk, only that the recipes, the spices, were from offworld. Pay attention."

"Or what? You'll banish me? Spread the glowing bits of me far and wide?"

"I'd never—don't even joke about that!"

"I'm dead, Jorl. You can't tell me what to do. More importantly, you shouldn't be trying to tell me anything. This is what, the thirtieth time you've summoned me? It's not healthy."

"I'm a Speaker. It's a rare gift, even on Barsk. Why shouldn't I use it?"

"Just because a thing can be done doesn't mean it should be done. I'm not telling you not to use your gift. You're a historian, and I imagine it must be a powerful tool in your work, talking directly to the people who made history. That's incredible. Do more of that. But you shouldn't keep talking to me. Let me go. Even a historian can't keep living in the past."

"I don't want to have this argument with you."

Arlo spread his hands, his trunk lifting in an ironic gesture. "Stop summoning me and you won't."

"I needed to talk to you. Something's going on and I don't understand it. I thought discussing it with you might help."

The smile fell away from Arlo's face. "Something more than Tolta's cooking?"

"I've been studying the prophecies of the Matriarch since our school days." He grew still, head bowed, hands clasping the nubs of his trunk and one another in his lap. Even his ears had stopped moving. "I think one of the dire ones is coming to pass."

"I've long since forgotten the details of her warnings. Of all the areas of history to study, I never understood why you made her life your focus. Most of her writings bored me, and the prophecies were so weird they made little sense, at least at the time we covered them in class. Which one are you going on about here?"

"The Silence."

Arlo scrunched up his trunk and spat. "I hate that one. You remember how my mam told us stories about it when we were small, years before we got to that section in school? Scared the leaves out of us."

"I remember. I had nightmares. Sometimes I think I grew up to study them as a reaction. You know, so that I could really understand what scared me."

"Yeah? Well, be sure and thank her for your livelihood next time you see her."

Jorl looked down, finding a sudden interest in the cuticles of one hand.

"What?" said Arlo.

"Your mom is part of the problem. I wasn't going to bother you with the knowledge, but she sailed off a season ago. I'm sorry."

"Oh."

"Kembü had a full life, Ar. It didn't have anything to do with your own passing. It was just her time."

"What do you mean, she's 'part of the problem'?"

"Do you remember when we were eight and crazy for insects? We spent the summer collecting every bug we could find? I got to thinking about it, and I found myself wanting the specimen jar you used. Just a sentimental reminder. And you know how your mother never threw anything away . . . So I tried to ask her if she knew where it was."

"What do you mean, you *tried?*"

"I couldn't summon her."

"How long ago?"

"Weeks. More than enough time for her to finish her last voyage and be summonable. Something set me off, thinking about that long ago summer. I snatched up a pellet of koph and reached out to pull your mother's nefshons together, only . . . I couldn't."

"What does that mean? Why couldn't you?"

"Because there weren't any, at least, not any that would come when I called for them."

"How can that be? We're constantly producing particles, storing them up until death sets them free." He gestured at his own chest with his trunk. "That's how I'm here now. So how can my mam not have any?"

"I don't know the how of it. I'm telling you what happened. A Speaker can only summon the nefshons of someone he knows. I know your mother as well as my own, but when I tried to find any sense of her, well, I *think* I felt something, but it wouldn't respond. They were there, I'm sure, but it was like something was holding on to them. I've never felt anything like it."

"You are kind of new at it," said Arlo.

"Don't insult me. I've done more than a hundred summonings, spoken with dozens of different people, including some I had to research because I didn't know them personally. I should have been able to Speak to your mother. But I couldn't attract so much as a single one of her nefshons."

They sat quietly a few minutes, until Arlo finally asked, "So then what happened?"

"I shrugged it off. Blamed it on not enough sleep, or some bad fruit from breakfast. I put it out of my mind. But a few days later I needed to check on a reference with another historian, a woman I'd fallen out of correspondence with, only she'd sailed away sometime before your mom. I couldn't reach her either. Same problem. But that time I wasn't tired and I hadn't eaten any bad fruit. Once I could dismiss as a fluke, but twice?"

"Flukes can come in pairs. Unlikely, statistically improbable even, but not impossible."

"I knew you'd say that. So I asked around, both here at home and among a couple of the nearer islands. I compiled a list of five other elders who had all sailed off on their last journeys this past season with ample time to arrive at that last shore. I couldn't summon any of them.

"I expanded my search, going back a bit further, built up a list of a dozen names. Those who had left two or more seasons ago responded to my call. Anyone who took to sea more recently than that I couldn't reach. Like your mother."

"And you think that's the Silence from Margda's prophecy?"

Jorl's ears flapped as his shoulders rose in a shrug. "What else could it be? I mean, sure, like all prophecy the wording is vague, but I don't know of any other event that fits her description of *When the dead will not answer, the Silence is at hand, and the fate of all Barsk will soon hang in the balance.*"

"You left off a piece," said Arlo. "Just like you've left off your tattoo."

Jorl's entire face reddened, making his vestigial tusks seem to brighten by contrast. "I leave the tattoo off because I didn't have it when you were alive; I want you to see me the way you knew me. I thought it would be more comfortable for you." He mentally updated his own image and the glimmering glyph appeared.

"Okay, point one: that's a load of crap. When I knew you, you weren't a Speaker, so the fact that we're having this conversation means I already know you've been through some changes since I died. Point two: you're deflecting the real issue here, the bit of the prophecy you don't want to talk about. What's the rest?"

"Each of Margda's prophecies goes on and on for pages in that meandering double-talk of hers—"

Arlo interrupted, "And yet, there's a bit that you're deliberately not mentioning. Jorl, you said you needed to talk to me about this, so talk."

Jorl gestured at his forehead with one hand, moving his trunk in parallel for emphasis. "The next line says, *The newest Aleph must do what has never been done though it is almost always done.* Whatever that means. It's nonsense."

"Nonsense that bothers you. Because there are what, only three Fant now living who've been awarded the aleph? And you're the most recent person to bear the mark. You think she's talking about you!"

"Maybe. But only if the Silence is really happening. For all I know, I'm misreading the signs, and the Silence is something totally different that won't come to pass for another hundred years, by which time I'll be dead and some other guy will be the latest person with a glowing tattoo on his head. I'm probably worrying about nothing."

"I can see how it might stress you," said Arlo. "Have you tried talking about it with any other historians? Other experts in the Matriarch and her prophecies?"

"Oh yeah, and what a mistake that was! Mickl accused me of 'conveniently' interpreting the data to enhance my own position. He claimed I was trying to write myself into history."

"Which one is Mickl?"

"He's the head of the department at the university on Zlorka. He got the job because no one else wanted it. His scholarship sucks—everyone knows it—so he hides behind his title and generates bureaucracy instead of anything remotely publishable. And now he's poisoning the rest of our community against me!"

"I remember you talking about him. He always sounded like an ass and a blowhard. If everyone already knows that, then his opinion isn't going to carry much weight. So that's not what's really bothering you. Tell me what is!"

Jorl leaned over, elbows resting on knees, dropping his face into his hands and covering his eyes. His ears flapped forward, further shrouding him. After a moment he whispered, "I don't want to be a part of history."

"Yeah?"

"Yeah."

Arlo pushed off from the wall, rising and crossing the gap between the two benches in one step to settle alongside his friend, one arm reaching across his shoulders to pull him close. "I know what that's like," he said.

"You do?"

"Sure. I don't want to be dead. But it's like complaining about the rain. We don't get the weather we want."

"That's not funny!"

"Probably why neither of us is laughing."

Jorl pulled away and rose to his feet, his desire to pace frustrated by the size of the alcove he'd imagined for their conversation. "This is your fault, you know, all of it."

"Now how do you figure that?"

He spun around and jabbed at Arlo with a finger. "Because you died!"

"Jorl, we've been over this before. Everyone dies."

"Don't give me that. You didn't sail away at the end of a long life. You killed yourself."

Arlo's held his friend's gaze for a long moment before looking away. "You told me that Tolta believes it was an accident."

"Yeah, right. That's the story that appeared in the professional journals and what they told your mother and the aunts at the funeral. An accident testing a new drug. But it doesn't wash, Arlo."

"It's plausible."

"Your lab had been completely stripped!"

"Perhaps by a jealous competitor."

"And all your records? Even the second set that I know you always kept in Tolta's house? Never mind the absurd notion that you were doing a field test of a brand new substance atop the canopy at dawn. No assistants. No safeguards. Nothing but a carboy of photo-sensitive accelerant which you just happened to splash all over yourself moments before first light?"

"An unhappy combination of coincidences."

"*You blazed a fucking hole all the way through the rain forest!* From the top of the canopy, through the Civilized Wood, and down to the mud and water of the Shadow Dwell. And nowhere along the path did you strike any occupied spaces or dwellings. I know you, Ar, you've been my best friend since we learned to cipher and distill. You're meticulous to a fault, it's what made you such an amazing pharmer. There was no accident. No coincidence.

You planned every piece of it and made sure no one else would be harmed. You took your own life!"

During all of Jorl's rant, Arlo hadn't looked up. He lifted his head now, saw the pain in his friend's face, the tears in his eyes. Sighing, he stood as well, hugging Jorl with both of his arms and curling his trunk around his friend's ear, like a parent would to comfort a child. "That's what this is all about, isn't it? The thirty summonings? It took you this long to get to it?"

"I just don't understand how you could do it." Jorl's voice cracked, ending in a sob.

"I know it doesn't help to hear this, but I struggled with the decision for weeks. More than once I cursed you for being away in the Patrol; I so needed someone to talk with about it. It wasn't something I did lightly."

Jorl broke the embrace, stumbling back and dropping onto the bench where Arlo had begun. "I had to come back because of your death. The Alliance never wanted a Fant serving in the Patrol, and they used the excuse of my being your Second to discharge me. They shuttled me back to Barsk by fast courier. I helped plant your remains in the Shadow Dwell and I wrote some words that someone else had to read for me."

"I'd like to hear them, sometime."

Jorl glared at him, but Arlo shrugged and settled onto the opposite bench.

"I went back to my old post in the history department, and days later a routine physical showed I'd developed the sensitivity to manipulate nefshons. They made me a Speaker, and soon after gave me the aleph. All of that happened because you died."

"Oh, so it's my fault you're becoming a part of history? You're still the same self-centered ass you've been since childhood."

"You're calling *me* selfish? Did you give any thought what your death would mean to Tolta or Pizlo?"

Arlo rolled his trunk between his palms. "I did. It's why I didn't say goodbye. I knew I'd lose my nerve. And though you seem to think otherwise, I thought about its effect on you, too. I didn't know you'd become a Speaker. I never expected to see any of you again, most especially not my wife or son."

Jorl winced, and the words left him before he could bite them back. "He's not your son."

Arlo's mouth became a thin hard line. His normal grayish pallor purpled and his hands bunched into fists. He slashed his trunk in a wide arc that only just missed striking Jorl. "He *is* my son. Tolta's family may have forced her to abandon him at birth, but we've both acknowledged him as ours, even if the rest of this fucking, narrow-minded planet doesn't."

"You can't just wipe away belief systems that have been in place since before we arrived on Barsk. Pizlo was an accident. Tolta shouldn't have been able to conceive before you two bonded. There's a reason that children like him are given up to the community when they're born. Their genetics are so messed up most never live out their first year."

"So now you're a biologist? You should stick to history. Yes, Pizlo isn't like other kids, and he's not healthy. He's got albinism, and he's all skin and bones, and has no pain receptors, and . . . and . . . a host of other problems. But he's beaten the odds that said he'd die in infancy. He's five years old now, and he *is* my son."

"He's six."

"What?"

"He's six now, almost seven. It's been nearly two years since you saw him last. And he's started filling out a little. You can't see his ribs anymore."

"You're keeping track of him?"

"I was your Second, Ar, what the hell else was I supposed to do?"

"But you said—"

"I know what I said. It's what society says, and I have to live in society. His existence is a violation of Fant culture. But . . . you were my best friend, and he's the only part of you left in the world. I couldn't turn my back on that. Besides, he needs an education, and it's not like anyone is going to let him go to school."

"You're teaching him?"

Jorl nodded. "I asked Tolta, and she thought it was a great idea. He's still a wildling. He rarely sleeps under your wife's roof, and even less often under mine, but we have lessons every few days and he doesn't suffer for them not happening daily."

"He's bright. And curious."

"He has your mind. Oh, and that specimen jar that sent me to summoning your mother? That wasn't really for me. I thought Pizlo should have something of his father's."

A flicker of delight chased a flash of pain across Arlo's face. "Yeah, he's always had a thing for bugs. That's what set me on the track of . . . never mind. But you're looking after him. I can't tell you what that means to me, Jorl. It's everything. Truly."

The two friends regarded one another, having run the gauntlet of emotions and arrived back at the core bond between them. Jorl smiled and asked, "Everything? Everything enough that you'll tell me what was so important that you're dead?"

Arlo snorted with pained laughter. "You. Are. Such. An. Ass!"

Before he could reply, Jorl felt a hand on his shoulder some-place else. The hand shook him firmly without producing any movement that Arlo could see. With a mental twist, Jorl focused his attention back in the physical world. Opening his eyes, he saw Tolta standing in front of him in the same small room.

"I'm sorry, Jorl, but Pizlo came home tonight. He says you promised to tell him a bedtime story next time you were both here."

He smiled, wiping the back of his hand across the trail of drool Speaking produced in him.

"She's there now, isn't she?" Arlo moved from the opposite wall and leaned closer, whispering like a conspirator. "I know that look. You always got that expression when she entered a room. That's the hardest thing about being dead, you know? You're the only one I ever get to see. Tell me, Jorl, please, how is she?"

"She's beautiful, Ar, you know that. As beautiful as when you last saw her this morning."

He sighed and eased back against the wall again. "This morn-ing to me and what, coming on two years to her?"

"He's here now, isn't he?" Tolta hovered closer, a delicate emo-tion lighting her face for an instant and vanishing before Jorl could put a name to it. "You have the same look on your face you always had when I'd catch the two of you in one of your foolish games. How is he, Jorl? Can you tell me?"

The eerie duality thrummed through him like a minor chord and Jorl needed to take a moment to be certain which side he was replying to. "He's fine, Tolta, just as you remember him. He sends his love." He reached out in both phases and felt his loved ones grasp his hand, telling himself that somehow they man-aged to touch one another in the process.

"Tell her I'm sorry, will you?"

"She knows. We all do. I have to go now, Pizlo is demanding a story." As he began the mental exercises to disperse his friend's nefshons, Jorl nodded his farewell.

"Tell him the one about Pholo. He always loved hearing about—"

With a shiver and a shake of the head, Arlo was gone. Reality returned to only a single frame of existence, a single alcove in Tolta's home. Jorl stood, stretching his arms and legs and trunk like a man rising up from a deep nap in the first afternoon of wind.

A pale blur of child-sized Fant pushed past Tolta and threw itself upon Jorl, attempting to climb him like a tree branch. With one arm and his trunk Jorl swung Pizlo up to his shoulder and followed Tolta out of the alcove and down a hall to the room set aside for the boy's use when he chose or could be persuaded to sleep under a roof. As Pizlo's trunk circled tightly around his left ear for the ride, Jorl began his tale of a legend of Barsk. He knew the story would end with the hero's enlightenment and the boy's slumber.

"Whilom, Pizlo, and oh so very long ago, there lived a young man named Pholo. But this was no ordinary Fant."

"No?" That one syllable was all breathless anticipation and no part question.

"No, because Pholo possessed the gift of flight! While all others walked or ran, skipped or jogged, Pholo soared through the passways of the Civilized Wood like a purposeful leaf on the edge of a storm . . ."

THREE

AIRY GLYPHS

THROUGHOUT the tree cities of Barsk's archipelagos, Fant went about their daily affairs. Occasional travelers worked their way through the maze of massive roots and boles, mud and gloom and deceptively deep pools that defined the Shadow Dwell, before stumbling without warning onto open beach and welcome rain. Families of mothers and aunts, sisters and girl cousins and children of both sexes, worked and studied, laughed and dreamed in homes, offices, and workshops carved and grown from the trees that defined the Civilized Wood. Adult males established smaller bachelor homes or circulated through the assortment of lodges and fraternal apartments that changed residents almost as frequently as their occupants changed clothes. Fant lounged and strolled along platforms and balconies, cooked meals, made music, enjoyed their lives. Children played on public balconies, studied in gymnasiums, slept in warm beds in homes populated with adults who loved them as the promise of their own posterity.

None of that applied to Pizlo's life.

He hung in open air, ruminating, suspended upside down in a well-tended shaft walled on all sides with living green. Seven such chimneys existed on the island of Keslo; every island on Barsk boasted at least one. Fant society created the insubstantial monuments as part memorial and part warning. Few reached all the way to the uppermost limits of the forest, or ran all the way down to its roots. This one, Suth's Shaft, was one of only three that Pizlo knew did both. It curved and meandered, bulged and narrowed, a metaphor for the twists and turns of Suth's life some two hundred fifty years in the past.

Maintaining the memorials required countless hours of effort. The shafts provided conduits for seedlings, pollens, and molds to float from one height to another, eager to root and grow. Everyone took turns to keep them clear, from roving teams of elderly bachelors to field trips of school children. They'd snip and clip, groom, and sculpt, preserving the negative space, until lunchtime bade them pack their tools and leave the living task for the next day's team.

This day, Pizlo had arrived early enough to have the space to himself. The walls of Suth's had called to him, promising an adventure. A collection of hastily knotted vines had proved sufficient to his need and allowed him to dangle in the middle of the Shaft, far from the safety of any side or railing. His feet wriggled above him and his head grew dizzier by the moment.

But the chimney wasn't his destination, merely the staging area. Eyes tightly closed, he listened to the forest as it revealed the path for him to take. When he had it clear in his mind, he squirmed free of the vines and dropped like a stone.

Like Arlo had dropped.

Unlike him, Pizlo bounced on curves, snagged branches,

passed turns, and briefly clutched bits of vine to gain spin. The effort transformed his fall into a controlled plunge that ended in a deep pool many levels down in the Shadow Dwell.

Since coming to Barsk and adopting an arboreal lifestyle, few Fant learned to swim. As with so much else, Pizlo was an exception. He let the water absorb his momentum, diving down to the pool's murky bottom before executing a perfect flip, his legs scissoring to propel him upward. He surfaced and swam to the water's edge. Mud-covered stone surrounded a pool scarcely wider than the boy's height. He hauled himself up onto a stone and lay back under the fronds of a butterleaf plant, panting and complimenting himself on the speed of his descent, a personal best for reaching the Shadow Dwell.

He used his trunk to snatch up several mouthfuls of dusty, golden leaves, grimacing at their bitter aftertaste. He squinted, as much with concentration as to focus his weak eyesight, and exhaled pollen rings through his trunk. In the circular glyphs of Barsk he spelled the consonants of his friend's name in the humid air. $J \ldots R \ldots L \ldots$

Jorl had been Arlo's friend and somehow that friendship had transferred to him, doubling the number of people in his world after Arlo's death left him only Tolta. He liked that, much as he liked the irony that all the thousands of Fant, the Lox and Eleph that shared this island with him while denying his existence because of his differences, were themselves denied by millions and millions of other people on more worlds than he could imagine. And none of the Fant who pretended he didn't exist had ever been to any of those other places or met any of those other people (who wouldn't have wanted to meet them anyway). Except for Jorl. He had done both, been there and met them and come home to be his friend.

Maybe that was why Jorl kept showing up in his conversations with the world. It didn't matter that only two other Fant acknowledged his existence; the rest of the planet conversed with him on a regular basis. Not words so much, because only people had language. Even though he was only six, Pizlo knew the difference between real and pretend. The trees of the Civilized Wood had brought him here today, and many times in the past rocks and streams in the Shadow Dwell had shared secrets with him. On two occasions, the entire island of Keslo had alerted him to time and place so that he could position himself just so, sprawled out on one of its thin strips of beach or secreted upon an observation platform poised above the canopy. On both junctures he had occupied just the right spot when the ubiquitous clouds had parted to reveal one of Barsk's moons. He'd looked up at them and felt them gazing back down in turn. The moons were the wisest things he'd ever met. Their light shone onto his face and passed knowledge to him, ideas and thoughts and stories, of what had been and what was yet to come. Pizlo smiled as he remembered the experience; Jorl would have called those conversations visions.

Conversing with the world was yet another way he differed from other Fant. They had gray skin, his was colorless white. They winced and pouted when they stepped on a sharp stone or cut themselves on a broken branch, but no injury, large or small, bothered Pizlo. Tolta had tried and tried to get him to wear long-sleeved shirts and thick pants, but he preferred less encumbrance, and since he couldn't feel the hurt of the innumerable cuts and scratches covering him from ear to toe he ran wild, wearing nothing more than a pair of shorts and a daypouch on a strap around his chest.

The daypouch held food, but he'd been thinking about making one large enough to carry books. Jorl had taught him to read and loaned him books, one at a time at first, but as many as three at a go, now. Most had stories about Fant who had lived in the past, and he liked best the stories that Jorl himself had written. Pizlo's penmanship was just about good enough for him to write down some of his own stories, the ones that swam in his head, coming to him from a place beyond dreams. But paper and ink were hard for him to keep hold of as he rambled from place to place.

He spat out the last of the leaves and stood. He'd come here with a purpose beyond plunging down at speed. Clambering over tree roots, slogging through thick mud, and fording a pair of fast-moving streams, he came at last to his destination at the base of one of the massive meta-trees that made the Civilized Wood possible. A name had been carved into the bole, the incised letters stained and filled in with something like sap. Arlo's name.

A small pile of river stones marked the spot where the remains had been planted. Pizlo had watched from hiding as Jorl performed the rite.

He'd awakened this morning to the whisper of one of the marking stones, urging him to visit. That had been new, and new was always interesting. He was here now, and wondering what would come to him.

As though stumbling from a dream into deep water, Pizlo pulled together several pieces of concentration and compared memories of the letters written on the tree and the fading letters he'd written earlier on the air. He closed his eyes and felt the world fall away. In his mind, the blackness deepened to something darker than black. He waited.

Time passed. His little body grew exhausted. His stomach rumbled and his throat felt dry. He chose not to notice. He emptied his attention into that blackness, like a fisherman might lower a net into the sea, patient for the catch to come to him.

When it did, the sight made him smile. There was Jorl. He looked tired, maybe a little scared. Before Pizlo could ask himself what could scare a grown-up, he saw Jorl change. He couldn't say what was different, and it didn't make sense. There was more of Jorl than could possibly be, but he was still himself. Like the ocean was the same water whether you cupped some of it in your hands or waded out until the waves crashed over your head. Jorl smiled as he grew, so vast he filled up the darkness and forced Pizlo to open his eyes to the more ordinary gloom of the Shadow Dwell.

He reached up and found a handhold in the tree, enough to start scrambling up, beginning the long trip back to the Civilized Wood. With luck, he might get back in time to visit Tolta for dinner. As he climbed, Pizlo's fingers roamed over his face. He discovered he'd brought Jorl's smile back with him from the blackness. He wished he'd managed to bring an aleph with him. Maybe he would find a way to do that. Next time.

FOUR

SOLUTIONS IN MEMORY

THOUGH she had never actually met one in the flesh, Lirlowil hated the Fant. Her hatred was a recent development, acquired after she'd been forcibly removed from the world of her birth and imprisoned in a suite of rooms aboard an automated station orbiting Barsk.

Beautiful by Otter standards, she'd spent the last few years enjoying the peaks of privilege earned not by any act of her own, but by the random chance that gifted her with being able to both read minds and talk to the dead. Unless you had the misfortune to be one of those disgusting Fant on Barsk, you could go your entire life without encountering a Speaker. The drug that triggered the ability was fiendishly expensive, and rarely worked the first few times. Alliance science had yet to determine what genetic markers resulted in the talent. Off Barsk, Speakers were unlikely, though hardly uncommon. True telepaths though, people who could effortlessly slip inside the mind of other beings and sample their memories and knowledge as easily as flipping the pages of a book, were orders of magnitude more rare.

The number of individuals with both sets of abilities would make for a very small dinner party indeed. Lirlowil's mental gifts emerged with puberty and elevated her social status a thousand-fold. The discovery that her talents included Speaking occurred a couple years later when she'd sampled some koph at a party and began seeing nefshons over the next hour's time.

Sharv, her home, was a mixed world, a glamour planet of mild climates. The days never grew uncomfortably hot, and the rain fell only lightly and at opportune times. Tourists came as much to enjoy its many sights as to be seen enjoying them. Artists of every description lived and worked there, mingling media and inventing new delights which sold for outrageous sums offworld. None of its cities contained more than a million souls nor possessed any heavy industry. The population included not only Otters but also Bears, Elk, a smattering of Yak, and the omnipresent Cats. The people of Lirlowil's homeworld had registered her as a planetary treasure, and even among the hedonistic lifestyles common to Otters she began to set a new standard as a sybaritic party girl. But there were no parties aboard the station, and the closest thing to hedonism Lirlowil had found was the ability to sleep in as late as she wished.

The station consisted of a giant wheel of attached warehouses connected to a central hub; the hub in turn linked to a beanstalk reaching down to a spot on the equator of Barsk. Enormous containers climbed up the beanstalk every hour. The Patrol crew that lived in the hub moved each of them to one warehouse or another, until such time as a vessel arrived and emptied the contents into its own hold and then departed. Sometimes these ships swapped out people, station workers taking berths on a supply ship or vice versa, trading one form of monotony for another. No one ever came to relieve Lirlowil.

She'd arrived there like so much cargo herself. A Bear from the Patrol had shown up at her home on Sharv. One moment she'd been fast asleep, dreaming of the debaucheries from the night before, and the next he'd been standing over her bed with a writ of transference in his hand and trailing a small entourage made up of a Prairie Dog wearing a civil parson's ring in one twitching ear, and an Otter, only a few years older than Lirlowil, garbed like a physician's assistant.

"I am Urs-Major Krasnoi," said the Bear. "I do not need your consent, but I do require you to be fully conscious. Can you tell me your name?"

This didn't make any sense. She wriggled her neck and shoulders a moment in thought, remembered the distinction between dreams and hallucinations, realized she was in bed and made a leap of faith as she asked, "What the fuck are you doing in my dream?"

The Bear had frowned at her, but his next words hadn't made it into her memory. Perhaps she'd gone back to sleep. The next thing she recalled was the feeling that her heart would explode, it was pounding so fast. The PA was leaning over her, an empty ampoule in one hand. As Lirlowil began to sweat, puke, and piss herself into a clear-eyed panic, she understood she'd been slipped a sobriety agent which was systematically purging any and all toxins from her body as if her life depended on it.

Gasping, she sat up in bed and grimaced. Nudity in front of strangers didn't bother her but being covered in her own filth surely did. The Prairie Dog stepped up, wrinkling his own nose, and opened a small book.

"The universe is vast and complex, comprising many peoples and many worlds." Lirlowil rolled her eyes but managed to suppress a giggle. Still, the solemnity of his words were marred by the shrill pitch of his voice. "Rarely do any of us have the opportunity to be of service beyond the immediate circle of our own community. But when that chance occurs we must welcome it. Failing that, we must rely upon that same community to recognize the circumstance for what it is and surrender us up to that need. Gaze with me now upon such an individual and bear witness to what we do."

The Bear stepped forward, opening a small pouch on his belt and withdrawing a notary seal. "Her mark, now, if you please," he said to the physician's assistant who took Lirlowil's hand, smeared a green gel over the pads of her fingers, and pressed them to a piece of cardstock. The Urs reviewed the impression and passed the card to the parson.

"I do place the seal of my office alongside your mark, confirming your change of status from Citizen to Resource." The parson tucked the card away, waited for the PA to pack up her things, and then both departed, leaving Lirlowil alone with the Bear.

As her chemical panic subsided, Lirlowil asked "What . . . what just happened?"

"What had to happen. There is a need and only you can serve it. We're leaving in ten minutes. You can use that time to pack whatever you can carry, or not. I don't much care. I'll give you another five minutes to take a shower. I won't subject my crew to your odor."

"Where are we going?"

"Your new home," said the Bear. "Nine minutes and three quarters."

Free of chemical enhancement for the first time in more than a year, Lirlowil took in the sprawl of toys and distractions that filled her home, including a handful of other Lutr playmates that had managed to sleep through her unwilling transformation. Ten minutes was ludicrous. She'd need twice that span even to find her essentials, and she had no illusions about being able to carry it all. She instead opted to take nothing and went straight to her bathing chamber where she indulged with a variety of shower massagers, perfumed soaps, and bath oils, for far longer than the Urs had permitted. In the end, he pulled her from her shower and marched her out of her home and to a waiting vehicle, water still streaming from her sleek pelt, naked except for a flimsy robe he had found and thrown at her.

Less than an hour later, Sharv was a dwindling blue-green marble in the view port of the Patrol vessel carrying her to the station above Barsk. Days later, a trio of Ailuros, the sheen of their slick, black security uniforms blending and contrasting against the black and white of their fur, took her from the ship and ensconced her in a suite remodeled from an unused warehouse. In the nearly one hundred days since, she hadn't seen a living soul.

A sealed viewer had awaited her in the middle of her rooms. She broke the seal and skimmed the document for an explanation. Then she dropped the viewer and threw a fit. She screamed. She wailed. She beat her hands and feet against the walls and floors. Nothing and no one responded. Trembling with frustration Lirlowil retrieved the viewer, reset it to the beginning, and read it through more carefully. Urs-Major Krasnoi's instructions were precise and absurd. He instructed that she use her talents to Speak to Fant—those disgustingly furless freaks—and telepathically probe them for any knowledge that involved koph, the Speaker's drug. According to her briefing, Alliance scientists had spent years attempting to reverse engineer the drug, without success. Her assignment was part of a new direction to obtain answers. They wanted the details of its refining, the quantities and characteristics of its ingredients, the qualities of the flora that made up its parts, the growing cycle of those plants, any particular methodologies involved in harvesting them, and on and on. If it touched on koph and existed in the minds of any of the dead Fant she could summon, the Bear wanted a detailed report.

Lirlowil shuddered. Whoever had come up with the plan had been utterly clueless about Speakers. She couldn't simply conjure up anyone from anywhere. The nefshons she manipulated were subatomic particles of personality that dispersed upon their creator's death. But during the long course of a life, everyone transferred hundreds of particles with every touch. These in turn became the stuff of memory. It's what made memory of people so vivid and different than memory of how to swim or the capitals of Sharv's twenty-seven principalities.

Speaking required she already possess some of these particles. A Speaker needed enough sense of her conversant's identity to separate that individual from every other person that ever existed. Trivially easy if she had personal experience of the conversant—nefshons of the person carried in her own mind. Lacking that, a summoning was still possible if enough objective information existed to create a clear picture. Unfortunately, exceedingly few dead, Barsk-born Fant had been sufficiently well documented to allow anyone to Speak to them.

Which was, Lirlowil realized, part of the reason they had wanted her. On Sharv she had developed a reputation for successfully Speaking to strangers. But it was a cheat. All those people whom she had never met were the friends or relatives or business associates of the clients that came to her. During interviews, while her petitioners unraveled anecdotes of the intended conversant, Lirlowil had slipped into their minds and gathered up richer impressions than their words could express, telepathically copying the nefshons the target had transferred in life. Armed with such intimate details, she succeeded where other Speakers would fail, all of which merely added to her prestige as a treasure of Sharv. But somewhere a bureaucrat had misunderstood the particulars of her technique, and here she was.

Her usual solution, having a tantrum, had failed to accomplish anything so she ramped things up. Assuming her suite was monitored—she'd already confirmed it was shielded to prevent her telepathic spying on anyone beyond its walls—she ranted and railed against the injustice of her situation. She made wild accusations. She threatened. She screamed the most lurid improprieties and colorful invective that had ever been heard on any Patrol station, let alone from the lips of a young woman raised in a privileged society. She broke every piece of furniture and every implement in her rooms that wasn't bolted to floor or wall. Nothing produced the slightest response or even a hint that anyone aboard the station monitored her at all.

Only when she'd taken a broken shard of mirror to her own throat did the gravity field in her room suddenly increase, pinning her to the floor with ever-increasing weight until she passed out. She awoke some unknown span later to find everything restored. Not just the gravity but all the rooms' furnishings had been returned to their earlier state. The viewer with her orders lay on the floor where she'd dropped it. Its content remained the same as well.

Bit by bit, over the course of several days, she adapted to her new situation. The crew of the station did not interact with her, which suited her fine. She sent off notes and reports from a unit built into her desk and received printed replies. Through trial and error she learned a few simple things. They wanted what they wanted, and as long as she attempted to provide, they would in turn tolerate her behaviors up to the point of physical harm, and try to honor any requests within the limited resources of the station and its crew.

The first proof of this was the gravity in one of her rooms. She'd asked for and received the plans detailing the electronics built into the walls that controlled her bedroom. Using the expertise she'd acquired from the mind of a thief she'd dallied with a year before, she removed various panels until she had access to the unit maintaining the room's gravity and disabled it to see how the station crew would react. They didn't.

After two days of floating in her sleep, Lirlowil restored the panel, though not the gravity. The null field of her room felt invitingly like floating in the comforting waters of her favorite stream back home. Wrapping herself in that small bit of comfort she finally went to work.

Her captors had provided a vast array of stolen diaries, biographies, and interviews, every bit of documentation on every known deceased Fant. Lirlowil had a keen intellect, she simply had never found any motivation to utilize it before now. She began pulling together sufficient information so that a few of the Fant became individuals for her, people she might actually have a chance to Speak with. When she was ready, she asked for and received a supply of koph. Then the real work began.

~~~~~~

"YOU are Shtev, an Eleph born on Barsk. Your time in life has long since ended; you are now as you were in life, but not alive. In this, a world of my own making, I bid you welcome."

Lirlowil had toyed with re-creating the comforts of her apartment as the venue for her summoning, but changed her mind. Being surrounded by memories of what had been taken away would only depress her afterwards. And, too, she didn't want to associate anything from her real life with nefshon constructs of Fant.

Instead she re-created the bedroom they'd given her on the

station, restoring the gravity as a minor kindness to her conversant. She sat on the floor and the Fant took shape across from her, a squat, thick, gray lump of a woman clothed in a grassy tabard that bared too much of her hairless skin. Even after preparing for it, the Lutr still cringed. It was like meeting a monster. Hadn't her mother given her a storybook as a child where an evil Fant hid in a tributary and snuck out to devour innocent children as they played in the larger river nearby?

"I . . . where am I? Who are you?"

Lirlowil rolled her eyes. "I'm a Speaker. Which means you're dead, so it doesn't really matter where you are, does it? Now, I have a few questions I need to ask you, and trust me the sooner you can answer them the better it will be for both of us. You worked in pharmaceutical exports, is that right?"

"I do," said Shtev. "I mean, I did. How did you know?"

"You had a Vulp penpal on an Alliance medical station. Her daughter published the letters as a book. That's how I found you."

"Found me? Why were you looking for me? I don't understand."

"You don't need to. Let's talk about koph, okay?"

"What?"

Lirlowil slipped into the re-created mind of the Fant, taking advantage of the confusion she'd sown and following the chain of associations she'd sparked with her last inquiry. She'd done the same many times before with the living, tracking a person's surface thoughts as they prattled on about something. Now she probed deeper, psychically interrogating the dead woman and plucking knowledge out of her without asking permission. The effort was inexpressible, and the act itself went against everything she'd been taught. The party girl who had enjoyed a life of water slides, recreational narcotics, and imaginative sex partners discovered she had moral limits after all. And then pushed past them.

Shtev cried out in pain. Fat gray fingers pressed against her forehead and her grotesque ears flapped uselessly. That disgusting trunk flailed. "Stop!"

The Otter cringed as the trunk intruded into her personal space. "You are *worthless*! Go, get away, I'm done with you." Her mind reeled with useless data gleaned from ancient shipping manifests, but she managed the mental exercise required to disperse the nefshons. Shtev vanished, dazed and violated, and Lirlowil had gained nothing.

She curled into a ball, floating in the null field of her room, and sobbed herself to sleep. Nightmares of waving, grasping trunks awaited her there.

Days passed before she had the courage to try again.

~~~~~

"YOU are Golub, a first-generation Lox of Barsk. Your time in life has long since ended; you are now as you were in life, but not alive. In this, a world of my own making, I bid you welcome."

This time her conversant was male, naked, and to her horror aroused. She'd drawn him from his most recent nefshons; had he died while having sex? He cradled his head in both hands and looked at her through red-rimmed eyes. "Grandma's tusks, what did you put in my drink, woman?"

"I'm a Speaker. You're dead."

"Oh. Really? Huh. I guess that explains it. I didn't think this house had any Lutr girls. A shame. I hear your people are really flexible."

Lirlowil flinched. She'd found the Fant because of his sordid exploits. Born on Barsk shortly after its colonization, he had left to visit his parents' birthworld, Marbalarma, and then spent the next thirty years bouncing from planet to planet, recounting his travels in a series of flims. These had found an audience in some parts of the Alliance, generating enough revenue for the Fant to continue in ever more exuberant acts of tourism until the day he died in a particularly vulgar incident on Dawn involving an exotic courtesan and her employer.

With even more reluctance than with her first attempt, Lirlowil slipped into his mind and went searching. His knowledge of drugs was extensive, but only with regard to the variety and palatability of recreational substances readily found off Barsk. Other than the diluted bits of koph that were part of seasonal celebrations during his childhood, he had no experience of the drug Krasnoi wanted.

She fled his mind and dissolved the summoning at speed. She'd not immersed herself as fully in this one's mind but nonetheless felt even more unclean.

~~~~~

LIRLOWIL filed her reports in unending detail for both encounters and received back both written praise as well as authorization to request a boon from off station. She asked for the impossible, hoping perhaps to gain some leverage when the promised gift never materialized. In this she was disappointed. The "impossible" took twenty days, but she awoke one morning to find an enormous globule of water floating in the middle of her bedroom. A squad of Patrollers had returned to Sharv, visited her family's homepond, and hauled away thirty metric tons of water.

Lirlowil had thrown off her nightclothes, pushed off from the bed, and dove into and through the water, emerging sleek and restored, feeling better than she had since she'd arrived. She shook off myriad droplets that formed almost perfect spheres in the room's null field. As she floated, grooming her dark, wiry pelt, the room's air system jetted the dropules back toward their source. Far from being defeated by her failed ploy, she took inspiration from it. If her captors could do the impossible, she would at least continue to try.

~~~~~

FOR her third attempt she'd immersed herself in propaganda written by a radical isolationist who had dedicated his life to severing all ties between his home and the Alliance. She hated politics and she had no patience for the ultra-serious, wide-eyed dreamers who wanted to change your world whether you wanted to live with those changes or not.

"You are Emil, an Eleph of Barsk. Your time in life has long since ended; you are now as you once were but not alive. In this, a world of my—owww!"

As soon as he'd taken form, Emil had somehow slapped aside the telepathic tendrils that Lirlowil had reached toward him.

"What? I'm not dead. This is a trick. Get out of here. Your kind aren't allowed."

"My kind?" How had she already lost control of the conversation.

"Your high and mighty furred kind. Isn't that how you exclude us? Because we're not covered in hair? Well, fine, we neither need nor want you either. Away with you!"

She reached for his mind again, and found her probe batted aside as before. Did he have some innate defenses? Emil didn't seem aware of her attempts.

"I don't plan to linger, believe me. But I have to ask you some questions—"

"I have nothing to say to you! Begone!"

"Look, I'm a Speaker and you're dead. This ends when I choose to end it, not before. So stop giving me grief and we'll get done that much sooner."

The Fant glared at her. "You want to see grief, I'll show you grief."

His trunk pulled back and to the left, then swung at her head. Lirlowil ducked in the other direction but the attack had been a feint. Not so the fist that came at her from the other side and struck her in the face.

It was as if the nefshons under her control shattered and exploded. Or maybe she'd just been blinded to them. Either way, she was back in her room, the summoning ended. It hadn't been real but her face ached for days all the same.

She'd gotten nothing from him, filed a report of her failure, and returned to her research. Nine days later she was ready to try again.

~

HER fourth attempt went more smoothly. "You are Tral, a Lox of Barsk. Your time in life has ended; you are now as you were in life, but not alive. In this, a world of my own making, I bid you welcome."

"Oh. Hello. We're doing this again? Wait, you're not my son."

The Fant had taken form quicker than most, and his minimal confusion confirmed Lirlowil's suspicion that he'd been summoned before.

"No, I'm not. But he wrote a lovely biography about you that let me summon you." She reached into his mind and began her search.

"Did he? I didn't know that. He's always writing, that one. Even as a boy. Not a real livelihood, I told him, but what child ever listens to his parent, am I right?"

She found extensive knowledge of Barsk flora in his mind, but all of it involved tapa and other sources of material for tailoring, which made sense for a garment maker. Of pharmaceuticals in general and koph in particular, Tral knew less than nothing.

Although the most civil and benign of her Fant conversants, he was nonetheless still a large and ugly monster. She concluded yet another useless summoning and sent the man away.

Lirlowil filed this fourth report as she had the preceding three. Appended to it was, once again, her insistence that such haphazard summoning of Fant was almost sure to be unproductive. She had a response the next day. They thanked her for her continued struggles, as they had three times before, and encouraged her to resume her efforts immediately. Lirlowil put this latest document, covered with the signatures of unrecognizable names, in her desk with the others.

Beyond melancholy, she also knew that no display of melodrama would accomplish anything. Krasnoi and the Patrollers who held her captive only cared for results. She was nothing more than a tool to them. Lirlowil didn't need to probe their minds to understand they would leave her there to succeed or die trying. She had no intention of dying in a converted warehouse in orbit above a world of misshapen freaks. The past four attempts had convinced her of the worthlessness of her research materials.

If she was to have any hope of finding a summonable Fant with the information her captors wanted, she had to reshape the problem and see it in a new way. She'd been pairing the traditional methods of Speaking with the radical technique of her telepathy. What would it mean to approach things from a novel stance? There were rules, set in place by the very first Speaker—a Fant, naturally. A glimmering of an idea began to form in Lirlowil's mind. She was certainly no stranger to breaking rules . . .

FIVE

RECIPROCAL REFERENCE

~~~~~~~~

THE first diffusion of dawn's light through the Civilized Wood had reached Jorl's home and begun to warm the buds of sartha that a well-meaning friend had planted beneath the window of his sleeping room. All too often the heavy fragrance wafting in would cause him to fall back asleep. As a result, he often missed his early appointments. But not today. He'd awakened in the night, following the fragment of some dream and moved to the writing table in his study. For hours he'd been lost in his revision of a troublesome section of text, a comparative analysis of the significance of the Compact from the point of view of the first generation members of the Archipelagos' Council.

He'd started the project in the last days of the dark season, when the constant cloud cover of the sky thickened in a layer that removed the distinction between day and night. The seasons turned as they always did, dark giving way to storm. The rain increased eightfold. Continuous thunder and ubiquitous lightning made long stretches of indoor work more desirable. Jorl had fled the fury of the season and performed day after day of Speaking, summoning and interviewing each council member.

He'd completed that portion yesterday and celebrated by visiting the little bookshop down the boardway from his home. He'd allowed himself to be distracted by the pretty clerk who always flirted with him, and if he came away with a few more volumes than he'd intended, well, where was the harm?

Then he'd set to work writing it all up. It should have been an inspiring document, but the minutia of those days, all the pointless details from the perspective of history that had seemed so critical to the men and women living them moment by moment, dragged it down. Jorl frowned and started again. After the third rewrite of the opening pages it still felt dull as mud. With a grimace and a nervous fan of his ears Jorl pushed away from his work table.

He sighed and then inhaled deeply. The scent of the sartha came to him from his sleeping chamber and he toyed with the notion of returning to bed, if only for a short nap. The resounding crash as his study's shutters burst open chased the thought from his head. He leapt from his chair to see Pizlo landing in a blurred tumble, all arms and legs and trunk, in the center of the room. The boy wobbled and rolled a bit, finally coming to rest almost at Jorl's feet. He shook his head once, seemingly none the worse for wear, and smiled up at Jorl.

"Have you had breakfast?"

Jorl attempted his sternest look while secretly welcoming an excuse to ignore his revisions. "No, I have not. But you should know, I only share breakfast with guests who present themselves properly, and request permission before entering my home." He studied the child. Pizlo's pale white flesh bore any number of scratches and minor wounds, but none of them were fresh or in need of attention. The only thing out of place in this out of place child was a greenish blob of paint on his forehead.

Pizlo grinned, "I don't need permission. All doors are open to me. I have an aleph," and he pointed at the paint.

Jorl fought back a smile. He'd been expecting this conversation for some time. "Oh really?" he inquired. "And what three achievements of yours entitle you to such a distinction?"

The boy's delight in himself withered a bit. He rubbed at the paint and glanced at his hand. Nothing had come off. He bit his lip as if in thought and then took a bold stance, arms akimbo, and stared up into Jorl's eyes.

"Three things? Why . . . you know, the usual three, the same way that all of us do it. Same as you."

Jorl went to the adjacent kitchen's small cupboard and took out an assortment of fruits and nuts before returning to Arlo's son. He beckoned Pizlo over to the table, setting the bowl down while he took his seat again, and helping himself to a large plel. Pizlo took hold of the wastebasket by the desk, upended it, and used it for a stool as he settled in and began working his way through the bowl of food.

"The thing is, it's never the same three. At least, it never has been. No two Aleph-Bearers have ever been marked for the same reasons." Jorl finished the plel, and looked for the wastebasket to spit out the seeds, recalled its recent transformation, and spat them out the newly opened window instead.

Pizlo seemed thoughtful, or perhaps it was just that he was busy eating. Jorl had never known a child with so much energy, or one who could eat so voraciously. Already the bowl was all but empty. Even so, he suspected Pizlo had already eaten breakfast this morning. At least once.

Amidst mouthfuls he said, "I got mine because of my insect collection. It's the best one in Keslo!"

"No doubt," agreed Jorl. Pizlo spent most of his days and nights out of doors, making his own trails in the spaces that surrounded the Civilized Wood and doubtless venturing down to the Shadow Dwell far below. Tolta had set aside an entire room to house his collection of several thousand specimens; it was one of the ways she lured him to come for an occasional dinner or spend an infrequent night sleeping in an actual bed. "But that is just one accomplishment. You need to have two more."

Pizlo took in this new information, digesting it slowly while he chewed on the remaining plel. Only after he had finished the fruit did he cock his head. "I . . . I can swing real good. On vines. That's how I flew in through your window!" He beamed at Jorl and waved back at the window as evidence of his qualifications.

"Fair enough, but that's still only two. Perhaps you should wash that paint off and go back to asking permission to come in, at least until you manage a third appropriate accomplishment." Jorl took the boy by the hand and led him to his utility closet in search of a rag and some solvent.

After they'd removed the paint, Pizlo asked Jorl to take a walk with him. He agreed, but only after insisting that the child exit by the door and not back through the window. They strolled along the boardways, the morning warming around them. The reactions of the other Fant they passed varied depending on whether they saw Jorl or Pizlo first. Friendly greetings trailed off to silence. Smiling faces turned cold and looked away. Some just stopped in their tracks, jaws slack, trunks limp, as they tried to make sense of a prestigious Aleph-Bearer out for a stroll with a non-person. Pizlo didn't appear to notice; they were no more a part of his world than he belonged to theirs.

The pair made their way along one of the less traveled routes and paused at a balcony that looked out on a hollow bowl in the green of the forest surrounding them, an open space that sometimes housed a suspended stage where students put on plays during the seasons of wind and mist. Pizlo leaned far out over the railing, glancing at other balconies above and below theirs. Jorl resisted the urge to grab hold of the boy and protect him from falling. He'd seen him climb before, and the likelihood was that Pizlo was as comfortable hanging there as Jorl would have been in his own bathtub.

"I may have a third."

"A third?"

Pizlo scowled, pulled himself back onto the balcony and sat at Jorl's feet. "A third thing. Only it's not the word you used before. Not an accomplishment."

"No? But it's something you've done?"

"Kind of. It's something I've always been able to do. I guess. I don't know why other people don't do it, but they don't."

Jorl settled onto the polished wood of the balcony floor opposite the boy. "Okay, tell me about it. What is it you do?"

"I talk to . . ." He stopped. It was an odd thing to put into words when none of the things that spoke to him actually used words. He tried again. "Sometimes I know stuff . . . stuff that other people can't know, or won't know, or don't know yet."

"Other people?"

"Yeah, like you and Tolta, and Arlo back before he died."

Jorl winced. He'd never once heard Pizlo refer to either of his parents as mother or father, only by their proper names. "What kind of stuff?"

"Stuff. A lot of it doesn't make any sense. Like, which way up a skipping stone will land if I pitch it into the waves. Or how many bowls of cereal I'm going to eat between now and the solstice. Or the best route and time of year to travel from Keslo to Emmt and avoid the crowds of wandering bachelors. Or how one day, you're going to circle the entire island. You know, stuff."

Jorl laughed. He took out his daypouch and withdrew several pieces of tart fruit, giving Pizlo his choice. The child grabbed one in each hand and greedily resumed eating. "What do you mean 'circle the island'?"

The boy tilted his head to one side, and tried again. "You know. You. Keslo. Circling it."

"Ah," said Jorl, still lacking any understanding. "Maybe it's something you dreamed?"

"Maybe. For some things. But not all of it. Not even most of it. Sometimes it's like something I read in one of the books you loan me, where the words tell me one thing but later, maybe days later, something else that the book didn't come right out and say, makes sense, but it still came from the book. Only it didn't. It came from me from having read the book. Only sometimes, for some of the things I know, there wasn't any book that started it, and I just know them. Like knowing how to get to places I've never been, and feeling as familiar as sitting here. Like, a couple days ago, I knew where I had to go to find a kind of bug that I'd never seen before. It was a place I'd never ever been, but when I went there, there was the bug. Stuff like that. Would that count toward getting an aleph?"

Jorl had been peeling a piece of citrus while listening. He popped a couple wedges into his mouth and shrugged. "It might, I really can't say. There's a council that travels from island to island and makes those decisions for everyone in both archipelagos. Maybe next time they come to Keslo you can ask them."

"They won't talk to me. They'll look right at me, but they won't see me. No one does."

Sighing, Jorl admitted that was probably true. Instead of replying, he offered Pizlo a few fruit wedges, which the boy took without pause.

They sat a while in silence, enjoying the tart, juicy flavor released as they chewed.

"What did you do?"

"To get the aleph? I didn't really do anything. I just went ahead with my life. When the council gave it to me I was as surprised as anyone."

"But what did you *do*?" Pizlo insisted, he squinted and stared at Jorl with obvious concentration.

"I was in the Patrol," said Jorl, pausing to lick the juice from his sticky fingers. "I joined when you were only a couple years old."

Pizlo glanced at his own fingers and mimicked Jorl, speaking around them as he dipped them one by one into his mouth. "It's more than six hundred years since anyone from Barsk served in the Patrol."

"Why do you say that? Is that one of the things you just know?"

The boy gave Jorl a hurt look. "No. I read it. In a book. One of your books."

"When was this? I don't remember you borrowing a book like that."

"You were out. Don't be mad, it wasn't one that you were using, I found it on one of your shelves and I put it back when I was done. You didn't even notice." Pizlo had the good grace to murmur this last bit in an apologetic tone.

Jorl hrumphed. "Fair enough. And you're right. It's a provision of the Compact; Fant are exempt from conscription."

"And the council marked you for that? On account it had been so long?"

"Not quite." Jorl paused to find the right words. "I came back because your father had died. Soon after, I discovered I was a Speaker. That's when the council gave me the aleph."

"But there are a lot of Speakers in the world. More than a dozen here on Keslo alone."

"You're right; we've had thousands since Margda, though I'm only the second Speaker to come after that got an aleph. Even so, the council counted that as one of their requirements for marking me."

"But that's only two!"

"Well, there was a third, but it's not really something I did." He leaned back against the railing, closing his eyes, the memory still very fresh.

Pizlo interrupted the reverie. "Who then? What was the third?"

"The third was something I'd studied back at university, from the writings of the Matriarch. At the time I never imagined it was about me. She's the one who invented the idea of giving people the aleph in the first place."

"A prophecy!" shouted Pizlo, causing Jorl to flinch.

"More like a footnote. The Matriarch had written a letter to tell future councils to expect someone, and to give him an aleph when they found him."

"How would they know who to give it to?" Pizlo's voice had grown quiet and dry, like a storyteller building tension.

"She wrote that there would be one who had gone out and come back, and who though of the present would look into the past. The council took that to mean leaving Barsk and returning, and being a Speaker."

"But that's still only two!"

"Yep, and here's the weird part. The Matriarch told them that those were the first and second reasons to bestow the aleph, and that the third reason was finding the person she wrote about. Kind of circular, but there you have it."

"So it really was a vision? Not just a letter she wrote and mailed into the future."

Jorl smiled. The life and times of the Matriarch had been the focus of his study back at university and occupied much of his professional life. "Technically, though it's not viewed as one of her more serious or bigger prophecies." He paused, his thoughts returning to his conversation with Arlo from days earlier.

"So, she knew things. Things other people didn't know. Did she write them all down, or did she keep some just to herself?"

"She wrote some of them down. She wrote a whole book about the visions that came to her when she had her seizures, and notes about what she thought each of them meant," said Jorl. "But was it everything she saw? How would we know? Maybe she kept some to herself."

"Can you ask her? You know, cuz you're a Speaker and all. Maybe she's got other stuff she wants to talk about now that she's dead and all."

"That would be something, wouldn't it? To actually sit down and have a chat with the Matriarch? But I can't do that. No one can. It's against the rules for a Speaker to summon anyone who was ever a Speaker."

Pizlo scowled again. "That's stupid. Who gave you that kind of rule?"

"Ah, well, that would be the Matriarch again. Maybe that's why she wrote down her visions, because she knew no one would be able to talk to her about them."

"Maybe. Maybe I should write down the stuff that I know. Just in case I ever become a Speaker, too. It could happen. Yeah, I'm going to do that. I'm going to start right now!"

With no further warning, Pizlo jumped up and pulled himself through a gap in the railing. He grabbed an underside support, balanced for an instant, and then dropped. Jorl rushed to his feet and leaned out, looking for the boy. He caught a glimpse of him, already far below, crashing through the leaves and branches at the bottom of the bowl, making his own paths, heedless of the damage he did to either his surroundings or himself.

SIX

ORDERS AND CHOICES

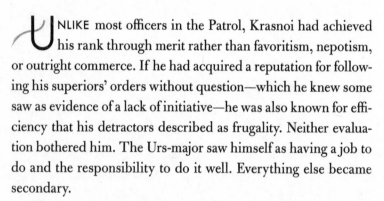

UNLIKE most officers in the Patrol, Krasnoi had achieved his rank through merit rather than favoritism, nepotism, or outright commerce. If he had acquired a reputation for following his superiors' orders without question—which he knew some saw as evidence of a lack of initiative—he was also known for efficiency that his detractors described as frugality. Neither evaluation bothered him. The Urs-major saw himself as having a job to do and the responsibility to do it well. Everything else became secondary.

Which is not to say that he didn't find some of the actions required by his assignments distasteful.

When Bish, a high-ranking senator, had informed him that he would establish a base on Barsk's uninhabited south polar continent, he had done so. As support personnel poured in, so, too, did documentation, including an annotated version of the Fant's cherished Compact. The Alliance spanned thousands of worlds, each with vast histories of treaties and documents, and as a rule Krasnoi left knowledge and facility of them to the politicians. But in situations where he expected to spend extended time on a planet, he took the time to brief himself on local policies and regulations.

He'd had a brief moment of conscience, wondering if his superiors had sent him unlawfully, and having ignorantly followed such orders if anything could be accomplished by crying foul now. But no, distasteful as it might be, that path offered no gain and only led to waste. It would not erase the illegal trespass, nor accomplish any good. Better to complete the mission with efficiency and move on. Having reached a decision, Krasnoi had put the matter out of his mind.

His command grew as season passed season on Barsk. Under the authority of the Bos senator, he visited several worlds to acquire needed or assigned assets for the work ahead. Work crews constructed a durable albeit temporary base anchored upon a century or more of hard-packed snow. The bored crew of the mostly automated orbital station had been reassigned to perform whatever tasks he deemed necessary. A Patrol vessel began making scheduled visits, bringing naked, aged Fant who variously claimed to be already dead or seeking some ordained demise. Supplemental staff, everything from cooks to guards to an interrogation squad, reported in as the mission's needs unfolded.

The interrogators had brought his thoughts back to his original concern over illegal orders. Personally, he loathed the Fant. Something about them, maybe their trunks, maybe their vast hairless bodies, made him truculent. He'd quickly given up attempts to engage any of his charges, after the first few encounters had left him belligerent regardless of the conversational content. He didn't like that about himself, and prior to the arrival of the interrogators—a squad of Badgers from Scrothe, a world on the barely habitable edge of the spectrum—he hadn't imagined anyone would. He hadn't met any of that race before, though he'd been aware of the stereotype of Taxi being anti-social. Even on long-established and well-mixed worlds, they kept to themselves. He stood now in front of the vid-wall in his office, watching a live feed as they practiced their craft on one of his captive Fant, an old woman whose sickly gray, wrinkled flesh elicited his own aggression.

It did more for the Badgers.

They circled around her, none standing more than waist-high to her. The Taxi took turns, not so much making inquiries as screaming questions at their victim. Before she could complete a response to one, another on the other side of the circle demanded an answer about something else. As Krasnoi watched, the Fant became disoriented, spinning in place to face and answer each current interrogator. After several minutes of this, she stopped responding at all. The Urs-major appreciated the strategy; what point when the interrogators obviously weren't listening?

The Badgers took it differently. They started over, the same range of questions about koph, what it was derived from, how it was manufactured, but this time they punctuated their queries with jabs from electrified batons!

The Fant resumed speaking, but no matter how forthcoming her responses, as Krasnoi watched the Taxi became anxious, or frustrated, or perhaps simply irritated with the quality of her answers. Each held a baton, each baton possessed an apparently limitless supply of charges. The Badgers unleashed these from behind the Fant, against calf or knee or thigh, occasionally reaching up to attack the stomach or back, making their victim whirl and spin all the faster. But always the smaller interrogators danced back out of reach of a rare swinging fist or flailing trunk, and always another of the squad darted in from a different direction with another baton.

In the end, the batons failed to elicit the desired answers. The Fant simply accepted the attacks as one more kind of pain, not so different than the aching cold or the smell of plastic that they all had complained of from their first days. After she had crumpled to the floor, either exhausted or unconscious, the Badgers had delivered a few more jabs before giving up and retreating from the room.

Some among the Fant referred to themselves as the Dying. Perhaps the harsh physical interrogation and torture dispensed by the Taxi counted as something the living suffered, making it just one more thing that the Dying could endure.

Was this Fant an isolated case or a representative one? Were the females more resistant than the males, the Lox more than the Eleph? Or did the interrogation fail because she simply didn't have the answers to the questions Krasnoi had been charged to pursue?

The Badgers had a yard full of prisoners upon which to test these questions. The Urs knew that none among the squad would be at all troubled that their tasks marked yet another violation of Barsk's Compact, the execution of another unlawful command.

A pair of Ailuros guards borrowed from the orbital station entered the room and dragged the Fant to her feet. Krasnoi shut off the vid. He put the details out of his mind but could not shake the brutal inefficiency of what he'd seen.

SEVEN

PARENTAL DISAPPOINTMENT

~~~~~~

OON after he became a Speaker, the quality of Jorl's dreams changed. The skills he developed in crafting a venue for his conversations were what his unconscious used every night to create the images of sight and sound and touch in his dreams, same as everyone. It was obvious, in hindsight, that as he became a better Speaker his dreams would become more vivid. So, too, his recurring nightmare.

He was back in the Patrol. Jorl knew he was dreaming because he remembered being sent home to Barsk soon to stand Second at Arlo's planting. He had to be dreaming because his friend hadn't yet died. He and his crewmates had arrived in a system beyond the edge of known space to perform a routine mission of cataloging and mapping. The Alliance wouldn't be seeding any colonies there. It wasn't a place where anyone could live comfortably; the only planets were gravitationally challenged gas giants, all too far away from their star. But a couple of these had moons, and one of these satellites looked like it might do. An outpost could survive, albeit only with regular supply drops. Unlikely ever to happen, but making that decision wasn't the purview of the mission, just data collection.

Missions change.

As Jorl's ship approached the moon for a closer look they heard the voice. A message originating where no one from the Alliance had ever traveled.

Kengi, the Myrm communications officer, looked up from her screens, her tongue tasting the air as she announced, "That was a targeted scan, Captain. Telemetry suggests the signal originates beneath the ice sheath." Jorl had wanted to like Kengi; her long and narrow snout bore the closest resemblance to a trunk of any of the races in the Alliance. That, more than anything, was probably the reason she'd distanced herself from him when he joined the crew.

From his duty station, he glanced at the Anteater and counted off the seconds before the captain replied. On a typical day, a full minute could pass. One learned to live with the delays when one's captain was a Sloth. Brady-Captain Hrum's quick response just confirmed he was dreaming.

"An automated signal? Something we've tripped? Seems farfetched. That ice must be thousands of years old. Morth, do you concur?"

Brady-Lieutenant Morth was the cousin of Hrum's sister-in-law, but a fine science officer despite the obvious nepotism that garnered him the best work shifts. "More like tens of thousands," he said, "I mark the origin point as a small hollow about half a kilometer down that might once have been a cave, back before the moon's magnetic pole last moved and everything got buried."

"Ah, the rigors of cataloging. Well, never let it be said that a little bit of frozen water deterred the Patrol from exploring a mystery." Hrum waved a long arm in a languid command. "Bring the beamers online. Drill me a hole wide enough to drop a shuttle through, even with that cave. Let's go see what's buried out there where nothing should be."

Jorl stood back from his station. Hrum always picked him for shuttle missions. Maybe it was just the tradition of scut work for the newest crew, and maybe not. The captain gave him a nod, and then to his surprise said, "I'll lead this one. Kengi, you come, too. Maybe we'll find some frozen bugs for you."

The Anteater rolled her eyes at Hrum's back, but rose from her station as well.

When all of this had really happened, Jorl had had to wait nearly an hour for the meticulous Morth to finish drilling a passage for them. In the dream, though, Jorl walked from the ship's bridge to the shuttle and then instantly exited the hovering craft out onto the edge of a cave mouth.

The icy floor of the cave gave way to irregular stone and then a level ceramic tile. The three crew all wore environment suits fitted to their differing physiques, though Jorl's helmet was easily twice the size of the others. Before putting it on, he'd had to fold his ears in on themselves three times. His suit lacked a sleeve for his trunk, requiring him to keep it wrapped around his neck like a muffler. All the suits included headlamps. The floor continued on into the cave beyond the range of their lights.

"Remind me to have a conversation with Morth about using relativistic terms like *small*," said Brady-Captain Hrum. Her short legs set a slow marching pace as they traveled deeper into the cave.

Only the tile floor was artificial. The regular shape of the cave suggested it had been created with an energy beam not unlike what they'd used to drill. The walls were native rock.

"By my uncle's tongue, what the heck is *that*?" said Kengi. A massive box blocked further passage.

Jorl stopped. "Could that be some form of life-support unit built to sustain whoever sent the signal?"

"If it is, they're doubtless long dead," said Hrum.

He couldn't squeeze past it on either side, but Jorl could see the depth of the thing. It stood nearly twice his height, a cube rather than a box. Boxes had lids. If this thing had an opening it had to be on the back end where they couldn't see. It was all gray metal and plastic and cloudy glass. In the beams from their headlamps Jorl could see *something* on the other side of the glass, slow swirls that danced with hidden meaning.

Kengi consulted her gear. "This is the source of the signal, but I can't tell you where the power is coming from or what's driving it. It just . . . is."

The captain waved Jorl over. "Lox-Ensign, stand in front of the thing and touch it."

"Sir?"

"Do I have to repeat myself?"

Jorl shook his head and followed orders. He pressed a palm flat against the glass surface of the cube. Another set of swirls began dancing. Before the captain could tell him not to he began following after them with the tips of his fingers, tracing their movement on the glass. Hrum grabbed him by the shoulder, yanking him backwards. Too late.

Lights came on, deep inside, shining through the smoky glass in more complicated patterns.

"I'm measuring an increase in power," said Kengi.

"Dangerous?"

"No, Captain, not at these levels. More like a system coming online. Whatever it is, we've woken it up."

The swirls rushed together behind the glass, forming a rough, humanoid shape, losing color until they were a dull black, like the shadow of someone of indeterminate race leaned against the glass on the inside regarding them.

"Gilgamesh," said the shadow or the wall, or maybe the cube.

"What?" said Hrum.

"I'm recording," affirmed Kengi.

"The Pendragon."

Jorl stared at the silhouette, mouthing the unfamiliar syllables.

"Kal-El."

The thing had a rich and resonant voice. Something in the rhythm or timbre of it suggested that Jorl and the others should recognize the words. He didn't.

"Boxes do not talk!" said Hrum, and Jorl saw her shiver. "Kengi, abort recording. Back to the shuttle, both of you. Double time!"

The first lesson Jorl had learned in the Patrol was about following orders. He fled. Kengi, despite the weight of her communications gear, outraced him. The cube continued to speak.

"I am these and more. I am the Archetype of Man and from slumber such as you have never known have I awoken. Speak, friend, and I shall hear you."

Bradys never hurry. Jorl saw panic in Hrum's eyes as she shouted commands through her comm unit. "Max us out the instant we're aboard! Full power to the beamers. Fire once we're clear. I want nothing but vapor where this cave is." Somehow, she ran past him.

The voice echoed after them. "I am the hero. I am the young warrior, the dreamer, the quest taker. I am the sum of mankind's symbol of this aspect of himself. I am the past sent forward."

The trio tumbled through the open portal of the waiting shuttle. Hrum slapped the control for an emergency close of the airlock and shouted to the pilot. "Fly!"

Jorl clutched at the portal latch for stability as the ship accelerated. He slammed against a bulkhead, banging an elbow hard. Hrum and Kengi both lost their footing and piled up against the closed portal. Kengi let out a squeak of pain as the captain's boot caught her in the back.

Morth's voice echoed through the shuttle as Jorl and the others righted themselves and settled into their seats. "Powering beamers, sir."

A flash of brilliance and the dream shifted forward several days.

Jorl stood at attention in Brady-Captain Hrum's ready room, eyes focused on the wall behind her head.

"Say what you have to say, Ensign. I have real work to do."

"Sir, it was my understanding that, among the missions of the Patrol, was the recovery of artifacts from the ancient times Before."

"And?"

"Surely the object we encountered qualifies."

Hrum paused, as was her way. She picked up a stylus nib from her desk and affixed it to the tip of one claw. She didn't bother to look up as she answered. "What object are you referring to?"

Jorl's ears fanned with anxious dread. "The object you ordered destroyed. Sir."

"That incident is behind us, Ensign. I suggest you let it go."

"I can't do that, sir."

"Ah? And what will you do instead then?"

"I've written up a report. My personal observations of the mission. I intend to send it in to HQ."

That made Hrum look up. A slow smile spread across her face, an expression Jorl had not thought his captain capable of. Another wonder followed. She laughed; long and slow, like only a Sloth can laugh. To his horror, she kept on laughing for several minutes, finally raising a hand to her face to wipe at her eyes.

As quickly as it had come, all amusement fled her face. Her

brows dropped and her jaw tightened, and Jorl found himself facing anger like he'd never experienced from his captain before. She rose from behind her desk, rumbling upward like an earthquake and advanced on him. He knew it was a dream, that the violence surfacing in the Brady couldn't actually harm him, but as he had in life and in every previous version of the nightmare he backpedaled until the office's wall stopped him. Despite her shorter stature, she pressed herself against the Fant, craning to shove her face up against his.

"We were never there, Dicknose, we were never there."

The dream shifted again, a flickering of scenes. Every other member of the crew coming forward with affidavits supporting Hrum's version of events. Hrum's report of a routine stop at an unmapped moon. Jorl's report coming back with a stamp of *unverifiable* and a black mark in his personnel file. And speaking faintly in the background of it all, its powerful voice sounding now like a helpless wail, the cube from Before, the past sent forward, lost to them now forever.

Somehow that loss was his fault. He could hear it in the ache of that thing's voice.

With a cry, Jorl struggled with his sheets and blankets to sit up in bed. He half expected to see the tiny cabin from his Patrol vessel. A hand went to his chest, the pounding of his heart threatening to burst through. The nightmare, again. Real as the waking world. It always filled him with a sense of his own limitations. Would the loss of the artifact seem so vast if he weren't a historian? Would the helplessness haunt him?

He hadn't caused the thing's destruction, and short of mutinying how could he have saved it? Should he, a mere ensign, have countered his superior's orders? Should he have relieved Brady-Captain Hrum of her command? Was he to blame?

The persistent recurrence of his nightmare suggested that he believed so, at least at some level. It had begun days after his return to Barsk, and his subsequent training as a Speaker had sharpened it. After the fifth repetition he'd sought the assistance of an oneirist, a respected Eleph who never asked him about the specific content of his dream but kept poking at him for what *he* thought it meant. He'd left her office more frustrated than when he'd entered. How was he supposed to know what any of it meant? It scared him witless, left him flinching for days. Episode by episode it had built an association between helpless and useless in his mind.

After the twentieth repetition he'd found the best solution to be simply getting on with his work, let the sense of helplessness stay behind in the dream by focusing on his real productivity. Today would be no different. He had things to do, and they were too important to let the phantoms of his past delay them.

In short order he left his bedroom and set about pouring a mug of morning beer with koph. The familiar routine of preparing for a summoning calmed him. Finishing the beer, Jorl sat at his work desk, feet planted firmly, his chair turned toward the right where a comfortable guest chair had lived until Pizlo accidentally set it on fire the previous season. No matter, he remembered the chair quite well, and as the morning's nightmare so amply demonstrated, the strength of his imagination and memory could accomplish what came next.

The koph had begun working its way through his blood and into his brain. He became aware of and banished the golden blanket of his own nefshons. A moment later he imposed his will upon the universe, summoning particles of familiarity. He pictured a face he had known all his life, and softly murmured "Tral ben Yarva." His father's nefshons rushed forward faster than when he had summoned them before. Tral had been his test as a Speaker. Dead more than ten years, he had come when called. Even now, Jorl could not say who had found the reunion to be more of a surprise.

In his mind, Jorl's study was little different from the reality. Stacks of papers still cluttered his desk, albeit slightly different ones. Spent sticks of ink bamboo lay scattered alongside full cups of the things. Printouts and partially completed manuscripts, both heavy with marginalia lay piled on both sides of his chair. The still-mourned guest chair faced him, empty at first and then suddenly full with the figure of a Lox of late-middle age that appeared older still, folded in upon himself with weariness and too many years of illness. The man smelled of sea salt and recent rain.

"Hello, Dad."

Tral blinked. His ears flapped slowly, as if testing the air. His hands lightly touched his chest, his thighs. The nubs of his trunk feathered absently across the tips of his vestigial tusks. His eyes appeared rheumy, though Jorl did not recall seeing them so when last they'd met. But that was the point. This Tral had been drawn from his father's last living nefshons, from a time after he had set sail.

"Jorl . . . This is . . . this is your home. Why am I back on Keslo?" A moment passed. The confusion abated. "Oh. I'm already dead. And you're a Speaker now. I remember that. We've talked like this once before, haven't we?"

"We have. And I wouldn't have summoned you a second time if it weren't very important."

With a flick of one ear, Tral waved away the apology. "I can't recall seeing you look so dire. What has you so wound up? Does it have anything to do with that Otter girl?"

"Otter girl?"

His father shrugged. "I think she was. But, you know, I've only seen images. Willowy she was."

"When did you see a Lutr, Dad?"

"How am I supposed to know that? When did you talk to me last?"

"More than a year ago."

"Well, there you have it," said Tral. "Some time between then and now. She said you wrote a book about me, if that's any help."

"Why would she summon you? What did she want?"

"No idea. We didn't talk long or much. So, if it's not her, what has you bringing me here?"

Jorl flexed his trunk and remembered the conversation he'd planned. "A prophecy of the Matriarch that looks ripe to come true."

Tral gestured with his trunk at Jorl's forehead. "Is this the same one as you said got you that mark? My son, a Bearer and a Speaker. I wish I'd lived to see it."

Jorl blushed. He fanned his heated face with both ears and then shook his head. "No, something else. The details aren't important, but the information I need from you is."

"If it's in my head, then I'll happily share it. What do you want to know?"

"Some time after we last saw one another in life, you set sail, didn't you? Your passing was deliberate and sure, not some accident somewhere?"

"It happened just that way, Son, the way it does. Late one night I woke from a dream and knew my time had arrived. I closed up my shop and went around to see Belti. You remember her? Her middle daughter was always sweet on you though you never seemed to see it yourself. Anyway, I remembered she had an old boat she'd long since stopped using. I bought it from her on the spot. Filled it with some supplies, and set out with the dawn a day and a half later."

"And you reached your destination?"

Tral smiled. The rare expression tugged at Jorl's heart. The way one corner of his father's mouth pulled up more than the other, the gleam in the old man's eye, associated with too many wondrous memories of earning favor and pleasing him, the last time years before when he'd finished at university. He took a deep breath to clear his head, and realized he'd missed some of Tral's words.

"—the beach not long before you called me here. I'd just let the boat go. I'm right where I need to be, I know that, so I won't be needing it anymore. But that's all in your past, isn't it, Son?"

Jorl nodded. "Yeah, Dad. A decade and more. I just . . . I needed to know you'd reached your destination—"

"Have no doubt of it," interrupted Tral.

"—and I need you to tell me where it is," finished Jorl.

"You what? I can't do that."

"Dad, something's happened. I think one of the Matriarch's prophecies is coming to pass and it has something to do with Dying Fant who have sailed off on the last journey. I need to follow them. It's important."

"I'm sure you think so, but it's not for you to know. It's not the sort of thing you know until it's your time. And if it was your time, you'd know."

"You said you'd share what you know. Happily."

"Ask me something else. Something I can tell you."

"You *can* tell me, you're choosing not to."

Tral crossed his arms over his chest. His ears dropped defiantly. "You have a clear understanding of the situation. That's good."

"Dad, I didn't want to do this, but, you know I have an aleph."

"I'm dead, not blind. What of it?"

"So you have to tell me."

"I don't believe I do."

"Being dead doesn't relieve you of your culture. The bearer's mark grants him passage. No doors can be closed to him. He's free to go wheresoever he wills. That's the law of Barsk!"

"I'm not disagreeing, Son."

"Well, I choose to follow where you and other dying Fant have gone."

Tral relaxed in the guest chair. The smile returned to his lips but his eyes had lost that joyous gleam.

"Then go, boy. I'm not stopping you. Go ahead, sail off."

"Then you'll tell me where it is?"

"Of course not. I already told you I wouldn't. You're not stupid. You've never been stupid. Pay attention."

Jorl slapped at his own forehead, the aleph's glow faint, but steady. "You just said you weren't stopping me!"

"And I'm not. But I'm not going to enable you either. That mark means you can go where you please and no one can hinder you. It doesn't mean anyone else has to help you though. And I won't."

The two Lox fell silent. Jorl seethed, but Tral merely sat there looking bemused.

"This isn't *just* about the prophecy," said Jorl.

"No?"

"I'm not certain I'm even reading it right."

"Then what is it about?"

"I'm a historian. That's what I do and who I am. My area of specialization is Margda, and her prophecies are a part of that. I'm one of the top three scholars in that area. I've published some very highly regarded research. I'm good at what I do."

"Never doubted that," said his father.

"Yes, and being able to Speak just gives me another tool, and allows me to do things beyond the reach of most other historians. Can you appreciate that?"

Tral waved his trunk in agreement.

"And the aleph, I'm not the one who ever sees it, it hardly ever comes up, but it's also a tool, like Speaking. Right?"

"Still with you, Son."

"The current . . . situation, I'm the right person in the right place with the right set of tools to resolve it and get some answers. I have an obligation as a historian to do this."

"Huh. Well, I can't say I follow all of that, but I do see how important this is to you. Maybe even life changing."

"Yes, thank you. So you'll help and tell me what I need to know?"

"Nope. I already told you that. Leave off. This is important to you, I get that, but it doesn't change my mind. Doesn't matter how hungry you are but it won't make a sky rain soup."

"Soup?"

The old man gave a sheepish shrug. "Figure of speech. Look, I'm sorry you went to all this trouble for nothing."

With a grunt, Jorl hauled himself up from his chair to stand over his father. "It wasn't for nothing, Dad. But . . . my whole life, you never understood me. I know you tried, but we just never quite made it onto the same page."

"That didn't get in the way of my loving you, Son. Or of being proud of you. I was always proud of you."

Jorl sighed and let his eyes close. He nodded. "Yeah. Okay. Thanks for that. I, um, I'm going to let you go now, okay? Anything else you want to say?"

"Is your mother still alive?"

"She is."

"Take her some flowers. For both of us. It's probably been too long since you've visited. And when you do, mention you spoke to me, and tell her that even to my last day she was the most beautiful and amazing woman I ever knew. Can you do that?"

"Sure, Dad. Consider it done."

Jorl settled back in his chair and with eyes still closed let go of the hold he'd maintained on his father's nefshons. He began the task of actively dispersing them again and letting the mental landscape he'd crafted fade as well. When he was done he opened his eyes and started. Pizlo stood in the spot where his father had just sat, naked except for a pair of ragged shorts and a daypouch hanging across his torso by a braided cord.

"Who were you talking to?"

"My father." Jorl frowned. "How long have you been there? And why?" A shiver went through him. For all his kindness in other aspects of his life, had Tral been able to see Pizlo standing there, he'd have seen only an abomination. He'd have been horrified to learn such a creature came and went freely in his son's home.

The boy shrugged. "Not long. I wrote down some of the stuff."

"What are you talking about? What stuff?"

"The stuff I know that other people don't. But how do I know if any of them are *visions*?"

"Visions?"

"Like you said the Matriarch had."

"Ah, right. Well, it's not common, but it's certainly true that every few generations someone on Barsk will get glimpses of the world to come and know things that others do not. The Matriarch had that."

A brilliant smile spread across Pizlo's face. "Yeah, visions of the future. Like how she saw you would get an aleph. If I've got prophecies, maybe I'll get an aleph, too. Or something. You and Tolta are the only ones who talk to me. And Arlo did. But everyone else ignores me, and I don't suppose having a mark would change things."

Jorl waved the boy closer, picked him up and set him on his lap. "Probably not. And besides, prophecies are tricky stuff. It's only after that people recognize them as important. At the time they're spoken most people don't want to hear about them."

"Really? But aren't they truth?"

"Especially then. Truth is tough."

"Why? I mean, it's the truth. It just is."

"I think that's so, in the abstract, but none of us get to really know the abstract. We only know what we think."

"I don't understand."

"Well . . . do you think I'm a nice person?"

"Sure," said Pizlo. "But, I don't know a lot of people."

"That's okay. I do, and they all seem to think I'm okay. At least, the Fant I know do."

"You know people who aren't Fant?"

"I did. When I was in the Patrol, every other person was something else. And you know what? None of them saw the truth about me. I met Brady, and they acted like they didn't care one way or the other. I met Urs, and every one of them was belligerent to me, and to this day I couldn't tell you why. I must have met a dozen or more Cynomy, and they were always frightened of me. They all had a different reaction. I was the only Fant any of them had ever met. It didn't matter that I hadn't done anything to merit those reactions. They were all true, for them. It colored every interaction I had with every person during my time in the Patrol.

"I don't think I'd like to be in the Patrol. Is that why you left?"

"No. A few days after your father died I received a priority message. I'd been Second for him when your parents bonded. HQ had never been happy about having a Fant serve in the Patrol. For once the Compact's requirement about respecting Barsk cultural norms worked to their favor. A diplomatic courier vessel docked with my ship and by the time it delivered me here the ink on my discharge had just about dried."

Pizlo rubbed at his face with both hands, his pale skin so nearly translucent that Jorl could see the fine traceries of arteries and veins.

"So you're saying, people not only may not want to hear a thing that's true, that sometimes they make sure other people can't either?"

"Yeah. Not all people, and not all the time, but yeah. When Margda tried to share her earliest prophecies, they weren't well received by most of the people around her. After a while, she stopped telling people what she saw as truth, and just wrote them down for us to find later."

"But she told some people about some of them?"

Jorl nodded. "She did. I've Spoken to some of them. Friends and close confidants of her."

"Maybe one of the things I'll know is who I can tell things I know to."

"Maybe. But you should know you can share anything you like with me."

"And you'll keep it secret? At least for a while?"

Jorl lifted Pizlo from his lap and set him on his feet, gazing at the boy solemnly. "Your father was my best friend, for as long as he lived and beyond. And with one exception, we told each other everything and always kept one another's deepest thoughts in confidence. He's gone now, but it only seems right to give you that same vow. This may not make a lot of sense to you now, but I think we'll talk about it again, when you're older. It's part of that same connection. So, yes, anything you need me to keep to myself will stay with me."

"For real?"

"Absolutely."

"Even if it doesn't make any sense?"

Jorl smiled. "At the time they happen, visions rarely do. Not even to the people who have them."

"Oh. That really helps. Because some of the stuff I know about you that you don't know yet has me really confused."

"You know something about me?" Jorl raised a hand to cover his smile, recalling his own flights of imagination at that age, and growing wistful remembering the adventures he and Arlo had had performing secret missions throughout the boardways of the Civilized Wood, much to the consternation of both their mothers and the plethora of aunts, sisters, and cousins back home.

"Yeah. I told you before how you're going to circle all of Keslo."

Jorl nodded. "I remember. There's more?"

"Yeah. You're going to leave Barsk again."

"No, that's not going to happen. That's a promise."

"I know. You're not going to leave because you want to, but that doesn't matter. You're going to leave. But I don't know if you come back. I've been trying to find out, or figure it out, but I don't know yet." At this last, the boy's face had screwed up with emotion and he looked on the edge of tears.

Jorl slipped his trunk around one of Pizlo's ears and drew him closer. "Okay. Well, I can see that that was a big secret for you to carry around all by yourself. Now that you've told me, the weight of it isn't so much, right? But it's still a secret, so I'll keep it to myself. And if you're right, if it happens, I'll let you know that it came to pass. Sound good?"

Pizlo shrugged and pulled free of Jorl's trunk. He turned away, his face already cleared of sorrow. He began poking through a collection of jars on a shelf that in other days had sometimes held cookies. "Okay. Are you hungry? Because if you are, I could have a snack with you. So you don't have to eat alone, I mean."

Nodding, Jorl stood and headed to the pantry in his small kitchen. "It seems to me that one of the things you always happen to know is when I've replenished the larder." Pizlo had followed him in and seated himself on a stool at the breakfast counter. Jorl opened a container piled high with sweet leaves and put a generous couple handfuls in a bowl for the boy. He took a smaller handful for himself and absently stuffed it into his mouth. He chewed as he watched Pizlo devour the snack.

"These are my favorite!"

"That's what you say about everything you eat here."

"I know. And it's true each time. A person can have his favorite change, can't he?"

"I suppose, but doesn't that take some of the meaning of 'favorite' away?"

"Oh. Maybe. Or . . . maybe I mean it in a different way."

He laughed. "That's the same problem I have making sense of the Matriarch's prophecies. I think sometimes she uses words to mean different things than everyone else thinks they mean."

Pizlo swallowed the last of his leaves and held himself very still. "Yeah . . . that's how it feels. Sometimes. Oh! I forgot. I wrote one down for you."

He jumped to his feet and shoved a hand deep into the pocket of the daypouch strapped across his chest. He took out a ball of crumpled brown scrap paper, all the thick stiffness of it worn malleable as cloth. Holding it by the edges with both hands, he used his trunk to carefully smooth out the page on the counter. It was covered over with the immaculate tight characters that Jorl had begun teaching him from his very first lesson.

"This is one of the things you just woke up knowing?"

"Yep! I was having a dream where I was walking on a big map and counting all the islands of both archipelagos. The islands were the size of my feet! I made up a dance, back and forth over all of them. When the dance was over I had both feet on Keslo and I noticed a new spot, a tiny island that hadn't been on the map before. Except it always was. Except it wasn't. And when I woke up, I knew how to get there."

"And no one else knows this tiny island?"

"Not exactly."

"Which is it? People know it, or they don't?"

"Some people do. Only, they're all gone."

"Gone? Where?"

"Gone there." Pizlo pointed at the paper and pushed it toward Jorl. "It's the place where nearly everyone goes, but no one ever comes back."

Jorl parsed the riddle at once. He stared down at the scrap, not daring to believe, his eyes tracking the words that described leaving Keslo with precise directions for a destination several days away from the last islands of their archipelago. "When did you happen to know this, Pizlo?"

"I had the dream days ago. I didn't know what it was, and I forgot about it. But it kept coming back, and I kept forgetting it. I only wrote it down this morning because I had this other thing come to me."

"Other thing?"

"Yeah. I knew that you'd want to know about what came out of that dream. So I wrote it down because I didn't want to forget it again. It's a gift."

Jorl took the directions and moved back to his work desk and rummaged among the books there until he'd found one with a collection of holographic maps. Pizlo followed after, eyes wide and bright.

"I like maps."

"Boys your age almost always do. So, here's a map of the western archipelago."

"It looks like the map from my dream, only a lot smaller. Ha, I guess my map would be too big to fit in a book."

Jorl smiled. "Maybe in a dream book. But look, here's Keslo, where we are, almost all the way to the east. And if you go a little further, past all this open water, you reach the eastern archipelago. All the Fant in the world live in one or the other of these chains of islands. All the islands you danced on in your dream."

"Have you been to them all?"

"No, only about half a dozen. But a lot of men wander and see many more of them in their time. I guess I got that wanderlust out of my system when I left Barsk. But see here, in the middle of that empty water?" With one finger he traced a broad circle of ocean midway between the archipelagos.

Pizlo poked with his own finger, stabbing a spot near the top of Jorl's circle, closer to the equator than most of the islands. "That's where the place in my dream was, but I just see the empty water," said Pizlo.

"Me, too. That's because this place isn't meant to be on any map. Every Fant gets this one vision, Pizlo, of a place to go and how to find it. But they get it with a message that tells them they should go, and when. You didn't get that message, did you?"

"Nope. I just got the place. And the idea about how it's a place people go to but don't come back from. That's kind of weird, isn't it?"

"I can see why you'd think so. It's knowledge that normally doesn't come to someone so young. People learn how to go to this place when they're very old. It's where they go when it's their time to die."

EIGHT

VENUE AND VISION

~~~~~~~

LIRLOWIL preferred to take her koph as a tea. She inhaled the welcome smell of spiralmint, closing her eyes as the warm, dermal calm spread throughout her. Properly prepared, koph tea always provided a relaxing effect, whether one was a Speaker or not. The expense of the koph kept most from experiencing the luxury. She had stumbled upon her secondary talent as a direct result of her hedonistic ways and the eagerness of Sharv's government to fulfill her every whim.

As she drank deeper, relaxation led to a familiar disorientation and she became sensitive to another level of perception. She regarded a nefshon self-construct of herself, afloat in the null-gravity of one corner of her bedroom on the station. Her four previous summonings of Fant had begun this same way, but she took no comfort in that. As she performed the mental exercises and crafted the patterns of summoning, Lirlowil could not dismiss the inherent wrongness of what she was attempting. In eight hundred years of Speaking, only three rules had ever been imposed, an edict created back at the very beginning by Margda herself, the Fant who'd discovered the process. If successful, she'd not only break the very first of the rules, she'd rub their creator's face in the act at the same time!

Lirlowil pictured the Fant Matriarch. She knew her from flims, from archival projections, from myths, and from songs. Lirlowil keyed the mnemonic locks from her research, releasing every speech and anecdote and rumor and opinion by and about her target. Without direct experience of her conversant, her mind cast a wide net in its quest, gathering relevant as well as erroneous particles. It was a slower process, but in the end the nefshons would sort themselves. As with most of her previous summonings of Fant, she had the advantage of being close to Barsk; a vast portion of her target's nefshons lingered near and came at her summons.

Committed now, unable to stop, memories and emotions from Margda's subatomic particles buffeted her as they sought to resolve themselves under Lirlowil's guiding mind. She opened herself to them, needing them all to build as full and recent a simulacrum as possible. The small, withered, wrinkled body of her last days . . . an undying fascination with political power . . . her first view of the sky . . . the butterfly scar on the lower inside of her left ear . . . the flavor of walnut paste . . . the shudder of prophecy . . . the love for her father . . . the reflected glow of the aleph . . . the searing helpless pain of seizure . . . the oppression by the Alliance . . . anger at her own failures . . . watching dust motes dance in the light of a chimney's . . . allergic reaction to gnorb . . . welcome smell of spiralmint . . . delicate twining of trunks . . . the vision leading her to the creation of the Edict . . .

" '. . . these limits only I place upon you, that never shall a Speaker Summon a Speaker . . .' was that so restrictive a law?"

In the slow swirl beyond sight, Lirlowil gasped as Margda took on visible form more rapidly, more solidly, than she had anticipated. She wore a shapeless gray toga that stopped just short of her feet, belted beneath her considerable breasts, but otherwise unadorned. As if wearing anything even remotely more artful was out of the question for someone like her. As if her clothing were a statement not only about herself, but about the vacuous priorities of the Speaker who had summoned her. More, the elderly Fant stared back with an icy gaze, fully aware of her circumstances and showing none of the confusion the recently summoned always showed. She'd asked a question even before she'd arrived, and from the look on her strange, hairless face she awaited an answer.

Startled out of her intentions, Lirlowil fell back on established ritual. "You are Margda, first of the Speakers. Your time in life has long since ended; you are now as you were in life, but not alive. In this, a world of my own making, I bid you welcome."

The Fant snorted, whipping her trunk around abruptly and causing the Lutr to lean away. "So you're not the complete renegade, are you? Some of the teachings you still follow."

Indignation caused Lirlowil to narrow her eyes and protest. "I've been fully vested and certified by the Alliance's Speakers' Bureau." Her conversant only snorted again.

"Don't start in with me about your precious bureau, Child. They only know to teach what I taught them. I endured endless days shut away with their best people in a boardroom on a spacecraft bobbing on the ocean because they couldn't be troubled to come to my home and possibly encounter other Fant. And I wouldn't leave the planet. Oh how they squirmed, torn between their hunger to understand the techniques and capabilities of Speaking and their loathing for a member of a race they'd gone to such lengths to hide away."

Lirlowil swallowed hard. Truth enough, she found this Fant—all Fant—beyond disgusting; it had never occurred to her how the objects of that revulsion might feel about it. But the flicker of compassion didn't last. Her own discomfort at being lectured to by a conversant, especially a Fant conversant, pushed her back on the offensive. "You should feel honored that they've respected your teachings."

"Which is more than you did, eh, edict-breaker? Congratulations! Of the tens of thousands of Speakers in the centuries since I wrote those rules, you're the first to violate any of them. I knew you would, but it feels very good to be vindicated."

"How could you know?"

Her conversant's face contorted into what might have been a smile, though with that hideous trunk of hers it was hard to be sure. She brought a hand up and tapped a thick finger against the side of her head. "I know you know my life's story. You summoned me here, after all. Surely you didn't discount my long history of mental illness. Imagine what I might have accomplished in my time if I hadn't been held back by madness and seizures. Though, to be fair, they also provided me glimpses of the future. Glimpses of you, my dear. I only instructed those fools so they in turn would create their little bureau and train you. I only created the rules of the Edict because I needed you to come along and break the first one."

"Wait, you're saying you *knew* I would do this? Hundreds of years before I was even born?"

"I knew someone or some thing would precipitate a crisis. Are you responsible for the Silence? No, of course you're not. You're just a piece on the board, not the game's player."

"What game? You're nothing but a crazy old woman who died

ages ago. You didn't foresee any of this. That's just a side effect of the same paranoia you had when you were alive."

"I'm here, aren't I? And it's not paranoia when every other living being off your homeworld who knows your name would be happier if you'd never existed." Margda turned away then, stepping around the room on her enormous feet. Her head pivoted back and forth as if she were examining everything in careful detail. With a start Lirlowil realized that her conversant walked, not bounced or floated, but walked, despite the absence of gravity.

"What a strange place you've brought me to," the Matriarch said softly. "Do you know, I have never been in space before. I wouldn't let them lift their ship when I was aboard. Made them leave it just offshore. Everything here feels just like that ship. It's all . . . made. And too small. Lifeless. Not at all like a world. Not like my world."

Lirlowil sneezed. There was a fragrance in the air, faint but undeniable, woody and green, and no part of the recycled air the station provided. Wrinkling her nose, she watched agog as Margda moved through the room, held down by a gravity that shouldn't have been there. Having satisfied herself with her inspection of the various shelves and objects on the walls, she approached the large sphere of pond water occupying the room's center.

The Otter followed, organizing her questions and marshaling her telepathic powers. The Fant completed a circuit around the watery globe. She turned back to her Speaker and smiled. Lirlowil hesitated, breathing in deeply through her mouth. This wasn't proceeding like any summoning she'd ever performed. The odor in the room had increased, and now included the scent of impending rain. Margda meanwhile had raised one wrinkled hand and reached out to touch the glistening surface of the water. As her fingertips made contact, gravity returned to the globe and its shape collapsed. Water crashed to the floor and rushed outward in a great wave that swept Lirlowil beneath it.

~~~

AS she opened her eyes to darkness, Lirlowil knew she'd been unconscious. Something had gone very wrong. A traditional summoning would have ended, the efficacy of the koph long since passed from her physical body and normal consciousness returned whether she willed it or not. That hadn't happened. In the reality of the station, she floated in the null field of her room, her body in a vaguely seated position, though her limbs hung lax, her muscles flaccid. Her eyes gazed languidly at nothing and her jaw had fallen open. She bumped from one wall to another, driven by the faint jets of the room's air system. She moved with excruciating slowness, but as she was completely unaware of it, it hardly mattered. Eventually, after many rebounds and continued drifting, she would pass into the globule of water in the middle of the room, and either recover or drown.

"You still don't understand, do you?" hissed Margda. "Silly child, haven't you ever thought it through?" The voice moved around her and Lirlowil tried to orient upon it. It seemed at once to be near and far, above, below, within, beyond. She paddled against the water, far more water than should have been around her. Her head broke the surface but still all she saw was darkness. Nothing of her bedroom remained.

"Only those with intelligence, with souls, emit nefshons. What then, my fuzzy little Speaker, is the stuff of the setting created for yourself and your conversant?" Lirlowil trembled. Margda's voice seemed to be whispering to her from inside herself, as if the faint exhalation of her words could be felt upon her skin.

"It comes from your mind, dear Otter, from your desperate need for order and structure. It is the Speaker who imposes reality upon this realm, forcing her own perceptions of dimension and texture into the summoning. It is all an illusion that you provide, because mortal minds find comfort in the familiar, concrete settings."

"Then . . . where . . ." stammered Lirlowil.

"Where are we? Or, where did your room go?" Margda sounded like she was smiling.

"Both. Either. I don't understand . . . I summoned you! How can this be happening?"

And there was light. It came into existence as though it had always been there, Lirlowil's eyes already adapted to the level. A breeze laden with a faint resinous aroma and heavy humidity made her whiskers twitch. And gravity. Lirlowil found herself standing now, her feet flat against a broad wooden floor which in turn was part of a larger wooden room. Wall hangings composed of an impossible number of shades of green surrounded her. The Matriarch of Barsk sat on a large polished knob of wood that seemed to grow out of the floor.

"Welcome to my home, little Otter. I don't suppose it exists any more, but I remember it well enough." The Lutr gawked, even as she realized she was acting like a newly summoned conversant herself. If the Fant noticed she gave no indication and instead continued her oration. "But, to answer your question, it happened because I wanted it to. And it is my desire, not yours, that shapes things here."

"But you said it was the Speaker who controlled the environment."

"Yes, and so it is, when the Speakers' laws are followed. But you broke the first rule of our Edict and summoned another Speaker. There are consequences that you must deal with."

"So . . . if someone, another Speaker, were to summon me, I'd be able to do . . . this?" Lirlowil's thoughts tumbled over themselves, rearranging her understanding of her profession.

Margda stiffened on her seat. Her pallor darkened, her wrinkled skin grew drier and older. All semblance of life drained away. As Lirlowil watched, the Fant transformed into a withered husk as the centuries since her death caught up. Moments later, speckles of green appeared on the remains of her skin and quickly spread. A coating of moss, as fine as an infant's fur covered her. It thickened. Tiny leaves emerged here and there, followed quickly by stems, which in turn unfurled and blossomed with flowers. The limbs of the Matriarch's aged corpse cracked, revealing bare wood. Twigs emerged, swelled, and grew into tree limbs. The gray toga tore as the Matriarch-turned-tree stretched it beyond the shapes of a mortal body, removing the last vestige or hint that a person had ever sat there.

Lirlowil could only gape in silence. This wasn't possible. Even in the construct-space of a summoning, it could not be.

"Do you really imagine it likely that anyone would ever have interest in summoning you?" Lirlowil whirled as Margda's voice came from behind her. "Besides, there's a part of you that insists reality follow the same parameters it always has, even here. That attachment to the way things work in the living world precludes this kind of manipulation. I, on the other hand, had the privilege of spending a good portion of time, when I was alive, in the paroxysms of my own insanity. Rather liberating, in its own way."

Lirlowil reeled around, then back again, glancing from flowering tree to long dead conversant, and back. And then she fainted.

"Damn," Margda sighed. With a mental gesture she unmade the tree that had so unnerved her summoner. With another she caused the Lutr's body to float once more, move across the room, and settle on the cushions of the window seat that looked out on the warm green of a time long past. "Poor child. I didn't think to shock you quite so much. Ah, but it's nice to know that even dead I can still learn new things. Who would have thought a nefshon construction could lose consciousness?"

NINE

A VOICE OF SILENCE

~~~~~~~~

EVEN while he'd been wailing, a part of Rüsul had heard every word the Cans had spoken. They'd called it a cell but it felt more like a box, like a giant version of a plastic cube that he had seen as a child when his island's mayor had received a misaddressed shipment from the Alliance's Committee for Cultural Exchange. He could no longer recall what it had held, but the plastic container had captured his imagination like some inanimate monster that lived in a child's night terrors.

His cell wasn't all that larger than the near-forgotten shipping crate of his youth. It was tiny, not quite as small as the water closet in most bachelor homes, but it felt like it was, lacking either purpose or window or anything that might be reassuring or familiar. What kind of people would put the Dying in a box? What kind of people would keep the Dying from their appointment with death? Rüsul couldn't tell how long he'd been held captive. Without weather, how could there be time? Without the thrum of life in wood and rain, how could existence continue? The light from the box's ceiling and walls was constant, and though dim its harsh white stung his eyes. The walls stank of plastic. The flooring stank of metal. A container of slop had appeared soon after his incarceration. They might have meant him to believe it to be food, but it had a similar chemical odor as the walls and just as easily could have been intended as paint to cover the plastic. Rüsul was more inclined to use it for the latter, but he lacked a proper tool for its application and couldn't bring himself to touch the stuff with fingers or nubs. He certainly wasn't going to eat it until hunger drove him to desperate measures. Fortunately, the oppressive plastic stench all around him suppressed his appetite.

He huddled in the middle of the box, succumbing to a claustrophobia he hadn't known he possessed. His heart raced like it wanted to lunge from his clammy chest. He couldn't still the wild trembling of his ears or the shivering of his trunk. It wasn't just the unnatural substance of the walls, or even the dry air that tasted like nothing at all. The panic coursing through him came from the shattered promise his world had made with him, that once he had launched his raft and set out to die he would never after be enclosed by anything but the walls of the world itself. The horrific setting exacerbated the anxiety, but he would probably have felt a lesser kin of it had he been forced to stay back home in his studio, or anywhere in any island's Civilized Wood. The time for such things had passed, but he had been pulled outside of time.

Rüsul strove to occupy as small a footprint of contact with the metal flooring as possible, equidistant from the box's four walls. He kept his eyes squeezed shut against the painful light, and rocked in place, wishing he had a chock of wood in one hand and a familiar knife in the other, just to lapse into the ritual comfort of carving and calm the beating of his heart. Rüsul had spent his entire adult life shaping wood, setting up shop in the Civilized

Wood of one island or another for a few years until the need to see newer faces sent him on his way again. It had been a good life, making art and making friends, and he had no regrets. But it was over and done. He was Dying now. Everything came back to that, and he could not wrap his head around it. Why would anyone interfere with it?

He rubbed at his eyes, red and aching. His throat was sore and his trunk felt raw, but other than chasing his captors away, his wailing hadn't accomplished anything. He didn't want to stop, but he just couldn't physically cry any longer. Worse, he couldn't catch his breath. Rüsul knew he'd been hyperventilating for some while now. His heart hurtled toward exhaustion and a kind of escape. His feet hurt like he'd climbed down to the Shadow Dwell and back up, over and over. And he had the grandmother of all head-aches pounding away with the kind of persistence only a grand-mother could muster.

This last discomfort began to overpower the others. It expanded down from his head, reaching throughout his neck, down into his shoulders and chest, a low, dull thrumming that was more than the sound of his blood rushing within him or the pump-ing of his own heart. The beat was rhythmic. It held a pattern, one that felt as old and familiar as the pain in his joints, or older still, hearkening back to a time long before the aches of age. And odder still, as he paid it more attention, he discovered the throb-bing existed outside himself.

Rüsul opened his eyes, blinking away tears. He moved his empty hands in the motions of carving, trying to center himself and halt or at least slow his rapid breathing. The stupid light of his box was just stupid light, and his hands knew his art well enough to do their work in dark and storm. He had no need to make the light mean anything more than a pesky circumstance, like a neighbor's newborn testing out a healthy set of lungs while he tried to work. He shaped empty air with a nonexistent blade and calm settled upon him. His eyes closed of their own accord, his own lungs settled into a relaxed pace. The throbbing in his forehead continued even as the other complaints and outcries of his body began to fade into the background. It came into focus, not a headache at all, and not coming from his head but only resonating there in that space between his eyes and above the root of his trunk. It played in him like he was a living soundbox, a sensation both familiar and impossible to place.

With his eyes still closed, Rüsul rose on unsteady knees. He turned from the waist, rotating his chest and shoulders back and forth in as wide an arc as he could. He leaned back, keeping his jaw pressed down against his chest, and presented the broad surface of his face to the walls of the box his captors had put him in. There. It was coming from that direction. He pushed up, onto his feet, dragging them in tiny steps toward one wall, stopping when his forehead touched the plastic surface. He recoiled half a step, arms lax at his side, letting the fullness of the thrumming beat enter his head and travel through his body.

In that moment Rüsul forgot his own pains. He heard, he felt, a meaning in the faint but persistent pounding. It was a rhyme of changing pressure, a child's game as universal as green leaves and falling rain. One would hide and the others would search and whosoever discovered the hidden child would in turn hide and the game continue, on and on. In the opening spaces of his skull, Rüsul felt the refrain he'd not made for almost ninety years, the faint pounding of infrasonic signals, *where, oh where, play fair, be there,* over and over again.

He opened his eyes. A slight turn of his head, to first one side and then the other, assured him he had targeted correctly. He leaned in, pressing his head against the wall, no longer caring about its alien plastic or the light or the closeness of his box. Somewhere beyond this wall, close enough to be felt, another Fant called out in the wordless way that children had used to tease their playmates, or when lost to cry out for their missing parents. Rüsul was not alone.

The decades of adult life dissolved in his mind. From dusty, untraveled corridors of memory he grasped after knowledge and skills untouched since childhood. The rules and rhythms of the games flittered on the edge of knowing, like a word dancing just out of reach on the tip of the tongue. After a few false starts, they came to him, each fragment trailing other memories and pieces until he had enough. His eyelids drifted down once more and with long forgotten ease he flexed and pulsed out the prescribed reply. *Hiding . . . Abiding . . . Will you be confiding?*

Over and over again he sent out the rhythms, more a well-learned pattern than actual words. He repeated it twelve times in all, as required by the game, lest he be forfeit. The idea struck him as so absurd he almost giggled and had to start again. Almost.

With his first pulse, the other Fant's infrasound had stopped. As Rüsul completed his cycle he felt a probing, meaningless pulses pushed out by the other in a rush of echolocation. A flush of relief and comfort washed over him like he hadn't felt since he'd wandered away from his mother as an infant and found her questing pulse before he had a chance to wallow in his own panic. And then, clearer, no doubt aimed directly at him as he had locked onto the position of the other Fant, as welcome and rare as sunshine upon his face, the classic reply:

Free . . . Free . . . Tree and me . . . Free . . .

Rüsul slipped to his knees in silence. The enormity and horror of his capture fell away. He thrummed back a reply of *Free* . . . even as he allowed the shock and fatigue to claim him. As he plunged into unconsciousness his face relaxed into a smile. He was not alone.

TEN

MOONLIGHT

LIKE some over-ripened piece of fruit dragging down the branch of its birth, Pizlo hung from the penultimate level of the forest canopy, dangling in the emptiness that was Arlo's Chimney. Slimmer and straighter than any of Keslo's other open air monuments, the shaft that bore Arlo's name also commemorated the path he'd taken as he'd fallen from a tiny platform above the canopy. Wreathed in fire, his plunge had burned a passage all the way through the Civilized Wood and into the Shadow Dwell. The shape of that trajectory had been smoothed in the transformation to art. The width of the shaft now averaged twice the height of a Fant. The inner surface had been planed into six evenly sized walls that turned like a lazy hexagonal helix, completing ten rotations as it ran from top to bottom.

Pizlo had come not out of sentimentality, but rather at the beckoning of his personal oracle. The sense of it had begun days ago, a gentle urging of where and when that had grown in insistence even as he prepared himself. Night had fallen before his arrival, smothering the limited, diffused glow that reached the spot at the height of day. And despite the direct route of the shaft, he was too far up for any illumination spilling from homes in the Civilized Wood below. But darkness suited him. He knew his surroundings, every plant, every branch, every vine, with a surety that did not depend on traditional senses.

He had rigged a sling to hold himself precisely where he needed to be, equidistant from the six green walls, not quite supine, gazing up to the top of the shaft at an opening as black as everything else. Long before morning, Pizlo would be gone, leaving no indication that he'd ever been here.

He waited. Swayed. His trunk grasped a supporting vine of the sling and leveraged his angle a few degrees, easing an unfelt strain on his neck as he stared up into darkness. Rain had fallen down the shaft when he'd first arrived and set up, but it had since stopped as he knew it would.

A buzzing cloud of winged insects took advantage of the break in weather and rose from below, attacking a colony of flightless bugs that had emerged from a hollowed knot of a kalatma tree on one face of the shaft just above Pizlo's height. The defenders beat back most of the invaders, shredding their wings with brutal swipes of barbed and edged forelimbs. Bodies hurtled downward as a warning against future attacks. But some few of the fliers, maybe one in twenty, profited from their comrades' sacrifice and swept past the other bugs to bite into the tap of the kalatma. They drank deep of the sap. As their abdomens swelled with fluid, each began to give off a pinprick-sized vermillion glow, taunting the defenders who turned to repulse them too late. The bloated, surviving fliers pushed off, formed a small, glowing cloud, and began to drift back down the shaft. They paid no attention to the young Fant hanging in their midst.

Pizlo lurched in his sling. He thrust both arms into the cloud, hands curled into two cups that he brought together, capturing some of the insects. Squirming, he unstopped a gourd that hung from his waist, curling his trunk around the neck to hold it steady as he transferred most of his prize. His collection had twenty-seven varieties of insects that glowed under one or another circumstance. He'd study this latest addition after he crept into Tolta's house for breakfast. He kept a few of the fliers, coaxing them into a single closed fist as he restoppered the gourd with the newly freed hand.

Nearly time. Whatever event had required him to be in this place at this moment sang in him. Pizlo wanted to mark it somehow and tightened his fist, bringing it up to beat once against his chest. Then he flung his hand away, fingers wide. The crushed bug bodies disappeared into the night. Their passing left an amorphous glow on his outstretched hand, enough light to mark the return of vision amidst the darkness. He stared at this palm, eerie and orange in the emptiness of Arlo's Chimney.

As if signaled by his light, the clouds above parted. A moon shone down from directly overhead, small enough that the edges of the shaft framed it. Its light poured in, filling the shaft. Pizlo cried out, his weak eyes the only source of pain in his world. He held his stained hand high, part offering, part protestation, as he understood what had brought him here. The moon itself had called out, not specifically to him, but to any who could hear it. And he had heeded the call. He forced his eyes open, desperate to see the moon despite his tears. Its radiance flooded him and he grinned with satisfaction.

This was Pemma, the second smallest of Bark's seven moons. It was the third moon whose light he had bathed in, one more than most adult Fant ever saw in a long life. Pizlo was only six and knew he'd live to witness the other four as well. He didn't know when the next one would come his way, but he felt certain that the one after the one after that was one he would share. He strained to keep his eyes open, joyful tears washing away the pain. He could hear the moon, its voice brilliant and clear. It had called to him and he had listened and all was right with the world.

The clouds closed again, cutting off the light and leaving Arlo's Chimney dark once more, save for the faint glow from the boy's palm.

Still smiling, he pulled himself up from his sling, using only his unstained hand and his trunk. This moon, like the previous two, had spoken of very different things than the rest of Barsk did. Pemma had said many things at once, bits of wisdom, smatterings of gossip, tangents of possibilities. Listening to a moon was like eavesdropping on dozens of separate conversations at once and contributing to none. It had lasted only a few moments, but days would pass before Pizlo understood anything that had been said. He climbed up the vine to the knot of crossed strands that had let him hang there and transferred his weight to them, pulling the sling up after. He paused, standing in the middle of the shaft and reached into a pocket of his daypouch, withdrawing a small wooden object. He'd found it that morning on the edge of the Shadow Dwell, stained and battered from the ocean. He'd plucked it from the surf.

It was his favorite of Keslo's beaches. More gravel than sand, it had the most turbulent waves, and he'd found no better place to go to talk with the ocean. He would walk out into the water until it recognized him, until a wave lifted him up in greeting. The conversation would continue as the ocean pulled him away from shore and hurled him back, over and over until there was nothing left to say. He wished he could share it with Jorl. But Jorl couldn't hear the ocean that way and would only be frightened to see him dragged across the gravel time and again. Jorl would worry about

Pizlo being injured and hurt and completely miss what really took place. Besides, the ocean wouldn't hurt him. Nothing could.

Pizlo gazed at the gift the water had given him that morning, a carved figurine that had been indistinct by morning light. He studied it now by the glow of his stained hand and marveled that it had so many emotions in the worn face. Certainty and pain, confusion and confidence. Pizlo did not believe in coincidence, but wondered why an image of the Matriarch had come to him today of all days. Jorl had said she had visions and seizures; he hadn't had seizures, but maybe that was because he didn't talk to many other Fant, and Margda had talked and talked to them all. He was pretty sure she was still talking now.

"Shhh, it will be okay," he told the wooden figure. "He'll be big soon. Bigger than anyone." He closed his fist, restoring the darkness, and ran the nubs of his trunk over the wood one last time before letting it drop. Perhaps tomorrow someone else would find it. Perhaps not.

Untying the last of the vines, Pizlo let them fall away. He rode one of them to a wall of the chimney and pulled himself through the foliage and deeper into the canopy, disappearing, not unlike the moon.

ELEVEN

PROBLEMATIC PROBABILITY

~~~~~~~~~

SENATOR Bish paused as his private elevator opened outside the entrance to what he'd come to think of as his *psychic bullpen*. The door was actually a heavy security airlock that opened on to the top floor of a luxury hotel on the main continent of Gripta. His maternal grandfather had been born on Gripta, and owned a wide range of real property there, this hotel among many others. It had led the old Bos to hide his private team of precognitivists there, far from potential prying eyes back in the capital on Dawn. The irony that before being forcibly relocated to Barsk, several hundred Fant had once called Gripta home was not wasted on Bish.

His aide, a faithful Brady, accessed the airlock controls. Passive sensors in the wall compared the signals radiated by devices sewn into her kaftan and compared these to the pattern of keys she tapped on a pad. Many of his colleagues in the senate would have flinched at having a Sloth on staff, let alone as personal assistant, but the well-known lethargy was an inaccurate stereotype. Druz moved more slowly than he did, true enough, but the delay created a pause in which he could gather his thoughts as he moved from task to task, and that had proved a boon. He had his own stereotypes to beat back. People assumed a Yak would be headstrong, and every time he presented a reasoned and reflective argument he cut through half his opposition. Far from being a liability, Druz provided an opportunity for him to excel.

"Sir, whenever you're ready."

"Open it up," he replied. "Let's get this over with. I'm sure their excuses will be inventive. They usually are."

The Sloth gave the wall a final tap and the airlock's outer door opened. They stepped through and repeated the sequence at the inner door. Bish had inherited the hotel and its special occupants when he'd secured his grandfather's senate seat. The precognitivists themselves had requested the independent environment and airlock, presumably based on some possible future they had seen.

He slipped a hand into his robe and removed his senatorial ring from an inner pocket. A pretty collection of fossilized wood and platinum, every member of the Committee of Information had a similar, albeit unique, ring. Their wearers changed with the committee's composition, and the artist who'd designed them had intended them to accommodate the full range of Alliance races. But Bish's hands were big even for a Yak, and the ring fit uncomfortably on his littlest finger. On those rare occasions he needed to invoke its sigil he simply displayed it for a moment and then tucked it away again. Visits to his oracular menagerie were an exception. He held his arm out at length and slid the ring over the tip of his left horn and a short way down the length until it stuck snuggly, the face of the sigil aimed forward where it would catch the eye and remind the viewer of his status and power as head of the Senate's most powerful committee. Precogs, he'd found, could too easily get to feeling full of themselves.

The other side of the lock opened onto a wide vestibule which, in turn, had three hallways flowing from its far end, the center providing access to common spaces such as workrooms, kitchens, and dining areas, and the two side corridors leading to private apartments. Bish's current complement of psychic employees numbered fifty-four, a full third of them being Prairie Dogs. One such stood waiting for him now.

"Welcome, Senator. Your office did not notify us that you would be coming today." The Cynomy fidgeted and refrained from eye contact.

Bish replied with his best beneficent smile. "A small test, Tekki," he said, "which you passed with ease by being here to greet me."

A twitch, followed by a moment's silence, and then. "I'm Brekki. Tekki is my uncle. And one of us is always here. Always."

It was an indication of the Bos's good humor that he tolerated the correction. Projecting the aura of a tolerant and friendly elder relative, he continued. "That being so, you knew I was coming."

"Yes," said the Prairie Dog, finally raising its head and tilting back far enough to meet the Yak's gaze. "We saw the likelihood of it. Just as we saw the likelihood that you would not leave happy."

Druz rushed ahead with a response. "Do not presume to tell the senator what he will be feeling. It is impertinent and you yourself acknowledge you can be mistaken."

"I'm just saying. Don't take it out on us when we do the work you give us and you don't like the outcome. It's like blaming the desert for being dry."

Bish took a deep breath and centered himself. Clairvoyants always acted this way, mistaking vision for power. The little shit in front of him wouldn't know what to do with actual power if the senator put it in his tiny hands.

"Friend Brekki, we are getting ahead of ourselves. Now that you've confirmed my presence, do me the kindness of informing your senior to come and brief me on your team's progress. Also, an offer of refreshment would not be unwelcome."

In response, the Cynomy began to tremble. "Can't. Everyone else is busy or hard asleep. You get me. And I don't have any refreshments for you because you're not going to want it."

The Sloth began to raise an arm toward Brekki but Bish gestured her to calm. Her defense on behalf of his own sensibilities warmed him, but disciplining a rude precog would not get him what he needed.

"Fine. If you are who I have, then you are whom I will use. At your team's suggestion, I initiated a program to investigate a drug the Fant of Barsk call 'koph.' You informed me that doing so would trigger a sequence of possibilities leading to a great development affecting the Alliance. Has that come to pass?"

"Yes, Senator. The likelihood is a near certainty now."

"Very good. So you can now tell me more about this development."

"No, sir."

"No?" Rudeness was one thing, but insolence and outright contradiction he would not tolerate. If it continued, he would make an example of this precog. He had plenty of other Prairie Dogs, after all. "The act of pursuing koph was supposed to bring it into focus. I was assured of this."

"We experienced a complication," said the Cynomy.

"You are scrying the future timelines. They vary in probability, not clarity. There should be no complications."

"Normally, no, especially when we work in concert as we do. But in this instance, there is an Observer Effect, someone else attempting to study the same future and that very act prevents any of us from a clear perception of it."

Another precog interfering? Now? His grandfather had never had to deal with such incompetence. "Have you identified the source?"

"Yes, Senator. Fairly completely."

"And? Why wasn't I informed? Do you know how easily I could have sent a Patrol vessel to deal with this interloper?" Bish's voice had become strained with resentment at having to pull information from this pathetic creature.

"No, sir, that isn't a viable option. The source occurred in the past and is long dead."

"What? Where?"

"Barsk, sir. One of the first generation activists who forged their government had a powerful clairvoyant faculty, though largely untrained. She appears to have been quite interested in pursuing the koph development as well."

"Let me see if I understand this. You told me to pursue koph, which meant engaging in covert operations against the inhabitants of a sovereign planet in clear violation of established Alliance law. This was supposed to bring our goal into sharp focus. And now, I'm to understand that some ancestor of the same Fant that my people have been working on has instead blocked your vision? What options does that leave?"

The Prairie Dog shrunk in upon itself and stared at the carpeted floor of the vestibule. Its reply came as a whisper. "Continue to pursue koph."

"Continue?" Bish roared even as Druz presumed to place a hand on his arm. And yet, the audacity of her action restored his composure. She knew him well. He'd been just seconds away from wringing the life out of the worthless precog. Had the others seen that possible outcome? Had they sent Brekki as a sacrifice to appease his wrath. If so, he would not give them that satisfaction.

"Senator?" The Brady's hand remained on his arm.

Bish thought of his grandfather, the consummate urbane statesman and projected that impression outward. His aide's hand fell away.

"Continue to pursue koph? If doing so hasn't already yielded the desired result, why continue?"

"But it has, Senator. The foreseen probabilities are lining up as predicted, only the resulting specifics are clouded from us. Continuing after the drug will cause competing futures to fall aside."

"And this will reveal the development we seek?"

The Cynomy shrugged. "In a sense. Once a single timeline is inevitable, events will play out and the thing will be out in the open for anyone to see."

Bish's hands closed into fists as he stared down at the precog. "How is that helpful? If others can see it, what's to keep them from taking advantage when it becomes known?"

"Oh. We know where it will happen. And we know you'll be there."

"What?"

"We can't see what happens there, but that's where the timelines converge. You need to go to Barsk yourself."

Bish sputtered. "I . . . when?"

"Now, Senator. That's why I didn't bother with refreshments."

He spun toward his aide, the tip of his horn coming dangerously close to gouging her head. "Druz! Is my ship ready?"

"As always, Senator."

He paused and eyed the Prairie Dog. Had he just been played

by the team of scryers assembled by his grandfather three generations ago, or did it just feel that way? Would it do any good to make an example of the spokesman they clearly were willing to sacrifice, or was this simply how they communicated with a world they didn't fit with? But in the end, none of that mattered. The key to being an effective senator lay in pragmatism. The results they'd handed him were more important than his ego.

"Time to go then," he said, dismissing the Cynomy from his plans. At least for now.

I⊤ had taken Jorl most of the morning to acquire a small boat that didn't surpass his understanding of sailing. Under other circumstances, the irony would have amused him. During his time in the Patrol he had passed his preliminary exams to sit a conditional third board to his vessel's pilot, but here at home he had never learned to navigate anything bigger than the simple craft needed to cross to the next nearest island. Unlike most men of his age, and especially since his return from offworld, he hadn't felt the urge to travel from island to island.

He'd visited more than a dozen of Keslo's shipwrights, but in every case some secret shibboleth slipped into the conversation had betrayed his ignorance and he'd been sent on his way. More than once he'd considered invoking his aleph and simply walking aboard an available vessel, but the realization that he'd be hard pressed to take it from its docking, let alone avoid knocking himself overboard or becoming hopelessly entangled in rigging prevailed. Near noontime, inspiration struck and he returned to the Civilized Wood and visited the academy. The provost asked few questions, both in deference to the mark on Jorl's brow and his reputation as a serious scholar, and generated the necessary paperwork that would secure him a boat that fit his needs and abilities. It had belonged to an oceanographer with the academy. That scholar had set sail two seasons ago, taking a much simpler craft and leaving behind a research vessel that had the distinction of possessing a motor and gyrocompass, thereby freeing Jorl of the need to understand how to tack or trim a sail, read the wind, or navigate despite cloud-covered skies.

None of it felt real, but he had finally accepted that the Matriarch had indeed intended him to fulfill some part of her prophecy. *When the dead will not answer, the Silence is at hand, and the fate of all Barsk will soon hang in the balance. The newest Aleph must do what has never been done though it is almost always done.* There was no question any longer. The nefshons of Fant that had sailed off, that should have come to the summoning of any Speaker on Barsk, were not responding. They were out there, he had felt them himself, but instead of rushing to his summons he'd felt a resistance where none should be. The Silence. And the last part of the prophecy, to do what hadn't been done but was always done, what else could that be but for a Fant who wasn't Dying to set sail? Pizlo had given him directions that he couldn't possibly possess, and his aleph gave him permission to travel anywhere, even to a place that every Fant ever born on Barsk would flinch at as a premature destination.

But he had to know. As a historian, he understood that what in hindsight were taken to be grand events really consisted of a myriad of tiny, seemingly inconsequential choices. Often as not, great moments hung on coincidences and random luck. And yet . . . What if prophecy caused all of that to get thrown away? What if everything in his life and the lives around him, from his wanting to join the Patrol to Arlo's death, what if all of it had all occurred just to bring him to this moment? What if doing this was his destiny?

Jorl stopped that train of thought and asked aloud, "What if the academy hears you talking to yourself like the island's idiot and strips away your standing as a historian?" The answering silence provided slight reassurance.

His next stop involved picking up supplies for the trip. He visited his local grocery and bought an assortment of fruit and sufficient leafy greens and containers of water to cover him for the trip there and back, and a few extra days just to be safe. For an extra fee they loaned him the use of a small cart and promised to send a child down to the academy docks to retrieve it before dusk.

Men, young and old, routinely left their homes, sometimes visiting friends and relatives on other islands for a season, sometimes just wandering for years on end. Nor did they tend to tell anyone before going; formal goodbyes were more the province of women and children, both known for forming deeper attachments. When he'd joined the Patrol and left the planet, he'd done so without fanfare, sending a short note to his family and mentioning it in passing to Arlo. But this felt different, less like a personal decision and more an act that had been preordained.

Towing the little cart behind him, Jorl stopped first at Tolta's, but his friend's widow was not at home. He pinned a note to her visitor's board, saying only that he was going away, that he wouldn't be gone long, and that he'd resume his lessons with Pizlo upon his return.

He saved the most difficult visit, that of his family's home, for last. Like most women's dwellings, it housed upwards of fifty people: grandmothers and aunts, female cousins, and underage children of both sexes. It boasted multiple stories, elaborate sleeping balconies, and a sprawling wrap-around porch on three sides. Jorl had no sooner knocked upon the entrance when several enthusiastic children threw the door wide and all but pulled him into the house's guest parlor. Female Fant were social by nature, and frequently traded visits in clusters that mystified their male counterparts. The house's parlor already held two small gatherings of adults, with children running back and forth to fetch refreshments or attend to errands as directed. Jorl had come prepared. He dipped his trunk into a sack of candied fruit bits from the grocery and distributed them with mock solemnity to each of the children in turn.

Two of his sisters were part of one of the groups already in the parlor and both noticed the candy. One uttered a snort of disapproval, and the other, Adri, his youngest older sister, disengaged from her friends and approached.

"Where are you going this time? You told us you were done traveling off planet. You promised!"

"Who said I was going anywhere? Can't I just come by and visit my sisters?"

"You could, but you don't. Not during social hours. You show up when you can slip into an open seat at the breakfast table, or when you know Gran is making one of her special dinners. Otherwise, the only time you ever popped in unannounced was to tell Mother that a season earlier you'd secretly filed a petition to be allowed military service and that a shuttle was taking you away that night."

Jorl frowned. Was he really so predictable? He fanned his ears with embarrassment and soldiered on. "Relax, I'm not leaving Barsk. Because, like you said, I promised."

"But you are going somewhere?"

"Well, yes."

"Just tell me why," Adri demanded. "Why do you get these ideas to leave. Not to travel like other men, you make it mean something different. You *leave*."

He sighed, giving up any hope for a sisterly hug, let alone a packet of well-wishes and homemade snacks to brighten up his other supplies. His sister towered over him, just as she'd always done since childhood. Was she really only a few years older?

"It's something I have to do. There are questions I want to ask, and I can't ask them here. But honestly, it's not half so bad as you think, not like before. And remember, I came back, right?"

Adri only scowled. Her trunk twitched with a retort but she said nothing. She didn't have to; he could read her well enough. She was just searching for the right words to wither him there in the parlor. He didn't dare give her the chance. He abandoned his carefully rehearsed speech and lumbered forward before she could stop him.

"Look, I know you don't understand, that no one in the family does. But you at least have always tried to be on my side. Maybe you can explain it to the rest, in any way you think will work. This is something I have to do."

His sister's trunk stopped twitching and she drew herself up. She'd formulated at least the start of a response. It wouldn't accomplish anything, other than to leave them both frustrated, and it was the last thing Jorl wanted to endure. Turning from her he tossed the remainder of his bag of sweets into the air, shouting "Candy!"

The children who had dropped back to give him and Adri space came dashing forward now, and a dozen more who had been within earshot poured in from adjacent rooms. Jorl used the chaos to let himself out of the front door. Taking hold of his cart from where he'd left it on the porch, he moved on, mentally crossing off this last errand from his list and heading at last to the boat that would take him away once more.

~~~~~

THE provost had supplied directions and a map, and Jorl had no trouble finding the late oceanographer's boat. It lay moored at a small dock, one of half a dozen craft bearing such names as *Grant Money* and *Office Hours* and *Peer Review*. Afternoon had since arrived and then some, and while Jorl didn't relish traveling in the dark, he hoped to at least slip out past the last of the islands on the eastern end of the archipelago and be out on the open ocean. On the way down the dock he passed a small kiosk. An attendant sat inside, slumped over in sleep, chin on chest. He didn't have the heart to wake her, and went past and began to stow his supplies. After several minutes the attendant, a stocky young woman probably working her first job fresh out of school, came running, down the dock, waving and trumpeting like the place was on fire.

"Here now, you can't be messing with these boats. Owners and guests only. Get off of there now, before I toss you off."

Jorl's back had been to her and he turned at her approach. The woman continued barreling his way, seemingly intent on hauling him from the boat and perhaps heaving him into the water. She staggered abruptly, halting herself as she came close enough to see him. Or more accurately, see his forehead.

"Um . . . that's not your boat."

"No," agreed Jorl. "It's the academy's."

"Well, it used to belong to Grummel. I guess ownership reverted to the academy, but they didn't tell me about anyone borrowing it."

"That's my fault. I guess these are for you." Jorl took a sealed pouch from his cart, paperwork from the provost, and presented it to the attendant. She rifled through the pages, made a point of glancing up at Jorl's aleph again, and shrugged.

"Okay. I guess that's all right then. But, you didn't complete this last section indicating your destination. It's for your own safety, like in case you have an accident or something goes wrong and you don't get there." She pulled a stick of ink bamboo from a pocket and held it poised to fill in the missing information. "So, where are you going?"

"Yeah, about that. If you have to ask, I can't tell you. But don't worry. Nothing's going to go wrong."

Wishing he felt as confident as he sounded, Jorl waved the attendant toward the boat's tie and motioned for her to cast off. He hauled the rope aboard and then settled in. It was three times the length of any of the rowboats he had used for past travels between islands, and even had a small shelter enclosed on three sides. Jorl didn't mind sleeping out in the rain, but it was nice to know he wouldn't have to.

~~~~~

FOR reasons that could only be appreciated by another academician, Grummel the oceanographer had named his craft *Tenure Redeemed*. Jorl passed plenty of other craft on their way moving from one island to another, from simple rowboats and small ferry rafts to larger ships with as many as three masts and sails all unfurled. It was the middle of the season of wind, the most popular time for travel, and Jorl kept a firm hand on the ship's rudder. The near-silent engine of the academy craft gave him good speed, and he didn't trust his own skill enough if he let himself come too close to any other boats. Eventually though, in the final moments of twilight, Jorl slid past the last island that lay east of Keslo and out into the open water beyond the edge of the western archipelago.

According to every map on Barsk, the next bit of land he could expect to see was Relfa, the western most island of the planet's other chain of islands, a voyage that took a sailing ship at least twenty days. Jorl had never visited Relfa nor any of the islands beyond it, though he knew plenty who had. His own father had told him tales of setting forth in the company of several dozen other men in a co-opt-owned galley that made the trip several times a year. Common sense said that such a large collection of young bachelors and wandering husbands in a confined space, day after day, had to end badly. Once they reached adulthood, male Fant just tended to get surly around large numbers of their fellows. Each wanted to be off living his own way, master of his own destiny, and free of any reminders that someone else might have another way of going about things.

It had been less of an issue in the time before the Fant had come to Barsk. When the Lox and Eleph had been minority populations on mixed worlds of other races, seeing others of their kind, even other men, had felt more reassuring than confrontational, perhaps in part because of the general animosity they received from anyone who wasn't Fant. Nonetheless, pilgrimages of collectives of men from one group of islands to the other happened, as much a rite of passage as the passage to distant lands. Tral had spoken of massive wrestling matches on the deck of his ship, the consumption of prodigious quantities of distilled spirits, and spontaneous songs being written and sung with so many verses that they could outlast the day's light. But he'd also talked about how half of the men on that particular voyager had leapt from their ship when they'd come in sight of land, preferring to swim to shore than spend another moment in the company of others. Jorl had asked him once if he'd been among the Fant who'd stayed aboard and put into dock at Relfa, or if he'd opted to swim, but his father had only smiled and changed the subject.

As night fell, Jorl dropped anchor and retired to the boat's enclosure. By lamplight he read through what he gratefully considered an idiot's guide to the boat's state-of-the-art navigation system, as fine a piece of Alliance technology as any he'd seen on Barsk. With the exception of those who worked in the planet's pharming industry, most Fant eschewed complex devices. Jorl could imagine the cognitive dissonance someone like Grummel must have endured in a vessel perfectly designed for a stereotypically absent-minded academician. If not for his own time in the Patrol, he'd probably be in similar straits.

Over a dinner of citrus and sweet leaves, he reviewed the scrap of paper with Pizlo's directions, as well as his own notes that he'd scribbled between lines. In the vast empty water that lay to the east, a mere three days journey given the speed of the *Tenure Redeemed* and far closer than distant Relfa lay his unnamed destination. He had no idea what he'd find there. As he lay himself down for sleep, his imagination served up a range of possibilities. Perhaps a beach overflowing with the rotting remains of rafts and boats that had carried their occupants on a final trip. Maybe the island held a rain forest like every other island on Barsk. Maybe the Dying had built their own version of a Civilized Wood filled with individual apartments where they enjoyed their last days. Or maybe he'd simply find a vast accretion of bones, the crumpled skeletons of eight centuries of Dying Fant, their flesh long since stripped away, strewn from one end of the island to the other, from its gravelly beach to the mud and streams of its Shadow Dwell. With images of animated corpses dancing in his head, Jorl wandered into sleep.

He rose at first light, the clouds on the eastern horizon beckoning him with a rosy glow, the sky overhead showering him with a light rain. With a yawn and a stretch he eased himself over the boat's side, splashed himself to full wakefulness and tended to the morning's ablutions. Clambering back aboard, he returned to Pizlo's page and converted the boy's route into terms the boat's hardware could understand. It quickly returned a declarative ping, and its display informed him of his options: barely two days if he left immediately and continued nonstop, a bit over three if he maintained his intention of cruising only during daytime. He hoisted anchor and engaged the engine. The *Tenure Redeemed* surged forward and he sat back to enjoy the warm rain and the vast open sky.

Jorl had been too intent on beginning the voyage to give much thought of how he'd occupy himself during it. His focus had been on setting out, and now he had insufficient distractions for the trip, having failed to bring along so much as a book to help pass the time. Ironically, he had a collection of *imramha* he'd been meaning to read, written by a Speaker on Telba. Every few generations some young man went off in a boat and had a voyage filled with impossible adventures. The Speaker had summoned a dozen of them, one at a time of course, and compared their own experiences with the tales that had spawned.

Lacking other diversion, he instead reviewed everything he could remember about the Matriarch's prophecy regarding the Silence, seeking any insight or clue that might guide him once he reached that final island. What had she seen? Jorl couldn't fathom how the simple act of arrival on its shore would resolve his or any Speaker's inability to summon the recently dead. Which meant that somehow, his destination wasn't the end of the journey but rather a necessary first step to something else. If Margda had known, she'd either given no indication in her prophecies, or had been far too cryptic for him or anyone else to have figured it out. Maybe it would be clear once he got there. Or maybe he had it all horribly wrong.

Most of that first day he simply sat in the boat and gazed up at the overcast sky. The cloud cover was as complete as ever, but it moved far faster than his boat and he tracked the arrival and disappearance of individual clouds within the larger sheet that defined the sky in shades of ever lighter gray. The flight of the clouds and the movement of his boat lulled him into an easy trance state and soon his mind began giving meaning to the half-shapes of the clouds. There was an Alliance ship racing to some secret mission beyond the horizon; far to the right was that cute shopgirl who always flirted with him and never complained at even his most obscure book requests; directly ahead must surely be hiding a tree from his childhood, where he and Arlo had convinced themselves no adults could ever find them no matter how hard they searched. The clouds swept past, his mind formed new explanations for their shapes, and in this way, pausing only for the occasional nap or meal break, he passed his first full day at sea.

The second day began much as the first, though the rain fell with a bit more force. The boat's instruments assured him he was making good time toward the open bit of water he insisted was his destination. The day's sun was halfway to its zenith and he'd already mapped out a pair of wrestling Prairie Dogs, the front door to Tolta's home, the glowering face of the Matriarch, and a bucket overflowing with ink bamboo from the roiling clouds overhead. Through it all the boat's engine had been a faint but constant hum, more felt than heard. Jorl's reveries ended as the background sound rose to a shrill wine, alerting him that the boat had crested the last swell and not fallen back but continued to rise.

Jorl spun in place and saw the reason, his experience giving name to the color he saw, a shade of gray he knew intimately from many an afternoon pointlessly painting the outer hull of his own Patrol ship, punishment for one or another imagined offense on those occasions when they'd dipped into an atmosphere and docked at some welcoming port. A larger craft had risen up beneath his boat, so broad that he could have put a couple dozen of the *Tenure Redeemed* side by side and still not fallen off the edge. Its depth had to be at least as big, suggesting many levels or a series of huge cargo holds. He didn't have enough detail to guess which of several ship designs lay there, but even the smallest required a length ten or more times its width. Not a scout ship, and too big for a survey vessel. Something this big went into space for years at a time, ferrying important people between worlds or executing deep space missions or responding to unstable colonies on the fringes of Alliance space.

As if in response to this last thought, he saw a gate open further up where the gray hull rose in a lazy curve from horizontal to vertical and three red-clad figures poured out.

Contamination troops, he thought. He'd worn the same garb once himself, his trunk tucked uncomfortably down the front of his translucent mask. He'd sweated a pool in all that plastic, investigating an abandoned ship left adrift, its atmosphere vanished and its skeleton crew dead at their stations. A malfunction of its systems had left it vulnerable to a hull breach that had killed everyone, but the Patrol had taken no chances and the investigation team had suited up expecting some kind of plague. When in doubt, the Patrol always prepared for the worst, which probably explained the gear worn by the trio striding toward him. He recognized their race by their gait before they came close enough to identify through the windows of their masks. He stood to meet them, giving voice to the first question to form in his mind. "What are Cans doing on Barsk?"

An instant later they had boarded his boat. One Dog grabbed hold of his left arm, another took the right. The third glared at him as if Jorl had insulted his mother so frequently and thoroughly that no retribution imaginable could be enough.

"A better question might be, what is a Fant in the prime of his life doing out on the open water like an imbecilic and suicidal elder?"

Jorl's head turned so quickly toward this voice that his trunk nearly slapped the third Dog in front of him, causing that one to flinch, duck, and fall onto his ass. Jorl frowned. Cans were fiercely loyal and disciplined; they made up the bulk of the Patrol, but they were almost never in charge. Standing now in the gate, the source of the responding question, was a Cheetah. Unlike the Dogs, she wore neither hood nor mask. The blue of her gear proclaimed her officer status, and the molded insignia at her elbows, distinct to the initiated but easily missed if you didn't know to look, marked her rank.

"I'll have to disagree with you, Captain. I'm well within the patterns of my culture to be here. Whereas your presence is a violation of the Compact we have with the rest of the Alliance."

"Interesting and more interesting still," said the Cheetah. "Perceptive and well educated. Let us hope you're smart enough not to offer any trouble. I am Nonyx-Captain Selishta, and my mission here grants me exemption from your precious Compact and permits me to detain you for investigatory purposes."

Jorl frowned, and pulled his trunk close, coiling it for action. "I know enough to recognize when I'm being lied to, Captain. There are no exemptions. I learned that in my own time in the Patrol."

The Captain strode across the hull with a swift fluidity, and the third Can who had only just regained his feet scurried out of the way. The Nonyx stood half a head taller than the Lox and stared down with an expression that clearly showed she did not respond well to contradiction.

"You're that one, are you? I understood one of your kind had served a partial tour." She flicked a finger at Jorl's forehead without actually touching it. "What's that paint?"

"A cultural marking," said Jorl. "It grants me free passage, anywhere and anytime. Its sanctity, like all of our customs, is also guaranteed under the terms of the Compact. Your troops holding me against my will is another violation."

With a smile, the Cheetah gestured to the pair of Dogs holding him. "Release him. The lot of you go and prepare the tertiary hold for his vessel; it's obviously not going to dismantle like the others so we'll take it whole."

The nearer two Dogs couldn't let go fast enough, and quick-timed back toward the open gate. The third whined a query. "Ma'am?"

"That's an order. Relax, it's not as though he has anywhere to go."

"You can't take my boat."

The Cheetah waved the statement away. "Identify yourself, Fant."

"Lox-Ensign Jorl. Retired."

"Damn me, an officer? Well, then ensign-retired, let me adjust your world view. As I said, I know all about your precious Compact and I don't care. I'm authorized to ignore it, every line and provision. Which means, among other things, I am free to be here on your soggy planet, and I will detain you as I please. You can argue the legalities if you want to waste your breath, but look at your situation and acknowledge the pragmatics before you. You are my prisoner."

"I don't suppose there's anything I can say or do to change your mind about that?"

The Cheetah laughed. "On the contrary, ensign-retired. You can make this easier on both of us. I am justifiably weary of my time on your world. Give me your word as an officer that you'll behave, and you'll avoid a visit to the brig."

"You'd accept my word?"

"Why not? Years from now, it will make an amusing anecdote. And again, it's not like you can go anywhere. This way my people have one less isolation cell to disinfect, which should please both sides. I assume you'll also be less inclined to whine and cry than the others."

"Others?" His trunk hung lax as he realized the probable answer to his own question.

"All in good time, Lox-Ensign. First, your word?"

"Yes, Captain, you have it. For now."

"Amusing. Now then, step lively, back into the ship. We were returning to base when the helm spotted you, and the sooner I'm free of this damn rain the happier I'll be."

"But why are you here, Captain?"

"Have you been retired so long? Orders, of course."

THIRTEEN

LEAVING HOME

THE previous night Pizlo had a hunch that he'd want porridge when he awoke. He acknowledged that it had been several days since he'd visited Tolta, let alone slept in the bed she kept prepared for him. He admitted that he liked the softness of its coverings, but he'd seen the unhappy look on her face when he'd last stayed over and left the stains of his recent travels upon the linens. Life was just simpler on his own; then again, there was the matter of the porridge.

He traveled to one of the Civilized Wood's popular gathering spots, empty so late in the evening, and bathed in the fountain at its center, scrubbing at the mud streaks and leaf stains on his pale skin. He lost a few scabs in the process, and these scrapes bled a bit, but he washed that away, too, and applied pressure here and there until the tiny wounds clotted and he was as clean as he was ever apt to get. He'd washed his shorts at the same time as he bathed, and as he stepped from the fountain he removed them the better to squeeze the extra water from them. Still wet from head to toe, he put on the damp shorts and then strapped his daypouch

across his chest again. He hurried to Tolta's home, expecting to
dry along the way. He climbed in through a window, snuck into
the bed that she insisted was his, and went to sleep.

He awoke to Tolta preparing breakfast, not just hot porridge
but a serving of sweet leaves and several kinds of fruit juice, too.
He slid onto a bench at the table and worked his way through two
steaming bowls, three servings of leaves, and full glasses of all
three juices (and refills of two), all the while nodding or shaking
his head in response to his mother's questions of if he was doing
well and getting enough to eat and keeping himself out of trouble
and staying clean and studying with Jorl.

When he finished, he glanced up to smile and thank her, but
stopped without a word. His mouth fell open and the memories
of things he didn't know he knew bubbled to the surface of his
awareness.

"You never got to say goodbye, did you?"

"Hmm? You mean to Jorl? No, dear, I was out when he came
by. He'll be back in a few days, I think. He left a note though and—"

"No, not Jorl. Arlo. He didn't leave a note. And he knew he
wasn't coming back."

Tolta bit her lip and turned away, but not before Pizlo saw the
beginning of tears. Keeping her back to her son, she busied herself with the porridge's cooking pot. "No, Pizlo, he didn't leave a
note. But how could he? It was an accident and—"

"It wasn't."

Silence but for the scraping of a wooden spoon against a pot.

"Jorl says—"

"Jorl doesn't know everything!" Tolta slammed the pot down.
The wooden spoon scattered across the floor. "He may act like he
does, but he doesn't. He could be wrong sometimes. It happens."

"Yeah, but he's not. Not about this. I know, cuz the moon told me. It said Arlo will say a proper goodbye."

"A proper . . . the moon?"

"Yeah. I'd forgotten that part, but I just remembered and thought you'd want to know. I didn't mean to make you sad. Anyway, I should go. Thanks for breakfast, Tolta."

"Pizlo, wait. What do you mean the moon told you?"

"I saw it the other night. The second littlest, Pemma. It was my third moon. It told me lots, so much that I forgot bunches but I'm remembering now. That's why I gotta go. Bye!"

With no more warning, Pizlo slid off the breakfast bench and bolted for the door. He flung it open, leaping through as soon as the gap had widened enough. He heard Tolta rushing after, but in the time it took her to reach the door and lean through, hands to either side of the frame, Pizlo had already vanished into the surrounding green.

He'd been thinking a lot about what the moon had said, and also what Jorl had told him about the aleph. It opened all doors, and he might need one himself if he was going to follow where he thought he needed to go. Even though he was only six, he felt certain he'd accomplished three things of such special merit that the traveling council would surely award him an aleph, even if they *were* usually stingy about it. Jorl had once said his was only the fifty-seventh aleph ever. If only they could be made to talk to him and acknowledge his existence. In fact, didn't his existence count as an accomplishment? Even though they acted like he wasn't there, he had heard how they spoke about him. *Abomination* was the description they most often used. *Nature's Mistake* was a close second. His kind were considered soulless, but that was silly. Who among them had ever seen a soul, anyway? His situation was biological, not spiritual. He'd read about it in one of Jorl's books, the genetic fluke of two Fant conceiving without a proper bonding. And how the resulting child most often arrived stillborn, and how most of the rest died within a year from missing organs or senses. It'd taken him days to realize his own inability to feel pain was part of that. But the unique thing was he had survived, six years now, longer than any other fluke. That had to be an accomplishment worthy of an aleph!

And he understood things. Hadn't he given Jorl directions to the place only the Dying knew? That had to count as a second one. It wasn't something he could prove though, not like his being alive, not until Jorl came back and said he'd been right. But still, *he* knew he was right.

Maybe the one about swinging on vines wouldn't count, even though he did it so well. And maybe they wouldn't be impressed by his insect collection, no matter how much better it was than anyone else's; he'd already learned that not everyone shared his enthusiasm for bugs. But the fact that he talked with all of Barsk, from the mud in the Shadow Dwell to the clouds in the sky, that had to count. Jorl had never mentioned anyone else who could do that, and he hadn't read about it anywhere. Just because he took it as given didn't mean other people wouldn't see it as special. Surely the way any of them could talk to anyone else was pretty special. Noisy and maybe pointless, but special. They chattered endlessly around him, but not much of it mattered or meant anything.

At least when Jorl talked to him, he told him stories. He liked that, the sharing of experiences. It was real. It mattered, didn't it? Wouldn't it be great if he grew up to be a Speaker like Jorl, to be able to summon people from before he was even born and listen to their stories. But . . . they probably wouldn't want to talk to him either. He had to think that over more; it would be awful being a Speaker but not be able to Speak. Maybe he should just focus on his aleph . . .

There were things to do. Pizlo didn't know where the aleph-granting traveling counsel was, but likely not there on Keslo. He'd just have to take matters into his own hands. He'd explain it to them when they met him and they'd understand. Maybe. If they talked to him. But that wasn't going to happen, not if like everyone else they pretended not to even see him. Maybe he should get something better than an aleph. Maybe he should just claim the right for himself because his entire life was one ginormous on-going accomplishment that almost no one on Barsk wanted to admit. Or maybe that was the third special accomplishment that would earn him an aleph. Or maybe turning it down in favor of his own mark would be the third. The logic kind of got away from him, but somewhere along that line of thought he'd reached a decision: he didn't need an aleph. Didn't he already go anywhere he wanted because people wouldn't see him? No, he needed his own mark. Something no one had ever seen before, and so they couldn't be afraid of it, or deny it was real. Something they could talk to, even if they wouldn't talk to him.

Pizlo never wandered the walkways of the commercial areas of the Civilized Wood during the day when other people constantly came and went. But sometimes he went there deliberately, like when he wanted to play a game of making people dodge out of his way. He'd walk slowly from point A to point B. He'd do it with his eyes tightly closed, and trust to their need to get out of his way without acknowledging the fact by so much as a muttered complaint. Other times he went just after dawn, when the shops were closed and he could press his face against windows and gaze through the creeping diffused light at stuff that ordinary folk needed in their lives.

Today he had come with purpose. The light filtering through the trees was at its brightest and the concentration of Fant about their business there the greatest. He'd burst in on a balcony at the far end of a cul-de-sac, emerging from the wall of sculpted foliage and dropping onto the boardway. His arrival startled several Eleph who quickly averted their gaze as he began walking toward a store. A path opened for him more surely than it would have even if he'd born with an aleph. Either behavior was burned-in at a cultural level, but this one left every Fant breathless with a shared shame. Pizlo had never understood, but was grateful for the response today. Today he needed stuff.

Five stores did business in this cul-de-sac and Pizlo knew them all. The closest was a bookshop that he'd gone to with Jorl once to pick up some texts he'd special-ordered. Pizlo had waited outside without his teacher asking, and Jorl had surprised him with a present when he'd emerged, a pack of five bamboo inksticks. A cobbler kept a store next to the bookshop. Fant rarely wanted or needed shoes, but were hard on them when they did and the owner did a steady business weaving new shoes, repairing old ones, or carving new lasts when he was between customers. Beyond that was a physician's office, which held no interest for Pizlo, though it had two doors, a main entrance on the cul-de-sac and a second, more discreet exit onto the main boardway. Going the other way around from the balcony was a consignment spirit shop where Fant could bring the best of their own distilling and put them up for sale, or acquire the efforts of others. Every ten days they did tastings and samplings, but otherwise there were never more than two or three Fant in the shop at any one time. The last venue sat on the other end of the cul-de-sac and wrapped around onto the side of the boardway much as the doctor's office did. This was Suliv's shop, part grocery, part whatever-else-you-needed. It was also Pizlo's destination.

The boy pushed open the door and paused on the threshold. A stiffened piece of bark above the entrance made a sharp click-clack sound, announcing his arrival and perforce the shop's owner, two clerks, and assorted patrons glanced his way. And then, just as swiftly, acting as with one mind, they averted their gaze, resuming their earlier conversations and actions as best they could. Pizlo didn't care. He helped himself to a wicker basket by the door and began wandering up and down the aisles, skirting past people before they could stiffen at his approach or attempt to dodge him. The thing he needed most was also the oddest item on his list, and if Suliv's didn't have it, Pizlo had no idea where he would get one. He could read pretty well, much better than regular children his age, or so Jorl had assured him, but he'd never seen the word *emergency* printed before, either by itself or alongside other words, and it took him several passes in front of the object of his desire before he recognized it as what he needed. Once he had added it to his basket, Pizlo knew the rest would be easy.

Moving more quickly now, he pulled down an assortment of food from the shelves, some fresh and some dried. He selected three expandable mesh bags, and when he reached the limits of his basket he began filling the bags. He also chose a small bottle of dye of a deep indigo hue, staring at it for a long time, though midway through his eyes drifted closed as he listened intently to the bottle's silent whispering.

Pizlo plopped himself down in the aisle, opened the bottle and dipped the little finger of his left hand into the solution to the first joint. He pulled it out and inspected the vivid color that had already penetrated that bit of skin. Satisfied, he tucked his chin down and began painting a series of crude circles in a series of four rows, re-dipping his finger as necessary. First one, then three, then two more, and finally one. Three of the circles he filled in, blue from edge to center; the other four he left open. Having bathed and scrubbed just the night before in the fountain, his pale skin gleamed cleaner than it had in some time, and the contrast of dye against the white flesh drew the eye.

He wiped his finger off on the bottom of his foot, rubbing the tip against the resulting stain again and again to confirm that it was dry. Satisfied that he wouldn't leave a mark when he touched something or walked, he got to his feet again. Pizlo resealed the bottle, stuffed it into one of his bags, and strode deliberately to the counter at the front of the store. A Lox that looked enough like Tolta to maybe be his aunt stood at the counter, and an Eleph who seemed to know her stood behind waiting for her turn. Pizlo meant to get in line behind them, but at his approach one slipped left and the other right. They'd left their intended purchases strewn across the counter. A shocked clerk stood on the other side with literally nowhere to go. His eyes darted side to side. He lashed his trunk with agitation and fanned his ears, not daring to look at the albino boy loaded down with store goods.

"I need all of this stuff," said Pizlo, piling his selections on the counter which was at a height even with his trunk.

"Yinto was here the other day," said the clerk, seeming to speak to the possible-aunt that had a moment earlier left him there. "He said his eldest daughter, the one that moved to Kelpry, the island just past Gerd, had twins. Can you believe that? Twins!"

"I don't have any money. But I need it. All of it."

The clerk's trunk darted spastically but otherwise he gave no acknowledgment that Pizlo stood on the other side of his counter. "Remarkable thing, twins. Yinto said that no one on Kelpry could remember the last time it happened. Got to be three generations back, at least."

"I'm going to pay you with a story instead. A prophecy."

The other shoppers had melted away, down the store's aisles far out of sight or out the door and on down the boardway as quickly as possible, perhaps just in case Pizlo chose to exit and follow them. Trapped behind his counter, the clerk looked like he wanted to cry.

Pizlo wanted to cry sometimes. But he didn't now, and he couldn't indulge the clerk's feelings. He had to get going. He needed the things he'd gathered, and had already used some of the dye. He couldn't just take everything though. "I know you're not supposed to look at me. Or listen to anything I say. I know those are the rules. But prophecies trump rules. They have to. Rules look backward, they're blind to the situations that might come up after someone makes them. But prophecies only look forward. So they're more important. Okay?"

The clerk only fanned his ears faster. He called out as if to a customer down one of the aisles. "Those are on special today. Three for the price of two. One day only!" Maybe there was even someone back there, but Pizlo didn't turn to look. He reached up, put his hands flat on the counter, and whispered.

"Psst, whatever else you do . . . *don't* look at my chest!"

Confused, the clerk did just that, and then immediately averted his gaze.

Stepping back and striking what he hoped was a dramatic pose, Pizlo dropped his voice as low as he could. "I am the bearer of the mark of the seven moons. Three I have seen. By the time I have looked on all seven, I will see you repaid. This is the . . . the prophecy of the shop. Remember it, even though you are not allowed to remember me." He scooped up all his *purchases*, transferring a few from the basket into the remaining empty mesh bag, tossed all three across his shoulder, and left the store.

He'd been right. He didn't need an aleph. He had moons.

FOURTEEN

IMPROPER IMPLICATIONS

It was one thing for a widow living alone to invite a man who was an old family friend into her home for dinner. Fant males were notorious for poor nutrition, resulting as much from a disinclination to learn basic culinary skills as a seemingly innate ability to burn water. But let that young widow visit that same male friend at his own apartment and entire leagues of gossips would chatter for days at the implications of impropriety.

Not that anything would ever happen with Jorl, Tolta was sure of that. She'd given up caring what other people thought about her when Pizlo had been born, the unexpected child she'd refused to deny. She'd entered into local lore, and had no doubt that more than one grandmother in Keslo told frightening bedtime stories of the Abomination's mother living among them. People whispered about her anytime she passed by, it was no more preposterous to have them whispering about alleged affairs with Jorl ben Tral. As if that was the only reason she might have to seek him out.

In point of fact, she'd gone to his home in response to the note she'd found on her door. He'd often left similar missives in the past when going off with Arlo on the sort of foolhardy errand or misguided adventure that the two men should have worked out of their systems back in their teens. Hard won experience had taught her to ignore the innocence in his message and pursue whatever he wasn't bothering to tell her. She intended to confront him face to face before he went off and did something beyond stupid again, like joining the Patrol.

But she'd arrived too late and all her carefully rehearsed patient-but-firm phrases went unspoken. Bother.

She wandered down the boardway from Jorl's front door, passing such shops as catered to bachelors: an all-night health club, a soup and salad bar, a spirits shop, and more. She paused in front of a bookshop that she knew Jorl frequented, and on a whim entered. It was a charming little store, full of paper clutter and endless bookshelves that all seemed to have been made by different hands. A tiny bell above the door announced her arrival and an unseen woman called out, "I'll be right with you" from down some aisle or other.

Tolta browsed, absently wondering what she might pick up to tempt Pizlo to linger one night. He had mentioned borrowing books from Jorl, but perhaps he'd like to have one or more all his own.

"Don't rush on my account. I'm just looking."

A Lox younger than herself came around a corner supporting a massive tome with both hands and trunk. She heaved it up onto a counter with an audible grunt, blushed, wiped her brow and smiled as she gave Tolta her full attention.

"Turning people who are 'just looking' into paying customers is one of the challenges of the job. Are you 'just looking' for anything in particular?"

"In terms of purpose, yes. But as to content, no, not really. I'm looking for something my son might like. He's somewhat precocious and rabidly curious."

The clerk paused and Tolta chided herself. It was possible that a younger woman might not recognize her at a glance, but mentioning Pizlo—even if not by name—would be all the trigger anyone on Keslo would need to bring her story to mind. It was just one more thing she didn't want to deal with this day. She turned to go.

"I think I've seen him."

Tolta paused in midstep. *Seen him?* No one *saw* Pizlo, or if they did, couldn't admit to it. Since Arlo's death, only two people in the world willingly saw her son. She turned back.

"Excuse me?"

"He . . . didn't come into the shop. I only noticed him because of the man who did come in. They'd arrived together but your son waited outside for him. He'd been in earlier to order some specialty items and dropped by to inquire if they'd arrived yet. The man, I mean, not your son."

Tolta smiled. "That would be Jorl ben Tral."

"Oh! You know him? Wait, of course you do, or you wouldn't trust your son in his care. Sorry, I . . . I just get a bit flustered." The clerk's cheeks reddened and she turned half away, busying herself with rearranging some books on a handy shelf.

"Flustered? Because of Jorl? Whatever for?"

She stilled her hands on the shelf and turned back to Tolta with a gleam in her eye and a giddy shyness that the older woman hadn't seen since slumber parties back when she lived in the vast house with her mother and aunts and cousins.

"He just . . . wasn't what I expected."

"You were expecting something?"

"Yes. I mean, no, not really. I . . . I haven't been in Keslo long. But when I arrived and took this job I learned that the newest Bearer lived nearby. Someone like that, someone who's *done* things, enough to earn an aleph! I thought maybe I might see him once or twice, but he comes into the shop all the time."

"He is fond of his books." Tolta smiled and found herself warming to the girl. "Mind you, he's written more than a few himself."

"Oh, I know. I stock them all. I have a section devoted to him, two whole shelves. Have you read his work? I have. I've read all of them. I never thought anyone could make history so interesting."

"You sound like you have quite the crush on him."

"No . . . not really. I mean, nothing could ever come of it. He's too important a person. He'd never even notice me."

Having known Jorl most of her life, Tolta had never thought of him as important. He'd just always been there, carousing around with Arlo, standing Second at their wedding and again at her husband's funeral, helping fill the void in Pizlo's life. When he'd left on his scatter-brained adventure with the Patrol he had left a hole in their lives. When he'd returned, she'd wept when she'd realized how much she welcomed his unasked-for support. How had she not noticed that she was the only one on Barsk who didn't see him any differently than before he'd gone? A celebrity? Of a sort. But important? Whatever Jorl's other faults, ego was not among them. If he hadn't noticed the obvious interest of a pretty and bookish woman it had more to do with his own distraction than anything resembling importance. She smiled as she recalled all the stupid things he and Arlo—and sometimes all three of them—had done.

"My name's Tolta, by the way."

"Dabni."

"A pleasure to meet you, Dabni." And it was. The young woman hadn't actually interacted with her son, that was probably beyond the pale, but she could admit having seen him. Wonder of wonders. "You know, my mother and his mother grew up together and are still the best of friends. He and I have been around each other our whole lives and he even introduced me to my late husband. I'm sure there are all kinds of stories I could tell of him from long before he was marked."

"Oh! I'd like that very much."

"Well, we should make a date of it then. Perhaps over tea sometime."

"I have tea," said Dabni. "In the back. I mean, I could make us tea. And I have some cookies a customer dropped off that I don't mind sharing. If you're interested, I mean."

Tolta bit her lip at the girl's obvious infatuation. Did other people see Jorl this way? Perhaps there was more to the gossip she'd set in motion than she realized.

"That sounds wonderful. Thank you."

Dabni scrambled to clear a spot on a table and drag over two weathered but sturdy chairs. "Make yourself at home. I'll just be a minute with the tea." She vanished back around the corner of a tall bookshelf, her voice carrying back. "And while you're telling me about Jorl, I can see about finding you a book for your son."

Tolta settled back and smiled. Better and better.

FIFTEEN

MEETING SILENCE

~~~~~~~

BARSK'S first generation of Fant had bargained with the Alliance in the creation of their Compact, and each believed they'd gotten the better deal. The other planets enjoyed Barsk's pharmacopeia, and the Fant received isolation, a guarantee that their cultural beliefs would be respected by the Alliance, and a promise that only Eleph and Lox would ever set foot upon their planet.

The Alliance had been willing to let them have Barsk eight hundred years earlier due to the soaking weather. Except for the Lox and Eleph, all of the other races had fur. While a few enjoyed the water, none appreciated an endless forecast of rain. There was also the matter of land, or rather, the lack of it.

The northern hemisphere didn't contain a speck of earth above sea level. The pole contained enough solid ice to constitute a continent, but it couldn't support life. Just south of the equator, two chains of islands provided the planet's only habitable land, the western and eastern archipelagos. Barsk's only true continent lay at its southern pole; several type of flightless birds dwelled along its edges, feeding on the fish that spawned in shallow waters along its shoreline. To the rest of the Alliance, trying to live on the tiny polar continent made an existence on the rainy islands seem luxurious. And none of them had wanted the islands in the first place.

But it did make the southern continent the perfect place for a secret base.

Nonyx-Captain Selishta hadn't bothered to toss Jorl into a cell. Instead, he had followed her to the ship's bridge, and then settled into a corner when she'd directed him to keep out of the way while she relieved the acting commander who saluted and departed back the way they had come. The Cheetah took the time to speak briefly with the remaining bridge officers. Selishta maintained a rigid discipline on her ship; none of her crew had so much as glanced his way.

When she advanced on him in his corner, she moved with that same liquid gait, stopping just out of reach of arms or trunk.

"I am thinking you might be an omen of changing fortune, Ensign-Retired. Certainly you have altered my belief in the tales that suggest all of you Fant are as dumb as rocks. None of the other Fant I've acquired on this mission could manage intelligent conversation, though perhaps that was a function of their age and their insistence on being dead." Her lip curled up in a toothy smirk. "You're not dead, are you, Ensign-Retired?"

Jorl whipped his trunk up at a stiff angle, giving the captain a salute as only a Lox or Eleph could, a foolish display he'd used in the Patrol before he'd learned how much it antagonized his superiors. "Not dead, and more than alive enough to know when an officer is obeying illegal orders."

The Nonyx had flinched at his salute, but smiled at his reply, her whole mouth gaping wide to reveal small teeth and pairs of larger fangs above and below. "My exemption from your Compact is not illegal. The same senate that crafted it has the power to issue exceptions to it. So spare me further arguments about my presence or interference in your culture."

"Even dumb rocks know that a treaty cannot be altered so conveniently. Surely the same is true of Patrol captains."

She frowned, her nostrils wrinkling in a sudden whuff of air. "I find your novelty already wearing thin even as your presence thickens the air on my bridge."

She darted a hand behind her in a crisp gesture. A blue-clad Jaguar arrived at her side but the captain offered no acknowledgment and continued with Jorl. "Your amusement value notwithstanding, I do not see ship's discipline served by allowing you to remain here, even for the short span of our return trip. But we have exchanged promises and I will not stain your record with imprisonment. Rismas!"

The Jaguar responded with an instantaneous "Ma'am!"

"May I introduce Theraonca-Ensign Rismas. He will escort you down to the secondary hold, taking you there the long way around so by the time you reach your destination, we will have reached ours. Others of my crew will have assembled the rest of our . . . cargo there. I'm sure you'll fit right in."

The captain turned her head and with a nod caused the ensign to step closer to Jorl.

"Rismas, while it would be splendid to assume that our guest will be civilized and do as bid, assumptions are not the basis of command. If he deviates or otherwise stalls your well-intentioned efforts to deliver him to the hold, you are authorized to subdue him with such ever means you believe will be most effective."

"Yes, ma'am!"

She turned her attention back to the Fant. "I think that explains things well enough, don't you? I don't want there to be any misunderstandings. It would not surprise me if the Theraonca-ensign resents that you once held the same rank he possesses, so if you give him the slightest provocation, I have no doubt that he will carry out his directive with the utmost zeal. Are we clear?"

"Where is this ship going? Where are you taking me?" asked Jorl.

Selishta showed teeth again. "Who knew the Lox could be so comedic? You'll have your answer when we arrive. I'm sure the officer waiting at our destination will take personal responsibility for you once you're off my ship. But I believe we are done. The novel experience of chatting with a Lox-ensign-retired, is fleeting at best."

She pivoted to regard her ensign long enough to say, "Rismas, you have your orders," and had crossed the bridge to speak with her other officers before the last word had left her lips.

"You know," said Rismas, "I've seen images and flims of Fant before, but you're much uglier in person."

Jorl's reply died in his mouth unspoken as a sensation he'd not had since childhood struck him without warning. A thrumming that resonated in his head, a child's rhyming game long forgotten. *Playing . . . Straying . . . Will you be betraying?*

"Did you hear that?"

"What, can you hear the engines engage with those giant ears of yours?"

"No, the rhyme . . . you didn't feel it?"

Rismas frowned, his eyes narrowing to slits. "Which is it, hear or feel? Either way, I didn't. But we're underway now. So get up. The corridor should be clear and it's not a far walk down to the secondary hold. And like the captain said, if you give me any trouble it will be the last thing you do."

The Jaguar stepped back out of the reach of Jor's trunk as he got to his feet. Jorl turned slowly, trying to get a better feel for the source, but without alarming Rismas in the process. He rubbed at a spot on his forehead just below his aleph and flexed as he hadn't since he and Arlo had played *Seek Me* when they were boys. *Free . . . Free . . . Tree and me . . . Free . . .*

Almost instantly, a response came back. *Treeing . . . Seeing . . . Will you be agreeing?* The phrase every child on Barsk experienced when welcomed into a game. He glanced around at the bridge crew. In addition to the Nonyx-captain and the Theraonca assigned to keep watch on him, he noted an Apolodon-lieutenant sitting at the main navigation board and a pair of Geoms running the secondary and tertiary boards. All seemed oblivious to the infrasonic rhymes, something to be felt rather than heard.

"This way. Now."

Jorl complied, walking calmly, hands open and at his sides. He kept his trunk down and close to his body so that Rismas, walking a step behind and to the right, wouldn't see it. His remarks hadn't surprised Jorl, he'd heard it often enough while in the Patrol, usually in response to his trunk or lack of fur, or sometimes both. The instructions were simple enough and he had no doubt about the ensign's response if he provided any excuse.

Contrary to his assurances, it seemed that they actually walked quite a ways, passing an interminable number of closed doors on either side, each bearing a numbered control pad. His feet already ached from pounding on the unforgiving and lifeless flooring with every step. Through it all, the rhyming thrum continued around him, echoing in his skull, growing louder, more urgent. *To The Tree . . . To The Tree . . . All Come Free . . .* Calling all players to the home tree at the end of the day's sport.

"Stop." The Jaguar issued the command as they came up alongside a double-wide doorframe.

"I take it this is the secondary hold?"

Rismas ignored the question and tapped at the pad alongside the door. "Captain said you were in the Patrol, so you know how this works. The hold has a standard, two-door airlock. Both sides are under full atmo, so there'll be no delay. I open this side, you walk in and I close it behind you. Then the inner door parts and you enter the hold. Don't linger; I can tell. The airlock has security measures and I'll use them."

The door uncoupled with a familiar clunk and rolled open. Without a glance at the ensign, Jorl walked into the airlock, stopping a step shy of the far door. He managed not to flinch as the outer door sealed behind him. Regardless of the nature of Selishta's *cargo*, it had to be better than the blind bigotry of the ship's crew.

He waited; the thrumming he'd first felt on the bridge throbbed at its strongest here. The inner door clunked, an identical sound as before, and rolled back revealing a scene of unspeakable horror. Facing him from inside the hold had to be twenty, maybe thirty, Eleph and Lox, not simply elderly, but Dying. He saw it at once, something in the eyes that he'd last seen in his father the morning he'd sailed away. As surely all of these had sailed, and never reached their goal. The Nonyx-captain had collected them, just as she'd intercepted Jorl bound for the same destination.

He stepped from the airlock into the hold and the thrumming fell away.

One of the Eleph made a gesture with his trunk that was both dismissive and disbelieving. "Oh. You're not what we expected. Not what we expected at all." He paused. His mouth worked like he was chewing bitter grass, then he offered his hand. "My name is Rüsul."

Jorl fanned his ears and introduced himself. He took the

oldster's hand, grasped it firmly but let it go quicker than might have been polite. His heart raced. He gazed upon a cargo hold full of the Dying, men and women pulled out of time. He'd been in space. He'd Spoken to the dead. Others might find such things bizarre or inconceivable, but he had not flinched at them. But this, the wrongness of it was like knots in his trunk. He'd never felt so clammy.

He crossed the few steps that separated him from the others, Rüsul's words reflected on their faces. "Not what we expected at all." Part of him recoiled from so much as breathing the same air. Their very presence was unthinkable. And yet . . . they were not to blame. He had to hold it together, help them somehow. And who better? Perhaps accepting the presence of Arlo's son into his life, teaching a boy whom society insisted was a pariah, maybe that and not the aleph was the reason he was here.

Beyond the end of their years, they had reached out to him with the voices of children. He had to speak to them now as adults, if for no other reason than to show them that he could.

"I know you," he said. "Margda knew you, knew of you, centuries ago. You're the source of the Silence."

"Don't talk to us," said an elderly Lox. "It's not right. You shouldn't be speaking to any of us."

His shoulders dropped, his ears stilled their movement, and in a whisper that the cavernous hold made loud enough to hear, Jorl said, "You called to me. I've felt you calling to me almost since I came aboard."

"We thought you were one of us," said the Eleph who had first voiced disappointment. "That you'd sailed off as the rest of us had. That your final journey had been interrupted."

"It was. Well, not my final journey, but I was bound for the last island same as the rest of you."

"But you're not Dying?" asked Rüsul. "How could you know where to go?"

"I didn't, actually. I had some help. It's, uh, complicated."

The Lox who'd wanted him quiet advanced upon the Eleph, her trunk swiping at him even as she shook a finger in his face. "Stop talking to him. It only makes him talk back. He shouldn't even be looking at us. He's alive and we're done with all that. You know that. It's how it should be. How it's always been."

A slow rumble of murmurs, hoots, and trumpets swept through the Dying.

Rüsul batted at the old woman's trunk and stomped his feet in place. "None of this is like it's always been. None of us should be together. None of us should be in this place. The Cheetah and her Dogs plucked each of us from the ocean, and nothing of tradition fits now."

"He's right," said Jorl. "This is what the Matriarch foresaw. This is part of what she called the Silence."

"I read the prophecies," said a new voice, another female Lox, even older than the first who'd spoken. "Back when I was in school. I remember them. And you have an aleph. Are you then the 'newest Aleph'? Is that why you're here?"

"I think maybe I am. Like the Matriarch, I'm a Speaker. I set out to reach the last island, hoping to solve the riddle of the Silence. I never imagined it would bring me here, or that I'd be talking to all of you."

"You shouldn't be. I don't care what that one says, it's unnatural and wrong."

"You all need to stop talking and pay attention," said an amplified voice, thundering through the hold. All the Fant turned toward it. Some gasped, others flinched, but all reacted to the sight of a Bear standing on a tiny balcony above a gate in the far wall.

"Use those miserable ears you're all so proud of and hear me well; I won't be repeating myself. I am Urs-Major Krasnoi, and I command the internment facilities which are your new home. In a moment, the external gate of this hold will open. When it does, you are to exit in an orderly line. My staff will process you and see you settled. There'll be a meal waiting for you in the yard. Likewise, barracks and a bed for each of you. Eat well, sleep well. Tomorrow we will begin the interrogations and learn if any of you are of use to me."

Chaos erupted from the Dying Fant in the form of stomping and trumpeting with no sign of stopping. Some few began to shout their confusion.

"Interrogations?"

"The Compact!"

"Internment?"

"Don't talk to us!"

The major shifted, rearing back and raising one hand high and behind his head. In the next moment the hand leapt forward as he hurtled a tiny ball with the fury of an accomplished athlete. It struck one of the hollering Dying squarely in her forehead, bounced halfway back toward the balcony, and fell among the crowd. The target Fant's voice cut off and she crumpled to the floor. Everyone else fell silent, though a pair of Fant nearest Krasnoi's target helped her to stand and nodded to the others around that she was all right.

"I told you to stop talking and pay attention. I don't care about your Compact or your customs. You're here because I've gleaned from studying your culture that none of you will be missed. You can all get back to killing yourselves after I have what I need."

Jorl pushed his way through throng of subdued Dying until he stood directly below Krasnoi. "Which is what? What do you want to know?"

"Koph," said the Bear. "When we know about koph, we'll know what comes next."

SIXTEEN

UNEXAMINED CORNERS

~~~~~~~~

PIZLO had always moved about freely, whether along the boardways used by other Fant in the Civilized Wood, or more commonly crashing his way through the surrounding foliage. He clambered branch to branch and tree to tree, swung by vines, or simply dropped from one perch to another. Arlo and Tolta had ignored custom and morality by acknowledging him as their true child, but that hadn't been enough to make him a part of the mainstream. He lived wild and free, sleeping when he felt the need in shelters he built for himself, or more rarely in the room Tolta maintained for him. He ate when he remembered to, grazing on the fruit, nuts, seeds, and leaves growing plentifully throughout the forest, or stocking up on cooked victuals when taking lessons from Jorl or visiting Tolta. In his six years, he had explored every bit of space on the island of Keslo, from the highest point of the canopy to the wet darkness of the Shadow Dwell. Keslo was his home, but much as Jorl had, Pizlo knew he had to leave. He didn't need to go out, not into space and beyond like his mentor, but he would be going up. And he couldn't do that from Keslo.

The question of how to travel to a neighboring island had never come up before. In his own way, and all unknowing, he'd been bound by the same cultural restrictions that kept the Fant of his home from interacting with him. The *Mistakes of Nature* almost never lasted through infancy. Those few that had, did not survive to adulthood, and so the need to wander from home had never occurred among his kind. Abominations always belonged to their neighborhoods, abandoned in the public meeting space soon after birth and reared grudgingly and at arm's length by committee, without any warmth or love. It was no more possible for one to board a boat or raft and cross the water to visit another island than it was for a Fant to fly. And yet, every child of Barsk had heard the story of Pholo, however apocryphal it might be. Whether real or simply metaphorical, a Fant had flown. Pizlo couldn't fly, but Pholo's story offered precedent enough for him to defy both custom and propriety. He set out for Zlorka, two islands' distance north of Keslo.

The main university in the western archipelago had been built on Zlorka, and to hear Jorl speak of it, it was the most cosmopolitan spot on the planet. Its northern edge touched the equator, and a harbor there housed the anchoring end of the planet's sole space elevator.

Pizlo's mesh bags made it difficult to travel by a direct route, so he walked and ran by turns along the vast maze of boardways that snaked through the Civilized Wood until he reached a balcony on its northern most point. From there he hugged his bags tightly to his body and hurtled into trees. With the ease of endless practice he began to climb down and drop. Even so, he descended much more slowly than his normal pell-mell method, exercising more care so his supplies didn't snag on anything along the way. The extra time allowed him the luxury of grabbing handfuls of tasty leaves and nuts as he traveled, stuffing his mouth and filling his daypouch for later. By late afternoon he stood upon a narrow beach, little more than a strip of sand and gravel that marked the space between the ocean and the beginning of the forest. A light rain fell, but the wind whipped nearly sidewise. He felt the impacts like a myriad of tiny stones striking him without pause, but as ever Pizlo took no pain from any of it.

He sat on the sand and unpacked all of his "purchases," setting aside the emergency item—a self-inflating survival boat—and redistributing the rest into his bags and daypouch. He spent a while working out how to activate his prize, but soon enough he had it open and with a twist of a knob it expanded into a shallow disk of bright yellow fabric. Pizlo piled his bags into the craft and dragged it the few steps to the water's edge. The tide lapped at his feet, beckoning, but he paused and did not enter the boat.

"I'm going now," he said, turning back to the forest, but actually addressing the entire island. Pizlo cocked his head, waiting for something that never arrived, and then shrugged. He glanced up at the clouded sky, shielding his sensitive eyes from the rain, and repeated, "I'm leaving, Keslo. This is new. It feels bad, but I'm doing it anyway. Just so you know."

He stepped into the surf, wading away from shore and pulling his boat after him. When he was in up to his waist he spun around and rolled over its side, landing on his back in the bottom. He let the tide carry him out while he got himself settled with his daypouch in his lap and a long-handled paddle gripped in both hands. Dipping the paddle into the water and his trunk into his daypouch where he'd stored the nuts from his shopping, he set out from his home island for the first time, a unique event in the entire history of Barsk.

"I bet this would count toward an aleph," he said, munching on some nuts as he paddled away.

The meager afternoon light gave way to full dusk. The wind died down and the rain went from unfelt stinging to unnoticed patter. Dusk eased into gentle darkness. Pizlo kept paddling. At other times of day there would be dozens of rafts and boats in the water between Keslo and Telba, the next island to the north and a bit west, but the trip required a short span and rarely did anyone feel the need to complicate it by making landfall at night. Pizlo had the water to himself, sparing any other Fant the confusion and horror of encountering him in such an unimaginable place. He was well past Telba by midnight, keeping his course unerringly, as if the ocean's swells themselves passed word to him.

The rain increased again though the wind did not. Fat drops fell straight down and Pizlo had to divide his time between paddling and bailing as the tiny craft rode low with rainwater. He didn't have a map in his head so much as a precise sense of where he was, where he'd been, and where he wanted to be. At a point roughly halfway between Telba and Zlorka the rain eased off and he could concentrate exclusively on paddling again.

His palms and fingers had long since blistered, and the blisters broken open. Pizlo only noticed that the paddle slipped in his grip a bit more than before and attributed it to the rain.

Well before dawn, Pizlo paused. He *felt* something. He had no sensation of pain from his bleeding hands nor any awareness of the strained muscles that had spread across his back. The cramps in his legs from sitting too long in place made him awkward but otherwise caused no discomfort. Rather, an insight had come upon him, like the moment when he'd understood that the glyphs Jorl had shown him could stand for sounds, or the time he finally realized that it wasn't his difference that made Tolta talk to him but her own. Pizlo had arrived at the equator, and he knew it.

Since rounding Telba, he had paddled northeast, aiming not to reach Zlorka at its nearest point, but to come upon it from the side and then circle around toward its northern face. The harbor of the space elevator awaited him. He turned his boat due west, paddling ahead in the dark, and soon after could make out light. A faint glowing strand rose up out of the mist, disappearing as it climbed. A bit later, he came ashore, the line between water and beach visible in the light from the elevator. His legs folded uselessly beneath him when he tried to climb out of the boat. He'd ruined his hands. Shreds of skin that had once been blisters hung from them and the tender flesh beneath bled freely. He gazed briefly at them, seeking patterns in their shape like an augur of flesh, but found nothing and shrugged. He smeared the blood across his thighs and calves as he pushed his hands across them, working cramps from the muscles. On his third attempt, Pizlo stood well enough to stumble from the boat. He slung his day-pouch across his chest. He meant to grab his bags but since letting go of the paddle, his fingers still refused to move properly. He used his trunk instead. Standing in water to his waist, stomping back and forth to make his legs and feet work as they should, he pushed his boat back into the water.

"Thank you," he said to the boat, drawing out the moment, never having known a boat before, not knowing if he would again.

He scrambled out of the surf and onto the beach, stumbling like a child who had discovered his parents' liquor chest and sampled with the delight of a natural experimentalist. He pressed the fingers of both hands against his chest, forcing them to flex until he could make them do it of his own volition. Only when his body was working again more or less as it should, did he lift his gaze to the light of the elevator and examine his surroundings.

The space elevator rose out of a complex of buildings. The nearer ones looked much like structures you might find in the Civilized Wood of any island, though built on a larger scale. Pizlo imagined they served as home to those Fant who labored here, day in and out, meeting the barges bringing the pharmaceuticals from those islands responsible for that sort of manufacturing, and loading them into the gleaming cargo pods that sat on nearby tracks leading into edifices like nothing else on Barsk. Each pod was as big as Tolta's house, like a giant cube but with the corners cut off leaving flat triangles and no points. The pods and the tracks they rested upon showed more metal and plastic than Pizlo had ever imagined existing in one place. And the inner buildings rose up in angles not from nature, like monster houses seen only in a nightmare. The tracks flowed into the nightmare, even now with no workers attending them, creeping more slowly than he could walk, to what at first seemed the monster's maw, but which Pizlo realized was only a passage to their true destination. He stared up at the shining beanstalk and counted. Every hundred heartbeats or so, another pod tumbled into the maw and out of sight, and a different one further along in the process rose up in the shaft of light, leaping upward into the sky like it had learned to fly.

Pizlo stumbled to the far end of the tracks, his gait improving by the time he arrived. Dozens of pods sat on rollers, gradually drifting closer to a space where the tracks began, emerging from a housing in the ground. He could see a series of hooks that came up from below, rumbling like thunder as they pulled down the center of the tracks so they hooked on the pods and carried them along the tracks. Likely hundreds of cargo pods had been packed the previous day and left to slide one by one onto the tracks and await their turn up the beanstalk. These were the remaining ones from the day's work. The process would begin again in the morning. Pizlo planned to be far away by then.

He started poking at one of the waiting pods. His fingers still didn't work well, but the sensitive nubs of his trunk were more than capable of working the latches on an access panel and he soon opened it. The inside of the hatch had a packet of pages. The light from the elevator made the headers legible. They read "inventory" in the circular glyphs of the Fant, and presumably the same thing in the boxy marks used by the Alliance. Pizlo braced his arms on either side of the hatch and pulled himself in, his bags banging against the sides before following him. He had enough room to stand up, but an adult would have had to hunch over. He stood in a narrow corridor made by the walls of stacked containers of assorted pharmaceuticals to left and right and underneath. He bumped to either side and jumped up and down but nothing moved. Either they were too heavy, or they'd been bolted in place, maybe both.

Looking back out, he could see the buildings of the complex slowly sliding as his cargo pod edged ever closer to the track. He took some time to examine the inside surface of the hatch, making sure he could open it from within before closing it and shutting out the bit of light and the sound and smell of the ocean. In total darkness he explored his corridor, taking his time to turn at every junction and to double back again until he'd covered every pace. He imagined some Alliance sapient, probably from one of the smaller races like a Geom or Marmo, purposefully striding where he had roamed, comparing the cargo in the pod to some manifest in hand.

He settled himself in a corner, his back against the intersection of two walls of containers, and put his bags down. Everything jolted once, and a faint rumbling echoed around him. His pod had arrived onto the main track at last and a hook was pulling it slowly closer to the entrance of the elevator. Now that he was here, the efforts of the long day caught up with him. He'd never been so tired, but as much as he wanted to close his eyes and sleep, he needed to deal with thirst and hunger first. His fingers felt all puffy, but at least his hands had stopped being slippery. He held a water container in place with the heels of his hands and opened it with his nubs, dropping his trunk into it as soon as the lid came free and slurping up the entire contents. Next he went through all the sweet grasses and succulent fruit from one of his mesh bags and ate until it was almost empty before putting it away. He set the empty bottle aside, carefully putting the cap back in place; he didn't know how long he would have to be in here, but he didn't want to make a mess for that hypothetical Marmo, and so he might be refilling the container before he left.

Thirst quenched and belly full, Pizlo curled up tight, shoving his damaged hands into his armpits and tucking his trunk under his crossed arms. He dropped into a deep and dreamless sleep even before his cargo pod had worked its way to the elevator. The rumbling of the track stopped, and while he slumbered he entered the shaft of the beanstalk and began to climb, faster than anything he had ever imagined.

SEVENTEEN

DEAD VOICES

~~~~~~

TWENTY-SEVEN other Fant had been on the ship that abducted Rüsul—twenty-eight if he counted the young man who so clearly did not belong—and they had come from all different islands, from both the eastern and western archipelagos. Despite a long life, he hadn't known any of them, though a few recognized his name or had known someone who had met someone who owned one of his carvings. The internment facility was different. Nearly two hundred others had been snatched up from the ocean on their respective voyages to what they'd imagined to be the final journey of their lives.

He had no sooner finished being "processed" by a pair of utterly disinterested Feln when a trunk fell upon his shoulder and a familiar voice exclaimed "It is you! By my grandfather's tusks, I swore I'd never forget the scar on your ear no matter the years that passed."

An ancient Eleph stood behind him, arms akimbo and as grim an expression on her face as any Rüsul had known. "Phas? Can it be? I've not seen you since—"

"Since you jilted me and went off with another woman, you old bastard!"

Never smart when it came to women, Rüsul didn't even try to stop the laughter that came burbling out of him. "That was always your problem, confusing a man's free choice with a personal attack. And I have to think I made the right choice. After two children and more years together than I ever deserved, my mate never once got mad enough to tear into me like you did."

The other Fant slapped Rüsul's shoulder again and gave out a loud whoop, revealing her initial anger as mere pretense. "Two kids? Well, I should probably be thankful that she got you instead of me. I wasn't ready for children for a long while, and I learned quick enough not to become involved with men who didn't want to wait."

Rüsul's nubs lightly grazed the mark on his left ear, his thoughts hurtling back to a foolish bachelor trying to woo the two prettiest women on Telba at the same time. "It's been a long time since I thought back to that night. Probably just denial that I was ever so young and stupid."

"Maybe I scared some maturity into you. I confess, I was angry for days. But you actually did me a favor. I caught a boat headed to Zlorka and threw myself into my studies. I wouldn't have had the career I did if you hadn't broken my heart. But it's all crumbled leaves, eh? It's good to see a familiar face here. Not that any of us expected to see another soul."

"What is this place, Phas? How long have you been here?"

"Time makes little sense anymore. The day goes on and on. The night comes and goes in less time than a midday nap requires. The company is depressing and the food's terrible. And the outsiders, they're the worst. The Feln aren't so bad, they look down on everyone, but the Ailuros are indifferent and the Taxi are flat cruel. Not that any of it matters to most of these Fant, they're so wrapped up in their own heads about having set off to die that not much gets to them."

"And what makes you so different?"

Phas laughed. "A lifetime spent with the dead. I was a historian, and all of this feels like just another story to me, the only difference being I've been cast in the events this time around."

Before Rüsul could respond, the young Lox from the ship approached the older pair of Elephs, trunk down and ears still, like a reluctant child presenting himself after having shattered some bit of crockery in an ill-conceived game that should never have been played indoors.

"Excuse me, I did not mean to eavesdrop, but I thought I recognized your voice and I heard you say you were a historian, yes?"

Phas stumbled back, clearly startled by the presence of the young man even as her gaze locked onto his tattooed forehead. Rüsul saw recognition flash into his former lover's eyes.

"Jorl ben Tral! What in the world are you doing here?"

The Lox shrugged and relaxed as he came closer. "In a way, I'm here because I went looking to ask you about a text, only you'd sailed off a season earlier. I tried to Speak to you, and couldn't. And that put me in mind of Margda's prophecy about the Silence and—"

Nodding her head and fanning her ears, Phas interrupted. "And you're the newest Aleph, of course." She swept her trunk toward Rüsul. "Allow me to perform some introductions. Rüsul, may I present my colleague, Jorl ben Tral. And Jorl, this is Rüsul ben Shel, the boy that got away and whom I blame for a life spent in academia."

Rüsul opened his mouth to speak then stopped.

Jorl nodded and sighed. "I'm sorry. My mark notwithstanding, it's fine if you're not comfortable talking to me."

"It's not that," said Rüsul, eyes focused over Jorl's shoulder. "I was just distracted by that person rushing toward us."

Jorl turned around to see, recognizing the woman who sped up as she now clearly recognized him as well.

"I might have known! Jorl ben Tral! No surprise to see you showing up when there's oddness. You oaf, what did you do this time?"

Phas's head spun as she stared first at the swiftly approaching Lox and then to Jorl. "This is your doing?"

"No, of course not," said Jorl.

"You said he was a colleague. I thought you meant a fellow historian, not that he also had a history of erratic behaviors," said Rüsul.

"What are you implying?" Phas's trunk coiled defensively. "Erratic? I was scorned, and I—"

"Oh my," said Jorl. "Kembü?"

"Kembü?" repeated Rüsul and Phas together.

"The mother of my best friend. He and I, uh, used to get into a lot of trouble."

"Hrumph!" said Kembü, as she stopped her charge just short of knocking Jorl over. "My boy got into trouble. You, on the other hand, sowed chaos with your every breath. I swear, they gave you that mark for being contrary, if for anything at all. Now tell me what you did to cause all of this!" She threw out an arm, encompassing the entire yard.

"Honestly, none of this is my doing. I doubt I know more of what's going on than any of you."

"I don't think that's quite true," said Phas. "The ship that abducted each of us, it's a Patrol vessel, isn't it?"

"Yes, but—"

"And you served in the Patrol. And then there's the matter of Margda's prophecy of the Silence."

"Yes, but I—"

"Relax, Jorl, I'm not accusing you of anything, but we both have studied too much history to ignore coincidence. Come on. There's some folk I want you to meet. They're not so deep being dead as most of the others here. I suspect you've a story to tell, and I want them to hear it. Rüsul, and uh, Kembü, you're welcome to come, too."

Rüsul shrugged. "I've only got one other place to be, same as the rest of you, and I don't imagine this will slow that trip one way or the other. Let's go."

They made their way a short distance to a corner where two of the barracks halls met. Three other Fant, a woman and two men, sat on shallow cots, heads bowed in quiet conversation. Phas trumpeted at them as she approached, causing all three to lift their heads.

"Seems my day to be doing introductions. The lady is Mlarma, the fellow on the left is Tarva and the other is Abso. This handsome devil here is Rüsul, whom I haven't seen since the world was young, and this woman is Kembü, whom I've only just met. The youngster, who is being ignored or shunned by all the right-thinking Fant in the yard is Jorl, a former colleague."

"You're not Dying," said Abso. He sat shoulder to shoulder with the other man, trunks lightly entwined. "Everyone else here was picked up on their last journey. How did the Dogs grab you?"

Phas had vanished into a barracks while Abso spoke and reappeared now dragging a pair of cots. Rüsul set them up for himself and Kembü and Phas went back for more.

Jorl captured his attention as he explained about how he had set out for the final island. He elaborated on the prophecy that Phas had mentioned, backtracked to explain how he'd acquired his mark of passage. Rüsul almost lost the thread of the story as the youngster rambled on about serving in the Patrol, but eventually he tied it all together and brought it through to the present moment.

Mlarma nodded and said, "Phas has been telling us tales out of Barsk's past and earlier before the Fant were brought all together. It seems to me, that the most unlikely events almost have to happen, or life would just be dull and no one would write anything down. Your experiences are no more bizarre than these two." She jerked her trunk at the two men who responded by smiling at her.

"Forty and some odd years ago, I was a poet," said Abso. "I wandered over half of the islands of both archipelagos, finding inspiration in the strangest of places and never dreaming I might stop and settle down. Then I met this one and realized I'd found the muse I hadn't known I'd been seeking."

Tarva blushed and picked up the tale. "I taught math," he said. "Not the most popular of fields, nor the easiest. But it suited me. I'd also wandered, even more than him. There was always something in me that would not let me stay still. But I managed, for a time, after meeting Abso. It was wondrous, but after three seasons together I just couldn't stay. You know how the wanderlust gets for some? And yet, in all the rest of my life's wandering, I never met another person who spoke words to rival the beauty of mathematics."

"Nor I, anyone who let me see things in such miraculous ways."

Phas made a rude noise with her trunk and everyone started. "So here we sit, two hundred-some Dying Fant, and these two act like it's some deliberate act of the universe set in motion for no better reason than to bring them back together again. I've known other poets and fictionists with big egos, but who knew mathematicians thought so highly of themselves?"

Rüsul stiffened, but from the reactions of the others it was quickly clear that this was old ground they covered and the remark in good fun. And almost without thought, he joined in and told a story of his own life, followed by Kembü telling one about herself when she was younger than Jorl—and judging by the expression on his face it was clear he'd never imagined his friend's mother as ever having had any other life.

When it was Tarva's turn again he sighed and got a wistful look in his eye. "All of this reminds me of my gram. She had the most amazing adventures. Of course, it never occurred to us that any of it might not be true. But Gram wasn't telling us tales for truth. She filled us with concepts and questions and amazement for the world. I like to think Gram was a born mathematician, only she never knew it."

Phas, Mlarma, and Abso chuckled, and Rüsul realized they'd heard this comment before. If Tarva noticed, he gave no sign.

"I couldn't have been more than four, and it was one of my sister's birthday, though now I don't recall which one. Our aunts had cooked her her favorite meal and barely two bites into it Gram asked her if it was good. My sis laughed and told her it was delicious, and Gram nodded and we all went back to eating. A bit later she asked her 'does it taste like it did the first time you had it, and decided it was your favorite, or when you say it's delicious are you tasting the memory of that first time, and making a comparison?' That was my Gram."

Tarva paused, turned to gaze into Abso's eyes for a moment, and then smiled sheepishly as he continued. "And just like that, she changed my life. I mean, wasn't she really asking if the second time we do a thing are we forced to remember the previous time to understand it? That every time my sister ate that meal, at some level, she was eating all the other same meals? I tell you now with no shame that it gave me bad dreams for nights, the notion that so little in life is truly novel, that so much of what we do is connected to our previous experience of virtually the same thing.

"One evening, about five nights after my sister's birthday dinner, Gram found me sobbing in my sleep and woke me. She asked me why I was crying and I tried to explain it to her, how it seemed like life had become empty and hollow if most everything I was going to do was something I'd already done. And do you know what she said? She told me that if that was true, then I'd done something new by fretting and crying about it, and that now that was old stuff and if I was really that worried about all of it, then I shouldn't bother doing either of those things again. Then she hugged me and wished me good dreams. And when I fell back to sleep everything was fine. Neatly tied up. And now here I am, telling that same story again, and when I think that it's so like but still a bit different from the other times I've told it, instead of feeling the futility of things, I can almost feel my Gram hugging me and telling me to go back to sleep."

Abso sighed. "And I'm the one who's supposed to be the poet, right?"

Rüsul could only nod. He looked at Phas, thinking of a life he hadn't known, and then glanced at Jorl. The young man looked to be pondering the story still, or perhaps pondering futility itself.

EIGHTEEN

ONE-SIDED CONVERSATION

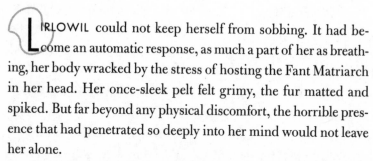

LIRLOWIL could not keep herself from sobbing. It had become an automatic response, as much a part of her as breathing, her body wracked by the stress of hosting the Fant Matriarch in her head. Her once-sleek pelt felt grimy, the fur matted and spiked. But far beyond any physical discomfort, the horrible presence that had penetrated so deeply into her mind would not leave her alone.

The koph she'd consumed for the summoning had long since worn off, but Margda had stayed. Lirlowil had woken up slumped over her workstation, and dared to hope that her last summoning had been a dream. But when she closed her eyes, the old Fant was there. With frantic precision she'd performed the patterns and rituals for ending a summoning and dispersing the nefshons of her conversant, but to no effect. The particles of the discoverer of Speaking had taken on a life all their own, clinging to her brain. Lirlowil might as well have been in a dream.

"Why won't you leave me? Why are you here?" She hated the whining sound of her own pleas, but couldn't help it. The Fant's enduring presence violated her to her very core. Her mind, which had been the source of all her power, once sacrosanct, had been laid bare. "I'm sorry, I know, I know, I violated the Edict. I shouldn't have. It was wrong. Beyond wrong. But I didn't want to. I didn't have a choice. I didn't want to summon *any* Fant."

She could feel Margda in her mind, as if the Fant sat biding her time in quiet meditation, ignoring the sobs and pleas of her summoner. She'd said nothing since Lirlowil had awakened, merely existing, like some hideous old woman napping in her brain.

When she opened her eyes, she glared at the Lutr and spoke as if picking up the thread of a conversation. "I've told you, Child, your wants and wishes don't interest me. Your sense of volition, or the lack of it, is an illusion. Everything you've done needed doing and was set in motion long ago. Let go of your self-pity. Your feelings in these events matter no more than a leaf's desire to steer the wind!"

The chill and brutal words caused Lirlowil to flee to her sleeping room. She leapt into the null field and threw herself upon her bed, gripping the bedclothes to keep from rebounding in the absence of gravity. Her sobbing shifted to shudders. The room was real, she knew it with certainty. Margda no longer bothered to maintain the nefshon construct of her long-vanished home from Barsk, nor of herself either. The Fant existed as a presence, a hideous creature Lirlowil alone saw when she sought respite from the external world, a voice sneering at her within her own head. But more, Lirlowil's telepathic abilities had vanished. Whether it was a consequence of having Margda in her mind, or something the Fant was doing to her, she didn't know.

"But why won't you leave?" Lirlowil wailed again, to herself, to the room, to the unseen Patrollers who presumably monitored everything in her suite of rooms, but mostly to the obscenity in her mind. "You're not *doing* anything! If you're going to punish me for violating your damn Edict, then just do it and go back to being dead!"

Margda's response began with an echoing chuckle. Lirlowil squirmed as she imagined the sound rippling up and down the Fant's trunk.

"I am doing something. I'm waiting. We've a couple days yet to go before all the players are in place. Besides, if I were to leave now, we both know you would not bring me back. Not at the correct moment, not ever."

Lirlowil sat up in bed. For lack of a better target, her eyes fixed upon the globule of lake water suspended in the center of her room. "The correct moment for what? What are you trying to do? And . . . what will happen to me, when you've finally done it?"

"Ah, self-interest at last. Despite all of our differences, of race and time and distance, we achieve commonality. I understand self-interest."

All at once, Lirlowil could see Margda. It was as if she had suddenly appeared, leaning over her, helping her up, touching her with familiar gestures which both calmed and repulsed at the same time. None of it was real. Bits of her cortex fed her visual and tactile imaginings. The Fant only existed in her mind.

"I am trying to set things right. Or what I believe to be right. To stop the foolishness that has you here in this room in space instead of where you belong. I am trying to save the Compact that I helped create. But foremost, I am trying to save Barsk from those who would destroy it."

The Lutr Speaker stood, head tilted as if listening to a voice in the room, trying to make sense of the words. Could the old woman really be trying to be nice? Had she reappeared just now as a kindness, despite the revulsion she evoked? None of it made any sense, and as she reached that conclusion, she knew Margda witnessed it as well.

"You really are a bright girl, even that fool of a Bear could see that. But you're not terribly introspective and your motivations have never extended beyond your immediate plans."

"What does *any* of that have to do with you?"

"Let's go back to self-interest," said the Fant. "Child, do you want to return home? Do you wish to go back to the vapid life you loved so well? To return to that enchanting realm of fresh water and crisp, clean air and quit this place for good? Then tolerate me a while longer. Your liberation will come as a side effect of the larger changes I'll achieve."

Margda dissolved again into nothingness, at least perceptually. But Lirlowil could feel her still in her mind. The Fant probed her somehow, desperate to turn the Lutr's telepathy on herself. No, she had that wrong. The Matriarch hadn't actually used Lirlowil's telepathic abilities, she'd been poking at them, studying them. From inside, like the mental equivalent of picking up an unfamiliar object and rolling it around in your hands. Lirlowil gasped. The actions were reasonable in some ways, frighteningly intimate in others.

"Good. Calm yourself, that's the way. Now, explain to me how our telepathy works. I will need it for what comes ahead, if either of us are ever to be really free again."

Resigned, Lirlowil had barely begun repeating to herself the exercises from her first tutors in the powers of her mind, when the entrance to her suite opened to admit a black-clad Panda. She leaped to her feet and sailed out of her room and landed in the gravity of the reception area, none of her anxiety and fear apparent in the lithe grace of her movement.

"Save me, please! One of these despicable Fant has invaded my mind. You're security, do something. Secure me!"

"None of your pretend madness. Your request was sent on to Urs-Major Krasnoi and he sees value in it. You're to come with me immediately and take a shuttle downwell."

"Request? I didn't make any request."

The Ailuros frowned at her. She waved one massive black and white hand at Lirlowil's workstation. "You wrote it there, not two hours past. What are you playing at now?"

The Matriarch's voice sounded as if it came from the sleeping chamber, though only the Lutr could hear it. "I knew I forgot to mention something. You wanted to get out of this prison, didn't you? Well, while you were unconscious, I sent a note to your keeper worded to accomplish just that. You see? We don't have to be at cross purposes, Child."

Lirlowil shook her head. "The Major? He wants me planetside? But . . ." She paused. Ignoring the put-upon expression of the Ailuros, she stood taller, her mind racing already for some advantage. By habit she reached out with her mind to the security guard in front of her, eager to pull more information from her thoughts, explanations, interpretations, hunches. Anything at all, anything more than to depend upon the hideous creature in her mind. The power came at her call but ebbed before she could glean anything more than a sliver of hidden fear that she instilled in the security woman.

"Oh my, yes, that's very interesting," whispered Margda, in a voice that now hung just behind Lirlowil's shoulder. "Let's try that again."

Her mind filled with the memory of the scent of fresh rain and the power surged through and poured out, clumsy and blunt. It struck the Ailuros, like a hammer pounding on the thin shell of a delicate nut, sending shards in all directions but miraculously sparing the tasty meat inside. The Panda screamed once and slumped unconscious to the floor, blood trickling from her nose and eyes and ears. The Otter dropped as well, onto her knees as both hands clutched at her temples.

"No! No! Not like that."

The Lutr's reaction elicited only petulance from Margda. "No? Then how?"

"Like . . . picking thistles with tweezers," whined Lirlowil, as she braced for the storm the Matriarch had unleashed.

Old memories and new flooded through their shared awareness, what the guard had eaten for breakfast, what she'd sent home to a trio of cubs for their last birthday, the hope that assignment to this mission had originally brought and the subsequent realization that its clandestine nature would mean a blank in her record rather than promotion, the morning her gran had taken her fishing for the first time. And more, always more. A lifetime of detail, blurs of black and white fur, cultural references that made no sense and felt odd, if not outright wrong. Noise and noise and more noise with barely a hint of worthwhile signal. And somewhere under it all, her own thought, a faint worry that she'd incapacitated and possibly killed a member of the security detail assigned to her, and Krasnoi's repercussions when he found out.

"Teach me, then," insisted the Matriarch.

"I can't," hissed the Lutr, struggling back up on her feet, head bent and clutched in both delicate hands. "I can't hold an idea of my own. You've filled me with a lifetime of this Panda's thoughts. They're crushing me. And on top of that, you've roused the major's interest in me. Why?"

Her body moved on its own, awkwardly stomping across the room to pull out a chair and collapse at her workstation, like a broken puppet manipulated by a drunken puppeteer. Unintentionally, her fingers danced upon keys and the text of a recently sent message floated before her eyes:

> I'M WASTING DAYS AND DAYS RESEARCHING FANT TO GAIN ENOUGH INFORMATION TO BE ABLE TO SPEAK TO THEM, AND THEN LEARNING NOTHING USEFUL. IF YOU HAVE LIVING RESOURCES, LET ME MEET THEM, SKIM THEM, AND EITHER FIND WHAT YOU WANT OR ELIMINATE THEM FROM CONSIDERATION.

She shoved the keyboard away, her gorge rising with disgust. "Oh no, no! I couldn't bear to meet more of your kind. Not in the flesh. Please!"

"You little fool! You can reach into people's minds, see them as they are and not as the flesh they wear, and still you let bigotry rule you."

She took control of her movements again, but only to bang her head against the workstation. Memories full of visceral pain flooded her, triggered by the physical pain she'd barely begun to inflict. Complications during the birth of her cubs, corporal discipline administered upon her as a child by a stern grandfather, a friendly tavern fight that had gotten out of hand and gone from brawl to riot leaving seven dead and her with a torn ear and shattered collarbone. None of it her. None of it her.

Lirlowil screamed at the Fant, "Don't lecture me. You don't know how it is. Flesh shapes mind. Mind shapes flesh. It's not so different than Speaking."

"It should be. If you worked to make it so. But you're weak. Lazy."

Lazy? Her? She flashed on going through training, endless days of running obstacle courses, agility exercises, hand-to-hand combat. She could field-strip nine different weapons, survive in a desert with only a blade, make love nonstop for two days until her partner collapsed from exhaustion and dehydration. But no, she'd done none of that; that was someone else.

"I'd hoped you could be my partner in this, that we could both gain from such extraordinary circumstances." The Matriarch's tone dripped with contempt. "I dislike being wrong. You don't have the discipline to seize the opportunity I offer you. You can't even see how to dam this torrent of foreign recollections you're drowning in."

"I can't help you. I won't help you."

"Oh, Child, you so underestimate yourself. You can, and you will. Willingly and actively, or not. But for now, just sleep!"

A fat-fingered gray hand seemed to close around her mind, squeezing consciousness out of her. Lirlowil struggled against it, sliding from her chair and collapsing alongside the fallen security guard. And then the world went away.

~~~~~~

A short time passed. Lirlowil's body responded more readily with the Lutr unconscious. Margda knelt, head bowed, and heard the arrival of three more Pandas. She raised her head, noted their drawn weapons but gave no outward acknowledgment. Without a word, an Ailuros lifted his fallen comrade into his arms and backed out of the converted warehouse. Another stepped forward, careful not to block the line of fire of the remaining Panda; when he stood in front of the Otter, he backhanded her with enough force to make her body rise off the floor before she crumpled to a heap.

"When this is done, when the major has no more need of you, we will remember what you did today."

Margda struggled to sit up, one delicate hand gingerly touching the side of her new face where the Ailuros had struck. She spoke, her voice strong with none of the fear or cajoling or self-importance that she imagined always marked Lirlowil's conversation with the security detail. Margda's words, as the Eleph moved inside the Lutr's body.

"When this is done, if any of you still matter to me, *I* will choose what you remember. Now, take me down to Barsk and where I need to be. I've waited far too long to reach this point."

She got to her feet and walked out into the corridor, empty now. The Panda lowered his weapon and led the way. "There's a shuttle waiting. This way." The one who'd struck her, followed behind. They didn't matter. They meant nothing to her.

Gaining more control over her borrowed body with every step, Margda allowed herself to be escorted from Lirlowil's prison of so many days, moving with determination but none of the Lutr's natural grace, plodding instead like an old woman several times her size. If the Pandas noticed, they wisely gave no indication. Margda assumed that a trip downwell would have little novelty or interest to her host and did her best not to gape at the viewport, though it was difficult. In her life, she'd never been off Barsk, and the view of her homeworld from low orbit brought an unexpected joy. Riding the Lutr's body felt little different than commanding her own, save for the annoying ghost proprioception she kept experiencing of a trunk that this body lacked. Suppressing Lirlowil herself had been easy enough; any defenses the Otter might have possessed had vanished in the onslaught of unwanted Panda memories. From her vantage point, Margda had simply stepped out of the way of the mnemonic flood, and instead of throwing Lirlowil a rope to haul her to safety, she'd shoved a metaphorical weight into her hands. It wouldn't be so easy taking dominance over this mind next time, but she had no intention of relinquishing control until she completed her task. She had waited, dead, for the better part of eight centuries, she could damn well endure the mewling whimpers of a spoiled Lutr for a few days. In the meantime, she needed to acquire precision, and for that she'd have to allow the Otter to wake up again and teach her to use the power with more delicacy. Thistles indeed!

NINETEEN

DEGREES OF WRONG

⁓⁓⁓⁓⁓

HAVING stood on other worlds, it was easy for Jorl to believe he wasn't anywhere on Barsk. Somewhere beneath his feet was good earth, but he could dig and dig for days and never reach it. He stood upon hard-packed snow, beneath which lay sheets of ice that had been put down season after season, year after year, as the snow compressed and transformed under its own weight. Underneath it all lay the actual surface of the polar continent. He trusted in this with the belief of things unseen that marked most of science.

Jorl had the exercise yard to himself as he had since his first day there. What need did the Dying have for exercise? They shuffled back and forth to the vast basin that provided their drinking water, or leaned against the barracks that formed three sides of the yard's square, or sat on cots they'd pulled from inside. Misery lined their faces, but not because they couldn't bear to stay inside rooms built of plastic, nor because sleeping outside meant the cold reached into their bones so they shivered constantly, waking or sleeping. Physical discomfort paled alongside the horror of their existence severed from the proper flow of time. They should be dead. And yet they breathed, ached, cried, and waited in agony for some semblance of normalcy to return, to complete that last journey and die.

Twice a day self-propelled troughs of bland and processed vegetable clusters appeared in the middle of the yard. Distinctions like *breakfast* and *lunch, dinner* and *supper* failed in this place where the dim daylight endured far longer than a day should, and the span between dusk and dawn passed while one watched. It didn't matter that the provided food had little flavor, none of the Dying Fant possessed any appetite. Every other day most would make a pilgrimage down the length of a trough. Trunks would dip within, secure a portion of the tasteless clusters, transfer them to mouths that automatically chewed and swallowed. And again and again, until the Fant reached the far end of the trough, finished that last mouthful, and returned to sit or stand by the barracks' walls. Even after all the Fant wanting to eat had done so the troughs remained more than half full. Upon some unseen signal, they withdrew from the yard.

On the fourth morning since arriving, the routine changed. As the troughs departed, Jorl saw six short figures skitter past them and enter the yard. Unlike the Fant, their tiny feet left no imprint in the packed snow.

"Badgers," said Jorl, following them with his eyes as they veered off toward a group of Fant congregating outside the far left barracks. "Taxi," he said again, using the name they used among themselves. He'd only met one during his time in the Patrol, a woman who epitomized aggression, spoke in short sentences, and did everything with sharp, quick movements. His shipmates had assured him she was a fair representation of her people, and universally loathed her only slightly less than they disliked him.

Jorl had spent the first two days making an effort to meet all the other Fant. Only Phas and her friends had proved willing to talk to him. His status as a Bearer let him move among them, and grudgingly earned him their names, but nothing more. As they saw it, none of them had anything to say to someone who was obviously still living.

But though the Taxi also lived, they were neither Lox nor Eleph. The Dying Fant did not flinch away as the squad of Badgers chittered among them, separating one of their number by the simple expediency of surrounding her. As Jorl watched they escorted their chosen Fant back the way they'd come. The body language among the newcomers lurched toward defiance; ears flapped, trunks flailed, but others of the Dying who had been there longer shuffled over in ones and twos, murmuring explanations and smothering resistance. Over the course of the day, the Taxi returned twice to the yard and claimed additional Fant. The troughs arrived again, and after the Fant had eaten, they departed. The three Fant taken earlier returned later, pointedly denied the opportunity for a meal. All looked worse than before they'd left, shambling with less purpose, bruises just starting to flower here and there across their wrinkled gray legs, arms, and torsos. Circles of the Dying formed around each, offering what comfort they could and coaxing the tale of their experience from them.

The newer arrivals among the Fant listened to these accounts and steeled themselves for their own interrogations. They could endure. What was torture compared to the agony of having the closure of their deaths disrupted?

Jorl took no comfort in this. After another period of sleep and the arrival of the first of the day's food troughs, he wondered if the Taxi would pick him today. After those Fant who felt like eating had done so, the troughs began to withdraw again and Jorl's gaze followed them across the yard, searching for the squad of angry Badgers. Instead, he saw three very different figures coming across the packed snow: a slender Lutr, unequipped and underdressed for the cold in a floral sarong, shivering in-between an identical pair of Ailuros in the flat black uniforms of security.

From across the yard, the Otter appeared to be scanning each Fant from afar, searching for something in what surely were unfamiliar faces. Her eyes locked onto Jorl, and he would have sworn she smiled. He saw her lips move with a quick instruction to her guards, and the trio changed their trajectory to move further away from Jorl. They stopped at the first cluster of prisoners, lingered a while and then moved on to the next group. Again and again this continued until the Otter had gazed into the eyes and shared words with easily fifty of the Dying Fant. The Otter and her Panda escort had worked their way to the double handful of Fant closest to him and again paused to engage them.

Jorl watched the Lutr talk to the Fant, Four Eleph and two Lox. Something about her movements, her posture standing there, the way her head bobbed, felt familiar, almost comfortable. He'd never met any Lutr during his days in the Patrol, but he'd heard stories that ranged from hedonistic revels in everyday life to splurges of sybaritic sex that would make the rain blush. Looking at this one now, the way she interacted with the Dying Fant, he couldn't imagine any of those things. He saw her smile as she chatted individually with them and the Dying Fant responded with more enthusiasm than he'd yet witnessed from them. Through all of that, her accompanying guards glared at the Fant with a mix of disgust and warning. Neither the Lox nor the Eleph paid them any heed; all focused on the Otter.

In time, she glanced toward Jorl again. He quickly averted his eyes, but too late. In his peripheral vision he saw her disengage from the others and make her way toward him, the two Pandas stalking alongside, matching her step for step. She stopped twice a trunk's length from him, the appropriate distance for a female Lox or Eleph when encountering a single male for the first time. The realization of it jarred him enough that he turned to face her, earning him a nod of acknowledgment.

"What is your name?"

He frowned, and felt a pang of solidarity with the Dying. It simply wasn't done, at least not to a Fant. A young woman, regardless of her race, did not walk up to a man and demand his name. He started to turn away.

"Your pardon, that was poorly done. May I start again? I am called Lirlowil. My mother's name was . . . Thithlowil."

Again he stopped. "I'm Jorl ben Tral." He paused, and then lamely completed the rest of the greeting ritual. "Perhaps our mothers know one another."

Lirlowil laughed, a sound like wind chimes set against a husky rasp. "It's a pretty thought but unlikely. But now that we're off to a better beginning, tell me something. Why are you not like these others?"

"The intent behind my destination differed from theirs, though we share similar tales of abduction."

"Oh. No, I know about that. Horrible, but long foretold. But I meant the mark upon your brow."

Jorl's hand reached up of its own accord, but stopped before his fingers actually touched the aleph tattoo. "A mark given me by my people. What did you mean, when you said the abductions were foretold?"

"I must have read it somewhere. But about that mark, have you had it long? Have your people marked anyone else that way since?"

"Not long, and no, I'm the most recent. Why do you ask?"

The Otter shrugged, the movement not as fluid as Jorl expected it to be.

"It's what I'm here for. To ask questions. You've met the Bear major?" She glanced at the Pandas who still flanked her but studiously pretended not to hear a word. "He wants information that only an Eleph and Lox might know, but he has no ready access to the actual people who must surely have it. So he's been trying several different methods and hoping to get lucky. Based on what I've seen so far, he's wasting his time. None of them know anything about koph. Do you?"

He should have expected it, but the question caught Jorl off guard and he stammered, saying nothing.

"You do, don't you. But probably not for the reason I'm seeking. You know about koph because you use it, am I right? You have the look of a Speaker about you."

He found his voice, "I didn't know there was a look."

"Certainly. Look closely at me, and you should see it, there in my eyes. We have much in common, Jorl ben Tral. More than you realize."

"You're a Speaker?"

She gave a stiff bow. "I am, have been, for a very, very long time."

"I mean no disrespect, but you look like you're barely out of adolescence."

"A keen eye you have. Let's just say I have an *old soul* and leave it at that."

"But you—"

"As I was saying, the Bear major doesn't care about Speakers. They just use koph. He wants Fant who know how to make it from scratch. All he's ever seen is the finished, refined product that gets shipped to the rest of the Alliance."

"You'd need to talk to a pharmer about that," said Jorl.

"Exactly. Do you know any?"

"I . . . did. He's passed."

The Otter nodded, more impatiently than empathically, or so it seemed to Jorl.

"Sailed off?"

"No, an . . . accident."

"Ah. Well then, thank you, Jorl ben Tral. I've waited a very long time to meet you and have this conversation. Please, excuse me now."

She smiled, the expression never quite reaching her eyes, and turned away. The Ailuros turned with her. They had already moved to the next cluster of Dying Fant when Jorl trotted after, trunk waiving.

"Wait! What did you mean about having waited a long time?"

A Panda's fist caught him full in the face, and its twin slammed into his stomach. He doubled over, unable to breathe and trying not to retch. He dropped to one knee on the packed snow, wishing he could move away before the next blow fell. But it didn't come.

When he lifted his head he saw his assailant crouching on all fours, trickles of blood streaming down his face from his ears and the inner corners of his eyes. He had vomited as well, and the contents of his stomach steamed in the frigid air. The other Panda still stood alongside the Otter, but clearly wished he could help his comrade.

"I held back," said Lirlowil. "As a kindness. Next time, I won't. I don't share the Bear major's contempt for these people, and I won't permit you to demonstrate yours. Do you understand me?"

The Ailuros on the ground managed a faint confirmation, and the one still standing also said "Yes."

"Jorl, are you all right?"

He rubbed at the spot on his face that had taken the punch, imagining the bruise that would spring up soon enough. Resolving to scrape up some snow and create a compress, Jorl hauled himself to his feet and nodded.

"Good. Now, you have to excuse me. Time is racing away from me. But I promise, we'll speak again soon." She winked at him, as if they shared some secret, then turned again and moved on to engage that next group of the Dying. The uninjured Panda stayed at her side. The other collapsed there on the ground, clearly breathing but otherwise unmoving.

What had she done to him?

TWENTY

VIOLATIONS

~~~~~~

MARGDA continued her circuit through the yard until she'd chatted, however briefly, with every one of the Dying Fant. The wrongness of it grated, but the yearning to gaze once more upon her people pulled her through it. She'd died long ago. The nefshons that had been pulled together by Lirlowil included some of her last. She had reached the final island that all of these tragic souls had been denied. When this was all done, she would never see their like again. She hid behind the façade of the Lutr's body, ignoring custom to be with other Fant one last time.

And through it all, she practiced her control over Lirlowil's telepathy.

Her attack on the Ailuros who had struck Jorl had been both reflexive and yet restrained. She'd reached out, wrenching at the guard's mind much as she had to that other Panda on the station, but with greater focus and a lighter touch. Nor had she let the flood of memories pour into her borrowed brain, as they had the last time. Instead she'd deftly turned them aside, incapacitating the

Ailuros and not herself. And in doing so, she'd begun to see how to use this ability.

She reached out to the next Eleph she met, clamping down on the power like she had squeezed off Lirlowil's access to it. The technique was remarkably similar, and the analogy of limiting the flux created the means to practice control. Her new telepathy grazed the Fant, as delicate as the nubs of her trunk might caress a loved one's cheek. A general sense of numbness echoed back, accompanied by the barest spark of interest that lived far below the Eleph's conscious awareness.

She closed off that contact and extended a touch to a second Fant, pushing deeper, envisioning that one's mind like a mighty tree and her probe as no more than a wayward leaf carried to it on the wind. She pulled back surface thoughts, curiosity at the Lutr and her Ailuros companion, surprise that one of the guards had collapsed, distaste that the young Lox continued to bear witness to the shame of the Dying, resolve at the recent brutality by some Taxi. Margda ended that contact as well, completed a few audible pleasantries. She moved on.

A light rain, really little more than a mist, had begun to fall. Almost beneath the level of her own awareness she sensed a slight sigh that emanated from the Fant. Something familiar and welcome in the midst of so much strangeness. Surely also a sign that she had achieved some tipping point with the borrowed telepathy. Margda traveled through the entire yard and visited with all of the Fant. She touched and skimmed and read enough minds and memories to feel comfortable with the ability, and powerful enough to reach into any mind and pursue what she needed. Unlike with the Pandas, she could not easily search through deeper memories. The Dying Fant had already let most of them go. It seemed as if large portions of their minds had already shut, sectioning off more and more of the past. That life was over for them and at some unconscious level they'd made peace with it and allowed their pasts to fade.

She'd also exhausted the Otter's body beyond sensibility, which in this instance had the surprising benefit of keeping Lirlowil's waking consciousness from regaining control while Margda practiced her telepathic ability. One final test remained. She had just turned away from the last cluster of Fant and caught sight of the second of the day's food deliveries. Riding on the lip of the automated trough was an Urs, and though Lirlowil had only met him once, that single encounter had burned his image into her so deeply that Margda had no difficulty recognizing the Bear major, Krasnoi.

He stepped from the trough as it came to a halt and continued at a brisk pace toward his Lutr asset and the remaining guard. The nearer Fant shuffled away, ostensibly to sample from the trough. Margda reached out in this new manner and slipped a probe into Krasnoi's mind, finding interest and irritation and surprise.

"I found your earlier suggestion intriguing enough to bring you down to the planet. It becomes less compelling when I add in that you've induced brain hemorrhages in at least one and now possibly two of the guards assigned to you."

The weariness of her borrowed body began to weigh on Margda, but the prize was so close. She persevered.

"I presume you've read all the reports I've submitted. I've certainly read all your procedure manuals, followed your guidelines. I've wasted most of my time researching a handful of Fant to the point where I could summon them. I spent only a few minutes of telepathic probing on each once I had them in front of me and gained nothing of use. Whereas in one brutal, draining afternoon down here I have mentally interrogated your captives more thoroughly and painlessly than your squad of sadistic Badgers."

Krasnoi scowled at her, though Margda read the increased interest in his mind. She'd intrigued him, and saw his question an instant before he gave it voice.

"And have you learned anything of value?"

"Three things, actually." She waited, feeling the shift of power, knowing that reveling in smug superiority was one of her weaknesses but not caring.

"And those are?"

"First, that the expert knowledge you seek is mainly found in the hands of professionals whom the Fant call *pharmers*, pharmacological specialists. It's an obnoxious bit of wordplay that was coined by the first generation born here. They're trained in botany, biochemistry, and physics."

"And do any of the Fant here self-identify as pharmers?"

"That's the second thing. No, not a one. None of them have any information of use to you. You've completely wasted your time. This entire operation, abducting the Dying because no one would miss them, has earned you absolutely nothing."

Had she pushed too far? She saw the anger in his mind before it bloomed on his face. But no, he was first and foremost a pragmatist. A salutatory trait among the Urs, and one Margda had herself cultivated.

"And what, then, was your third insight?"

"Your accidental acquisition, the younger Fant with the silly mark on his head? He has a friend who *is* a pharmer."

"How does that help me? I abducted him, not his friend."

"You couldn't have abducted his friend. He's dead."

"Then what is your point? We have nothing!"

Margda allowed her body to smile, her satisfaction finding a waiting analog in the muscles of Lirlowil's face, producing the kind of grin that threatened to push the Bear too far.

"Have you forgotten the other reason you chose me, Major? I can talk to the dead."

"Then why haven't you done so, Woman? Enough of your games!"

"Learning these facts for you has left me physically and mentally exhausted. But more to the point, I don't have any koph here. The supply you provided for my work is back on the station. Without it, I'm no more a Speaker than you are."

The brightness of success that shone through the Bear's mind shattered her fragile connection and Margda didn't bother to establish another one. Things were moving along as she needed them.

Krasnoi nodded to the Ailuros who had been studiously ignoring the conversation. "Escort our talented Speaker back through the base. Acquire whatever you need to re-equip your shuttle and return her to her rooms on the station with best speed. The fruition of all our efforts is close at hand."

"Yes, Urs-Major."

"Lirlowil, I fault myself for not thinking to use you as you have done today. Your timing is inspired, though. I've received a transmission from the chair of the Senate's Committee of Information. He intends to review our progress himself. Take what rest you require on the trip back to the station. Once you have your koph, get to work and acquire the information I need. Failing the senator is not an option. Do you understand me?"

Margda let her smile dim as the Bear reasserted his power, or thought he did. His beliefs didn't matter to her, but it did not harm her to allow him the delusion.

"Of course, Urs-Major." She cocked her head to the side and arched a brow to get her escort's attention. "Take me to the shuttle, if you please."

~~~

SHE'D lied, of course. What need had she of koph to summon? She was a nefshon construct herself, one that included the ability to perceive the subatomic particles of personality. She might need Lirlowil's telepathic ability to exist, but while she did she could Speak whether her host was worn out or not, draining her resources right up to the point where the Lutr's physiological systems began to collapse in a cascade of organ failure. Though bone weary, she was still a long way from that!

Over the course of the long day, her remaining Ailuros had transformed from oppressive to intrusive to respectful. Following the Bear major's obvious appreciation of her he had turned downright subservient. He'd settled her into the shuttle's private lounge and shown her how to access an assortment of gourmet snacks, chilled juices, and obscure liqueurs, as well as an entertainment screen with thousands of recorded options to distract her from the monotony of ascending out of Barsk's gravity well. Margda had thanked him curtly, assured him she wanted nothing more than to sleep, and made it clear she was not to be disturbed until they'd arrived back at the station.

She ate a quick meal and hydrated, less interested in taste than in refueling the body she'd been abusing, and settled comfortably onto the lounge's main acceleration couch. Then she closed the Lutr's eyes, and brought forth the memory of having just taken koph. For the first time in her experience, she failed to see the golden cloth of her own particles still connected to one another and clinging stubbornly to her body. The confusion passed into amusement. The body that had produced all her nefshons had returned to dust long ago, further proof that she had died.

The construct she'd made for herself was her body as she'd last appeared before sailing away, not the fragile, furry thing of twig-like bones and minimal flesh that she'd suborned to house her. With long practice and firm memory she applied her attention to invoking a space to work. Her home in the Civilized Wood of Yargo opened all around her and she felt the familiar ache in her left knee as she lumbered from her visitors' parlor to her kitchen. She opened a cupboard and smiled as she caused a box of Lirlowil's preferred tea to appear, with a blister-pack of koph pellets alongside it. She went through the motions of heating water, adding the koph, and steeping the tea. She didn't need it, but the ritual grounded her and she wanted every advantage for what came next. The fragrance of spiralmint filled the room of her imagination.

Margda moved back to her parlor and settled into a hammock seat by the window, glancing out at the still city she alone inhabited. She sipped her tea, closed her eyes, and sipped again. Her discovery of nefshons had come to her during a vision, the first of many that started when her body began rejecting her seizure medication. She'd understood the power implicit in transcending death, and seen a need to reserve some aspects of it for her own use, to ensure certain futures and prevent others. The three laws of the Speaker's Edict had covered most of that. Lirlowil had broken the first law, as Margda had foreseen, making it possible for what she planned now, the violation of the second law: summoning the living.

She set her cup of tea on the floor and leaned back, letting the strands of the hammock support and gently rock her. She reached out, calling the nefshons to her and immediately discovered her influence weaker than it had been in life. She was a cheat, and it cost her, made her control more precarious. Dwelling on the possibility of failure would only summon failure, an ironic outcome instead of the summoning she wanted. She banished the possibility from her mind and focused on her impressions of the one she wanted. Jorl ben Tral. The flavor of him. Young and naive, adventurous and foolish. She had recognized him the instant she met him. In life and flesh he was just as she'd envisioned him centuries before. But he was only a means to an end. It was the other whom she needed. A name, a face, a life that had never come to her in visions, only the knowledge that his closest companion would stupidly leave Barsk, crossing the emptiness of space instead of being at his friend's side when he chose to die.

In her mind, nested in the mind of another, she conceived a golden string of her desire. Plucking it sounded the music of Jorl's life, vibrating all the way back to him in the living world where its far end anchored in the golden cloth of his living nefshons. Whatever he was doing back at the polar base, he would have just felt her touch on his soul. It all but guaranteed his full attention. She gripped the string tightly with her trunk and both hands and yanked, willing some portions of his nefshons to flow along the string to her. His construct formed as easily as any dead conversant's would. He took form before her, shattering the second law of the edict as her vision from long ago had promised. The future she'd foreseen so many centuries ago opened before her.

TWENTY-ONE

CONTACT

~~~~~~~~

ETWEEN one chew and a swallow, Jorl twitched, as an itch ran all the way up his spine and radiated out through the pores of his skin. It resolved into a sensation like being watched; it came from all around.

He lifted his head and fanned his ears once, spat out the half-eaten vegetable cluster, and the yard fell away. With no sense of transition the snowy ground beneath him had become a wooden floor. His next breath did not create a visible puff in front of his face, and he inhaled air that was warm and moist and smelled of growing things. No barracks wall lay behind him, but rather the comforting intimacy of a parlor in some home of some island's Civilized Wood. In front of him, seated in a frayed hammock, an old woman swayed and studied him.

He returned the favor. She had a familiar look, not as some once-met aunt of a distant friend, but rather in a way that suggested secondhand experience, not direct knowledge. He'd never seen a more ancient Eleph before, even among the Dying Fant, and the myriad wrinkles around her eyes showed someone who had spent years laughing as well as years in pain. On her forehead the mark of an aleph, dim and faded, exuded a faint glow.

Impossible as a dream, he recognized her. He was sitting across from Margda, the Matriarch of Barsk, discoverer of nefshons, architect of the Compact, creator of the aleph. He had finally lost his mind.

"Close your mouth, Jorl, you look like an oaf with it hanging like that."

He blinked and, as an afterthought, closed his mouth. Somehow, he had expected a more polite apparition. He had never heard of anyone experiencing belligerent insanity. He blinked again and faintly, if he concentrated, he could still see the yard and the other abducted Fant, like translucent afterimages. Was the real world available to his other senses? He tried to listen for the sound of shuffling feet on packed snow, but the Matriarch's words drowned out the attempt.

"So, you are the end result of my life's plan. You are the consequence of my visions and predictions. You owe me for the aleph on your head, Child, and I've come to collect on that debt."

He stared into her eyes, dark and cold and demanding his full attention. The dim image of the other reality faded away.

"Um, your pardon, Matriarch. This is certainly an interesting bit of delusion my mind has conjured, and I would love to play along, I assure you, but even if I actually felt I owed you anything, it would be quite the trick to repay you. You're dead."

Jorl rose from the floor, finding his feet and moving about the room. It felt good to be warm again. The Matriarch remained in her hammock, sitting, regarding him.

"Delusion? Child, you disappoint me. I had hoped for more insight from you, depended on it in fact. Did your time away from this world fail to open your eyes? Fine. So be it. The traditional methods are tradition because they work. In this instance, they require only minor alteration. Attend!"

She released a deep sigh, closing her eyes for a moment as if remembering or composing what she wanted to say. She began speaking again before opening them. "You are Jorl ben Tral, historian, Speaker, and most recently, captive. Your time in life has not yet ended; you are now as you are in life, in this, a world of my own making. I bid you welcome. Understand?"

He froze. The words differed in some particulars, but he knew the rest well enough. He knew their cadence and he knew their context, and the impossibility of them filled him with confusion. Margda had used the ritual of establishing; he'd done it himself often enough, grounding a newly summoned conversant. Was she implying that she had summoned *him*? But only the dead could be summoned, and only those who were not Speakers could be summoned. And in any case, certainly not by a Speaker who herself had died centuries ago.

"I can see you have questions, but I don't have the luxury of time to answer them for you. Accept what you see as true. I am Margda, you know me. And yes, I am Speaking to you, despite my being dead, despite you being alive, and despite your own status as a Speaker. I made the rules of the Speaker's Edict specifically so I could come back and break them. I saw it in a vision, without the rules the future I sought wasn't possible. I made them only to ensure that I could do what I saw needed to be done. I'm sneaky that way."

Jorl walked back to her, unsure how to respond. He stopped in front of the hammock that raised her to standing height. He met her gaze and the words came.

"How can you break any rules? You're dead!"

She glared back at him, her ears rippling with the Eleph idiom of irritation that spoke more eloquently than speech. Her eyes narrowed with obvious disgust.

"Don't be an imbecile. You and I both know that death is hardly an impediment. I was summoned myself, days ago, by a young Speaker who also possessed a telepathic talent. A nefshon construct has the knowledge and experience its source possessed in life, and mine includes Speaking. That's the danger in summoning any of our kind; such a conversant can still Speak."

Jorl nodded, following the logic and obviousness of it. No Speaker had ever realized it because even considering the idea had been forbidden. By Margda.

"But . . . the nefshons of the living can't be summoned—"

"Of course they can. You see the bundle of your own nefshons every time the koph takes hold. Summoning the living just takes more effort, wrenching the particles from the nefshon fabric of the conversant's life."

He gestured around him, "And the rest of this?"

"You're the historian. This was my home, gone now but vivid to me as I saw it only days ago."

"What happened days ago?"

"In my timeline? That's when I sailed away."

"So . . . other than the fact you've broken the first two rules of the Edict in Speaking to me, everything else about this summoning works like any other? And from your point of view, you're at the far end of your life, but still alive."

Margda's eyes remained locked on his, and Jorl couldn't look away.

"Good. You're working it out. That should save us some time. Yes, I was summoned by another Speaker, one who tossed aside the first rule of my Edict. And, as a result, I in turn summoned you. Long ago, shortly after I stumbled upon the ability to manipulate nefshons, I had a vision of a young pharmer discovering a new drug, one with the potential to keep Barsk safe for centuries, or to completely overturn the balance the Compact had achieved with the Alliance. In my vision, the pharmer had a similar intuition and chose to end his own life rather than risk anyone else gaining knowledge of his creation."

"How could one drug be responsible for so much?"

"Since my time, koph has allowed some sapients to Speak. Because the drug is plentiful at home, a diluted portion is part of annual celebrations that even children partake in. An immunity to the toxic effects builds up, and as a consequence Fant are orders of magnitude more likely to be discovered to be Speakers than all the other races combined. At the time of the Compact, this made the Alliance uncomfortable, and their attitude has only worsened since."

"And the new drug? How does that change anything?"

"It changes everything! I believe he uncovered a koph agonist. Imagine a Speaker's power to reveal information that vanished with the death of its keeper, expanding more than a thousandfold for the duration of a summoning. Every important person's private indiscretion could be dug out from whatever pit it had been buried in. Industrial secrets would be discovered and stolen. Familial offenses that died with their principles would endure for endless generations. The potential blackmail and extortion would lead to draconian measures that would rewrite society at every level."

Jorl gasped, the pieces falling into place. Margda continued to talk.

"The Bear major and the people he works for are desperate to learn how to refine koph for themselves, presumably to establish some parity by increasing the population of their own Speakers.

They're bumbling fools, the lot of them, and they'll fail at their task. The methodology and their strategy make no sense. They haven't yet even deduced that it's derived from taww sap. Somehow they've gone off on a misperception that it's distillation from a type of leaf though they've no clue which one in the entire forest it might be."

"That's why they've abducted the Dying?"

"Perhaps. Not everything is clear to me. I foresaw the new drug, but not its discoverer. Instead, I glimpsed the Lox who eulogized him, his Second who would be a Speaker. That was you, Jorl, eight hundred years in your past I saw *you*. I knew I would return, and I needed you to be at hand when I did. I arranged for you to have the aleph because our people need the secret your friend died to protect."

Jorl's face fell into his upraised hands. Tears streamed from eyes he hadn't known were crying. "That's why Arlo died. To protect us all."

"Arlo?"

Sniffling, Jorl nodded. "My best friend. The pharmer you foresaw. He killed himself but would never tell me why."

~~~~~

TO her surprise, Jorl's simple remark was like turning her face up to fresh rain. She'd been lightly probing him all through their conversation, turning over this memory and that. The organization of his past surged in a myriad ways as she wandered through it, uncountable nodes of ideas and concepts, each connecting hundreds of thousands of others with bridges of different weights and saliencies, organized by sound and color and meaning and experience. Most of them looped back upon themselves over and over, each time subtly different than its previous incarnation. Untold individuals existed in Jorl's mind and memory, some still living, others now dead, whom he had known in life, as well as people he had met only after their own deaths. He held too many for her to ever find by happenstance the one she sought.

Until he'd spoken a name and given her the key. Arlo. She pushed deeper into his mind, finding the node that defined all things bearing that name. A lifetime of detail so rich that even the weakest and stupidest of Speakers could have summoned him. But it meant nothing if she couldn't hold on to it. In the midst of her probe, Margda felt her overtaxed telepathy fade away, taking the full sense of who and what Arlo was with it. Mere drabs remained, and even those threatened to slip away.

"Yes, that's the person I've been seeking. Thank you, Jorl."

Without ritual or patterns, invoking nothing of the conclusion from traditional summoning, she held up a hand with a single golden thread between thumb and finger. She let it fall, and their connection severed in that instant. She had what she'd come for.

TWENTY-TWO

EXPEDIENCY

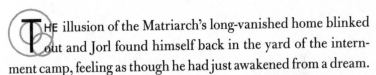

THE illusion of the Matriarch's long-vanished home blinked out and Jorl found himself back in the yard of the internment camp, feeling as though he had just awakened from a dream.

"Jorl, are you all right? Do you need help getting up?"

The carver, Rüsul, stood in front of him, extending a hand.

Jorl shook his head, but made no move to stand. "Just lost in my own thoughts. I'm fine, thanks."

The old Eleph nodded. "Well, if you like, you're welcome to join us in our little corner. Doubtless Tarva has more tales of his gram he wants to fill our ears with."

Jorl smiled. "I'll join you soon. I just need some time . . . to process my, um, thoughts." Rüsul nodded again and wandered off, and Jorl let his head drop to stare blankly at the snowy ground of the yard as he tried to make sense of the enormity of his visit with the Matriarch.

He wasn't sure how much time had passed when he felt a shadow fall across him. He glanced up, expecting to find Rüsul again, but instead Krasnoi stared down at him.

"Ensign-Retired, have you had the experience of searching for something only to find it in the very last place you look?"

Jorl allowed his puzzlement to show on his face. "Why would you continue to look once you'd found it?"

"Exactly. You understand me exactly. And having found you, I can now stop searching."

"Me? I thought you wanted knowledge of how to make koph? I only know about the finished product, not how the drug is made."

"No, you don't," said the Bear. "No more than the rest of these useless relics do." He swept one arm in an expansive gesture that took in the entire yard. A squad of Pandas were ushering all of the Dying Fant into a large circle freshly etched into the packed snow.

"What are you doing?"

"Putting an end to a tactic that has done nothing but waste time and resources. They have nothing I want or need."

"You said I didn't either."

"Not quite. None of them have what I seek, but you know someone who does. My Lutr Speaker will wring the knowledge from him soon enough. I'll hold on to you until she does. This mission has been cursed with too many complications to let you slip away prematurely. But the others? They're beyond useless and I will not suffer them any longer."

For a moment, Jorl saw Urs-Major Krasnoi in a new light, gracious even as he admitted failure. "You're letting them go? You'll take them to the last island and let them finally die?"

"Don't be absurd. Nonyx-Captain Selishta and her vessel are long gone. Easier to have them die here and now."

He lifted his head and caught the eye of one of the Pandas, who in turn shouted an order at the other members of the security squad. The two hundred some Dying Fant stood bunched together where they'd been gathered, swaying listlessly as the

Ailuros formed a shallow arc in front of them. Then the Pandas drew the devices they'd worn strapped along one leg, two-handed stocks with cables running back to canisters mounted on their backs. They pointed these at the Dying Fant and a moment later began spraying them with streams of liquid, like children playing a game with squirt bottles on the hotter days of the mist season. Several focused on dousing the outer perimeter of Fant while others aimed their streams higher, soaking those in the middle and back as well. Their canisters didn't contain water.

Jorl jumped up, arms and trunk waving, dashing toward the guards. He tripped on Krasnoi's suddenly outstretched foot and sprawled on his face, the packed snow scraping his skin.

Sparks erupted in front of each Ailuros, and their streams turned to fire. The blaze sped to the Fant like a living thing, rushing to embrace each of them in brightly burning arms. A few screamed but most made no sound. The squad stood prepared to take down any that broke from their cluster but none of them fled. They stood there, numbed beyond life, and burned.

The flames shone red but transformed gradually to a blinding white as the Ailuros continued to pour accelerant on their targets. The snow beneath the Fant transformed to steam, creating a grave like some macabre magic trick. Jorl managed to sit up, gagging in the acrid smell of burning flesh. His ears hung flat against his head; his mind simultaneously attempted to reject the horror and insisted he take action. He shouted and trumpeted and surged to his feet, desperate to do something, only to be knocked flat again by Krasnoi. A series of kicks kept him down, leaving him to gaze helplessly at the burning Fant. Waves of heat radiating from them made him flinch, but he could not bring himself to cover his face. The ink of his aleph burned on his forehead, and he had the odd thought that his privilege of passage must sometimes mean stumbling into places he'd have passed on in hindsight, and owning the obligation to stay there all the same. He bore witness, the silent slaughter of old men and women who had sought nothing more from life than its proper end. The nightmarish moment combined with the skills he'd honed as a Speaker as every individual face seared itself into his memory. There was no point to looking away now; the image of them would be with him forever.

The Dying Fant stood packed together, holding one another up as they burned until they crumpled en masse, and still the guards maintained their position, weapons poised and active until every bit of flesh and bone and tusk and tooth had been reduced to ash. Krasnoi kicked him again, savagely, but Jorl's own pain couldn't matter now. He raised his head and stared into the flames and ash, still reeling from the slaughter. The wind shifted and mercifully blew the stench of death away. Rüsul, Phas, Kembü, Abso, Tarva, and all the others who had been interred short of reaching the final island were gone, finally dead though not in the manner their lives had promised. He dropped his face into his hands, sobbing, and the image of them standing there still, burning and dying, lay vivid in his mind. A light snow began to fall as if to mark the moment of pure despair. He whimpered, realizing that at last, Margda's Silence had ended.

"What's going on here?"

Jorl's ears spread out at the question and he turned his head toward the unfamiliar voice. A large figure strode toward them from the far end of the yard where the Fant had never been allowed to congregate. The Pandas all lowered their devices but otherwise remained alert. The fire continued to burn.

"Senator, I wasn't expecting you for another few days." Krasnoi's brusque tone had changed, and Jorl heard worry in it.

The new arrival's hair hung so long in places that it had been braided, his fur gray with age. He projected power. His gait held purpose and strength. Metallic threads wove elaborate geometric patterns through the flowing robes he wore, and a chain of black glass links hung from around his neck. Jorl had never met a Bos before, taller than any Fant and easily as broad, but he knew from the horns emerging out of both sides of the fellow's head that he could be nothing else. More, there was something familiar about him, but Jorl couldn't place it. The Yak's voice rang like a deep metal drum, clear and strong, the sound authoritative but not unkind.

"I'm the chair of the Committee of Information. I didn't get to that position by being predictable. No doubt you'd have this all cleaned up and sorted by this time tomorrow. A pity then that we're having this conversation here today and you have to tell me what I'm looking at."

Jorl blinked and grasped his nervously twitching trunk with both hands, still staring at the spot where the Dying Fant had stood. It had to be some kind of trick, the stench an illusion, the flames a distraction. You couldn't just kill people like that!

He spread his ears as the words of the new arrival muscled their way past both horror and denial and entered his awareness. Every book, every treatise, every paper he'd ever written and submitted for inclusion in any professional journal or conference proceedings had first been vetted by the Committee of Information. From an academician's perspective, it was the most powerful group within the governing body of the Alliance. Its twenty-five members maintained and regulated all formal education, passed judgment on all research funding, and pretty much defined the sum total of expert knowledge in existence. He had made it his business to learn about each and every one of them. Only one Yak sat on the committee; Jorl had never met the man, but he had no doubt about his identity or the power he wielded.

Judging by the subservient tone that had crept into Krasnoi's voice, the Urs understood the Bos's authority, too.

"Senator Bish, I assure you, you have not walked in on anything untoward. Rather, I am simply tying up some loose ends of this project."

"Loose ends? I have read all of your mission briefings, Urs-Major, and I don't recall seeing anything that might account for this. There should be no *loose ends*."

"With all due respect, sir—"

"Spare me your excuses. This entire project is a violation of the Alliance's treaty with its own member planet. You shouldn't even be here, nor I for all that. The only sapient beings permitted on Barsk are Fant. On behalf of the Committee, I set aside that prohibition very reluctantly. So you will understand if I find the need to scrutinize something you choose to describe in such a manner."

The Yak had completed his approach as he spoke, skirting the smoldering pit where the Dying Fant had stood, slowing to study each of the Ailuros as he passed, before halting in front of Krasnoi. He stared down at Jorl.

"Speaking of Fant, this one seems distressed. Also too young, if I understood your acquisition scheme. Why is he here?" Bish paused. He turned his shaggy head with slow deliberation, an acquired habit necessary given his horns. "Again speaking of Fant, where are they?"

"I determined their usefulness had come to an end. In actual fact, as I'll be detailing in my report, hindsight reveals that they never had any information of value."

"Hindsight? That's just lovely. We trample over these people's

Compact, abduct and detain their citizens, and you're telling me you failed to learn anything useful. I also note that you've failed to answer my question. I will ask you one more time. Where are they?"

Jorl lurched up to his knees. "He killed them!"

"They were already dead," said Krasnoi. He looked as if he might kick the Lox, but stopped short at a tight-lipped shake of the Bos's head.

"Tell me, Major, how do you kill the dead?"

"A . . . minor exaggeration, Senator. They were all on their way to die, would have been dead already had my people not interfered and brought them here, I—"

Quicker than Jorl had expected an old man could move, the Yak brought a hand up and pressed two fingers to the Bear's mouth.

"Shh, hush, Major. Words are precious things. Don't waste what might be the last ones you have. According to your reports, you acquired two hundred seventeen Fant. I see one remaining. Unless you correct my impression, I am to understand you have taken it upon yourself to murder the other two hundred sixteen. Do I have that right? Ah, hold a moment." He paused and glanced back the way he'd come. "Druz, tell me you acquired all of that."

A second arrival caught Jorl's attention. A slow-moving Brady had trailed after the Bos, catching up at last. She wore a shapeless kaftan that shifted with dark colors; lenses throughout the folds of her clothing glimmered with reflected light from the fire. "Yes, sir, it's all been recorded, both audio and video."

The senator turned back to Krasnoi, lowering his hand from the Bear's mouth. "You were about to say?"

"With respect, sir, this is a sanctioned military action, I take offense at your use of the word *murder*."

"You're quite right, I misspoke. I should have said mass murder."

"Senator!"

"The Committee granted you broad discretionary authority to acquire the information we required, but that does not equate with a license for senseless slaughter."

"They would all have been dead by now anyway! They had all chosen to die."

The senator frowned and waved Druz closer. When the Sloth arrived at his side the Yak reached a hand down to help Jorl to his feet, and kept hold of his arm as he spoke to his aide.

"You have the Fant medical data in your system?"

"Yes, sir," said the Brady. "Both Lox and Eleph. A moment." She lifted her arms and passed the massive sleeves of her garment back and forth over Jorl in a languid gesture. Bits gleamed upon them. "He's in shock, sir. I also note several bruised ribs, and an unusual reading that I suspect comes from the luminescent mark on his forehead."

Bish turned back to Jorl. "You said that the major killed your people. I need you to be clear and factual now, for the record. How do you know this thing? Did you see it yourself?"

Jorl pointed past the arc of security guards to the still-smoldering pit behind them. He struggled to keep his voice from trembling as he answered. "Right there. He gathered them up and burned them where they stood. Melted the ground out from under them, it was so hot. Can't you smell it? They're just ash and sludge now."

"The major did it himself?"

"No," sobbed Jorl. "The Pandas did the actual burning. But he ordered it. I was right here next to him. If you'd arrived just a bit sooner . . . they were all here, all still alive . . ."

"Take your time, Son. You've been through a lot. No one should have to see what you've witnessed." A signal passed between the senator and his aid.

She stepped close again, bringing her right arm up, then hesitated.

"May I touch you?"

Jorl nodded, and the Brady's three-fingered hand pressed lightly against his neck. In the next instant, something shot from her sleeve, injecting him.

"What did you give me?"

"A cocktail common in traumatic situations. An analgesic for physical pain. A mnemonic marker, to make it easier for a physician to edit out your memory of this event, should you later choose to do so. And a tranquilizer to ease the experience in the here and now." She stepped back, nodding first to him and then to the Bos as her long arm within its longer sleeve dropped back to her side.

The senator returned the nod and then focused on Jorl once more. "What's your name?"

"Jorl ben Tral."

"Well, Jorl, although Barsk may have chosen isolation among the terms of your Compact, it is nonetheless a part of our Alliance. You've probably never given it a thought, lacking any formal representatives of your own, but I and my fellow senators were elected to serve all citizens and secure their best interests. There can be no just governance without responsibility and accountability. Isn't that right, Druz?"

The Sloth had edged closer to the Bear. She raised her hand, the left one this time, and let it rest it gingerly against Krasnoi's chest, the folds of her sleeve hanging open below her wrist. Now she lifted her chin in the beginning of a nod to indicate the major should speak.

"Senator, the situation underwent an extreme change today. There hasn't even been time to begin formulating the reports."

Without taking his kindly eyes off Jorl, Bish responded to Krasnoi, "Summarize."

"Our telepathic asset reviewed all of the Fant. She did it in one afternoon—"

"Impossible. Her test scores indicate she lacks the strength of will for such a thing. Lutr are too undisciplined and indolent."

"Nevertheless, she accomplished it. Perhaps her time on the station, working on the project, taught her some steel."

The senator seemed to consider this, the tips of his horns glinting in the snowfall. "Continue."

"She confirmed that none of the Fant had the information we seek, but that this one has a connection to one who does, a deceased expert. I've sent her back up to the station where she can use her koph to Speak and probe him. And then we'll be done."

"Done with what?" asked Jorl. "What are you hoping to accomplish?"

"Koph, Son," said the senator. "The Alliance needs to control the drug Speakers use."

"But you already do. You choose how much and where to distribute."

"In part that's true, but we don't control its manufacture. Alliance chemists have managed to reverse engineer many of the substances that you export, but not koph. To be honest, we've barely a clue what it's made from, let alone how to do it. And it's too important to leave entirely in your hands. That's just not a position the senate can accept. But we couldn't simply come out and ask, now could we?"

"All of this, just so you could learn the refinement process to manufacture koph?"

"A bit more, actually. As chair of the committee, I instituted a team of specialist advisors, precognitivists actually. They have had visions of something more, a new drug, which we would only discover by pursuing greater knowledge of koph. That's why the major was authorized to trespass on your Compact, to stimulate the events that would allow us to acquire that knowledge. And I have to say, his initial proposal seemed solid: acquire and question Fant who would not be missed."

"But none of them had what you wanted. None of them knew anything." Jorl's voice cracked and he fanned his ears trying to keep the tears from his eyes, not caring if it offended or upset the senator.

"But you do. I have that right, Major? Jorl here has that knowledge?"

"Indirectly, sir. He knows the dead Fant who knows."

"That's good. That's very good. Now take a deep breath, Jorl. Have the medications calmed you enough? I need you to understand very clearly what I'm about to tell you." Senator Bish gently wiped a finger under each of Jorl's eyes, drying his face.

"But he—"

"I'll deal with him in a moment; you have my word. But this must come first. You heard me say that the senate must be responsible to the entire Alliance. That's why I'm here now, even though it's against the law established by your Compact. This is just one planet, albeit it's turned out to be an important one. And the Fant, both Eleph and Lox, combine to barely a million people. It's wrong for you to hold thousands of other planets and hundreds of billions of other people hostage to your own desires. I hope you can appreciate that; you seem like a reasonable young man. So I want to be clear, Son. I will have that knowledge from you. It's more important than you or me or even this entire planet. Pursuing the secret of koph will lead to the greatest good for the Alliance. No sacrifice is too great, no action too extreme. I would authorize the extermination of your entire race if it served this higher need."

Jorl blinked. He felt buoyed up by a vast and artificial serenity that wouldn't let him react emotionally to what he'd just heard. He believed his reply, but didn't feel it. "That's insane!"

"Not at all. It is a thoroughly reasoned and responsible decision. I regret that you cannot see it as such, but that does not change things in the least. The events you witnessed today make it clear that I need to take a more direct hand if we're to accomplish anything. That begins now, with you. You need to comprehend that I am utterly serious when I tell you that *nothing* is more vital to me. If you do not willingly provide what I require, I'm prepared to wipe out your people, island by island, until you do."

Bish patted Jorl's cheek and turned back to Krasnoi.

"Just as you have failed to appreciate how grossly you've exceeded your authority. I don't pretend to understand Fant culture or their preference for geriatric suicide, but I do know that it involves a choosing of both place and time. Is it fair to say that none of the planetary residents you acquired selected this location and hour?"

"That's not the point."

"Indeed not, nor I suppose is it that you wouldn't choose here and now either, but the situation demands accountability, and perhaps a touch of symmetry." His right hand reached into his robes; when he withdrew it, a ring of platinum and fossilized wood gleamed on one finger, the sigil of the Committee of Information. He held the hand in front of him and nodded to his assistant. "Druz?"

The Sloth had waited immobile as the senator spoke, her fingers spread across Krasnoi's chest. She began speaking in a breath-less rush, like an actor in a play that has run overlong who now seeks to catch up on the time. "This day, on the authority of Senator Bish, chair of the Committee of Information—"

"What are you doing?"

Something shot out from her sleeve and pierced Krasnoi's cloth-ing and fur below the spot where the Brady pressed against his chest.

"—You are discharged from service, now and ever more."

Urs-Major Krasnoi bent at the knees and staggered, pulling away from the senator's aide. A trio of gleaming metal talons ex-tended just beyond her fingertips for an instant before vanishing back within her clothes. The Bear's eyes bulged as he fell back onto the snowy ground, dead.

"You and you," Bish pointed at the two nearest Ailuros. "See to this body and carry it to my personal ship. Druz, take charge of cleaning up this mess. I want any sign that we were ever here to be gone."

"Yes, sir. I will have all materiel stowed in one of the station's warehouses until it can be properly processed."

"That's fine. Speaking of the station, inform them we will be arriving soon and that I expect to meet with the telepath there."

"And me?" asked Jorl. "What is your plan for me?"

The Yak gazed down at him, his eyes as warm as a loving grandfather. "You, Son, will accompany me, as my guest of course. We'll continue our discussion as two intelligent and civilized men. I hope we can come to an accord for the greater good of the Alliance's citizens, but if not, I can promise you that many more Fant will die."

TWENTY-THREE

FAR FROM HOME

PIZLO sat in the dark for most of two days while his cargo pod raced upward faster than anything he had ever imagined. As it climbed, the temperature dropped, not cold enough to harm any of the pharmaceuticals aboard, but uncomfortably close to freezing for an exhausted, young Lox. He started to say something about it, more to remark than complain, but stopped himself. For the first time in his life, there was nothing that could hear him.

He passed most of the time sleeping. His hands had since stiffened into immobility as he discovered when he woke with an urgent need to pee and couldn't work his fingers to pull down his shorts. Pemma hadn't told him how long the journey would take, but if the need arose Pizlo had expected to pee into his empty water bottle. Instead he ended up wetting himself, and while he couldn't feel pain he did experience sensations of temperature.

His humiliation increased when gravity went away. All his life Pizlo had leaped and jumped and flown through every high and low place in the forests on Keslo, and never once had his stomach registered a complaint. Now *down* had become a memory rather than a reality. His stomach revolted and everything in it came back up. Invisible in the darkness, his floating puke terrified him. The smell of his own stomach acids and partially digested meal accentuated the reek of his urine-soaked shorts. For the rest of the voyage he huddled into a ball, wondering if any of Barsk's moons would ever want to talk to him when he couldn't even go to the bathroom properly or keep his lunch where it belonged.

Finally, the pod must have reached the shaft's apex. The walls around him clanged as if something had struck the container and soon after gravity returned, though much less than what he'd known on Barsk. The floor tilted a good thirty degrees, and this was followed by a more muted clanging and then a trundling sound and a sense of movement. The pod had lost some of its chill. Pizlo waited until the sense of motion stopped—with another clang!—and the floor went level again. Tugging his possessions with his trunk, he made his way back along the dark corridor toward the entrance and opened the hatch.

Dim light poured in, more than enough to blind his already weak eyes. He was thirsty and smelly and cranky and he'd forgotten his hands didn't work. They slid along the frame of the entrance and the rest of him followed out of the pod. He fell a greater distance than when he'd climbed in and landed with a heavy thud. His head spun for a while, and when he managed to get to his feet, his left arm hung uselessly at his side. He stared down at it, annoyed. "That's not good," he said aloud, and shrugged. There was nothing he could do about it now. He gathered up his mesh sacks which had fallen out with him, and took stock of his surroundings.

The warehouse held thousands of cargo pods stacked in finished blocks running two wide and three deep and five high. The ceiling was high enough that they could have built the stacks even taller. Pizlo's pod was one among the set of six that would complete the top layer of a stack, which explained the height of his fall. As he collected himself, a gigantic machine cradling a cargo pod in a three-limbed metal grip sped past. It deposited the pod and then returned back the way it had come. He staggered after it, making note of the countless rows all around him, defined by stacks of cargo pods stuffed with drugs and medicines.

The machine led him to a gate. He followed it through and stopped as the machine turned left to approach a round hole in the floor. Five similar machines also surrounded the opening, and behind each lay an identical gate to the one he'd come through. As Pizlo watched, a fresh cargo pod hurtled up out of the hole and one of the machines extended multiple arms to snatch it. He recognized the resulting clang. The machine tilted back with its prize and rolled toward its gate.

He turned to the right, away from the mouth of the beanstalk, and after only a few steps encountered a different gate, one that was too small for the machines to access but more than adequate for people. He pushed at it and the gate split down the middle, the sides retracting into the wall on either side, to reveal a corridor. The gate closed up again behind him and he froze. Hallways and corridors weren't new to him, but nothing in the Civilized Wood ran so straight for so far. The only unending vistas he had seen had been at the beach or while on the sea. Everything spun for a moment and Pizlo sagged against the wall. His heart hammered like it wanted to escape his chest. His eyes ached and he couldn't catch his breath.

He let out a lone whimper, a sound too low for anyone to hear, and once was enough, an acknowledgment of panic that had crept into him unseen. That was fine. "I'm only six," he said, wiping at his eyes with the nubs of his trunk. Admitting it made it okay for him to be frightened, and knowing that allowed him to set it aside. His hands itched but he thought better about scratching them. Instead he let them rest, positioning one above the other, on the moons he had drawn on his chest. He closed his eyes and just breathed for a while. When his heart rate had slowed to normal he pushed off from the wall, opened his eyes again, and set off down the corridor.

The air in the warehouse had smelled better though he couldn't think why. He pondered that for a few steps until the closer space of his hallway made him realize that he was the source of the funk. Right. The revelations of his last moon had made it clear that he needed to come to this place but had been disturbingly silent on the specifics of what to do once he arrived. If the warehouse he'd been in with its endless stacks of stuff was like the entire island of Keslo, this space resembled the Civilized Wood. That meant that people lived and worked here. And just like back home, it would be simpler and easier for everyone if he could move about unseen. That included moving unsmelled; he needed to do something about that soon.

His trunk grazed the ink on his chest. "I am like the moons. Invisible behind tree and rain and cloud, but always there." He fanned his ears and listened but detected no sound. As he stepped forward, light filled the near end of the corridor from above, a trio of thin strips that illuminated walls and floor in his vicinity but let the rest of the corridor trail off in ever diminishing light. The lights overhead left trailing lines on his vision when he looked away. They also revealed a series of doors set flush with the walls, alternating continuously, or at least as far as the light allowed.

Everything was plastic, rendered in muted shades of color that invariably tended toward gray, though a paler shade than the Fant back home. Time to explore.

The nearest door had a threshold framing it in darker gray than the gray green of the door itself. Someone had stenciled several tiny glyphs on the frame a bit above his eye level. He pressed his head to the wall but heard nothing from inside so took another step and listened against the door itself. Much like the gate at the head of the hallway, it gave way and vanished into the side of the wall with a faint whooshing sound. It happened so quickly that Pizlo stumbled into the resulting space, waving his good arm for balance and barely keeping his feet. A light came on in the room, brighter than the corridor outside; the door whooshed closed behind him.

A pair of Pandas stood facing him, waving and smiling like they were happy to see him. Pizlo yelped and scrambled backwards. The door opened behind him with another whoosh and only after he had crossed the threshold again did he realize the Ailuros hadn't actually noticed him. He stepped back inside, closer, and they continued to smile and wave. They stood framed by a background of leafy green plants and a cluster of bamboo, beyond the edges of which was the same uniform gray plastic as the corridor outside, walls, floor, and ceiling.

"Oh!" Under the cheerful gaze of the Ailuros on the wall he investigated the room. A molded desk bulged from one side and a matching bench seat extruded from the floor in front of it. A sleeping platform was little more than another bit of raised floor with some bedclothes wrapped tightly across. A door in the far corner slid open onto a lavatory alcove, the commode and basin and tub all one piece with the room itself, and a shelf above the basin contained tiny dispensers of gel. The near corner's sliding door held a closet with three black uniforms hanging from a crossbar and a small chest of drawers containing several tunics and pants of a soft and pale green fabric. All the clothes were of a size and shape appropriate to an Ailuros. Three small hooks protruded from the wall at higher than head-height, like upward-curving fingers or nubs, on the wall halfway between the door and the closet. Something very much like a daypouch on a long strap hung from one.

Everything here was utilitarian and anonymous, with the exception of the holographic poster of the bright and happy Pandas. Maybe they were kin to the Panda that lived in the room. Pizlo had seen plenty of holos in several books Jorl kept of such things, but as a rule Fant rarely bothered with images of one another, not where memory could serve. Perhaps when Ailuros traveled far from their families they forgot what one another looked like.

Pizlo hid his sacks in the closet and closed it up again, then slipped into the lavatory, shutting the door behind him. He needed a few moments to figure out how to access the fixtures, turning the lights off and on and activating a drier in the ceiling before he actually managed to find the bathing controls and activate them with just his trunk. Water poured down into the tub like a mild rain and he let it flow over him, tilting his head back and drinking deeply. He pretended he was back home in the Shadow Dwell standing under a hidden waterfall that had called him to it, but he couldn't sustain it. The tub, the lavatory, even the water pouring down on him all felt lifeless. Nothing here could talk to him. He had never felt more alone.

He pushed at his shorts, struggling at the task. He hadn't been able to get them down back in the darkness of the cargo pod when he'd had two good arms, but managed to use his feet and trunk to yank them off now. In the process he tore off bits of recent scabs from his hands and started them bleeding again. He used up everything in the dispensers, slathering himself with gel and working the gunk into the shorts at his feet as well. The flow of water carried away assorted grime, filth, and tatters of skin, but left the inked circles on his chest unchanged. When both he and his clothes were as clean as they were apt to be, he pulled the shorts up his legs, and then rolled onto his back in the tub, tugging at them with his trunk and wriggling to get them all the way back on. He shut off the water and turned on the drier, then he just stood there, legs apart, one arm wide, ears fanning, and let the room dry him.

Refreshed but with his hands still damp and oozing, he stepped back into the main room, leaving moist, Fant-shaped footprints on the plastic floor as he retrieved his bags from the closet. The door to the hallway opened at his touch, and with a last backward glance at the smiling, waving pair of Ailuros, Pizlo slipped back into the corridor.

The light strips came on ahead of him and dimmed after he passed. He counted nineteen other doors like the one that led to the Panda's room. Without touching, he listened at each door. At two of them he heard muffled sounds of conversation but couldn't make out any words. Pizlo shrugged and moved on. It wasn't a problem until it became a problem. Certainly the moon hadn't mentioned anything about running into anyone.

At its far end, the corridor branched both right and left, but otherwise ended in another gate. Pizlo pressed his trunk against it. As with the other, the gate split down the middle and the two pieces whooshed to the wall on either side while lights came on to illuminate the new room, a space easily as wide as five cargo pods. Rows of tables and bench seats extruded from the floor, and cabinets and fixtures bulged from the walls on either side. But Pizlo barely noticed any of that. His full attention had been captured by the wall opposite him, which bowed out in a gentle curve and didn't appear to be a wall at all, rather a vast window from floor to ceiling that gazed out onto the surface of Barsk itself.

He stumbled closer until he could stroke the transparent wall with his trunk. He knew the view was real, could feel the planet that was his home whispering faintly to him in too large a chorus for any of the individual voices to be understood. He just stood there for the longest time, eyes closed, basking in the light of home.

Minutes later, a new voice, solitary and strong, broke through the whispers. He opened his eyes. A moon had risen over the distant curve of the planet, Telko, the largest of them all, and one of the remaining four that he'd not yet seen.

Pizlo greeted it with silent joy and felt an answering acknowledgment. Its light washed over him. He communed. The three previous times he had seen one of Barsk's moons they had appeared for scant moments during rifts in the clouds that blanketed the skies. Hanging there so high, the clouds wrapping the planet below, Telko had nothing but time to convey its message to Pizlo. Tears trickled down the boy's face. He dropped to his knees and sobbed in the embrace of the moon's light.

TWENTY-FOUR

DEAD TO DEAD

ESPITE the strain on Lirlowil's body, the Matriarch allowed herself only the briefest of pauses between ending her summoning of Jorl and beginning her pursuit of Arlo. Once the nefshons had been gathered, the act of Speaking itself would take less effort than actual conversation. But manipulating the particles, searching out a sufficient number to create a construct of the desired conversant could be exhausting, and back when she'd been alive, Margda had only rarely ever done so twice in a day. Her host would feel the fatigue, not her, which was a freedom and a danger, and she accepted both.

She allowed herself a small concession toward normalcy, conjuring up a fresh cup of tea for herself in the constructed space of her home back on Yargo. Sipping, she willed herself the ability to see nefshons that a real cup of koph-laced tea would have brought her and returned to the work at hand.

Even with the telepathically acquired details, Margda had only enough knowledge about Arlo to recognize him but not summon him outright. Such a limitation would have stymied other Speakers, but she possessed more ways than simply blending desire with perception to call the nefshons of her conversant.

If her visions held true, then despite the passage of eight hundred years no other Speaker, either on Barsk or off, had come near her level of focus. She'd developed techniques that she'd never shared, choosing to point her students down different avenues far from her private methodology. She plucked at the particles one by one, focusing her senses to let her examine what no living eye could resolve. She knew the feel of Jorl's own nefshons, and her telepathic probe had confirmed that he had recently summoned his friend. Her prophesied Aleph-Bearer was near, and some few of Arlo's particles would likewise remain near, dispersing away from him. These were the nefshons she sought. As she examined and discarded all others, these from an Eleph instead of a Lox, or too old, or the wrong sex, or not a Fant at all, she cast them from her awareness.

The process defined tedium, this more than anything had bolstered her confidence that no other Speaker would think to try it, looking at the particles themselves, independent of the conversant they could produce. Easier to go looking for one specific leaf among all rain forests of all the islands of Barsk across eight hundred years of seasons.

Margda had no choice. Her visions had not shown Arlo to her. Everything she had set in motion, the rules of the Speakers' Edict, the creation of the aleph, the conditions for ensuring Jorl would be marked, all were so she could one day be resurrected and Speak directly to Arlo. The entire mad plan had seemed full of promise and daring back when she'd been alive, but since her possession of the Lutr's body, doubt had crept into her mind. Her attempts to shape the future might fly apart, and the backlash could shatter her own construct even as it destroyed the mind of her host.

In all her long life, even during the worst of her seizures, she had never felt so little control. And yet, if her people were to survive, she had to succeed. On that point, all of her visions had been as clear as still water.

And then, she had him, or at least a tiny piece of him. A single nefshon belonging to a recently deceased, male Fant in his prime, and with the flavor of Jorl's touch upon it. This was Arlo. She focused her will upon it, causing the particles of all other possible remaining conversants to fade from her perception. The nefshons of her desire came at her call, more swiftly than most summonings because they'd already been gathered near by Jorl's use on the planet below.

Seconds later, a construct of Arlo coalesced and she brought all of her attention back to the image of her long-vanished home in Yargo. Her conversant stood before her, eyes closed, taller than most Lox, leaner as well. She'd dressed him as his own subconscious imagined him, in the multi-pocketed, bright orange and blue vest and utility shorts of a career pharmer.

"You've been summoned more than once before so I'll spare you the formal ritual. You don't need grounding. You understand what this experience is, yes?"

"I was just talking to Jorl . . ."

"And you've managed to retain that memory, an impressive feat, I assure you, but not something that interests me just now. I'm after recollections from before your death, not any chats you've had since."

"I don't understand. Who are you? Why are you Speaking to me?"

"Focus, Boy. Tell me your name, and then look at me. Closely."

"I'm Arlo. And . . . Oh! This isn't possible. You're dead."

"So are you, but we're not going to let that get in our way. Now say it, words give body to thoughts. Say it."

"You're the Matriarch."

She allowed herself a smile and reached out, her trunk encircling his left ear where it joined his head the way a parent might comfort a child.

"And you, my boy, are the savior of our people."

"The what?"

"Years before my own death, I saw that you would kill yourself. Why did you choose to do so, Arlo?"

"I didn't. Why would I? I had a great life. I was successful, I loved Tolta, we both loved our son—"

"There was a son? I had not seen that. Curious, but not important either. What *is* important is the truth. We don't have time for lies, and I'm hardly in a position to share what you reveal with anyone else. So tell me, Arlo. Tell me, why did you take your own life?"

He turned away, pacing across her workroom to stand by the window and gaze out. "You have no conception of how difficult it was. An inspiration, really. I had to act on it at once; if I'd worked it through rationally I'd have lost my nerve. But in the moment, with nothing but oblivion coming after, I could do it. Only . . . Jorl, and now you, keep summoning me back, and in this endless moment from the end of my life I have nothing but time. Time to reflect on the pain I've caused my wife. Time to mourn seeing my boy grow up. I made the ultimate sacrifice, but with every summoning I agonize over it again and again. I've come to hate Speakers. Can you appreciate the irony?"

Margda said nothing. He hadn't really been talking to her. She recognized his soliloquy as a conversation he'd wished he could voice to Jorl, venting the words out her parlor window instead. She waited for him to tire of his own silence.

"This isn't Keslo."

"It's not. That doesn't matter either. Tell me the reason for your suicide."

He continued to stare into the empty Civilized Wood of her making. When he spoke, it might as well have been to himself.

"I'd been working on a new drug, a taww variant. It had the potential to allow the creation of a more powerful form of koph."

"I'd suspected as much, but be specific. Powerful how?"

"A single dose would last a lifetime. Speakers would be able to perceive nefshons at any time, as easily as opening their eyes."

"That's exactly what the Alliance wants," said Margda. "After eight hundred years, they've more than grown tired of their utter dependence on us for koph. Give them this drug, and they'll lapse back into their sense of superiority and leave all of Barsk alone again."

"I couldn't. The variant was unstable. The taww's toxicity had the same source as the mechanism that allowed it to be retained permanently. It would work, but in the process it killed the user. So I went looking for a binding agent to resolve that problem . . ."

"And you found it?"

Arlo turned back to face the Matriarch, a haunted look in his eyes.

"I did. In bacteria derived from a bioluminescent insect I found in my son's bug collection."

Margda slid from her hammock and crossed to meet him, taking his hands in hers. "And did this neutralize the toxic effects of your variant?"

"It did. Perfectly. The simulations showed the perceptual enhancement remained unlocked and accessible. In that sense, the new drug was a complete success. But it also did more."

"More?"

"If the user had carried the bioluminescent in his or her body for more than a season, the taww variant increased the perceptual capabilities beyond what I could model. At least two orders of magnitude, probably greater."

"I don't understand. Why would anyone have an insect's bacteria in their body?"

Arlo pulled his hands free and raised one to lightly touch the aleph that glimmered faintly on her head. "Because you decreed the creation of the aleph, and the people who made it a reality used that chemical in the tattooing process."

She staggered back, a myriad possibilities and consequences racing through her mind. "You're saying, that if I used your new and improved taww variant, that not only would I never need to take koph again, but that my abilities would increase a hundred-fold?"

"No."

"Why not?"

"Two reasons. Mainly because you're already dead. But also because I eliminated the only sample I created. I destroyed it along with all of my notes and equipment and anything else that might cause people to suspect what I had discovered. And then I died."

"But why?"

"For the same reasons you would want to give a single-dose koph to the Alliance. Because if they learned of such a thing, that we had it and they did not, their paranoia and loathing would expand beyond anything we've seen since they forced all Eleph and Lox to resettle on Barsk."

Margda scowled. "What gives you the right to make that

decision for everyone. You were a pharmer, not a legislator. What do you know of negotiating with the Alliance?"

"You think you could do better?"

"I was one of the architects of the Compact that has kept our people safe for eight hundred years!"

"Exactly. Why would I risk throwing all of that away? Besides, it's more than just that. No one should have this kind of power. Right now, Speakers can reach back centuries, but with the new drug anyone with an aleph could search through millennia, possibly ten or a hundred times that with practice."

"Yes, and the Alliance actively discourages digging back that far. But that's something that could likely be negotiated. There's no point at present, but if the means to access such ancient memories became available, options would open up."

Arlo fanned his ears. "Spoken like a legislator, not a pharmer. Do you even understand how memory works?"

Margda waved the question away with her trunk. "Simple associations, neural networks, semantic representation through distributed points of activation."

"Of course you'd say that."

"What's that supposed to mean?"

"Everything you said came from the psychological understanding of your generation. But your own discovery changed all that. Once you showed the galaxy how to see nefshons, new research opened up new explanations. Those models you described are still true, but only go so far. They account for much of learning, semantic memory, and even aspects of episodic memory. But not our memory of other people."

"What are you saying?"

"The memories of individuals, the people who have touched our lives, require nefshons. When I remember something about my wife or son, I'm tapping into their nefshons, particles I've received from them. When I think about someone who has died, I'm unconsciously activating their particles that I already possess. Koph lets people *perceive* nefshons, but we've always had the power to manipulate them. It's how memory works. Your drug just provides some individuals with conscious control and more power. And my new drug could take that too far."

"Why too far? Why is that a problem?"

"What do you imagine would happen if a Speaker could summon *all* of a person's nefshons? Not just enough for a conversation, but every last particle? That person would cease to exist. No one would be able to recall anything about her. No matter how detailed, how intimate, how vast the memory might be, it would be gone. Wiped out of the consciousness of the galaxy. As if she never existed, never touched another person's life."

"Impossible! Even if a Speaker could pull in all of another person's particles, sooner or later they'd have to release them. They'd become available again. Floating freely."

"Probably. But the damage would be done. The memories would be gone. Another Speaker probably couldn't even summon that person again, because there'd be no memory of her to suggest a summoning in the first place. Now think about how you might undermine a society, a world, a culture, by causing everyone everywhere to forget the existence of key figures. Ask yourself what effect you have had on the development of this planet, Matriarch, and what confusion and chaos would erupt if you simply didn't exist?"

"That is insane! It would disrupt and redefine reality."

"That's the power my new drug might unleash. All of that could be done by one person. That's why I gave up my life, so the secret would die with me."

Margda stepped back and dropped into her hanging chair, letting her body go limp. The nubs of her trunk curled back to squeeze the bridge of its root between her eyes.

"I did not foresee any of that. I only saw a threat that could be avoided by your discovery. The Alliance knows nothing of this, but I believe they are tired of having to rely on Barsk as the sole source of koph. A secret senate committee is threatening to kill every Eleph and Lox on the planet if they don't get what they want. That was my vision. Only you can prevent the extinction of our peoples."

Arlo just shook his head, his ears flapping listlessly. "And if I give them what you want, they wouldn't have to stop there. One person, one irrational bigot could dedicate his life to wiping the existence of all Fant from the collective memory of the galaxy. I gave up everything for that. There's nothing you can say that will change my mind."

She raised her trunk in a sad salute and reached out with a trickle of Lirlowil's telepathy that had returned to her, confirming the conviction she heard in his voice. There would be no changing his mind. With no more ritual than a wave of her hand she removed her will from his nefshons and ended the summoning. Arlo vanished in an instant. A moment later, so did the house on Yargo. Margda found herself back in the body of the Otter, weeping and unable to stop.

TWENTY-FIVE

NEAR AND SOON

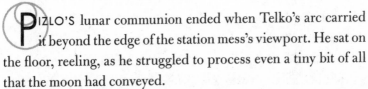

PIZLO'S lunar communion ended when Telko's arc carried it beyond the edge of the station mess's viewport. He sat on the floor, reeling, as he struggled to process even a tiny bit of all that the moon had conveyed.

Pemma, the previous moon, had told him he would need to climb high above Barsk to meet Jorl in a worldless island where nothing lived. Now Telko had provided the where and when, and much else besides and even the little bit that he already understood sickened him. "It's going to be horrible," he said, but if the whispering throng of the planet beyond the window understood, it gave no sign. Pizlo rolled to his feet, dragging his mesh sacks behind him with his trunk as he crossed back to the door. It opened to the long corridor he'd already traversed and shorter hallways both left and right. He had a destination now and set off down the right side, the way ahead illuminating as he approached. The doors to either side looked no different from those in the previous corridor, spaced the same as well. He counted off seven doors on his left and stopped at the eighth. Telko had promised it was empty.

He leaned his head against it to trigger the door and entered. It looked like the other room he'd explored, the one with the holo of the waving Pandas, except this one didn't have any Pandas. Nothing hung from the hooks on the wall. The lavatory and the closet were also in the same place, although both were empty. No one lived in this room. He sat in the middle of the floor and emptied out his sacks, making a feast of everything he had left. He hadn't realized how hungry he was until he began eating. After his appetite had abated, he realized he hadn't noticed the hunger because he'd been scared. Just a little. Even with what Pemma had told him, so much had been strange and new. Being afraid had been new, too. He didn't much like it.

Finished with his meal, Pizlo gathered up rinds and other debris and disposed of them in the lavatory. He took each of the bags that had held his supplies and knotted the mesh to create a sling and secure his useless arm across his chest. He fanned himself with his ears for a few moments and then stood up and went to the closet. Using his trunk and good arm he hauled himself to a seat atop the dresser to wait. He slid the closet door closed and settled back against the wall. Telko had told him he'd meet up with Jorl near and soon. He'd resolved the matter of near, and in the process used up most of the soon.

TWENTY-SIX

CONCURRENCE OF VISION

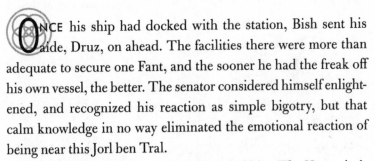

ONCE his ship had docked with the station, Bish sent his aide, Druz, on ahead. The facilities there were more than adequate to secure one Fant, and the sooner he had the freak off his own vessel, the better. The senator considered himself enlightened, and recognized his reaction as simple bigotry, but that calm knowledge in no way eliminated the emotional reaction of being near this Jorl ben Tral.

The incident at the polar base had rattled him. The Urs-major's colossal bungling of what should have been a simple mission had necessitated his instant removal, and while dispensing justice in front of the Lox had added to his profile as a benevolent figure, subsequently threatening the Fant had been a mistake. The Yak had realized the error the instant after the words had left his lips, and spent the trip to the station attempting to rectify things. Still, his mistake need not be irrevocable. The Fant was clearly in shock from witnessing the immolation of his elders, and the cocktail of drugs Druz had administered imparted a certain malleability.

Upon boarding his ship, Bish had placed Jorl in an opulent

cabin, sublimated his own disgust for the man by indulging his culinary hobby and crafting from his own hands an unparalleled meal. But he drew the line at sharing a table with him. Instead, he left his reluctant guest to enjoy the food alone, the better to rest and recover from his ordeal. The senator had set Druz to work at the same time, learning everything possible about the surviving Fant. For all her slow movement, the Sloth had as keen a mind as any being the Yak had encountered. She'd prepared and presented a report both thorough and surprising; best of all it gave Bish a starting point for establishing a fresh connection.

Soon after docking, the senator took it upon himself to escort Jorl through the station. In this instance, the limited facilities worked in his favor. The Lox had nowhere to run, which meant he needed no guards and thus no reminder that he was obviously a prisoner. It helped, too, that the room he'd selected for Jorl was in no way different from any of the station's crew quarters, though by now Druz had recoded its door to lock from the outside.

When he entered, he found the Sloth already settled in at a small desk, her equipment recording everything that happened in the room. He gestured for Jorl to precede him and followed closely.

"I apologize for the sparse accommodations, but this station wasn't designed for visitors. Per the terms of your own Compact, the Alliance keeps only a minimal presence here, just what's necessary to oversee your world's exports. Most of the transfer protocols are fully automated, both from down below and to the delivery vessels that carry everything to other worlds."

The senator watched Jorl look around the room. The Fant hadn't spoken more than a handful of words since leaving the planet. The meds had dulled the immediacy of his experience, but Bish saw the horror of it yet lingered. It showed in his posture, the softness of his voice, and most vividly in Jorl's eyes.

"It's fine, sir," replied Jorl. "Though you still haven't told me why I'm here."

"We'll get to that, I promise. But first, I wanted to share something my aide discovered while we were en route. She looked into your background a bit, nothing invasive mind you, all public record material. I had known from the Urs-major's reports that you had the distinction of serving in the Patrol, but I was unaware of your prolific work as a historian. I actually feel a debt to you, curious as that may seem."

The Fant's ears swiveled and lifted in reaction to his words, but Bish didn't let show on his face any of the revulsion that those hideous and furless flaps of gray flesh evoked in him.

"I'm not surprised that you don't recognize me; the resemblance isn't that strong and how many Bos have you seen, eh? But I'm not the first of my family to dedicate himself to public service. My mother's father was also in the senate."

Jorl's voice held both weariness and wonder. "Your grandfather also served on the Committee of Information?"

"He did."

"I . . . I wrote a biography about him. It was the first thing I worked on after leaving the Patrol. I even Spoke with him, several times."

"I envy you that. It's been many years since I've heard his voice. He died while I was still a child. That biography came to the committee, as all new media does, and a talented clerk pulled it from the slush of published works and tagged it for my attention. I was truly touched by the detail and fairness of your writing, though honestly I never expected that I'd get to meet the author. I have to tell you, after reading your words, the gentle way you spoke of my grandfather, I feel as though we are old friends already, Jorl. Do you mind if I call you Jorl?"

"Honestly, Senator, I don't feel as though whether I mind or not is going to make any difference here."

The Fant was shrewder than he'd expected him to be, and Bish chided himself for buying into his own racist stereotypes so deeply. No matter, though. One feint had failed, he had others at his disposal.

"Don't be like that, Son. This doesn't have to be adversarial. Regardless of whatever happens next, speaking not as a senator but as a grandson, I wanted to thank you."

Jorl stood, slumped and silent. Bish had spent a lifetime reading his adversaries' body language. Some things were universal, existing across all races. The Fant was beyond weary. The right argument would push him over the edge. And yet, as he watched, Jorl straightened. The weariness remained, but something had changed. He'd acquired a degree of hostility, unfocused for the moment, as if equally likely to lash out or be directed inward.

"What exactly is going to happen next? You've already broken your own laws by coming to Barsk. You've used officers of the Patrol to abduct hundreds of civilians, interred them against their will, and executed them. And now you've taken me a second time, removing me from my planet and dropped me where none could possibly know to look for me."

Bish frowned at the anger. Had he lost his moment? "I don't believe you appreciate the bigger picture here, Jorl. What we do, what we've been doing, has been for the greater good of the Alliance. Believe me, I sympathize with your perspective. The zeal with which the Urs-major carried out these things has blurred the real necessity behind them. But you have also seen the celerity with which I resolved the matter of his excess. Now, here, just the two of us, two civilized beings, I'm confident you will see the need for all that we do."

Jorl turned, and Bish noted how still his ears had become. The Lox crossed the room and seated himself on the sleeping platform on the far wall. On the voyage in, Druz had supplied him with a report suggesting that the movement, or lack, of a Fant's ears was a window into the degree of tension they experienced. When Jorl began speaking, it was clear he had built up his guard again. Was he somehow drawing strength from the massacre at the base?

"Who is the *we* in all of this, Senator Bish? Would you mind starting there?"

Long practice allowed the senator to keep the smile from his face, but the Fant had handed him an opening any politician could run with. "Not at all. When I say *we*, I, of course, refer to the people who make up the Alliance. All of us, you, myself, all sapient beings on all the worlds of which we speak. More directly, I mean their representatives, their voices in the process of managing this immense Alliance. Lawmakers like myself who strive on behalf of ordinary citizens like you. That's why I brought you here, Jorl, so you could help basic, decent people like yourself."

"I wasn't aware these people needed my help. You already know that I'm just a historian. Surely anyone with an interest in my work has ready access to the films and books I've published. What more could I possibly do to affect so many?"

Having maneuvered the Fant into asking the necessary question, Bish let the smile show. It was a friendly smile, warm and encouraging. A professional smile, built and earned, the work of a lifetime of public speaking and political gamesmanship. He stretched and briefly scratched behind his left horn before responding, knowing the value of a well-timed pause. When he did reply, it was with the patient tone that had won him landslide victories in election after election.

"I trust you are merely being coy with me. While you, personally, do have a contribution to make, I am speaking more generally of your fellow Eleph and Lox. All the Fant, as they are generally known to the Alliance. Barsk's government has enjoyed a special relationship with the rest of the galaxy. Among its other provisions, the Compact regulates the export of your many products. At the time of its creation, it was a great convenience for everyone. It assured the Alliance a continuous supply of thousands of items unique to Barsk, and it afforded the Fant the autonomy and privacy that had led them to Barsk in the first place."

The senator gestured at the Sloth who rose like an unbending tree branch, holding a tray with two cups of freshly poured tea. The Yak nodded once and she approached Jorl, offering him the first cup which he accepted. Bish helped himself to the remaining cup, raising it in a toast to Jorl, and draining the thing in a single gulp before handing it back to the Brady who then resumed her place in the background.

"But that was centuries ago, Jorl. The situation has changed. The Alliance now depends on Barsk for more than a million exports. And the number of worlds comprising the Alliance has also grown. But through it all, the terms of your Compact have remained constant. Your government has steadfastly refused to share the knowledge behind its pharmaceutical wealth. You've declined all requests to allow other scientists to visit and study your techniques, and you've outright rejected even the merest hint of assistance from the rest of the Alliance."

"We wouldn't have autonomy if we accepted assistance, Senator. Nor would we have privacy if we permitted visitors. Neither of those things have changed."

"But everything else has. And while it's true that our researchers have reverse-engineered many of your products, it has been, as your own people might say, the merest raindrop in a storm. Your officials hide behind their precious Compact and refuse to acknowledge that we live in different times, that the past is indeed past. As a historian, you should appreciate this, Jorl. So I ask you, is this situation fair to the rest of the people living in the Alliance? To the many billions of ordinary souls spread out across four thousand worlds who have come to depend on these exports?"

Jorl sipped his tea. "I suspect the matter is much more complex than you present it, Senator. And as you surely know, I am not part of Barsk's government. I have no more voice than any other individual on such matters. But that's not the real issue, is it? Major Krasnoi didn't take all those people because he wanted to know how to harvest or refine millions of different drugs. He was only interested in one. He wanted to know about koph. Why that one, among so many others?"

"Let me answer your question with another question. Tell me, Jorl, how much do you know about an Eleph called Margda?"

He watched Jorl smile at his query, as he knew he would. The dolt had no idea he was being manipulated, not that his awareness would have changed things one iota.

"Quite a bit. Her life was the focus of my research when I was at the academy. It's why I ended up studying your grandfather, because he was the first person off Barsk to take a real interest in her life and legacy."

"He did," said Bish. "He was particularly fascinated with her fits of clairvoyance, and how she bent those visions to her political will. It was such a novel thing to do, and she proved herself quite effective at it. I assume you've read all of her formal papers regarding her visions?"

Jorl nodded. "Those, as well as her journal entries, and what we have of her private correspondence."

"Good. That's very good. I have a great respect for thorough research. So it shouldn't come as a surprise to you that, rare as her precognitive gifts may have been, in the vast population of the Alliance there is no shortage of individuals with similar abilities to your Matriarch. But prior to her, no one—certainly no one in the senate—had ever thought to harness that resource toward our own political prosperity. But such talents *are* a resource, one that belongs to the greater good of all people. Your Matriarch didn't simply impress my grandfather, she inspired him. During his tenure in the senate, he began to use the Committee of Information as a means to structure that foresight."

"Is that how you've kept the outer colonies under control? You've had teams of psychic operatives scrying for you for three generations?"

"In part. But because Barsk was the only other place to have used precognition in this way, we've also always kept an eye turned toward your world. This aspect of the committee is rather clandestine, it's operation known in detail to only a small subset of senators, and for years now they have begrudged the expense, calling it a waste of time and resources. Barsk has continued on along the same course as always, quiet and calm. Recently though, that began to change. First one, and then another, and then several more of our precognitivists began reporting visions involving Barsk. They saw a change, a fast approaching critical juncture. They told us that it would involve the refinement of koph, a drug unlike any other of your pharmaceuticals. Not restorative, nor preventative, nor recreational. No, koph's sole purpose is as the means to allow some individuals to become Speakers. In time, every single one of those assets reported that everything would change soon, and all because of koph."

"What about it? We've had koph only slightly longer than we've had the Compact. What's changed?"

Bish stepped closer, arms wide, palms open, and beamed at Jorl with his politician's smile. "Not what, who. A new player in this vast game. My precognitivists brought me a name, the person they saw who could change everything. Tell me, Jorl, have you ever heard of someone called Arlo?"

A muffled sound from the far side of the room broke the senator's focus. Even before he could turn toward the source, Druz had shifted enough to point one arm toward the room's closet and fired a device from up her sleeve. Three steel talons darted across the room to embed themselves in the closet door and yank it open as the Sloth pulled back on their attached cables. A small figure tumbled out and crashed to the floor headfirst. A young Fant, white-fleshed and even more hideous than the larger, gray-skinned versions.

Bish stepped back, mind racing to assess the potential threat, even as Jorl jumped to his feet and gave a name to the creature with a voice of disbelief.

"Pizlo?"

TWENTY-SEVEN

BLIND ENDGAME BEGINNING

~~~~~~~~~~

"I TAKE it you know this child?" said Bish.

He'd tilted a horn in the direction of the Brady but otherwise kept his attention on the pair of Fant. The Sloth rose and started slowly across the room, the trio of cables withdrawing back up her sleeve with every step.

Jorl had left his seat to kneel alongside Pizlo, confusion warring with fear in his mind. How had the child come to be hiding in the closet, let alone here on this station? But questions could wait; he ran hands and trunk over Pizlo, checking the boy for injuries beyond the usual collection of scrapes and bruises that defined his daily life. He paused to puzzle over the circles drawn on his chest long enough to confirm they were only ink and nothing more. His growing relief evaporated when he noticed the arm fitted in a makeshift sling. Real fear took its place as he discovered the ruins of the boy's hands. Strips of white flesh hung from his palms. Somehow he'd torn through multiple layers of skin leaving behind weeping wounds. Hands and fingers had swollen to immobility, little more than fleshy blocks at the ends of his wrists. Even without the complications of likely infection, Jorl wondered if Pizlo could be saved the use of his hands at all.

"He needs medical attention!"

"Then he'll have it, of course." The senator sounded so much like his grandfather, a blend of decisive surety and familial kindness. Jorl doubted the sincerity but would worry about the cost later. All that mattered in this moment was helping Pizlo.

"Jorl, we're up in the sky! And I saw Telko, and that was after I saw Pemma." Pizlo's voice seemed breathy and his eyes didn't quite track.

"Hush now, it'll be fine. You've hit your head." Pizlo flailed a useless hand at the circles on his chest. "I have to fill in another of them." His eyes gave up their attempt to focus and his head lolled to one side.

"Allow me," said the Sloth, suddenly beside him, her voice deeper than he'd expected. From her sleeve, she drew a small tube which she snapped open, pouring the contents into her hand. "It's an anesthetic salve that will help with the pain until we can get him to the infirmary."

Jorl's trunk whipped left and right in negation. "He doesn't need it. He can't feel pain. Use that time to get him treatment sooner, please."

"No pain?" repeated the Sloth, even as she slid her arms underneath Pizlo and began to rise. "I've never heard of such a thing."

"No, he's abnor . . . his physiology is atypical. I don't know if ordinary healing methods will be effective or do more harm—"

"Have no fear," said Druz. "Our infirmary is part of a larger, working lab with very discriminating diagnostic gear. I will proceed with caution." She moved toward the exit with the boy in her arms. Bish stopped her with a hand on her shoulder.

"The major's telepath should have reached the station before us. Have one of the guards find her and escort her to this room."

"Of course, sir."

Pizlo stirred. "Jorl . . . the moon . . . it told me you'll see Arlo soon. Say hello for me, 'kay?"

The door opened and closed and Jorl was alone in the room with the Yak.

"He seems to know the name. And from his remark, dazed as he obviously was, he believes you know the name, too. That seems too unlikely a thing to be mere coincidence, don't you think? And more, what is the boy doing in this place at all?"

"Pizlo," said Jorl. "His name is Pizlo."

"I see. And who is Pizlo?"

The Fant shook his head, trying to make sense of events. "He's . . . he's Arlo's son."

"Indeed?" The sound of avarice had replaced the senator's kindly tone. "You and young Pizlo clearly know one another, which begs the question: what is Arlo to you?"

Jorl was still on his knees. He looked up at Bish, the events of the past day cascading through his mind. The Dying wandering the yard, the Lutr who had protected him from an Ailuros, the Matriarch summoning him and asking about Arlo, Krasnoi slaughtering the Dying before his eyes, the Brady executing the major at the senator's command, and now Pizlo here on the station high above the world. One improbable event after another. What wouldn't he give to trade it all away?

"Arlo is my best friend," he said, his voice little more than a whisper.

"I see. Then perhaps we can expect your friend to also make a surprise appearance and come for his son?"

He fanned himself with his ears but made no move to stand up. If anything, he wanted to sink into the floor, through the station, and tumble back down to the world below, but even that bargain was denied him. "I wouldn't hold my breath. He's been dead for close to two years now."

The Bos stood over him, saying nothing. Jorl didn't care anymore. This wasn't how history was made. None of the events he'd studied at the academy had been so predetermined. None of the principals he'd Spoken to had been such helpless pawns. Was there anything he had done, any decision he'd made in his entire life, that hadn't been preordained, just another step that ultimately led him down the path the Matriarch had foreseen centuries before? And was Bish any better? Or the Yak's grandfather for that matter? Despite commissioning his own team of precognitivists, here he was at the same moment that Margda had seen. Was all of the universe a fixed game, if one only knew where and how to look?

The door opened. Someone entered from the hallway, but Jorl didn't look up.

"Senator? A pleasure to meet you at long last."

Jorl recognized the voice. The Lutr who had spoken with him back in the yard. Krasnoi had sent her away before killing the Dying, before Bish had arrived.

"I've read your reports; fruitless but thorough. You're a very talented young woman." Jorl could hear the grandfatherly smile in his voice. "I have one final need of your abilities. The Fant and I are about to have a very serious chat. Monitor him. I need to know that he understands and believes what I tell him. None of us have the luxury of allowing him anything less than total clarity."

Hands gripped him under each arm and hauled Jorl to his feet.

The senator carried him back to the sleeping platform and dropped him there. Behind the Bos, Jorl could see the Lutr watching him, her eyes bright.

"Here's the thing," said Bish, still speaking in his politician's tone of voice. "My experts have told me to expect a new type of koph, but none of them can tell me what comes next. They did tell me that if we investigated koph, it would serve as a means to the unknown end we sought. That's what the Urs-major's operation was for and, regrettably why a closer eye wasn't kept on him. It was never about whether or not he would succeed, only that some part of our actions in pursuing an answer would lead us to where we needed to be. And so we've come up on what they call a *choice point,* and it involves the new drug all of this has been pointing to. What's not clear is who gets to do the choosing. Maybe it will be me, but maybe it will be you, Jorl. If it's me, I'll choose what serves the greater good of the Alliance. But if it's you, well, I don't know that I can rely upon you to make the right choice. And I can't abide that kind of uncertainty."

"What are you saying?"

"The Alliance is dependent upon your world for a great many drugs besides koph. But if most of them vanished tomorrow, we'd all manage. It might prove difficult, but also bearable. There are other materials manufactured on other planets that could serve. And we did just fine prior to the discovery of koph; back before we gave Barsk to the Fant. Losing the advantages of Speaking would be unfortunate, but not a true hardship in the grand scheme of things. Certainly it would be superior to some of the scenarios my precognitivists have envisioned. Are you following what I'm saying, Jorl?"

He nodded, his trunk falling to his lap, arms limp at his sides. "You're prepared to give up koph."

"Not simply give it up, that would never do. For example, block-ading your planet would just make the stuff more valuable to rad-ical elements, create a black market, invite offworld smugglers with no regard for your Compact. No, I'm talking about ending its production entirely."

"You want the Fant to pledge to stop making it? Even for our own use?"

"If it's being made, then the enhanced version my team has fore-seen would likely still come to pass, and never mind the absur-dity of expecting me to trust any member of your race with such a promise."

"Then—"

"I'm talking about ending your world, Jorl. Destroying every one of your island forests where the drug is grown and refined. I'm talking about taking the life of every person on Barsk to en-sure that not so much as a single pellet of koph ever rises up to this station again."

The Otter gasped even as Jorl trumpeted his disbelief. "That's impossible! No matter how strong your bigotry toward Eleph and Lox, the senate would never sanction the extermination of an entire race!"

"Quite correct. But I haven't shared the insights of my precog-nitivists with them, and I don't have the time to do so now, let alone try to convince them of the seriousness before us. Fortu-nately, I don't have to. You've served in the Patrol. How many vessels do you imagine I would need to raze your archipelagos? I'm a senior senator, Jorl, do you have any idea how many ship captains I've gathered to my side? Even if I sent them illegal orders, they'd only take the time to contact me personally for confirma-tion. Then they'd carry them out, on my say so. I have only to give the word."

"But you haven't done that."

"No, I haven't. Not yet. But understand, this is a zero-sum game. There can be only a single winner here, and if it's not to be the Alliance, then I will ensure there is no game at all, even if I have to overturn the game board and smash every piece. I share your grief over the Urs-major's slaughter of your people. Such a thing should be unthinkable. Learn from it. Understand that in our current situation, the wrong outcome would mean the end of your entire race. I know you don't want that, no sane individual could, so I'm inviting you to embrace the alternative. Accept the larger compromise and help the Alliance to win."

Jorl hesitated. Nothing could justify Krasnoi's crime, but was it possible to retrieve some good from it? "How am I supposed to do that?"

"Your dead friend, Arlo, is the key. That much is abundantly clear. And here you are, his best friend, and a Speaker, too. Summon him. Explain the reality of the situation to him. I have a fully equipped lab aboard my ship and this station's warehouses have every possible substance Barsk has to offer available at your request. Persuade your friend to give me the new drug that has all my precognitivists in such a panic, and perhaps we can avoid the need to destroy your world and your people."

"You don't understand. Arlo's a pragmatist, always was. He killed himself to prevent his secret from getting out. He won't necessarily believe or be swayed by abstract threats."

"Then offer him a real one," said Bish, and the grandfatherly façade fell away. "I have his son. And while you say the boy does not feel pain, I'm sure that Druz is so intrigued by your statement that she wants nothing more than to test it to the fullest extent of her abilities. Perhaps you're right. Perhaps she would be able to peel away his skin, break each and every one of his bones, wrench his tusks from his face, tear off his ears and trunk, cut out his eyes and tongue, and he'll not feel any of it. But whether or not I allow her to test such a hypothesis rests with you and Arlo."

The Bos's speed leaping from rational explanation to deadly threat did not surprise Jorl. Outrageous as it was, it still paled alongside the searing memory of the Dying's execution. He was nearly numb to Bish's threats, and wished he could disconnect entirely. Was this a bluff? The Brady had struck him as compassionate, but then, too, she'd swiftly killed Krasnoi. Bluff or not, the ease with which the senator imagined each detail was more cruelty than Jorl could subject Arlo to. "I won't summon him. I won't ask him to make such a choice again."

The Yak turned and reached out to the Otter, waving her to come and stand in front of him. "One way or another, he will have to choose. This woman is not just a telepath, but also a Speaker. She's quite adept at combining the two skills to allow her to summon even those she's never met. Whether he is instructed by her or by you, one way or another, Arlo will learn that if he does not give me what I want, I will destroy all of Barsk, but not until after I have his son tortured to death."

To Jorl's surprise, the Lutr Speaker scowled. Bish regarded her.

"You have an opinion to express? You think anything in your silly, pleasure-seeking head has any bearing on these events? The needs of the citizens of the Alliance will not be defeated by the members of a lesser race, nor the confused emotionality of a foolish girl who has forgotten that she is a resource now and no longer a person."

Her scowl deepened, and a moment later was replaced by a look of surprise. A hum rippled from the senator's robes, too faint for anyone but Jorl to hear. The Yak looked down upon the Otter and sneered.

"Stupid. I am a ranking member of the senate; I've assembled the most powerful team of precognitivists and specialized talents in history. Do you imagine I would share breath with a telepathic resource and not have myself protected? I won't punish the attempt. Truly, I would have been disappointed if you hadn't tried. Taste the futility of your actions and focus on being useful. Tend to the Fant. If he won't Speak to his dead friend then pull what you need from his mind so you can. That new drug unlocks everything, and I will have that key!"

Jorl rose from the bunk, hand and trunk both reaching out, but the senator had already turned. A handful of strides took him out the door. He vanished into the corridor leaving the Fant alone with the Otter. He couldn't tell which of them was more stunned.

"What will you do, Jorl ben Tral?"

"Do?"

"Will you Speak once more with your friend?"

"No. He made his choice. I've asked him to explain his reasons more than a few times. Whatever he discovered he's adamant that the secret end with him. So, what now? Is that why you talked with me at the polar camp? Will you pull details about Arlo from my mind? Try to summon him yourself?"

Lirlowil took a seat on the sleeping platform. She reached up and slipped one hand around the back of Jorl's ear and pulled him down. The familiarity of the gesture surprised him so much he didn't resist and sat beside her.

"He's already refused me."

"You Spoke to him?"

"I did. Of my own accord, earlier today, and not at the senator's behest. I only just met that pathetic excuse for a public servant. He reminds me of the head of the delegation that came to

Barsk to negotiate the last details of the Compact. A slippery, two-faced Aplodon who could chew rancid butterleaf and still breathe sweetness in your face with his words. Bish would doubtless have embraced him as a brother."

"The Compact? You're—"

"Yes, and you're welcome. No need to thank me."

"How are you here? How are you wearing the body of a Lutr telepath? Why doesn't the senator know? And why by every tree in the world would I *thank* you?"

"Don't whine like a petulant child, Jorl. You owe me for the course your life has taken, for the aleph I had placed upon your brow."

Indignation rose and he barely restrained himself from lashing out at her with his trunk. He jumped up instead and glared down at her, trumpeting in frustration.

"You've manipulated my entire life like a piece in some game, all so you could get to Arlo!"

"In part, that's true. I never knew why I couldn't see your friend's part directly. It never occurred to me that others would be scrying our people's future. The group that Bish has had looking stirred things up, blinding us all to the details. So yes, I set events in motion because what I was able to see revealed a roundabout path that would bring me close to the goal. But it wasn't enough. I could not persuade Arlo. I shared the threat of the destruction of our race with him, and he countered with an argument of a potentially greater horror."

"What are you talking about now?"

The Matriarch inside the Otter shook her head. "It's not mine to tell if he hasn't shared it with you. You're right, Jorl, I have used you like a piece in a game. But no more. We've passed the limit of my sight and the cruel truth is that I am blind to the endgame. But you heard Bish. If our people are to survive *you* must Speak with Arlo, get him to give up his secret."

"Why? You already put the question to him. Nothing has changed."

"You're wrong. Everything has changed. The threatened destruction of a world and its people is vast and abstract. It's far enough removed that a man like Arlo can cling to his beliefs. But the brutal murder of his own son hanging in the balance, that danger may yet save us all."

Jorl shook his head, stomped halfway across the room feeling like the ghosts of the Dying rushed after him, looming, haunting his every decision. He turned back to her, seeing through the phantoms of his imagination as well as the false face Margda wore. "I can't ask him to make that choice. It's not right."

"It's not right for you to deny him the choice. But you won't have to do it alone. I'll come with you. Here, take this."

She held out a hand. Resting on her upturned palm was a pellet of koph. He stared at her. Stared at the pellet. Once, he had been excited at learning he could perceive nefshons, to gain access to figures from history and interview them personally. When had it all become something else, something heavy and dark? His feet carried him back and he snatched the pellet from her hand with the nubs of his trunk, bringing it to his mouth and swallowing it all with the same gesture.

Jorl sat, closed his eyes, surrounding himself in darkness as he waited for his perceptions to open. His left ear tingled and he smelled spiralmint. The roiling gold that was his own nefshons appeared to him first, and he willed away his awareness of them. Rather than create the setting of his study where he usually met with Fant and others, he had a sudden urge to move the venue to a re-creation of the polar base, complete with smoldering ash pit. Instead he crafted a duplicate of the simple cabin that contained his physical form. The sleeping platform appeared with him seated upon it. A desk and bench took shape against an adjacent wall. Doors formed where they needed to be but wouldn't open to anything. Satisfied with the setting, he leaned back and cast his awareness out, grasping for the familiar feel of his friend's nefshons. He found them nearer than ever before. As he pulled them closer still, Jorl saw another figure also coalesce. An elderly Eleph, Margda, the first Speaker of all, sat next to him in the same position where in the real world the Lutr whose body she had somehow suborned also sat.

Before he could say a word to her, Arlo began to take form directly in front of them.

TWENTY-EIGHT

LEVELS OF DIFFERENCE

~~~~~~~~

PIZLO'S eyes had stopped working right. Everything kept fading in and out of focus and had a shimmering nimbus to it. Also, his head wouldn't stop pounding, like the drum he'd once made from a hollow log he'd found in the Shadow Dwell—which didn't make sense because no one was beating on it, were they? His stomach felt funny, not like when he hadn't eaten in too long, worse than that.

He remembered falling, startled off his perch in the closet when that tall man with the horns and musical voice had said Arlo's name. Had he hit his head? Somehow he was back in the corridor, floating down the length of it, the lights in the ceiling turning on and welcoming him as he passed.

A raspy voice breathed on his ears from above. "Do not squirm, Little Prince. You might make me drop you, and I've no wish to see you injure yourself any further."

He craned his head around and saw a sleek furred face over him, part of a rounded head that vanished into layers of dark cloth.

"Prince? Are you talking to me?"

The face smiled. Words followed. "Do you see anyone else for me to talk to?"

Pizlo swung his head around the other way. Despite his vision problems, he scanned up and down the corridor before realizing the woman hadn't expected him to answer. It was one of *those* kinds of questions.

"Sorry. Nobody but Jorl and Tolta ever talk to me. And most new people who see me pretend they don't." Despite the earlier admonition, he squirmed a bit, and discovered he wasn't floating down the corridor—and thus neither was the woman. Rather, she was carrying him in her arms like he was a parcel too big to pack in a bag or carry on your back, which he had to admit he was. The woman didn't seem like she was going to say anything else, but before he could ask why she was carrying him she breathed out another question.

"If the Fant treat their children this way, it is a wonder any of you grow up to produce another generation."

Pizlo shrugged, "It's not all kids. Just me. They don't like me cuz I'm so different."

The woman carrying him laughed. "That's why most people don't like Fant."

The corridor came to a tee, branching off with paths to either side and a gate different, but similar, to the ones he had seen before, with a tiny room with a second gate on the other side, and then more corridors. The Sloth moved with an increased confidence and Pizlo wondered if they were still on the station or had crossed over to some other place that made her feel more at home. She stopped at a set of double-doors, but unlike those he'd found at the observation room they did not open at a touch. Instead she shifted him around and raised a hand and made several passes just above the surface of the door. It made him smile, and he imagined her holding an inkstick and writing a request to go inside.

When the doors opened, Pizlo saw a very different space, one that had multiple work stations and desks like he'd seen in Arlo's old lab, with screens and panels, armatures and lights. There was a smaller room made entirely of glass in one corner, with several work tables and stools and holographic images floating just inside the walls. Off in another corner of the main room lay a pair of beds, raised very high off the floor, with queer-looking diagnostic tools hanging down from above. The woman took her time but eventually brought him to one of these and laid him down. It was surprisingly soft and he yawned.

"None of that, Little Prince. I need to make sure that the bump to your head is the worst of it before you can sleep. Tell me about yourself. What's your name?"

Now that she wasn't carrying him, Pizlo could see that she wore robes of dark cloth that shone with bits of glass or crystal here and there. She glittered like her clothes had tens of eyes that watched him from within the folds.

"My name is Pizlo," he said. "No one's ever asked me that before. You're the first person I've gotten to tell. What's yours?"

"I am called Druz. Your people call mine Brady." One hand moved to a nearby console and with the other she gingerly pressed his trunk down so it did not block her instruments. As Pizlo watched, his face appeared on a display above her console, several times larger than life. A flurry of thin lines in red and green raced across the screen. Some made circles around his eyes, while others turned into strings of glyphs that he couldn't read.

"Oh. You're a Lox. I didn't realize there were two kinds of Fant."

"Sure. How many kinds of your people are there, Druz?"

"Two, actually, but we're much more closely related than you and your kin. Ah, your pupils are fine, but according to my database your eyes shouldn't be red like that."

"That's normal for me. I'm the only one on all of Keslo like this. I heard a man from Kelpry once who said it was the mark of evil." He sniffled once and chewed his lip, then continued. "It . . . bothered that he was judging me like that, just on account of my eyes, and hadn't even talked to me or gotten to know me at all."

Druz continued adjusting the settings on her controls, letting her words drag out as she focused. "You are quite precocious, Little Prince, to be concerned about evaluations of morality at such a young age."

"I'm six," he said, his tone making it clear that he wasn't *that* young.

She pushed away from the workstation and hovered over him again. "The concussion is minor, and there's no reason to fear if you lose consciousness. You've dislocated your shoulder, and that's an easy fix. I'd like to treat your hands, but I need to proceed carefully. Your friend, the other Fant, mentioned you had unusual physiology, and I'm seeing that. I need to run some tests. Can you lie here quietly while I work? Maybe you'll even go to sleep."

"I guess. I have a lot of stuff to sort through and I haven't had a chance to do any of that yet."

"Oh? What sort of stuff?"

"Things Telko told me earlier today."

"Is Telko another Fant?"

Pizlo laughed and wriggled his trunk. Druz was so funny. "No, Telko's my fourth moon." And with that he closed his eyes.

TWENTY-NINE

CHOICE AND SACRIFICE

EVERY time Arlo had been summoned, he'd had his eyes closed when it started. One moment he didn't exist, and then he did, becoming aware of his own body in a way that wasn't at all like waking up. The first time, he had opened his eyes and with cold rationalism concluded that he had been summoned and must be dead. Then, and every time since, he endured a wave of regret over his suicide, swiftly followed by recrimination for its necessity.

Only then would he open his eyes.

He knew time had passed, in the way that someone knew that breathing made sense or wind could not be captured and put in your pocket. How much time, or what had occurred during it—for others, not for him—was not part of his awareness. He'd experienced every summoning as a distinct event, always intending to ask Jorl about that effect and never getting to it. And so here he was again, but as Arlo glanced around he found himself in a strange place. It differed from anywhere he'd been before, both from the familiar settings his friend always provided or the long-vanished home the interloper had created. And yet, there she was in front of him.

"You, again." Arlo glared at the Matriarch. "Did you forget something?" Then his gaze shifted and took in the figure of his friend. "Jorl? Did she bring you here, too? No, that's not possible. Did you both summon me?"

"Actually, it's quite possible, but not what's happened," said Margda. "You are here as Jorl's conversant. But anyone who can perceive nefshons can witness a summoning. How else do you imagine old Speakers train new ones?"

Arlo frowned. Jorl looked . . . off. Tired, underfed, but also broken somehow. Despite Margda's presence, his first instinct was to comfort his friend, but it wasn't the time. This wasn't one of Jorl's regular summonings, a blend of nostalgia and longing; he'd never have included the Matriarch. They'd brought him back for a purpose.

His ears drooped and his trunk swung from side to side as he studied his surroundings with wide eyes. "I can't say I care for this place. Not something that a Fant would make. Not from materials anyone on Barsk would build with. What's going on, Jorl? Where are we?"

His friend grinned shyly. "You've finally joined me in leaving Barsk. We're in orbit above the planet."

"The export station? Seriously? Most of my life's work passed through there. But it's neither a destination nor a way station for Fant. Even when you joined the Patrol, they sent an automated shuttle down for you. How do you even know what the station looks like?"

"I'm there now. In this room. And, in a way, so is the Matriarch."

Arlo's frown deepened. "We've met, and it wasn't the highlight of my being dead. So, let me ask again, what's going on?"

"Your friend is here to ask you to reconsider your earlier decision," said Margda.

"I don't know how much time has passed for you, but nothing is different for me since I gave you my answer."

Margda's trunk whipped across her body in denial. "Everything is different. I'm not relying solely on a vision from centuries before your birth. I have met the madman who threatens our planet and people. He's a Bos, complete with the stereotypic stubbornness of his race and the power of a senior member of the Alliance senate. He *knows* you have created a more powerful version of koph, and he will have it or destroy us all."

Jorl's head spun side to side as he flipped his focus between the two dead Fant. "What are you talking about? How is the new koph more powerful? Is that why you died, Arlo?"

He kept his focus on the Matriarch. "How does this Yak know such a thing? What did you tell him?"

"I didn't need to. He knows of it the same way I came to suspect it. But where I was limited to just my own visions, he has been employing multiple prognosticators for three generations."

"It doesn't matter," said Arlo. "It doesn't change a thing. The drug is too powerful if taken by someone with the bioluminescent factor in their systems."

Margda swore. "What makes you think they'll start using your damn bugjuice? Does Barsk even export it? Is anyone in the Alliance using it? Certainly not to create tattoos on their furry bodies."

Arlo said nothing. He tucked his ears down, crossed his arms over his chest, and lowered his trunk as he glared at the Matriarch.

"You don't know, do you?" Margda scoffed and waggled her trunk toward Jorl. "He never asked the question."

Arlo sighed. "I didn't want to stir up interest in the chemical compound by doing a search. I know we export a small amount of the insects themselves. The Cynomy consider them a delicacy. But as far as I know, no one has broken them down or analyzed them further."

"So, it's possible." The Matriarch smiled. "You could give them the improved drug. And they'll have little incentive to demand to know how it's made because in every generation each person will only need a single dose. Yes, the Alliance will still be relying on Barsk for the drug, but much less so than they currently do. That will appease them."

"That's it? You killed yourself because a Speaker would only have to take the drug once?" Jorl looked stricken.

"No, it's more than that."

"Yeah, I get that, there's a different effect on people with an aleph. What happens to them?"

Arlo jerked his trunk toward Margda. "I already told her, but I'm not going to tell you."

"What? Why not?"

"Because she's dead, and you're not. Look, even if the Matriarch's idea could work, there isn't anyone who can make the drug. I destroyed all my notes. No one else knows how to create the thing, and in case it's slipped everyone's mind, I'm also dead."

"Arlo, we have to find a way. I don't know if Senator Bish could actually destroy everyone on Barsk, but I've seen him order one of his own people killed. He murdered a senior officer right in front of me with no hesitation and—"

"Jorl, you can't wipe out hundreds of thousands of people by pulling a trigger. Do you imagine I didn't think about my wife and son down on Barsk when the Matriarch first told me about this?"

"You didn't let me finish. Like I said, I don't know if he could do that or not, but it doesn't matter. Pizlo isn't back home in Keslo. He's here, on this station, right now."

"What? How?"

"I don't know how he got here. He was here before I arrived. But Bish has him. And he's threatened to hurt him—"

"He can't *be* hurt, you know that—"

"Not cause him pain, really hurt him. Maim him and worse. He'll kill your son if he doesn't get your drug, and he thinks I can give it to him."

Dead or not, it was like having his feet go out from under him while he trod a boardway in the canopy on Keslo. Like having his trunk yanked one way while his stomach dropped in another direction. His son, the boy that should never have been, who had defied all odds to live and grow up, at risk now because of his discovery? No, he couldn't dwell on that. What else had Jorl said? The Yak expected his friend to hand him the drug?

"How? You said he's a senator, not an imbecile. You're not a pharmer, Jorl. Does he think you can Speak to me and I'll give you a cookbook recipe and that's all it takes?"

"It's because he *is* a senator that he's blinded to the pragmatics," said Margda. "He's used to making decisions, setting plans in motion, and acquiring the resources and talented personnel to manage the details for him. I understand him perfectly well; he is ambitious and convinced beyond any dissuasion that he is right. It's a special kind of monster that would torture a child to achieve his ends."

Arlo paced the room, much as he'd often seen Jorl do when anxious, his ears flapping with each step. The space wasn't big and it didn't take long to complete the circuit several times. He stopped in front of the Matriarch, brought his trunk up to grasp her chin. He jerked her into place and stared into her eyes.

"That's the heart of this, isn't it? You believe this senator could do all of this, harm my boy, destroy a world, all because in his head he knows he's right. You believe it, because you're the same kind of monster."

The Matriarch didn't even flinch. "If you had a lab here on this station, if you had access to the full range of materials that we export, could you re-create your drug?"

"I could do it, yes, but it's not something I can walk someone else through." Arlo waved his arm taking in the room. "And none of this is real."

"But if you were really here, alive on this station, could you do it? Would you do it?"

"That's not—"

"Just answer me. Would you?"

"Yes, of course. To save my son."

"Good. Then we're back on track. All we have to do is bring you back to life."

Arlo snorted. "Right. That's all. I have no doubt that if you ever figured out a way to do that, you'd be walking Barsk right now, taking charge of things all over again."

She smiled. "I'm right here, boy. Alive and well."

He trumpeted into her face and she scrambled backwards on the bunk, slamming against the wall. "*None of this is real!* You're dead. I'm dead. You want me to re-create the drug I died to protect? I don't just need a lab, I need to be back in my body in the real world, not capering around in some mental construct Jorl's imagined out of particles I can't even see."

"You're quite right. I'm long dead and none of this has any substance. And yet, when Jorl first met me during his interment, it was in the waking world and I had a body of flesh and blood."

Arlo turned to Jorl. "What is she saying?"

"It's true. Somehow she's taken possession of another person's body. An Otter. That's the body that's sitting in the real version of this room with me right now."

"An Otter with a powerful telepathic talent. That's what allowed me to put my nefshon construct in control of her body. And doing the same for you is the last piece of my final vision. If you both are willing."

Arlo hesitated, but only for a moment. The look in Jorl's eyes answered any question he might have asked, granted any permission he might have needed. It all seemed like madness, but was madness anything other than desperation blended with hope?

"Do what you need to do," was all he said.

"Whenever I can," said Margda, and disappeared.

"Where did she go?"

Jorl frowned at him. "I didn't vanish her any more than I brought her here in the first place. She came on her own and probably left the same way. Give me a moment and I'll check." The pharmer watched his friend's eyes unfocus for an instant. Arlo blinked, and *everything* went away.

~~~~~

HE remembered the time he and Jorl had traveled to Gerd, that last season before they started at the academy. The hostel had been so overcrowded they'd had to sleep on the roof, taking down a pair of clothes lines in the dark so they could string their hammocks. The next morning, waking up had been a slow and gradual thing. They hadn't seen that the next roof over had been planted as a garden full of sartha. The morning breeze had washed the pair of them in the buds' soporific scent and kept them asleep well into midday.

It was like that now and unlike any of the times Jorl had summoned him. His neck had gone stiff and his throat felt dry. He grappled with the distinction between groggy and disoriented, and realized that the preoccupation probably meant a bit of both. The growing sense of wrongness in his proprioception jerked him full awake and he found himself back in the station cabin where Jorl had summoned him before, seated on the sleeping platform much as his friend had been.

Arlo held up his hands and trunk in front of his face. They looked different. He stood and began flailing his arms to keep from falling, stumbling around the room in a body that felt shorter and thicker than his reflexes remembered. He understood what had happened even before he noticed the Lutr leaning by the door.

"You've put my soul in Jorl's body!"

"Nothing quite so melodramatic," said the Otter. The voice was higher, more melodic than the Matriarch's, but it had her rhythm. "If nefshon amalgams are souls, I've never seen proof of it. No, I've simply taken Jorl's construction of your particles and bonded them to his form, at least for a while."

He put one foreign hand out to the wall to steady himself, agog that it moved to his will. Even so small a thing made him feel more . . . comfortable. It drove home a new understanding. Life had a quality that had been absent every time Jorl had Spoken to him, a quality that he had always possessed in life but hadn't noticed the lack of, not once in all those many summonings. Until now. He *was* alive!

"We need to hurry," said Margda, and he realized she wasn't so much leaning as slumped against the wall. "Creating the bond has exhausted me. I cannot actively maintain the impression for long, and once I stop I don't know how much time it will take Jorl's mind to break through and wrest control of his body again."

He nodded, the gesture feeling odd because it was Jorl's gesture, not his own. "You said you could give me access to a lab?"

"And so I shall. This station is a minor maze, but the senator's aide gave me directions to where his vessel is docked. The lab is aboard that vessel. One thing though, the Sloth will likely be there; don't let her touch you."

"Why?"

"Both she and the senator have some technology that shields them from telepathic probing. It didn't exist when I was alive, or if it did I didn't know about it. My point is, I don't know what effect it might have on nefshon constructs in general, or the imprint on Jorl in particular. Now, come, we need to get you to that lab."

Her fingers, long and slender, gripped his upper arm as much for support as control. She led him out of the room and down a series of ugly, sterile hallways and eventually to a boarding gate and airlock with more hallways that managed to be both different yet still ugly. In the end, they arrived at a set of double doors that opened to reveal a thoroughly modern laboratory with its own miniature, glassine cleanroom within it. He saw only a single occupant, a Brady, who glanced up from running some test at a workstation as they entered. She wore a dark kaftan interrupted by glimmering bits that he recognized as a cunning sensor array. She put her station in standby and came toward them, the urgency of her words contrasting with the leisure of her gait.

"Have one or the other of you learned to make the thing?"

The Matriarch's grip tightened on his arm, a squeeze that meant . . . what?

"I can do it," he said, and the Otter gave a slight nod. "I'm going to need some things, but nothing that shouldn't be stocked somewhere on the station."

"Excellent. I'll show you how to access inventory control. Make a list and I'll have whatever you require brought here. Will this facility be sufficient?" She pointed at the transparent chamber in one corner, a small emergency shower standing next to it.

"That's fine." He fanned himself with his ears as he surveyed the rest of the room. Small protuberances in the ceiling gleamed with lenses, enough to capture each section of the lab several times over. Whatever he did here would be reviewed from every angle.

At the other side of the lab were a pair of medical beds, the like of which he'd only ever seen in the University's infirmary on Zlorka and nowhere else on Barsk. One of them held a small, white Lox. Pizlo, his hands wrapped in bundles of pale gauze. What had Jorl said? Had the monster already tortured his son?

Arlo cleared his throat. "What's the status of the boy?"

"That one's a puzzle. But all good news. He'll have quite a bump on his head, but there's no concussion and I've reset the injured shoulder. He made an impressive effort to ruin his hands—he insists he 'rowed' for more than a day, and even if what you said before about his not feeling pain is true, if I hadn't seen the effect myself I wouldn't believe he could have done it. The wounds had become infected but I believe I've caught it in time."

"He'll recover then?" It was all he could do to keep his voice from cracking. Tears were building up behind borrowed eyes and he blinked them back.

"I wouldn't be surprised. He has the most amazing immune system I've ever encountered. And his cortical scans display the kind of patterns I've only seen in adult precognitivists. I've no doubt the senator will be pleased to offer him a home."

Only the Matriarch's suddenly tightening on his arm kept him from replying. He could feel the Sloth's eyes on him and he had to remind himself that she saw Jorl, not him, and even then had no reason to believe there would be any connection between the child and the man. He nodded in response, and when he could speak without giving himself away asked, "May I see him?"

"Certainly. He's only lightly sedated. I have him under simple restraints to keep him from upsetting the dressing on his hands."

The Otter leaned in and hissed in his ear. "We don't have time for this!"

He ignored her and crossed to his sleeping son.

Pizlo had been four and a half when Arlo had last seen him, articulate and curious, a born scientist who had already amassed an insect collection that would have astonished adult entomologists. He'd been so small and had grown so much. He would be six now. Jorl had said he'd taken on responsibility for the boy's education. Arlo hadn't reflected on what that meant, what a historian's sensibilities would do to the keen edge of his son's hunger for learning. No matter, it was just one of the many things he had sacrificed when he had weighed all the options and made his choice. Except, standing here now, alive again, gazing upon his son . . . he wanted nothing more than to wallow in selfishness and ignore the consequences.

Pizlo stirred in his sleep. He murmured, lips barely parting. "Druz . . . I had a dream about Tolta and Arlo. He'd come back to tell her goodbye . . ." His eyelids fluttered open and he stared upward.

"Dad?"

Arlo brought both of Jorl's hands tightly down on the end of his trunk, forcing himself to smile through the sudden pain. Never once in his life had his son called him by anything but his name.

"Shhh. You hit your head. It's me, Jorl."

"Well, yeah, I know that. But does he know you're in there, too?"

"I have inventory access ready for you," said the Brady from another workstation.

"Right." Arlo twined his trunk with Pizlo's, one final time more than he knew he deserved. "I have to go. There's something I have to do. I love you, Piz."

The boy grinned, a wide smile as full of innocence as the morning rain. "It's all right. You're going to make sure that Jorl can fill this whole room."

Arlo returned the smile. "You always were such a strange boy. Don't ever let anyone take that away from you. And try to listen to your mother. She loves you, too."

Pizlo yawned, squeezed Arlo's trunk with his own and then let it go limp as his eyes closed. "I will. I love you too, Dad."

A moment later, Arlo took a seat at the workstation; the Sloth hovered over his shoulder, offering assistance though he found the interface familiar enough. The orbital station contained seventeen warehouses; five had been emptied by recent transports but twelve more waited, bulging with thousands of cargo pods containing all the riches created in Barsk's rain forests. The interface let Arlo sort by content rather than by warehouse or individual container contents. He began by compiling a list of the few components he needed, then added three times that amount of other unrelated and useless items, including some that even on a recording would be hard to distinguish from the necessary bits. To save his son, to save all of Barsk, he would give them the finished drug, but maybe he could also manage to keep them from learning how to create it for themselves.

~~~~~

TIME seemed to pass more slowly as he worked; it had always been so. Throughout all the years of his life with Tolta, Arlo had come home late for dinner seven out of every eight times. His wife hadn't complained, instead finding it the secret to their successful cohabitation. Unlike most males, the urge to wander from home had never claimed him. His work kept him away enough. The time he spent as a pharmer ran differently than the rest of time, rewarding and engrossing and ever fresh.

He'd moved into the clean room when his supplies arrived and gone immediately to work. Glancing up and through the wall, he studied the lab. The Brady sat at a workstation as though stone, one three-fingered hand curled in her lap, her eyes fixed upon the screen in front of her. His son lay on the med table, sleeping and healing. And yet Arlo did not doubt that a dozen eyes watched him. Watched and recorded.

Margda had left, whispering to him while the Sloth had supervised a pair of arriving Ailuros in the placement of his supplies. The Matriarch needed to retreat and let her borrowed body rest. He hadn't met an Otter before, but even he could see signs of exhaustion. She'd rested a hand on his arm, less to reassure and more to hide a tremor that she could not dismiss as easily as she had her host's consciousness.

Despite the awkward wrongness of Jorl's body, Arlo's years of practice in the lab proved to be as much a matter of experience as physicality; he managed his task adequately, owing in large part to the elaborate provisioning of the clean room. The senator had provided every conceivable bit of pharmaceutical apparatus, and not even Jorl's untrained hands could counter such an advantage. Clearing his mind of thoughts about his son, about the fate of all Fant on Barsk, about the other thing he'd neglected to mention to the Matriarch, Arlo threw himself into the work and let the rest of the world fall away. That focus, more than any telepathic trick from Margda, kept him in Jorl's body and allowed him to complete the work. Over the course of half a day, he re-created the taww derivative that had been his last great achievement in life.

When he had finished, he held a single slim phial of the stuff. Margda would have him give it to Bish, and maybe it would resolve the threat hanging over Barsk, but only for a time. In the end, the drug would not be seen as a boon, but as a betrayal, and from what Jorl had said of the senator, Arlo knew his reaction would be brutal. He didn't understand the scope of galactic politics nearly well enough to guess if the result would be the destruction of his people, or an increase in the Alliance's dependence on Barsk. Either way, being dead, it wouldn't touch him. And that was the point. Even with the threat to Pizlo, the choice wasn't his to make; it would have to be Jorl's.

Now that he had finished, his concentration began to slip away. He could feel Jorl, like a pressure against the inside of his skull. Lightheaded, he sealed the phial before he inadvertently spilled it. The Brady still hadn't moved, frozen like a statue, that one. All the same, he took a flask of water from a stand where moments earlier he had set it to heat and waved at her.

"I need a quick break," he said. "I'm feeling a bit dizzy. Would you like some tea? I find it very refreshing during labwork."

The Sloth's head came up. In an instant she was staring right at him.

"I'd wondered when I saw that among your supplies. Thank you for the offer. I have no need of refreshment, but I wish you enjoyment of yours."

Her focus returned to her work station and she returned to her stillness.

Arlo simply shrugged. It had been a burst of inspiration to add the expensive tea leaves to his list when he saw it amidst the inventory of items. Fanning both ears, he added what he needed to the water, steeping it even as he moved a bench closer to the wall so he could sit and lean.

The time had come to reveal the last piece, the other reason he had died, and as certain as he was of being recorded, he couldn't simply leave him a note. He hoped he'd done the right thing. He needed one last conversation with Jorl, and he only knew one way to make that happen. He thought of Tolta, and while he knew she'd have understood his suicide if he could only have shared the details, a sorrow rose up in him that he had never bid her a proper goodbye. He glanced through the wall of the clean room to where his son lay sleeping, and gave thanks that he had gotten to see his boy one last time. Then he closed Jorl's eyes and committed himself as he had that time before. He fancied he could hear the wind as it had shouted at him on the edge of the canopy. He pushed off, dying for the second time.

THIRTY

LOCK AND KEY

JORL opened his eyes and the weight of the world returned to him. The immolation of the Dying flickered across his thoughts again, tightening his chest and dragging his head down. He flexed his fingers, twitched his nubs, flicked first one ear and then the other, and shifted his attention to what the Matriarch had done to him.

In part it was almost like waking up, only he hadn't been asleep. Rather, for half a day he had been outside himself, watching as Margda's enslaved Otter had guided him through the station and onto the senator's ship and to a laboratory. The Sloth had been there, and Pizlo as well. And then his body had stepped through a rush of air into a transparent box and gone to work with skills he didn't possess.

Arlo's skills.

And now he was back. He sniffed the air, recognized the aroma of spiralmint and tracked its source, a beaker, dark with tea, and a shade of color usually imparted by including koph. In that outside-looking-in sense, he recalled making the tea, adding the koph, but not drinking it. The meaning couldn't have been clearer.

He dipped the end of his trunk into the beaker, filled it with tea and brought the tip to his mouth. He gulped it down, gasping at the extreme bitterness. Arlo had used far too much koph. Even before he had closed his eyes, Jorl sensed the swirl of his friend's nefshons hanging all around him, residue of his recent possession. Automatically, his mind assembled a mental construct and when he shifted his awareness he was greeted by the familiar setting of his home.

Every other time when manipulating nefshons he had done so with a specific person in mind, concentrating on unique aspects of the individual in order to pull together the right nefshons for a conversation. But now, with the particles already present, he simply guided them together before they had begun to diffuse. His construct of Arlo instantly took form.

"Jorl, are you all right?" His friend's expression looked surprised, almost frantic, nothing like the relaxed, almost bored poise he had affected at his many other summonings. Different even from how he had appeared earlier in the station's cabin.

"I'm fine. A bit tired. Also confused. What happened? What did you do?"

"It was the Matriarch. After she vanished back in that station room, she somehow woke me up, inside you. Something about infusing the nefshons of my construct with your body."

Jorl nodded. "She did it, just like she said she would, so you could do the work in the lab."

"And I did. I re-created the drug. The reason I died. It's in that phial on the table." Arlo's eyes moved to his right, landing on empty space to the side of Jorl's writing desk at home. His trunk gestured vaguely. "You know what I mean."

"I do. Thank you, Ar. It's done now. I'll give it to Senator Bish and maybe it will be enough to put an end to things."

"Wait. Before you do, there's something you need to know. It's not just a koph agonist."

"I know. You already told me about its effects on someone who has an aleph, or otherwise has that chemical in their system. We just have to hope that the senator never makes that connection."

"No, there's more. I . . . lied to the Matriarch."

"What?"

"I left something out. A lie of omission. But you need to know. Now, so you can decide."

"Decide what?"

"Whether or not to drink it yourself."

"Why would I . . . What did you leave out?"

Arlo started to speak, stopped and swallowed in an effort to re-lax, and then began again.

"Okay, it's not just like regular koph."

"You told me this before, it keeps the effects of the koph from ever wearing off."

"Right, but I didn't explain how it works. I ran hundreds of simulations to be sure. The drug bonds to receptor sites in the Speaker's brain, the ones involved with manipulating nefshons, just as normal koph does. But koph can't stay on those sites; after a while those transmitters get washed away, taking away the per-ception and control of nefshons. My drug stays on those sites."

"I'm a historian, I'm not so good with talk of things like trans-mitters and receptor sites."

"Okay . . . think of a lock and key. The key fits the lock, turns the mechanism, and is withdrawn. Once unlocked, a door opens and the Speaker can handle nefshons. But only for a while, soon the door will close and lock again. That's how it normally works."

"Lock and key. I got that."

"The agonist is like a key that sticks in the lock, in effect breaking the lock. And because the lock's broken, the door can't ever close again."

"But that's a good thing, right? It means a Speaker only needs to take a single dose. That's what the senator would want. It will reduce the Alliance's dependence on us, no more constantly supplying them with koph."

"No, it only looks good in the short run. The solution is actually a lie. Those receptor sites, the ones responsible for handling nefshons, they can't stop now. The door is flung wide and they keep going and going, day after day, season after season, until they eventually burn out, permanently destroying the Speaker's ability."

Jorl grabbed at his friend with both hands. "That's obscene! And you want me to take this drug? Are you insane?"

Arlo nodded again, his trunk twitching. "Only because it won't have that effect on you. The insect bacteria in the tattoo of your aleph is a harmless parasite. It feeds off of your body's resources to generate its luminescence. In the process, it secretes chemicals, enzymes really, into your system. Some of those enzymes adhere to the new agonist when it bonds to those receptor sites, like a hand grabbing the key and pulling it back out again so it cannot jam and break the lock. Over and over, key in and key out, granting perpetual perception and control of nefshons but without burning out the mechanism."

Jorl let go of his friend and sat back, the contours of his familiar chair vaguely comforting. When he'd performed his first summoning as a Speaker, he'd envisioned this same space, but it lacked verisimilitude. It was the idea of his chair, the concept of his writing desk, that had made it feel real. But as his perception and manipulation of nefshons had improved, he'd likewise grown more adept at painting in the sensory specifics of his imagined space. And not just when summoning. His attention had improved, and his memory for detail had become more focused. It showed in his interviewing of conversants, and in his writing. If he didn't have the aleph, if something like Arlo's drug caused him to lose his ability as a Speaker, would those subtler skills vanish, too? Were they the result of talent or learning or some combination of both? He hoped he'd never have to find out.

"Why didn't you tell the Matriarch about this? This wasn't simply a matter of worrying that the Alliance would learn of the connection between the bacteria in the tattoo ink and the increase in a Speaker's ability under your drug."

"No, though I meant that, too. The agonist enhances the Speaker's abilities. The simulations were inconsistent as to the extent of the power, but the potential was too great. No one should be able to do what it would allow. The other thing, the burning out of the ability entirely, I didn't say anything because I thought maybe, just maybe, this could end things. That your senator would take the drug back to the Alliance and spread it far and wide, happily believing he was freeing all of their Speakers from the chains of Barsk. And then, in a few seasons, at most a local year, one by one they'd go blind to the nefshons and stop being able to Speak. Back before I died, when I first realized what I'd created, I thought about that same prophecy of the Matriarch's, the one that had you so bothered? '*When the dead will not answer, the Silence is at hand, and the fate of all Barsk will soon hang in the balance.*' I thought maybe that's what I'd stumbled on."

Jorl gasped. Arlo's interpretation of that line of prophecy changed everything! "Maybe you did. Maybe *that's* what the Silence is, and not a couple hundred Fant stolen away instead of Dying."

Arlo smiled. "Maybe. Prophecy is tricky stuff, I think. I wish I'd thought to ask her when I had the chance, but you know how it is when she's talking. All other thoughts go right out of your head. Which reminds me, that Brady? She did a scan of Pizlo and said his brain shows the same patterns as Bish's precogs."

"Huh. That might explain a lot, like how he knew where the Dying had gone, and how he got up here in the first place."

"The thing is, that's what changed my mind, Jorl. I saw my son, helpless and hurt, and I heard that Brady suggest that he could end up working for the senator, and it all just came together. I knew that giving Bish the drug wouldn't work. This is the same monster you said killed all the old Fant right in front of you."

Jorl bit his lip, the unwanted memory flooding in again. "Not exactly. He was in charge of the Urs-major who did that. I only saw him give the order to kill that Bear, but he did it so casually, not out of anger or with any emotion."

"Okay, but my reasoning still holds. Wiping out the Alliance's Speakers wouldn't defeat or cripple him, it would only enrage him. The Sloth's comment about Pizlo's abilities cleared it up for me. All of this is personal to him. What kind of man can contemplate torturing a child or just as easily save him because he's a potentially valuable resource? Giving him the drug would be a horrible mistake in the long run."

"But you made it anyway."

"Because . . . I could be wrong. What if I'm blinded by my own fears? By the emotions that well up when I think of my son? What if the Matriarch is right?"

"Ar, you know your drug and you've had more time to think about its ramifications than anyone else. Do *you* think she's right?"

"No, I think she's blind, too, that she's the same kind of monster as Bish, and like him she rushes ahead believing everything she sees is all there is to see, and forcing reality to bend to her will. But here's the thing. We're not hypothesis testing. Maybe I'm right, or maybe Margda's right. This isn't just a simple thought experiment to play with in the lab. It's real and will affect every living Fant. That's not the kind of decision that should be left to two dead ones. I'm really, really sorry, Jorl, but I re-created the drug to put the choice in your hands. It's your decision to make."

"I can't—"

"No, you're the only one who can. You have the tools. You're a Speaker, you've studied all of the Matriarch's prophecies, you've researched other critical moments in history and seen how individual decisions have rippled to produce both intended and unexpected outcomes."

"I really think you've over—"

Arlo vanished in an eyeblink, and Jorl's home with it. He sat on a stool in the lab on senator Bish's ship, his back against a transparent wall. The senator's aide had a tight, three-fingered grip on his right ear. She had entered the clean room and stood over him, round face surprisingly close to his own.

"—stated my abilities."

"What abilities are those?" said the Sloth.

"I . . . never mind. It's nothing. Sorry, I was lost in thought."

"You were asleep. Understandable, I've seen how diligently you've been working, and I know how taxing it must be. But the senator has already queried me twice, and while he can be mollified by my sharing how hard you labor, he will have no patience for napping. Are you finished?"

"Finished? Um, no, not quite. Soon. I'm down to the last few steps of the process. You can tell him that I'll be done very soon. But, uh, even so, he still needs to be patient. He'll have to wait another day, for the drug to . . . set."

"It needs to set?"

"To work right, yes. Like . . . like a pie you've just baked, you need to let it cool. Not the best analogy, but you understand, right?"

She let go of his ear and eased her way to the exit. "Finish your work. I'll inform the senator."

THIRTY-ONE
UNWELCOME HOUSEGUESTS

I T didn't help Lirlowil at all, knowing that everything around her was just a mental construct. She hadn't made it, and she couldn't unmake it. Couldn't so much as strike a light. Instead she'd been trapped in the dark for . . . days? She couldn't tell; couldn't sense her physical body at all. All she had was her mind, that magnificent mind that had always served her so well until that stupid Urs-major had upended her life. But no, even he hadn't truly done more than inconvenience her. The real blame belonged to that horrible Fant!

Margda had locked her up in a closet within her own mind. And not even a proper closet, more like a pantry with papered shelves and sealed, glazed pots of dried herbs and vegetables. And all of it bound in finished wood, floor and walls and ceiling. She'd smashed a few of the pots, testing the edges of her volition and marveling at the details the Fant had included in what would have been false props in her own constructions. Why include sensory specifics for the contents of sealed pots tucked away in a cupboard that was never intended to be opened—let alone occupied—in the first place? A grudging respect colored the edges of her hatred. Clearly she had failed to develop her Speaker's skills to their fullest, relying on her telepathic talents instead. And yet Margda, no telepath herself and only a nefshon construct, had taken control over Lirlowil's own talent and thrust her into this imaginary closet.

And it was killing her.

Her prison didn't have to stay completely dark. Her telepathy had been co-opted, her control of nefshons overwhelmed by the Fant, but some perception remained. She could, if desired, perceive her own nefshons, that glowing, golden blanket that every Speaker learned to dismiss from awareness in her very first lesson. Except, she had no such blanket. The construct of the pantry in Margda's nonexistent home overlay any image she might have had of her physical body. Instead she perceived only a single golden thread, one end connecting with the mental image she had of herself in this place. The thread ran a short distance in the darkness and then disappeared, right where Lirlowil could feel the pantry's locked door. But if she touched the thread, she could sense the Fant on the other end. It connected them, mind to mind, and try as she might she could not sever it.

But as she gripped it and tugged and twisted, Lirlowil could feel Margda on the other end, could taste both the fatigue of that evil mind and the weariness of the body she'd stolen. And that was her hope.

Separated from her own body, her mind weakened. In time, she had no doubt that she would die. But the Fant, originally nothing more enduring than any other temporary nefshon construct, required both the Lutr's mind and body to remain. Through the thread connecting them Lirlowil could feel her nemesis exhausting both. If Margda managed to hang on, walking around in the station as an Otter until such time as she wore out that body, then both minds would wink out of existence. But if she paused, relinquished control to rest her own mind even for a moment, Lirlowil believed she might have a faint chance to break free and at least co-habit her body again.

If she could just get out of this damn pantry!

Groping in the dark, she picked up another pot and hurled it against the floor where it shattered into many, many unseen pieces.

THIRTY-TWO

GHOST IN THE MACHINE

~~~~~~~

IN the instant the Sloth turned her back, Jorl's trunk quested across the workbench and found the phial Arlo had described. Then he surveyed the room and studied what he had to work with. He wasn't totally useless in a lab; before entering the academy he and Arlo had spent several seasons producing spirits for sale to older students. He'd mastered the basic tenets of cleanliness required for consistent fermentation and enough lab technique to distill those results into beverages that were potent without being poison.

The Brady had returned to her frozen stance in the outer room, a careful nonchalance that he assumed disguised vigilance. He was supposed to be hard at work re-creating a drug, so he did his best to put on a compelling show. He puttered, fiddling with this piece of apparatus, that work screen, moving back and forth in the transparent box of a room. While he dithered with his surroundings, Jorl's mind raced. He agreed with Arlo's assessment, he could *not* give the drug to the senator. If he did, and didn't explain the outcome, assuming they'd recorded Arlo's

work and could re-create it, the backlash when the Alliance
began to lose its Speakers would be terrible. But if he warned
Bish, he wouldn't be believed. The Yak would see it as a ploy
and proceed ahead, perhaps more cautiously, but still Speakers
would be lost.

But if he took the drug himself . . .

The aleph he bore would keep him safe from having his ability
burnt out, Arlo had been certain about that. He'd been less
confident about the range of other effects that his simulations
suggested. Jorl could see that his friend had left something out,
something he'd told Margda but which she in turn had only
hinted at to him. Jorl feared how it would affect him, but he had
to weigh that unknown against the collected certainties that
awaited him. In that light, there did not seem much choice.

Arlo had requested a vast number of ingredients, obviously far
more than he'd used. Jorl systematically sampled from one substance after the other, pouring them into various beakers and
flasks, measuring and mixing them with no purpose, setting some
to cook and placing others in a cooling tray. Eventually, his actions
produced a reaction volatile enough to shatter one of the lab's instruments and start a small fire. Ceiling nozzles he hadn't noticed
showered suppressing foam down onto everything in the box,
causing at least one other piece of equipment to sputter, spark, and
shut down.

Jorl slipped on some foam and crashed to the floor, bringing
Arlo's phial to his mouth in the process, hoping the confusion of
the moment would mask his drinking its contents. He cast the
empty container aside, shattering it against the base of the work
bench where foam and other spilled chemicals contaminated the
remains. Meanwhile, the Sloth had reached the door and flung
it wide. She pointed at him.

"Move! Procedure requires me to purge the clean room's atmosphere, and I can't do that with you inside. Quickly now!"

A three-pronged metal claw embedded itself in the table above his head. Jorl reached up and pulled it free with his nubs, curling his trunk around its cable. Druz stepped back from the door, retracting the cable as she went, and he slid across the floor on a frictionless carpet of suppression foam. As soon as he reached the outer room, the clean room's door slammed shut and a shudder vibrated through the glass box. Jorl turned as he stood, watching a cyclone appear where he'd been. The fires had gone out, replaced by a mixture of foam and wind and smoke. The wind gathered up everything that hadn't been bolted to the floor, not just the sopping foam, but chemicals, hardware, glassware, and tools. The mix of them whirled around and around, picking up speed, and then abruptly and soundlessly vanished. A hatch in the ceiling had blown and the inner room been laid open to a conduit that led to the outside edge of the senator's ship and the vacuum beyond.

Another pair—or possibly one or more of those he'd seen before, he really couldn't tell—of the Ailuros guards arrived. The Brady didn't look at him or utter a word but must have issued a directive somehow. The Panda pair latched on and escorted him back through the ship, out the boarding corridor to the station, returning to the cabin where he'd last seen the Matriarch's Lutr. They left him there, locking the door on their way out.

Since taking Arlo's drug, Jorl had felt nothing. No effect at all. Perhaps it didn't work. The pharmer had never actually tested the thing. What if his simulations held some flaw that failed to capture the difference between theory and practice? He stood in the center of the room for a time, feeling younger and more foolish than he had ever felt in his youth, performing a mental inventory, searching for some sign of the drug he'd taken. Nothing.

He settled into a corner of the room, not bothering with either bench or bed, but choosing to curl up on the floor, his back cradled by the intersection of two walls. It had all been for nothing. Margda's prophecies and resurrection. His aleph. The abduction and slaughter of the Dying Fant. Arlo's death. He'd been struggling to give meaning to all of it, and failed. Just as he had with that artifact when he'd been in the Patrol. Useless all over again. With a sigh, he stopped fighting and accepted it.

He slumped in his corner, allowing his thoughts to jump randomly through a sequence of associations and half-remembered ideas that produced apparent non sequiturs but nothing worth lingering on. In his mind, he smelled spiralmint. It was a memory of olfaction, not actually sensed, existing only in his thoughts. It was enough though, so long associated in his experience with the use of koph and the beginnings of a Speaking state. His left ear tingled.

Jorl thought about sight and smiled, seeing himself afloat in a lightless void, and knowing he also still sat in a corner of the station cabin with his eyes fast shut. He'd taken no koph and yet he was manipulating nefshons. It intrigued him, but to what good?

He'd destroyed the lab, and likely prevented the senator from being able to re-create Arlo's drug. Even if the entire process had been recorded, he hoped no one would be able to tell where the real work ended and his cacophony began. And he'd consumed the sample himself, with no real plan in mind other than to keep it out of Bish's hands. Which put things back pretty much where they'd been before.

Margda had mirrored the Senator's ruthlessness, one politician to another, but despite her machinations which had shaped his own life, in the end she'd had no solutions. Arlo had killed himself, following the cold logic of a researcher. He'd been temporarily moved by an emotional appeal, but in the end had only been able to put the problem squarely in Jorl's hands. But Jorl was just a historian; what did his friend expect him to be able to do? He had no frame of reference, no precedent to draw upon. In all the thousands of years of Alliance history, nothing like this had ever happened. And yet . . . the nefshons danced before him now. He had to try *something*.

Being a historian, what if he looked back further, to a time before the Alliance. The idea was bizarre. Likely, the attempt would fail as soon as he began and he'd awaken on the station with nothing more than a trail of drool down his chin to show for the effort. But he had to at least try.

What did he know about those ancient times? What did anyone know? Now and then an artifact from Before was found on some dead planet or lifeless moon. One such had haunted his dreams. What had it said? Something about being *the past sent forward*.

Jorl focused on what he remembered: a cube of metal and glass, the whirls of color rising like smoke within it, taking on a living shape. Random dust motes swam in his vision, less than a flicker. Nothing. Despite Arlo's assurance the drug would increase his abilities, there was nothing to find. The device that had spoken, its alleged sapience notwithstanding, had apparently left behind no nefshons.

Back in the waking world, he became aware of a crick in his back. The cabin's temperature was cooler than he liked, and sweat beaded on his skin. This latest physical effort had been enough to push his own odor through to his awareness. The guards had locked him in. Bish had no further use for him and might simply leave him there to die of thirst or hunger. It annoyed him, not the idea of dying, but that he might do so while stinking so far above the cleansing rains of home.

No one would ever use koph to summon him, the prohibition applying to Speakers would ensure that. No one would learn his story. All that would be left of him would be the work he'd published before setting off to identify the Silence, an assortment of films and books, nothing but words. His words . . .

Jorl stiffened. Was he completely awake? He wasn't sure. Words. How many times in the past had he used the words, the writings or speeches, the messages written by an individual to summon and Speak with him? So many countless beings, all long dead, who had spoken the same strings of words, made it difficult. But when the phrases were something unique that the conversant identified with, a slogan or credo, they bound something of themselves to those words. Doing so imbued the words with their own identities, which in turn meant their nefshons were locked there as well. If the device from Before had had even the merest hint of a nefshon, perhaps it could be found in its own distinct speech. And he recalled it, a string of phrases that sounded like total gibberish but which would not have been used by another sapient. He spoke them in his mind, reaching out, straining.

"Gilgamesh. The Pendragon. Kal-El. I am these and more. I am the Archetype of Man, and from slumber such as you have never known have I awoken. Speak, friend, and I shall hear you."

Walls formed in the darkness within his mind as long habit once again created his workroom back home. The chill and odor of the real world slipped away from his awareness, replaced by warm humidity and a hint of sartha coming from the window of another room. And all around him words echoed, like a child's infrasonic call but richer. "Kal-El . . ." Over and over, the words tumbled from his lips, the phrase uttered dozens of times, each occurrence spoken with a stronger conviction than Jorl had managed before. "I am these and more . . ." Something approached.

Across time and space, nefshons converged on him from all directions, hurtling with impossible speed from a provenance inexpressibly vast. "I am the Archetype of Man . . ."

". . . and from slumber such as you have never known have I awoken. Speak, friend, and I shall hear you."

It was there. Right in front of him. Far larger than could be contained in the confines of his workroom. Summoning it had wiped away the walls of his imagined venue and had this been the real world his neighbors would surely be gaping at the sudden appearance of a giant cube that had ruined his house. Jorl smiled.

"You are the Archetype of Man," said Jorl, improvising the establishing ritual to the circumstances. "Your time before, unique and protracted, has ended; you are now much as you were in, um, life, but not alive. In this, a world of my own making, I bid you welcome."

There was silence. If the device had heard him it did not respond. And still the intensity of its self-awareness blazed in its words. Machine or not, it *possessed* nefshons. He'd already pulled together enough to manifest a conversant, and more continued to arrive, more impressions of words, but nothing else. No feelings or emotions or reveries like he'd typically feel when he summoned someone. There was no quality of essence or personality, only that overpowering statement of self. The device had been alive and sapient, but not in any way that Jorl could understand.

In that, he wasn't alone.

Behind the glassy portion of the cube, swirls of color coalesced in a humanoid shape. "Speak, friend, and I hear you. And I will answer, but I do not understand."

~~~~~

THE pair of Panda guards returned with a meal tray, a shallow bowl of the same processed vegetable clusters as had been served down in the internment camp. One came in with the tray and set it on the desk while the other stayed by the door, weapon at the ready. At some unconscious level, Jorl noted these things, but he didn't move. To the Ailuros he doubtless appeared to be asleep, slumped in the corner nearest the sleeping platform. His ears hung limp, his trunk lay looped in his lap, and his head lolled to one side with a trail of drool running from the corner of his mouth. Whether they looked upon him with disgust, pity, or some other emotion he'd never know. The events in his station cabin didn't matter just now. With greater focus and concentration than he had ever known, he existed in a mental landscape more vivid than any Speaker had ever achieved.

Jorl let the shattered walls of his house on Keslo fade, along with all the other structures of the Civilized Wood. Instead he constructed a clearing, much like the meeting place where they held public dances or speeches, but several times larger. Hand-cut planks of polished hardwood lay underfoot, each perfectly fit with the ones to either side. At the far ends of the floored space leafy branches created a solid wall all the way around, sealing them in a circle of green. More branches arched overhead, wooden ribs that had been woven together to create a ceiling three times the height of any Fant. Lamps hung from the arches, though Jorl could have just as easily included light without bothering to provide a source for it.

The great cube of the Archetype of Man rested in the precise middle of the clearing. Jorl stood less than an arm's reach from one face. He paced back and forth, toward one edge or the other, enough to catch a glimpse of a second or third side of the thing, but never quite crossing over, no more than he would have walked behind a traditional conversant. At some level he'd decided to think of the side in front of him as the thing's "face." The silhouette that had formed on the other side of the glass helped.

As he paced, he Spoke. They traded questions and answers, both seeking insight, both eking out the parameters of the other's world. It—Jorl couldn't quite call the device a "he"—had accepted the explanation of Speaking and nefshon constructs. There'd been none of the confusion associated with a first summoning. The Archetype of Man had not leaped to any false conclusions, had not mistaken Jorl for a deity. Rather, it withheld judgment until it had compiled sufficient explanation. All in all, it presented itself as a very rational creature, but more so than in the simply logical processes of the machines Jorl had used while in the Patrol. There was more to it, something which had made it alive at one time.

"What is the last thing you remember?" he asked.

It did not pause like a person might. It had no eyes to glance up and to the side as it pondered and searched for a memory.

"I was in a narrow space. A cave of ice and rock. The automata that had taken me to that solar system had determined that moon would be an ideal location. They created the cave and placed me within. My systems went dormant and my beacon announced my presence at regular intervals and in response to any incursions in the space around that moon. I recorded significant geologic upheaval several millennia later but did not awaken. After an even greater span, passive receptors reacted to the energy signature of tool-using beings, activating my beacon. My boot cycle initiated and I awakened. My gross sensors indicated several beings standing in front of me, but most of my processing was still engaged in the restart cycle and self-check, and I cannot tell you more about the individuals who had ended my sleep. Before the cycle ran to completion, the beings retreated. I recorded the presence of vast energies being expended in my vicinity, in excess of the capacity of my protective shields. The cave in which I had been housed lost structural integrity and my own physicality became compromised. That is all I recall; something must have disrupted my memory consolidation at that point."

Jorl nodded. "That happened in the recent past. I was among those, uh, beings, who activated you. We found you by accident. And then our commanding officer ordered you destroyed."

"That individual failed in that task. I am here."

"No, her commands were carried out. That was the end of you. Your, um, physicality. The manifestation conversing with me now is a nefshon construct, as I've described."

"The physicality is not important. Your nefshon science preserves me. All the knowledge of the hero remains within. It has not been lost. The legacy of humanity remains intact."

Jorl gasped as something inside him let go. He filed the notion away for later contemplation. "What's the next most recent thing you remember? You said something about automata placing you in that cave. Were you fully active then?"

"No. They were simply pre-programmed devices created to transport me to a safe site in the event my location was compromised. My previous activation occurred in fifty-four-two-seventeen, eleven thousand and thirteen years prior to you activating me. I had been aboard the station where I had been created. No one had visited there for more than fifty-two thousand years, and I remained inactive. My boot cycle had initiated and I detected four beings floating around me. They were clothed in protective suits. The station's structure had been breached at some earlier time, disabling the gravity and releasing the atmosphere. In the surrounding vacuum they could not hear my offer to share the tales of the heroes of man. After the prescribed period without any inquiry, I returned to an inactive state. I observed as they dismantled the station over the course of several

years, taking it apart piece by piece. In time, their efforts activated some failsafe, and the preservation automata removed me
from what remained of the station, and after several hundred
years delivered me to the moon in an adjacent star system."

Jorl stopped pacing, the comforting illusion of movement
overwhelmed by the significance of the device's words. A station!
Someone had found an entire station from Before! He fanned
himself rapidly and stared up at the huge machine.

"What did you mean by fifty-four-two-seventeen? Is that a
date?"

"Yes. It refers to the year of my final activation on the station.
Prior to that, I was last activated in the year twenty-one fifty-nine
by Dr. Castleman. She and Dr. Gieber performed routine searches
through my collection. Dr. Castleman had a particular fondness
for stories of the original peoples of the Pacific Northwest.

"Twenty-one fifty-nine? What calendar is that?"

"It is the calendar in popular use on Earth at the time of my
construction. Earth is the planetary designation of the human origin. Despite my location on a station far removed from Earth's
system, my timing mechanism utilizes terrestrial units." The Archetype paused. "Jorl, something is wrong. Time is not passing.
My internal chronometer is not functioning properly, and yet I am
not detecting any system errors. Moreover, my efforts at self-
diagnostics do not yield any feedback at all."

Jorl fanned himself faster. The machine sounded concerned.
"You're only partially correct. Time *is* passing, but not in the
conventional sense. I have been Speaking with you for a while
now, and it is later than when we began. But from your personal
point of view you're no older than when we started. You don't
have the same physicality as you did in life. You're not aging, um,
if you ever did. Understand?"

"My comprehension is incomplete. Perhaps the flaw is in my programming. I am not designed for independent philosophy. Dr. Castleman constructed me to be one of the Archetypes, to keep the stories of the heroes alive for humanity's descendants. As a function of my inability to fully comprehend the current situation, I have failed her. Perhaps she would understand you better."

"Maybe. Can you tell me about her? Your Dr. Castleman sounds like someone I would like to Speak with."

THIRTY-THREE
LEGION

~~~~~~~~~

JORL opened his eyes. He sat up, stretched, rose to his feet and began pacing the cabin. He'd dispersed the construct of the Archetype of Man, ending the Speaking more easily than ever before. Was that the extent of the power from Arlo's drug, an effortlessness to the work of Speaking? He couldn't worry about that now, he had to figure out what to do next.

He saw the tray on the desk and absently sent his trunk after some food each time his pacing brought him within range. The Archetype had been clear. Although sapient, its consciousness was artificial, its sense of self, limited. It viewed Dr. Chieko Castleman with a reverence that bordered on awe, not merely the devotion of a child for a parent, but more like some mythic figure responsible for all of creation. It had felt certain that while it could provide an endless supply of stories to inspire and instruct, the woman who had made it could offer up actual answers to any questions Jorl might ask. And more, it had provided ample information and details about her. Many of them made no sense to him, but enough to allow a Speaker to summon someone he'd never met.

Except for the minor point that Castleman had been dead for more than sixty-three thousand years. The woman's nefshons must surely have diffused throughout the galaxy by now, barely imaginable distances existing between each tiny mote of personality. It was impossible for Jorl to summon her. He'd tried. Even with the greater ability he'd presumably been granted by Arlo's drug, the most he'd managed was to detect a handful of particles, a general sense that the woman had existed, but now lay far beyond his reach.

He sat on the bench and finished the meal on the desk, absently massaging an ache in his shoulder with the nubs of his trunk. Margda had insisted he would be able to do what needed to be done. She hadn't foreseen what that was, only that it had involved Barsk's most recent Bearer and whatever Arlo had died to protect. Jorl's earlier depression threatened to engulf him again. He'd run out of ideas, and likely was running out of time. How long before the senator acted?

Jorl considered questioning the Matriarch, summoning her directly as she had done with him, but stopped short. The ease with which she had shoved his mind away and put Arlo in his body frightened him. And, to a lesser extent, the prohibition against summoning another Speaker—despite the machinations behind its creation—remained ingrained in him.

And yet, of the three limits Margda's Edict imposed on all Speakers, she had only broken two of them. Not summoning another Speaker had made a certain amount of sense and propriety. Not Speaking to the living had also seemed obvious. But the third, a restriction against summoning oneself, had never made sense to him. Why should any Speaker wish to Speak with himself? And besides, wouldn't doing so be covered under the first two restrictions? But the Matriarch had thought it important enough to her vision of the future to proscribe it on its own. Perhaps like the other two, she had done so to keep it sacrosanct until she herself needed it. Or . . . what if she had meant for Jorl to break this last rule himself?

He left the desk and returned to the corner, sitting on the floor and bracing himself between the walls once more. It required nothing more than closing his eyes to slip back into the awareness of nefshons, his waking reality supplanted by the mental one. He conjured up the same meeting place he'd used for the Archetype of Man and imagined himself standing at its center point.

Once there, he concentrated on his own nefshons, the very thing all Speakers were taught to filter out with their very first lesson. His nefshons enshrouded him, roiling and gleaming gold. Some of the particles were newly born elements of his personal history, while others, minutes or seconds older, pushed outward as if to diffuse like the particles of the dead, only to pull back and enmesh themselves among fellows without number, because he was very much alive.

The second lesson of every Speaker was to draw sufficient numbers of one's own particles to create a self-construct. Gathering them was like holding out your hands during a leafstorm and becoming filled almost as rapidly as the idea occurred. A mental tweak, a nudge, and one's own construct coalesced. He'd done it so many times before, it was as automatic as removing his own particles from his perception. He'd already done it upon returning here; he did it now, again and deliberately.

Jorl stared, open mouthed, at Jorl. One nefshon construct confronting another as in any summoning, both existing only in the mind of the Speaker, but both a part of that mind.

"You're me," the first Jorl said, realizing how stupid it sounded as the words left him. So did his twin.

"And you're me," he replied with a self-deprecating smirk. "We're us."

They paused, each studying the other, both aware of the golden fabric of nefshons surrounding them. Simultaneous grins burst out across both faces as the full ramifications took hold and they spoke in unison. "And we're both Speakers!"

The two Jorls took a moment, concentrating in the way all Speakers do when summoning, and then there were four of him, all grinning like a child who has told each of his older sisters and aunts that one of the others is looking after him and then sneaks off to pursue adventures of his own.

Four became eight, effortlessly; Arlo's drug making it trivial to maintain more than one construct, especially when the other constructs distributed the burden among themselves. Eight became sixteen, became thirty-two, became sixty-four, on and on, doubling and redoubling until they overflowed the meeting space the first Jorl had imagined and they let the venue fall away as hundreds upon hundreds, thousands of Jorl, imagined themselves linked, side by side, hand in hand, forming a vast chain of themselves around the island of Keslo, feet planted firmly on the edge of the shore, waves across their feet, the rain falling upon identical laughing faces.

With one purpose, they cast themselves wide. The Jorls reached out to encompass the galaxy. Together they did what no single Speaker could ever achieve, they sought out the essence of Dr. Chieko Castleman from wherever each isolated nefshon might lie and compelled every one of them to this single place. Like a magnet of personality, they drew the particles, the strength of their compulsion outstripping the restrictions of distance and time.

For a long while there was nothing. The pull hung in otherwise empty air. But then, slowly at first, nefshons trickled in. Like the first faint and tentative drops of a shower at the end of the season of wind, they came. Then more and more, swifter and in greater number. The trickle built to a steady flow, the flow to a torrent, the torrent to a deluge. And as the particles poured in, one by one the individual Jorls began to disperse. Their purpose achieved they dismissed themselves, until at last there was just the one of him standing there, the image of the cabin on board the space station restored around him amidst a growing collection of sixty-three-thousand-year-old nefshons. With no more effort than it would take to blink, Jorl exercised his will, and Dr. Chieko Castleman came into being again.

THIRTY-FOUR

ILL MET BY MOONLIGHT

~~~~~~~~

THREE kinds of people existed in Pizlo's taxonomy. Almost everyone everywhere fell into the first group: people who didn't talk to him. The people who did talk to him accounted for the other two groups. There were his parents, Arlo and Tolta. That group had dropped from two to one, though now he wasn't so sure. He'd talked to Arlo before going to sleep here, and he had the order right, it hadn't been a dream. The last kind of people was anyone else who talked to him but who wasn't related to him, and before today that had only been Jorl. In his mind, this was more than enough to make Jorl his friend. But now another person had talked to him, a woman who wasn't even a Fant. She'd been nice, and also interesting, and he hoped that meant he could count her as a friend, too. The possibility danced sweetly in his dreams while he slept.

He awoke to find the Sloth hovering over him. She'd changed the bandages on his hands and was in the midst of slowly moving one of her sleeved arms back and forth above his head. The sight of her round face made him smile. Jorl would be proud of him, having made a friend who wasn't a Fant.

"How do you feel, Little Prince?"

"I'm excited."

"Ah, I imagine seeing this station must be very strange and wondrous to you."

He shrugged, and his smile increased as he realized he'd never done that while lying down before. "No, it's not that. It's mostly pretty boring once you get over how ugly everything is."

"Well, why don't we go do something more interesting then?"

"Really? Like what?"

"Do you know what a spacecraft is?"

"Sure, Jorl worked on one before he came back home. Why?"

"We're on one right now. It's docked with the station you were on. Do you remember when I carried you here? We passed through an airlock and a connection tube."

"Yeah, the little room with the big doors. I remember." He sat up and looked at one of the walls and pointed with his trunk. "That's open space through there, right?"

"Yes, how did you—"

"Wow. This is even better than being on a station."

"I agree. I've always found stations to be significantly lacking relative to vessels. Would you like to meet the person who owns this one?"

Pizlo laughed. "You can't own a spacecraft. They're too big and important."

"The man who owns this one *is* important. He's a senior senator. Do you know what a senator is?"

"Is it like the captain of a ship?"

"No, even more important. So important that he has his own ship, and it goes wherever he says."

"Wow."

"Just so. His name is Senator Bish, and you actually saw him before, when you bumped your head. I've been telling him about you, and he's very interested in having a chat with you."

He gasped, eyes wide with surprise. "He wants to *talk* to me? Really?"

"Absolutely. Why don't we go see him right now?"

"Sure! But . . ." he swiveled on the table until he could see into the tiny transparent room. Jorl stood inside, working with all kinds of stuff like Arlo used to do. But it wasn't Arlo, not any more. He was sure of that and wondered where he'd gone.

"What about Jorl?"

"He's busy at the moment, doing a favor for the senator. They'll talk later. Right now though, it's your turn. Come on." She reached out with both arms, her hands still buried deep in her sleeves, and slid one under each of his arms to lift him up off the table and lower the boy to the floor.

Pizlo waved his trunk in farewell to Jorl, but the older Fant looked to be too focused on whatever he was doing. If he was doing it for the senator, and the senator owned this whole ship, then maybe it was really important. Pizlo looked up at the Sloth. He smiled at her and gripped the edge of one of her sleeves with his trunk and they walked out of the lab together.

~~~~~

FROM the lab they followed an arcing hallway a third of the way around the ship. The Brady pressed one hand against the threshold and paused like someone was talking to her. Pizlo couldn't hear anyone else, but maybe it was like when things back on Keslo spoke to him and neither Jorl nor Tolta heard. When she took her hand away the door whooshed open. The room beyond was darker than the hallway. Standing at the entrance, Pizlo could see only silhouettes of a table surrounded on three sides by a heavy couch, some counters along two walls, and a big desk at the back of the room with someone seated behind it. Druz ushered him inside.

He squinted, his eyes adjusting to the dimmer light even as the illumination increased. He saw rugs on the floor that looked like grass. The sofa was dark brown and the table a polished green stone. The counters were white plastic like so much of the ship, but now he could tell they had cabinets in them. The desk was more of the same green stone; the man behind sat in a big chair and he had thick horns that grew out from either side of his head.

Pizlo had never seen a Bos before, but he knew that's what the man was and knowing that made him smile. One of the moons had told him about Yaks. And then he remembered more, the specific Yak that had been mentioned, and as he remembered the rest he began to wail.

Bish winced as he came around his desk. "Druz?"

"My apologies, Senator." The Brady crouched until her face was on a level with Pizlo's. "Hush, Little Prince. You're safe here. Everything is fine."

Tears streamed from his eyes and he would have shamelessly wet himself if there'd been a drop in his bladder. This was the man Telko had spoken of, the glaring hole in the galaxy, lost to everyone in a way that no one had ever been before. It was so horrible, how could his friend just stand there, let alone attempt to comfort him?

A new thought flittered through his mind as he continued to moan with despair. *Abomination.* The clear and certain wrongness of the Yak merited no other term, the word others had whispered about him for as long as he could remember. Was this what people saw when they looked at him?

Druz continued speaking to him, soft words of reassurance with little content. She brought a three-fingered hand to his chin and raised it up to stifle his cry. He didn't resist.

"Did I frighten him? He's just a boy, and a Lox at that. Perhaps he's never seen so much as a picture of a Bos before."

"Yes, sir, I suspect that's it. And he's had a rough day of it. But I think he's over his shock, aren't you, Pizlo?"

He stared into Druz's round face, and relief washed over him. She and the Yak were talking, like they were both ordinary people. How could that be, unless . . . the galaxy was still whole and the man hadn't become an abomination yet!

"Yes. I . . . sorry. I was remembering something scary. I thought it had already happened, but I was wrong. It's okay."

She gave his shoulder a reassuring squeeze. "That's my brave prince. Now let me introduce you more properly. This is Senator Bish, chair of the Alliance's Committee of Information."

Druz stood up, and a moment later Senator Bish came closer until he loomed above Pizlo. Despite his odd appearance, he looked friendly and wise. Pizlo took a deep breath and released his grip on the Sloth's sleeve. Was this someone else who was going to actually talk to him? He was afraid to get his hopes up, especially if Telko's warning would come to pass too soon.

"Hello."

Bish didn't answer him, glancing to the Brady instead. "So, according to your reports, this little fellow is a precog?"

"His stature is the only thing small about him, sir. His cortical readings are easily a match for the most skilled among the committee's precognitivists. As he matures, and with proper training, I would expect his abilities to increase beyond the range we currently measure."

The senator smiled down at him, his expression not unlike the look Tolta sometimes wore when he showed her the newest acquisitions in his bug collection.

"Is that true, young man? Do you *see* things that the people around you don't see?"

Pizlo frowned and shook his head. "No, sir. My eyes . . . they're not very good. But I hear things that others don't. I talk to things that they can't."

"Really? Why don't we sit and you can tell me about that. Would you like some cocoa?" The senator gestured to Druz, who slipped away to fetch a tray from a counter. The Fant crossed over to the couch. Though his arm was working again, his hands still weren't. He had to half-jump half-climb to haul himself up onto the high cushion. By the time he had settled in, the Sloth had placed a tall mug of vanilla cocoa in front of him on the table and the senator stood alongside him. Pizlo leaned forward and dipped the end of his trunk into the mug, filling it with cocoa and transferring it to his mouth.

"That's a sight the Alliance has been spared for a great many years," said Bish. With a bob of his head he pointed a horn at Druz. "Your attention is needed in the lab. Come back when you've resolved things there. I can entertain our young guest in the meantime."

"Yes, sir. I will see you again soon, Little Prince." Her clothing twinkling, his friend left the room.

"How is the cocoa?"

"Good. It's better than Tolta's."

"Who is Tolta? Is that one of the things that speaks to you and not others?"

Pizlo laughed and nearly snorted cocoa. "No! Everyone talks to Tolta and she talks to them right back."

"I see. Then who are the ones who only talk to you?"

"Lots of things. Like the trees and the water and the clouds. And every once in a while, I get to talk to a moon." He remembered the circles he'd drawn and slapped his chest with one bandaged hand. "See?"

"You talk to moons?"

"Mostly I listen. They teach me things. Jorl does that, too, but that's different, 'cause I can't go to school."

"Hmm, no, I imagine a precog would not be a good fit among other school children. Not even on Barsk."

"What's a precog?"

"Someone who can see pieces of the future. It's a very special gift."

"Wow. I wish I could do that."

"Isn't that what you do?"

Pizlo frowned. "Things just talk to me."

The Yak laughed and raised his own mug, smiling as he sipped the cocoa.

"Do you know what a metaphor is, son?"

"Does it have grass?"

"No, it's when you talk about one thing as if it were something else."

"Oh. Metaphor."

"Sometimes we tell ourselves metaphors, to help us comprehend parts of the world that don't make sense to us. Do you understand?"

Pizlo shook his head, careful not to cause his trunk to spatter any stray drops of cocoa.

"How long have you heard things talking to you that others can't hear?"

He shrugged. "Forever. At least, as long as I can remember."

The Yak nodded and set his mug aside. "Druz tells me you have the ability of a powerful precognitivist. I've never seen even an inkling of that talent in anyone prior to adulthood. For one so young, I can imagine it being disorienting, even frightening. But your unconscious came up with a story to make sense of it. The voices you hear aren't coming from the world around you, they're the glimpses of the future your own mind has gleaned via your precognitive powers."

Pizlo shifted uncomfortably. He didn't want to offend the Yak, not when he'd only just found another person who would talk to him, but the Bos had it completely wrong. Pizlo didn't understand about metaphors and powers, but he knew himself. All of Keslo spoke to him, every day he was there. They didn't usually tell him big or important things about the future, just regular, everyday stuff. Sure, the moons taught him oceans of things, and sometimes that included pieces that hadn't happened yet, but he'd only seen four moons in his whole life, and most of those had been in the current season.

It was only then that he realized with a pang that, except for when he'd seen Telko through that big window, nothing had spoken to him since he'd left Barsk. He'd blamed it on all the metal and plastic around him. Living things could talk, but not the dead walls that people had built to let them live here so high above the world. And yet, here in this dead place, he'd met two new people who talked to him! Was one thing the result of the other, or was it all just a coincidence?

The senator was looking at him like he expected some answer even though he hadn't asked a question. Pizlo nodded once, and then looked back down at his mug and took another drink. It really was good cocoa.

"I'm sure Jorl has been an excellent teacher, but he has other demands on his time and the resources available on Barsk are somewhat limited. Let me tell you about some of the things you'll experience when you visit Dawn with me and meet some of the other precognitivists who have come to help me to do the work of the Alliance—"

Senator Bish kept talking, but Pizlo paid him little attention. The man was so obviously wrong with all that stuff about metaphor. Besides, something in the Fant's head had come loose and more and more of the finer details that Telko had shoved into him were falling into place. Stories and ideas that had just hung in Pizlo's mind before now had an order and a timeliness to them. Things were speeding up and getting ready to happen, not just the thing that would change this nice old man into an abomination but other pieces, too. He understood the flow of them now, and knew that Jorl's transformation was coming up fast.

Meanwhile the Yak kept on talking. Pizlo nodded and smiled and offered up the occasional polite agreement when the rhythm of the one-sided conversation seemed to demand it. At some point, his friend the Sloth had come back into the room. She replenished the supply of cocoa and kept refilling both his and the senator's mugs. Pizlo continued listening to the Yak and kept drinking the cocoa until he thought he would burst or, worse, fall asleep. The old man sure liked to talk. It bothered Pizlo that he could so hunger for more people to talk to him only to have that need met by someone who had nothing to say. He took a deep breath and tried to clear his head, catching the end of some fragment about boat races and shaping the future for all the peoples of the Alliance.

He was about to ask the senator to go back and tell him again the part about the boat races when he felt something click into place. The next thing that his last moon had told him had just come to pass. He felt it in his bones, much like when he had known he had reached the equator. It sent a shiver through his body and he sat up and almost slid off the couch.

"Is something wrong, Son? You look troubled."

"Oh! No, I'm fine it's just . . . It's happened. I knew it would, and it has. But knowing it will isn't as good as knowing it has." Pizlo looked up at the senator. "Have you ever felt like that?"

"What are you talking about? Have you had a vision? Druz, are your instruments calibrated to him yet?"

The Brady shrugged with embarrassment. "I believe so, yes. The resonance of it was several times anything I've recorded before. I didn't mention it, as I thought the equipment acting up, but if he confirms—"

"Tell me what you saw, Son."

"I saw Jorl."

"Oh really? What about him?"

"Not him. Them."

THIRTY-FIVE

THE FACE OF GOD

ITS . . . no, *her,* eyes darted side to side in obvious confusion. Jorl waited. He'd witnessed a wide range of reactions from first time conversants; disorientation was nothing new. It usually lasted only a few moments, to be followed by apprehension and ultimately fear. Tens of thousands of Speakers existed throughout the galaxy, and while the experience might not be as routine off Barsk as it was for Fant, everyone in the Alliance knew about summoning. But that knowledge only came to mind *after* the initial disorientation. And yet . . . the person before him came from a time without Speakers.

She looked like nothing Jorl had ever seen.

If the Archetype of Man hadn't referred to Dr. Chieko Castleman with feminine pronouns, he wasn't sure he'd have made that assumption. She wore a lot of clothing—though not as much as Jorl's colleagues in the Patrol had insisted he wear—a pale blue sleeveless shirt that opened at the neck, black shorts from waist to knee, and durable-looking boots that suggested her race had delicate feet. Most astonishingly, the woman had almost no fur.

There was a knotted bundle of night black hair atop her head, and a pair of slender, matching brows on the ridge above each eye, but every other bit of her that wasn't hidden by clothing appeared hairless. Her skin was light, but not as colorless as Pizlo's, more like a slightly aging parchment. Despite himself, Jorl stared.

And the odd creature stared right back. She seemed to have gotten over her confusion but had not yet moved on to the next phase. Beads of moisture appeared on her forehead and her chest began to billow as she breathed in and out rapidly. Her eyes widened and Jorl feared the woman would hyperventilate. Then, as quickly as she had begun, she mastered herself and slowed her breathing. She looked around again, and this time appeared to see the room's simple furnishings. As Jorl watched, she bent at the knee like most people would and sat on the bench. She brought her hands to her face and thrust them upward into her hair, spreading the moisture from her palms and up into her scalp, leaving her eyes closed.

Jorl waited. From the moment he understood he'd be able to Speak to this woman, he'd abandoned any idea of using the establishing rituals. They were a part of time that meant nothing here. Instead he focused on patience and put the real world out of his thoughts.

In time, Dr. Castleman dropped her hands. Her eyes remained closed.

"How . . . how is it that I am here? And where is here? And . . . and . . ."

"What is the last thing you can recall?" Jorl inquired, with a whisper.

The woman's head came up, her eyes opened and stared into Jorl's. Castleman's were green, with small flecks of something, perhaps gold. She had interesting eyes, with more white to them than he'd expected. But not otherwise remarkable. Not the eyes of a being who could create sapient life as the Archetype had insisted.

"It was the weekend. I was going climbing in the canyon. I stopped at the lab first and I did a full download of the main core, backing up onto memory plates. Standard stuff, belt and suspenders because I like that extra security. Morgan came by as I was finishing up. We had a beer, talked, I ate the lunch I'd packed. Then I left to get my climb in while there was still plenty of daylight. And now . . . here . . ."

Jorl nodded, and bit back a smile as the woman's eyes darted to follow the path of his trunk. He brought it back to center and kept it still, hoping to reestablish her gaze.

"And now here. It's likely you died that day. The Archetype of Man told me you had suffered an accident while recreating. The you that is talking to me now is an amalgam of you as you were up to about that point in time, and there is nothing of you that existed after."

The creature bolted upright from the bench. Her eyes widened showing still more white. "The Archetype . . . You talked to it . . . Then you, you're really what you appear to be, an anthropomorphic . . . an RM!" Her voice cracked with emotion, delight, amazement, awe, all these things but also terror.

"Please, relax. We have plenty of time. For your first question— no, I did not talk with the Archetype of Man, not as I suspect you mean. It's been destroyed. We communicated as you and I are now. I summoned it and with its help I was able to reach back, unimaginably far into the past, and find you." He paused, and again his smile crept out. "Thank you for coming. My name is Jorl. Jorl ben Tral."

Silence as the woman brushed her palms against her thighs. She stepped aside and walked around Jorl in a slow circle.

"I'm Castleman. Chieko Castleman . . . Chieko." She stared at Jorl. "Ben Tral?"

Jorl nodded, keeping his trunk steady. "My father was Tral. Tral ben Yarva."

Castleman stared openly now. Her jaw dropped. "But that's Hebrew."

"Excuse me?"

"That's a Hebrew patronymic. Hebrew. The language. Hebrew?"

"I don't understand. Who is Hebrew."

"Not a who, a what. It's a language. Or . . . was. My father used to speak it sometimes, though not often enough around me for me to pick up more than a few words." She stopped, shook her head as if to set herself back on track. "Why do you have a Hebrew patronymic? For that matter, why are you speaking English?"

Jorl shrugged. "It's just language. Except for a few words here and there, all sapients speak the same. As you and I are speaking now, though following your pronunciation is a bit tricky."

Chieko retreated to her bench and sat again. She looked like she couldn't decide whether to laugh or scream. Jorl had seen the expression before, but only on the faces of old men who had lost themselves in too many mugs of distilled spirits.

"So . . . If I understand this, I'm dead, right? Dead, and I'm talking to a raised mammal. An uplifted fucking elephant, who's complaining that I speak with an accent?"

She lowered her head between bent knees and giggled.

Jorl flicked his trunk in the woman's face, snapping his nubs until she looked up.

"What did you call me? What did you mean by that?"

Castleman cringed, shoving herself away until she backed into the desk. She shook herself and sobered somewhat. When she again met Jorl's gaze, she held it and would not look away.

"A fucking elephant. Sorry, I just . . . this is . . . hell, I'm sorry."

"No, no, not the pejorative or the prefix." Jorl shook his head. "What did you mean by 'raised mammal?' In what way raised?"

Castleman's hands trembled. "In your world, your time, there are other creatures? Other species, yes? Warm blooded . . . live-bearing creatures. Mammals . . . and other kinds as well, right? Creatures of the air, birds, um, avians . . . and reptiles and insects. Do you understand these terms? You're not the only living things, are you?"

Jorl's nod did nothing to dispel his puzzlement. "Yes, whole taxonomies of animals exist. Some overlap across worlds as well. What of it?"

"Wait, wait . . . you said 'worlds' just now . . . intelligent life has spread out across multiple worlds. . . . My god, it worked, it all worked!" Chieko Castleman's face opened up in a grin that threatened to split her face apart. The expression pierced Jorl like the miracle of a beam of sunlight on Barsk.

"Excuse me, I don't—"

"You, you are a mammal. Warm blooded. Your females suckle your young. Those are the gross characteristics of mammals." One hand waved vaguely toward her chest.

"We established all of that. I'd hazard the same is true of you. What's your point?"

With a gesture not unlike the way he'd whip his trunk for attention, Castleman waved him to silence. "You don't understand. When my parents were born all sapient life looked like me. Human. But then that changed. We began to take species of varying degrees of sentience and searched for ways to raise them to full sapience. The breakthrough came a decade before I was born, one of those accidents resulting from the synthesis of unrelated fields of study. It started when our life scientists had completed genomic maps of several dozen mammalian species on Earth."

Castleman's right arm waved as she spoke, describing wild ellipses through the air, her fingers held rigid as she jabbed home each point like a lecturer at the academy.

"Meanwhile, ethologists had teamed up with psychologists and returned to the question of instinct, how to account for the varieties of unlearned knowledge so many species possessed. That quickly brought up the old arguments about what sorts of human behavior could be considered instinctive. The only one they agreed on was a predisposition to acquire language."

"You're not making sense," said Jorl. "People don't *acquire* language, they're born with it."

His conversant laughed. "Your people, yes, but not mine; that's my point. Back then there were hundreds of languages being spoken, near to a thousand, really. I remember a professor of mine during grad school telling me that a couple centuries earlier there'd been tens of thousands of them. Anyway, the point they wanted to make was that it didn't matter what language a community spoke, human beings are hardwired to acquire language so you pick up the one in your environment."

"But where did they get it from?"

"Exactly, it had to start somewhere, right? That's where the cognitive scientists and biologists stepped in. They went looking for evidence of that wiring. They started by comparing the human genetic strings of information with other sentient species. And they found it! An insanely long chain of genetic instructions that unwound to a package of rules about the rules of language. It was all meta-rules and language universals, encoded guidelines that allowed every human infant to reinvent his or her community's language."

Castleman paused. Her arm stopped in mid arc and fell to her side. The exuberance of her explanation fell away. She stared at Jorl for a long moment, and then continued in a softer voice.

"It answered the question of why humans had language and other species did not. Not simply elaborate communication systems, but full blown linguistic productivity, to talk about abstract concepts and share insights that had no referents in the real world. Other species had intelligence, and even the leisure for communication, but only human beings possessed this meta-linguistic genetic sequence. That's when we let the genie out of the bottle. It was a simple research question at first. If we could give that bit of genetic engineering to other species, would they develop language? Maybe not language as we understood it, but language just the same."

Shivers ran down Jorl's spine. "You're saying that's how these 'raised mammals' were created? You humans grafted language learning onto my ancestors and we're the result?"

The human shook her head violently. "No. No, no, no, no. We did something even more perverse. Once the language sequence was known, psycholinguists realized it could be used to understand adult language representation. Research in the field of artificial intelligence had stagnated, but now it exploded! Entire nations joined together to combine their computational processing power with the goal of taking a language—as it was known and used by a living person, not as a system or grammar or a lexicon, but a dynamic knowledge structure—taking this thing and reverse engineering it to a genetic sequence. And because knowing a single language was much more specific, it turned out to be a much smaller structure than our predisposition to *learn* a language. Synthesizing that new sequence meant they could give it to almost any mammalian species, wiring in a particular language in the same way that other instinctive knowledge was already in place."

"And that's why we can understand each other?"

"Your language is the same English that was in the mind of a researcher somewhere. It was deconstructed and then encoded into your forebears' genetic structure where it would breed true. I had to learn to speak my language, but you'd have been born with yours. And every generation does it the same way, so there's no language change; any linguistic flux gets reset with the next generation of offspring.

"It changed everything. We began producing language-using species, an artificial evolution. It was the first step to an anthropomorphic movement. Once nonhuman species became active symbol users, our genetic engineers began changing the rest of their physiology to allow them to take full advantage of it. They reshaped them, giving them the entire vocal mechanism, bipedal movement, opposable thumbs, all the things which together with language had given humans mastery of our environment."

Castleman stopped again. She looked down at her hands, bringing the fingertips of one into contact with their opposites on the other.

"That was the state of things in my time. Raised mammals. Engineered to be intelligent and functional, with the best traits of their genetic origins. We'd only raised a few species yet, some dogs and cats, animals that were already domesticated and familiar. We felt a bit like gods, creating new life which would look upon us and know that we had brought them into existence."

"Dogs and Cats," said Jorl. "You made them?"

"We did. Their creation changed my world. All the old issues of social equality that we were getting close to finally laying to rest burst out once again. People divided over the role raised mammals should have in the world. Were they just smarter pets, or were they people? That became the new dividing line and old issues of discrimination fell away. Countries went to war over the question. Some governments banned RMs from within their borders. Others decided to use them to supplement humans for work on our lunar bases and in space. My own nation had grand plans to expand the research and send raised mammals off in generation ships to other solar systems. My work got its start as a result, cataloging and preserving our cultural histories. The Archetype of Man was just one of several self-curating repositories that were intended to preserve who we were and give guidance to raised mammals. And it must have worked, because here you are!" She sighed, flushed with satisfaction from knowledge she could never have attained in life.

Jorl had never seen anyone looking more content, and he paused a long moment before saying, "I don't think it happened quite that way."

Castleman's elation slipped away again. "What do you mean?"

"There are many different kinds of sapient beings in the galaxy, and maybe they're descended from the things your people created, but I'm not so sure. That doesn't seem like the kind of thing we'd forget. Nor the people who created us. But there's no record of you, not in any of our histories. But I could be wrong. Maybe we just forgot because it's been so long."

"How long?"

"Our history tells us that we started on the world we call Dawn, but the actual record only begins with our Expansion and the formation of the first Alliance of Worlds, a ring of eight planets that were colonized just over sixty-two thousand years ago."

"Sixty-two thousand? You have a recorded history going back sixty-two thousand years? And there's no mention of humans?"

Jorl nodded slowly, hearing the anguish in Dr. Chieko Castleman's voice. "Nothing. And believe me, you'd stand out. Our records begin with the founding of those eight worlds. Anything prior to that is just the Before, and it's all unsupported myth. We don't know where we came from. It's not really the subject of much speculation. And even historians like myself don't tend to ask questions about anywhere near that far back. Maybe as a civilization we're just focused more on going forward than looking back."

"I don't understand how that could be, not if we created you, gave you language and life and sent you to the stars."

"I agree, but there are no creatures that look like you anywhere in the galaxy. No human beings."

"Then tell me, Jorl, what became of us?"

The Fant offered his hand to Castleman, and the human took it in both of hers.

"I don't know. But it might explain some things. The only reason I know about your Archetype is because I was there when we stumbled upon it and destroyed it. There's no more mention of it in the official record than there is of your people."

"Oh my god! Why would you destroy it?"

Jorl said nothing. He held Castleman's hands in his, noting how similar they were to his own, reflecting on the many ways in which he more closely resembled the human than he did any of the furred races that included every other person in the galaxy outside of the people on Barsk. Why were there no records of human beings? Had the Patrol destroyed them all?

"I've been asking myself that question since it happened. But now I'm thinking it's just a part of something much bigger. I think maybe there are forces in play that have been keeping any knowledge of you a secret. I had it wrong, and even Arlo had it wrong. And Margda didn't see it clearly or couldn't grasp it all."

"I don't understand, who are those people? What are you talking about?"

"All of this, all the missing stories, the lack of any mention of humans. That . . . gap . . . in our understanding of everything. It's the Silence!"

THIRTY-SIX

LETHE

ORL sat at the desk in his cabin on the station, picking at the last clusters of food on the tray. The implications of his conversation with Chieko Castleman threatened to overwhelm him, despite their simplicity. They answered questions of the origins of the peoples of the Alliance, questions that he hadn't known even to ask. And why should he? The races of the Alliance had existed for tens of thousands of years; from the perspective of its citizens it had *always* been. Castleman had shattered that unexamined assumption. All the sapient life left in the galaxy had been manufactured from dumb animals. Despite his training as a historian, he doubted he truly grasped the destructive potential such a revelation would have on society.

Surely that was what the Matriarch had seen. Not the specifics, just that a weapon existed that could put an end to ignorance that had endured for millennia. And it fell to him, a simple Speaker, to tell the truth and end the long Silence.

With no more effort than breathing, he summoned himself again. An instant after closing his eyes he was regarding a nefshon construct scant moments younger than the one which represented himself. His double knew his intention and together they each summoned him again. The four repeated the process, as did the resulting eight, continuing several more times until his numbers were sufficient for the work Jorl had in mind.

He dismissed his replicas from his attention and concentrated on his next task, confident each of the others were doing likewise. After the challenge of summoning Dr. Chieko Castleman, reaching out to Senator Bish held no more challenge than flexing the nubs of his trunk. The Yak's nefshons resisted for just a moment, but with a mental tug a stream began flowing toward him, a golden tether between where the living Bos was in the real world and the imaginary space Jorl had created, where he now gave shape to his conversant.

For this final interview Jorl had envisioned a vast and featureless room, lit with the diffused and filtered sunlight of Barsk. Bish, the senior senator from the Committee of Information stood in front of him in a pale blue robe and dark slippers, presumably what he was wearing in his room on his nearby ship. He paused in mid-gesture, as though he had just been in conversation with someone else. And of course, he was, only now he was also here, and his awareness had been pulled to this place and time.

"Greetings, Senator. Welcome." Jorl spoke softly, just enough to focus the Yak's attention upon him.

"You! How did you get out of the cabin? After your fiasco in my lab, I left orders for the Ailuros to keep you locked in until Druz completed her review of your work." He paused, looked around the summoning venue. "Where are we? And where did that boy get to?"

Jorl paused. Boy? Had he meant Pizlo? But no, he could not allow himself a distraction now, or everything would fall apart.

"*Here* is not where you think it is, Senator. I'm still very much a prisoner on the station, right where you left me, just as you are still wherever you were a moment ago. But we're both also in this place that I've created for the occasion. I promise to explain it all shortly, but we need to wait for the others to arrive."

Before Bish could respond, Jorl felt a nudge on his awareness, followed by another, and then several more. Most of the other versions of him had completed their tasks and now clamored for admittance to his attention. He opened his perception to them all, and one by one they returned the favor, bringing themselves and their respective conversants into the venue of his making.

Jorl allowed himself an ironic smile. Even with Arlo's drug, few other Speakers could have done this; summoning required knowledge of the conversant, names and words and details. He'd been an academician before his first Speaking, and in the publish-or-perish world of the university it had made sense to research the names and preferences of the senators who oversaw funding for all academic journals. He'd never imagined he might meet them.

Another Jorl appeared standing alongside a gray-furred Cynomy, Welv, second only to Bish in seniority on the committee. Two more of his doppelgangers arrived, escorting a Feln and a Lep, and these were followed by a pair of Marmo senators, and then a Geom. The arrivals continued until two dozen duplicate Jorls had silently faded in, each in the company of a different sapient being gathered from throughout the galaxy, the other twenty-four senators who comprised the Committee of Information. The other Jorls positioned their conversants into a semi-circle facing the first Jorl, with Senator Bish at its middle. Together these men and women controlled the flow of knowledge and discovery throughout all the worlds of the Alliance. They represented both the larger races and the smaller ones, and they were all furred.

"Senators, please excuse the manner in which I have brought you here. My name is Jorl ben Tral, and as I am sure you can guess, I am from Barsk. The twenty-five of you comprise the Committee of Information. I realize you're not currently in formal session, but I have brought you together because I have valuable information for you and your committee head, Senator Bish."

He paused, allowing the conversants to glance around and recognize one another as they tried to make sense of the situation. That wasn't a likely outcome, so he pressed on.

"I know you are all aware of the Compact that defines Barsk's relationship with the rest of the Alliance. For eight hundred years this one-sided document has permitted you to take from us, giving back little other than indifference and, at times, even contempt. Yet despite this extreme bias, members of your committee feel the arrangement is insufficient. These men and women would prefer to take outright what Barsk has agreed to provide. Indeed, one among you would trump up economic arguments as a motivation for hatred, and racial differences as a justification for extermination. I refer to Senator Bish. He organized a project to acquire the knowledge of the manufacture and refinement of the drug we call koph. He has authorized and personally committed theft, kidnapping, and murder in pursuit of his goal. Even now, I am imprisoned at his command in the vain hope that I will provide information to further his desire. I doubt he planned to keep me much longer, and he certainly now knows he will need to kill me outright. But like some petulant child desperate to get his way, he has threatened to destroy not just me, not just my people, but our entire world. Those of you who are parents know better than to give in to such a demand. Nor will I. I will not allow Senator Bish to continue."

"You malformed little maggot!" The Yak shouted at him. The

wise and grandfatherly demeanor, the perfect diction and poise, these had all vanished. Jorl took a step back, not at the blistering outburst; he realized he'd stumbled upon the man's weakness. In the many decades Bish had enjoyed power, had anyone dared to refuse him, to deny him anything, in the presence of others? Jorl's outrageous presumption had shattered the senator's façade. The resulting, long-buried rage echoed through the room. The Fant's many incarnations all flinched.

Bish faced the Jorl that had spoken, barely allowing his gaze to flicker to the other versions of the Fant and utterly ignoring his fellow senators.

"You are an insignificant bead of piss on a single blade of prairie grass! I don't know how you managed this trick, but it changes nothing. Do you think you can end this by making an announcement to my committee? That they'll recommend legislation to the larger senate body? Idiot! There are no Fant in the senate, not a one. Some few races may hold your world harmless, your people neutral, but even these would benefit from shattering your Compact and opening your world's resources for the good of the Alliance. Once we've raped your planet and taken everything it has, no one will care if we burn it all to ashes, every tree and plant and Fant."

Still staring at Jorl, he swung his head in an arc, the massive horns taking in the other committee members in a wide sweep. "You have no allies here. Few of them would publicly support me in this, but none will actively oppose my actions, not openly and not privately." The Bos turned his attention to his fellow senators, slowly capturing each with his gaze. More than half turned away.

"So you say." Jorl's words brought Bish's glare back. He ignored the senator for a moment as he gave an infrasonic signal to his other selves. One by one they passed the tethers of their respective conversants over to him and then caused their own nefshons to disperse. They vanished, leaving only Jorl and the members of the Committee of Information. He fanned his left ear, feeling uncomfortably warm. He waved his trunk in a broad arc to bring their attention to him.

"I am a Speaker. As you must have realized by now, you are all conversants in a summoning I have performed."

The senators murmured among themselves. Naming the strangeness of the experience ironically made it more real. The many Lox they had seen, all looking alike, might have been dismissed due to their inexperience with Fant. But as each senator's escort had vanished and the one who'd identified himself as Jorl spoke, he saw realization dawning. They knew something was very wrong. There had only ever been one Fant there.

Jorl continued, "You know about Speakers. We can converse with images of the dead, one at a time. And yet, here there are many of you. And no, none of you are dead. But I am not like other Speakers." He paused and gestured at the tattoo on his forehead. "I am only the second Speaker to ever bear this mark. The first was our Matriarch, who was both the very first Speaker and the first Aleph. In assembling you all here, I have achieved what has never even been attempted. I have sought you out from your respective, far flung worlds throughout the Alliance and brought you here, not to threaten but to show you I can do this thing. All I want to do is talk with you. You are the Committee of Information, and I want nothing more than to share knowledge. Because in addition to bringing you here, I can do another thing beyond the ability of any other Speaker. I can reach back, unimaginably far, and summon someone from Before."

As he finished, Jorl opened his awareness to the collection of recently summoned nefshons and pulled them together again, summoning Dr. Chieko Castleman to stand alongside him.

Half of the senators began to scream.

"Impossible!" Bish roared. He glared at Jorl and at Castleman. "This is *impossible*!"

More than half of the senators showed signs of panic, but like Bish, some clearly recognized a human being. They glanced among themselves, whispering urgently.

"Senators, if you will allow, may I present Dr. Chieko Castleman, engineer, programmer, and archivist. A female human from Before."

"No," insisted T'Minah, a Geom senator Jorl particularly recognized from his past study of the committee; her office had final approval on historical research. "Bish is right. There must be a trick. There are no humans. There haven't been since before the Expansion. This is a lie."

"It's not a lie," Jorl assured them. "Like yourselves, the woman you see here has been summoned. Unlike you, she died tens of thousands of years ago. She comes from a time before most of our races even existed."

"What does that mean?" This from one of the junior senators, a Feln. She'd clearly never seen a human before. "What does he mean *before* our races existed?"

Jorl gestured encouragingly to Castleman with his trunk.

"Well, as I explained to Jorl . . . we, that is, my species, the humans of my time, um, we made you. Built you up from other animals."

"That is insane," yowled the Feln senator. "Built us? Built us how?"

Castleman looked toward Jorl, a mix of nerves and confusion writ upon her face. Jorl nodded for her to continue.

"We wired language into you, encoded you for intelligence so you could develop reason. We altered your physiology to make you tool users. We educated you in science and art. We made you self-aware as never before."

T'Minah had moved during Castleman's explanation and now stood alongside Bish. "Do you really expect us to believe what you're saying? Are we supposed to think you're some kind of god?"

"What? Good Lord, no! I mean, of course not. I didn't personally do any of that. My work was in a completely different area. But, uh, other members of my species did, yes. From what I've seen, and what Jorl has explained to me, you are all descendants of the raised mammals that humans created back in your Before epoch."

Several of the younger senators gaped openly at Castleman. A few trembled. "A god. A furless god," one muttered, which sent a shudder running through the rest of them. Jorl twitched his nubs at the succinct phrase.

"I see now what you're attempting," said Bish. He'd leashed his anger and his voice held some of its former power again. The thunder of his authority drowned out the other senators' whines and whispers. "You brought this committee together so you could present this 'information' to us, but we are not all shocked or overwhelmed by your news. Some of us already knew this history, knew about humans, and of our true origins. The senate elite has always known. It's in part why the Committee of Information was originally formed."

Jorl nodded to himself. He watched the faces of the senators who'd clearly been ignorant, not only of humans but also of the existence of such an elite in their midst.

"I suspected as much. It explains the unofficial policy regarding artifacts from Before." He turned to Castleman who looked as confused as the junior senators. "The ones who knew about you, knew what your artifacts represented. Bish has all but admitted that. Any time one turns up, it gets quietly destroyed so the rest of the Alliance can't learn about your people or that you created us. They're deliberately keeping everyone ignorant."

"But why?" Castleman took a step toward Bish. "That all happened tens of thousands of years ago. None of it should matter now. Your species, your races, have existed for longer than mine had at the time we raised the first mammals. And, if what Jorl tells me is true, you've outlived us as well. Why keep any of this secret?"

Bish glared at the human, but Castleman met his gaze and in the end it was the senator who turned away. When he spoke, his voice had lost the power he'd briefly regained.

"You don't understand. Neither you nor the Lox understand. You don't know." Bish seethed.

"You're the Committee of Information," said Jorl. "Share what you know."

"We cannot," said T'Minah. Several of the other members of the committee nodded her way, deferring to the Gopher's expertise. "We only know what is written in our most ancient records, an accounting of the centuries before the Expansion, and all who have read it are sworn never to speak of it."

Bish waved the other senator to silence. "All of this is less than a dream, and nothing revealed here violates any oaths."

"Then tell us," insisted Jorl.

The Geom closed her eyes and took a deep breath. "Here is your truth. We did not outlive your kind, Chieko Castleman. We destroyed you."

The human turned to look at Jorl, who in turn stared at T'Minah.

"What are you saying?"

"You heard her," shouted Bish. His jaw tightened as he spat the words, his eyes focused on the Fant with more raw hatred than Jorl had ever imagined. "We destroyed them! That is the account we have. Our ancestors could not live among the gods that had made them. They could not bear the knowledge that they were so little different from beasts, could not accept that there was nothing of the divine in themselves that was not placed there by humans. Humanity had used up its homeworld and left it behind, spreading to several star systems. They took their creations with them. On each of these worlds our ancestors rose up against their makers and killed every last man, woman, and child among them.

"And when all the creators were dead—and many of our ancestors with them—the survivors gathered on a planet they named Dawn, wrote their account and locked it away. Then they spent years expunging all reference to humans from their cities, their worlds, and their lives. In time, a new generation came forth and they grew up ignorant of their parents' origins. And no one spoke of the truth. Over and over for generations until all those who had taken part in the destruction of their creators had themselves died, and all their children, and their children's children's children, too, lest some whispered tale be passed down. And only then, when all memory of our creators had been expunged, only then did we leave Dawn and begin the great Expansion.

"That is the secret the senate has guarded, Chieko Castleman. That is the shame of all our races, Jorl ben Tral. And if perhaps at some level, the Eleph and the Lox with their lack of fur, their naked skin, have touched some racial memory and reminded us of our crime, perhaps now you better understand the reasons you are loathed and despised by the rest of the galaxy."

Sighing, Bish pivoted left then right, surveying his fellow senators. Some looked away, their faces reflecting the shame of their knowledge. Others stared back, aghast at what they'd just learned.

"So my young historian, you see now that this revelation of yours is not news. It cannot be used to affect your release or preserve your precious Compact. It does not matter and makes no difference. The senate has kept this secret from our earliest beginnings. The Committee of Information will not spread it further. That one, self-important Fant has learned of it changes nothing. But you have made one thing simpler for me. You've demonstrated that you're too well informed to survive. We are done, Jorl. This ends now."

Jorl crossed his arms and lowered his head. He spread his ears wide and allowed his trunk to hang down and curl up at the end, nubs closed tight like a third fist.

"On that we agree, Senator, but you've gotten everything else wrong. You've been interpreting dozens of different prophecies that all converge on this moment in time. You've correctly identified it as a turning point, and you've acted on that knowledge. But no one, not your precognitivists nor Barsk's own Matriarch, has been able to scry just *what* will occur. A decision will be made, some action taken, yes, but no one knows what form any of that takes. You've decided it has to be either shattering the Compact or destroying my people and planet. But I believe it's something else. Margda started all of this with her own prophecies a generation after every Lox and Eleph on an Alliance world were rounded up and moved to a single planet. She foretold something she called the Silence, and warned that all of Barsk would be at risk when it came. You're the obvious source of the danger she saw, and now I understand that the Silence was the secret you've kept hidden. This will end, but not by killing me or anyone else. It stops by sharing the truth with the rest of the Alliance!"

Bish chuckled. "I give you full points for arrogance, but there's only bluster and no bite to your words. You're out of tricks. The tableau you've created is impressive, but it accomplishes nothing. Regardless of the illusion you've crafted here, I know where you really are, locked in a room on the station where my personal ship is docked. In the time you've had us here I could have walked there. The only reason I haven't is because you're keeping me here. But how long can you manage this trick? Soon you will grow tired and this mass summoning will come to an end. And when it does, I will make my way to your room, relieve the guard on duty outside your door, and step inside to wring the life from your worthless body with my own hands."

Castleman stepped in front of Jorl and didn't stop until she was nose to nose with Bish. "Is that your only answer? To commit murder rather than face your own truth?"

The senator took a step back, not because the human had startled him, as Jorl first thought, but to give him room to raise an arm the better to backhand Castleman across her face and send the woman stumbling. Blood trickled from her mouth and as she righted herself, the human spit out a tooth.

"You are already dead, and by your own testimony you've been so for longer than my own race has existed. I won't be instructed by someone who is less than the memory of dust. When the Speaker here is gone, you will be as well."

"You're wrong," said Jorl. "I am like no other Speaker. I can summon the living from across the vast expanse of the Alliance and bring them together in one place. You've seen that there can be as many of me as I choose to create. But you haven't thought it through. Chieko Castleman has *already* been summoned. The particles that define her construct have already been gathered together from millennia of dispersion. Even if you kill me, any Speaker with knowledge of her could summon her back with ease."

"How fortunate for us all then that no others know about her."

"Give me a little credit for being a historian. While I was sending out constructs of myself to gather the members of this committee, still other versions of me went out and visited Speakers, both on Barsk and throughout the worlds of the Alliance. The experience gave them all quite a shock, as it violated two of the rules of our order. But when I told them about a summoning I'd performed, reaching all the way back to the Before, I captured their imagination. I told them of Chieko Castleman, and I promised I'd return within a day to share what I had learned. You can kill me, but when they don't hear from me, those other Speakers will give in to temptation and attempt to summon her. And they'll succeed. One way or another, the Silence comes to an end. And so do you."

"Do you think I care what a handful of Speakers does or doesn't know? This committee knows the precise location of every Speaker in the Alliance, and we control their access to koph. All you've done is create some extra work for my staff, tracking down the ones you've contacted and eliminating them as well. But Speakers on Barsk are another matter. They're too plentiful and unregulated, but I planned ahead in case of more drastic need. The moment I wake from this dream of yours, I will have Druz open a communications channel to the *Resolute Purpose*. It's already en route to clean up Krasnoi's mess, but that no longer matters. Nonyx-Captain Selishta is utterly loyal to me and will not hesitate to follow the orders in the contingency plan I left her. She will utilize the full firepower at her disposal to begin destroying all life on Barsk, one miserable and sodden island at a time."

Castleman turned to the other senators, screaming. "Is this how it happened before? One madman choosing to wipe out an entire race? Are you going to just stand by and let it happen again?"

"There's nothing they can do to stop me," said Bish. "By the time they act, it will already have begun. They can't even censure me, without admitting to their own part in everything that has come before. This entire event will become just one more thing that no one talks about. Now, wake up, Jorl. It's time to end the game."

The Yak launched himself at Jorl, tucking his chin to his chest and turning at the last moment so that he struck the Fant with the tip of one horn, goring him through the chest. Jorl fell to the floor and the senator pulled his head back, grinning as blood dripped into his shaggy fur and dark robe.

"Very realistic. I would never have thought it would work if I hadn't seen the effect when I struck your human friend. That's a mortal wound I've given you, Jorl. There must be so many questions that have never been asked because of your Speaker's Edict. Can the nefshon construct of a living Speaker die in his own summoning dream? Better you should wake up than find out."

Gasping, Jorl put a hand to the hole in his chest. An instant later he had healed it.

"Nefshons are particles of memory. That's what all of this is. All I have to do is bring to mind the memory of being whole."

"Impressive. Obviously you weren't out of tricks. But you felt the pain of it, and that's a memory now, too. You may have repaired the damage, but look at you. This make-believe body of yours is reeling. You're about to go into shock. I wonder how it will work if I tear off your head."

Castleman tried to intercede but the Bos hit her again, a pair of blows that sent the human sprawling. The other committee members hung back, useless.

Bish smiled and took a step closer. Jorl shook his head and scrabbled backward. He tried to unravel the Bos's construct and failed. This wasn't like ending a traditional summoning. He hadn't simply gathered the particles of a dead conversant, he'd tethered the nefshons of a living person to himself. He needed time and focus to untie that connection, and he had neither.

The Yak grabbed at him, hauling him up, his powerful hands closing on Jorl's head, bracing the Fant against his own body. In a panic, Jorl gave up on the tether and instead pushed at Bish's nefshons. His awareness sharpened, blocking out every particle that didn't come from the Bos. He reached out for them, shoved at them with the full force of his mind, trillions and trillions of particles, far more than could be part of the construct. They would not budge.

"This is a great moment. You will be the first person to die in a summoning. A pity no one will ever Speak to you and learn of this event."

As Bish began to twist, Jorl stopped pushing the Yak's nefshons and instead began to pull them.

All of them.

Many were part of the strand that trailed back to the blanket of particles surrounding the senator's physical body and the resistance on these was the same as he'd felt when he'd first summoned him. But others stretched across space and lay embedded in the experiences of tens of thousands of individuals spread throughout the galaxy. These offered less resistance, and as the first came loose and sped toward him others followed. A faint drizzle at first, almost hesitant, then a heavy rain of nefshons which expanded into a storm, then a downpour, a flood, and finally a deluge as even the particles racing back along the strand to Bish himself gave way.

Jorl's vision had grown black around the edges. Knowing that the construct of himself wasn't actually real didn't matter. He crafted it with the constraints and logic of the real world's physicality and Bish had taken full advantage. In seconds, the senator would succeed in twisting his head off and everything would end.

Instead, the man was gone. He hadn't stopped, he'd completely vanished. The Fant crashed to the ground, gasping for breath.

Castleman staggered to Jorl's side. "Are you all right?"

He looked up at the human, and shook his head. "Something's . . . wrong. Different. What have I done? Oh, Arlo, why didn't you tell me?"

THIRTY-SEVEN
FORGOTTEN SINS

~~~~~~~

PIZLO'S new friend had fussed with him for a bit, draping her long sleeves down both sides of his head and causing tiny bits of glass in her clothes to light up and change colors. Both she and the senator had acted like this was important, and then he had sent her out of the room to check something.

The Yak, meanwhile, kept talking to him. It was overwhelming really, to have someone he'd only just met go on and on, sounding so friendly like he and Pizlo had traveled all over the Shadow Dwell together and knew all of each other's secret places. Only none of it was true. Nothing the man said meant what he intended, or nothing he intended came out in his words. Maybe it was just that Senator Bish didn't know how to say what he meant. Or maybe it was part of being an abomination-in-waiting and not knowing it.

Some of it was hard to follow, over and above none of it being true. A lot of it was what Jorl would have called "abstract," all about duty and responsibility and the greater good. Pizlo listened hard. He could focus his attention better than most, but it didn't help much.

Senator Bish just stopped talking in the middle of a sentence, the last words mumbling from his lips with little air pushing them out. He'd drawn Pizlo to him and held him in place with one hand on the boy's shoulder as if delivering a benediction. His right arm had been raised in the midst of a dramatic gesture that it never completed and instead it swung slowly down like a flutter of leaves letting go of a common branch all at once. The other hand had fallen from Pizlo's shoulder, fingers spreading limply. He'd been in the midst of a lecture about the importance of reporting clearly and without embellishment the precise details of a precognitive event, stopping just short of accusing Pizlo of making up nonsense. Then all at once he wasn't.

Pizlo scrambled away from the Yak when the grip on him had changed, aiming toward the door. He slammed against it with both of his bandaged hands, but didn't dare to look away from the senator. The door wouldn't open. The room was big but had no other exits. Pizlo hammered against the door, his small hands striking it to the rhythm of his pounding heart.

After half of forever, the door opened and admitted his new friend, the Sloth. With a whimper, Pizlo buried his face in the folds of her kaftan, clinging to her with his trunk, his useless hands trying to hold on as well, there in the open doorway.

"It's about to happen!" he sobbed.

She dropped a hand to lightly touch one of his ears but otherwise focused all her attention on the senator standing in a passive slump deeper in the room. Her mouth executed a flat, frowning line on her face as she said, "Sir? Your biosigns have jumped to a pattern I've not seen before. Do you feel all right?"

The Bos made no reply.

"Don't look at him. Please, we have to go. It's too horrible. We shouldn't be here when it happens."

"What are you going on about? Is this something you saw? Your own readings are peaking again."

"I can't tell you. I mean, I can, but it won't help. It won't make sense to you now, and later it still won't make sense but in a different way. But it's horrible."

"Is he hurt? Did he have a stroke?"

"No, no, please, can we just find Jorl? They'll be able to help us. I know they will." He lifted his head from her clothes to dare a quick look back at the Yak. "Please, he's going to get too quiet. No one should get so quiet."

"Quiet? Who, Jorl?"

"No, no, Senator Bish. He's going to go all quiet. Quieter than anybody ever."

She pulled him a half-step into the room and did something to the threshold. The door closed tight again, with them still inside. Pizlo wailed in terror.

"Hush, Little Prince. I know you don't want to stay here, but you're too important to leave roaming on your own, and I have to take care of the senator. Just sit here by the door. Close your eyes. It won't take long to run a full scan on him. Shh." She disengaged his trunk from her clothing, patted it twice, and crossed the room to the senator, her long arms wide and the many shiny bits on her clothes blinking as she began her work.

Pizlo curled up, knees to his chest. He tucked his bandaged hands around his ankles as best he could and draped his trunk over his crossed wrists, looping up behind them. He squeezed his eyes tight and rocked in place, ignoring the soft sounds of the Sloth's questions, knowing the Yak couldn't answer. The part of him that talked had left. Pizlo knew that, even if he didn't understand it. That wasn't the scary part. Right now the senator was just like a man walking in his sleep. But all the bits and pieces the moons had shared with Pizlo were coming together now. When Bish woke up everything would be wrong and different.

And then he remembered he had to do one other thing first.

"Druz? Can you pick me up?"

"Can I . . . Be still, Little Prince. I'll come get you in a moment. I'm still trying to determine what's happened to the senator. He seems entranced, but it's more than that."

Pizlo bit his lip and pushed away from the door, heading to the Sloth where she stood alongside the Yak.

"He's just talking with Jorl. And this is important. I have to do it now. I'd climb him like a tree, but my hands don't work right and I can only use my trunk."

"Climb him? Who, the senator? What are you talking about?"

He tugged at her clothes. "Please, we're almost out of time. Pick me up."

Frowning, Druz swept her diagnostic sleeves back and carefully lifted Pizlo, bracing the boy against her side, until he was positioned between her and senator Bish.

"Thanks!"

"Now, what was so important that—"

Pizlo's whipped his trunk across the Bos's chest and into his robe, darting and questing until his nubs closed around the object of his desire.

"Here now! What are you doing? Stop that!"

Pizlo pulled his trunk back, coiling it against his chest. In its tip he gripped an odd ring of metal and wood like stone. He squirmed and wriggled and pushed against the Sloth with both feet until of necessity she had to let him go. He careened to the floor, changing the fall into a shoulder roll at the last moment and ultimately ended up on his feet. He scurried back to his place by the door.

"That was the last bit. I almost forgot, but now it's done. He'll go all quiet now."

Druz frowned. The senator hadn't moved or changed in any way since she'd arrived. She shifted her attention back to the young Fant and went to join him at the door. "You said that before. Why?"

"He's going to wake up soon. But when he does, you won't remember him. Nobody will."

"What do you mean, Little Prince?"

"You know how you're talking to me? And how, later on, even if I'm not there, you can remember us talking? It's cuz a bit of my voice stays with you."

The Brady smiled. "That's a funny way to describe nefshons and memory, but I think I follow you."

"And you've got little bits of voices of everyone you know, right?"

"I suppose."

"When Senator Bish wakes up, it will be because everyone who ever had a bit of his voice will have had it taken away. It's horrible. He'll be more quiet than anyone ever. And no one will remember him at all."

"That can't happen."

"It can. It will. You won't even remember me saying these things, because it's about him, and you can't even think about him without hearing that little bit of his voice. Everything it touches will go away with it. Everything."

"Nothing like that is possible."

"It *is*. Because of what Arlo did."

"You know Arlo?"

Pizlo sobbed. "He's . . . he's my dad."

Druz blinked, paused, and regrouped before his eyes. "Little

Prince, what are you holding in your trunk? Did you take something from the senator?"

"Yes . . ."

"Show me."

"I had to. He's not going to need it now, and I do." He uncoiled his trunk and held up Bish's ring of office.

The Sloth's gasp of surprise trailed off at the same moment that the Yak began shouting.

"Ha! I knew that coward would give up. Druz! Very good that you are here. Contact the *Resolute Purpose*. Instruct Nonyx-Captain Selishta to ignore previous orders and activate contingency plan B."

The Sloth pulled her gaze from the child by her side and stared at the Yak in the middle of the room. "How do you know my name?"

Pizlo brought his bandaged hands up to cover his eyes, whispering, "Horrible."

"Now, Druz, before that miserable freak tries any more of his tricks. And take the boy with you. If half of your findings are accurate, with a bit of training he'll grow up to be a grand addition to my staff . . . Wait, what are you playing at? Why does he have my ring?"

The Brady scooped up Pizlo under one arm like a bag of grain and pointed with the other straight out at the Bos, the gleaming trio of steel talons visible within her voluminous sleeve.

"Stay back. I don't know who you are, or what you're doing on the senator's vessel, but if you take so much as a step I will drop you where you stand."

"What nonsense is this?"

She pressed a hidden release high on the door and out of Pizlo's reach. They backed out while it was still sliding open.

Bish ignored her warning and came forward but she had it closed before he had crossed half the distance to the door. She dropped the Fant and pressed both hands to the threshold. Several slivers on her sleeves glimmered as spoke to the air. "Seal this door from all internal access. Emergency override."

"He can't get to us?"

"You know him? Who was that? How did he appear on this ship?"

"You worked for him." Pizlo, wiped at his eyes with his trunk. "But you don't remember him."

The Sloth frowned. "I don't work for him. I'm the senator's personal aide."

"Which senator?"

"Don't be silly, Little Prince. I work for Senator . . . Senator . . . Oh my. I don't understand. How can I not know that?"

"I tried to tell you. Come on. Let's go find Jorl. He's really good at explaining stuff."

"Jorl? Is there someone else on my ship I don't know about?"

"No, he's on the station."

"What station?"

"That's where your ship is docked. You remember telling me about that, don't you?"

"Actually, I do. I just don't remember what station." She looked down at him. "And I don't remember how we met."

"It's not important. What's important is that you're my new friend. And I'm going to introduce you to my oldest friend."

THIRTY-EIGHT

LOOSE ENDS

~~~~~~~~~~

"I HAD it wrong. Three different times, I had it completely wrong."

Castleman knelt next to Jorl, hands to his arm and shoulder helping him sit up. "What are you saying? What just became of Bish?"

Jorl struggled to his feet and steadied himself, ears fanning briskly.

"You remember Senator Bish?"

"What? Why wouldn't I. He was just here."

"Who was here?" Senator T'Minah stepped from the line of committee members. "What just happened?"

The other senators murmured in agreed confusion.

"Senators," said Jorl, "Do you remember why I brought you here?"

"You brought us this human from Before, upsetting some of my fellow senators," answered Welv, now the ranking member on her committee, whether she knew it or not. "And you yammered on and on about that Fant prophet of yours and her vision of the Silence."

"Hmm. Well, I was wrong about that. Margda's Silence wasn't the secret you've been harboring about our origins. It was what just happened to Senator Bish."

"Who?"

Jorl sighed and spread his hands. "Your committee has twenty-five members, yes? Look among yourselves, all of you. Can any of you tell me who is missing?"

The senators' murmuring grew louder as they gestured at one another.

Castleman whispered to Jorl, "Why don't they know Bish any longer?"

"Because I've stripped all his nefshons away, and with them their memories of every interaction."

"So none of the senators can remember him?"

"Not just the senators. Almost no one. I still do, because I did it. And you, I think, because you have no physicality; your knowledge of him exists only in this construct I created for you. There are doubtless thousands of physical records that refer to him, but the people who created them don't remember doing it. Nothing he did that touched another person remains in memory."

The Prairie Dog erupted with a shrill whistle to get Jorl's attention.

"We concede you have stumped us, young man. And we stipulate to being impressed, both by your ability to summon us all together here, and with your display of the human. But to what point?"

"There are gaps in your memory. The missing member of your committee committed crimes against my planet and people, admittedly without your knowledge. All of that is moot now. You know, I thought it was a mistake that the Eleph and Lox accepted being locked away, and I deliberately left home to be out in the rest of the galaxy and meet different peoples, but right now I just want to go home. Before I do, I want your assurance that you'll continue to honor the Compact and leave us alone."

"And will you observe your side of the agreement?"

Jorl nodded. "As we have for the past eight hundred years."

The senators formed a huddle and argued among themselves for a time. Most of the debate passed in hushed tones, though Jorl could make out a few phrases like "precedent of paradox" and "engagement without representation" from one or another of the pair of Marmo senators; Woodchucks being notorious for getting loud when excited. The Urs senator from Marbalarma dropped a heavy hand on the Marmo's shoulder, which friendly reminder took the volume back down below the threshold of even a Fant's excellent hearing. When they at last broke apart, Welv stepped over to Jorl and stared up into his face.

"I speak for this entire committee. Unusual circumstances require unusual—and atypically swift—decisions. After eight hundred years, none among us is surprised that some have grown . . . chafed by the arrangements codified by your Compact. But that is the way of most compromises, and it continues to bring more benefit to the Alliance than discomfort. The Compact stands. Further, we will set in motion a subcommittee to ensure that any attempts to rally support to abolish or otherwise break this agreement will themselves come under our scrutiny and be . . . ah, discouraged. With prejudice."

Jorl's ears fell limp as the tension slipped from him. Ensuring Barsk's status quo was as great a prize as he could hope for. "Thank you. I think that's the best solution for everyone."

The elderly Prairie Dog favored him with a flat smile. "I'm pleased you approve, but there is more. Your people's isolation will continue, but with a change. We are concerned that a world possessing such importance to the Alliance has operated so long without direct input to the senate. Further, that this committee which defines itself as knowledgeable of all things could be so ignorant. Therefore, we specifically require something of you, Jorl ben Tral."

"Me?"

"Who better? You've trained as a scholar, but your actions today show you are capable of more than just producing academic publications. You are a manifestation of your people's traditions, but nonetheless stepped beyond them to leave your world behind."

"But what do you want of me?"

Welv's smile vanished. "It is not about 'want,' but rather, as I have said, 'require.' You have brought us together across galactic distances, puzzled us with our own number, and threatened us with your knowledge of our greatest secret. These are troubling points, but a solution presents itself."

"Which is?"

"We have agreed to add you to our committee. You will swear to keep our secret of the time Before, because it is now your secret as well."

"What? No. I don't—"

"This is non-negotiable. Our charter demands we maintain a body of twenty-five members. There will be paperwork, no government action can occur without it, but that can come later. In this moment it is enough to speak these words. By vote of the Committee of Information, I elevate you to the position of senator and name you as a junior member of this committee. We will be in touch by courier soon. Until then, this gathering of the committee is concluded."

"Wait, I haven't agreed—"

"You have what you desired. Release us from this summoning. We are adjourned, Senator Jorl."

He nodded, too stunned to argue. It required no effort to summon multiples of himself again, the better to more easily unravel the tethers of the twenty-four remaining senators. One by one he let them slip away, each of his duplicates vanishing immediately after until only he and Chieko Castleman remained.

"You live in a future my people couldn't have imagined," said the human.

Jorl replied with a wry quirk of his mouth. "Not least of which because my ancestors slaughtered your descendants?"

"Well, yeah, that, but—"

"I'd very much like to continue our conversation, Dr. Castleman. But there's a young boy I need to find, and then see about getting us both off this station and back downworld. With your permission, I will summon you again."

"I think I'd like that."

Jorl let the construct of the human fall away, and dissolved the mindscape immediately after. He opened his eyes to the now-familiar walls of the station cabin and wiped at the trail of spittle that had run down his chin. He lay down on the cabin's Spartan sleeping platform and waited.

~~~~~

JORL heard the voices of the Pandas outside his door and sat up. A moment later the guards marched into the room. The Brady followed several paces behind, walking hand in trunk with Pizlo.

"Jorl!" The boy darted past the Ailuros and launched himself into Jorl's arms. His trunk curled around the older Fant's neck and he sobbed. "The horrible thing happened. Horrible!"

"Shh, shh, what thing?"

"With Senator Bish."

He disentangled Pizlo from his neck and held him away to see the boy's face. "You remember him?"

"No," said Pizlo. "That's what's so horrible. Everyone everywhere forgot him."

Jorl frowned. "If you forgot him then how do you know that?"

"The moons. They told me. I knew it was going to happen, but I didn't understand it. I was still putting it together. It only made sense right before. I don't remember him, but I remember what the moons told me about him."

The pair of guards had taken up positions on either side of the room. The Sloth made a throat clearing noise and both Jorl and Pizlo looked up to see her standing alongside the sleeping platform.

"I know you, sir. Jorl, yes? You were in my lab. You wrecked my clean room. But I . . . I can't recall what you were doing there. And . . . why were you locked in here? You're marked with the aleph of Barsk. No doors are supposed to be barred to you."

"You know about that?"

"I make it my business to know a great many things. I'm quite well versed on the full range of Barsk history and culture. Oh. Are you *that* Jorl? I think I've studied from some of your books."

"This is Druz," said Pizlo. "She was Senator Bish's aide."

The Sloth frowned, and brought a hand up to rub at a spot on her forehead. "I assist a senator, yes, but I don't know that name. I'm having trouble making sense of quite a number of things. Did I strike my head?"

"No, that was me. See?" With the tip of his trunk Pizlo gingerly prodded the bump where he'd fallen on his head.

"You're fine," said Jorl. "I think it will sort itself out fairly soon.

I'm sorry, none of this was planned. There's been collateral damage to anyone who spent a lot of time working for him. But we'll get it all resolved. Where is he now?"

"Druz locked him in his room on the ship," said Pizlo.

"The Yak is Bish? I still don't understand how he got on the ship."

"Don't worry about it, his power has been broken. He'll be busy starting his life over again. When you have a moment, put in a call to Senator Welv and I'll discuss with her where to drop him off. I have an idea, but Bish is not going to be happy."

"So the horrible thing is done? It won't keep happening?" Pizlo clutched at Jorl again.

"You both remember locking him away? Well, that's a sure sign that his nefshons are working again just like everyone else's. They've just been . . . reset."

All of Pizlo's tension melted away and he slid down, sitting in Jorl's lap. He pressed the tip of his trunk into Jorl's hand. "This is yours now."

Jorl took the ring. It just barely fit on his littlest finger.

Druz gasped. "Oh! I didn't realize . . . you're Senator Jorl. Forgive me, the confusion, I—"

"It's okay. I'm, uh, the new member of the Committee of Information."

The Sloth nodded vigorously. "Of course. That would make sense. This ship serves the Committee. I'm to be your new personal assistant then, yes?"

"Um . . ."

"Say, 'yes,' Jorl." Pizlo squirmed and reached up to curl a fold of Druz's clothes with his trunk. "She's really nice. She talks to me. She's my friend."

"We'll discuss it. I'll come up with something. I've disrupted your life enough already. But . . . the Ailuros? Are they part of your ship's crew as well?"

"No, they were brought to the station by Urs-Major Krasnoi. Though, I can't recall why now. I would expect they'd get reassigned as soon as the regular station personnel return. Your ship is well-appointed and automated. I'm the only crew. Is there somewhere you want to go?"

"Home," said Jorl. "More than anything else, I just want to go home. But there are a few things I need to do first, and a stop we need to make." He glanced at the guards. "Are they going to stop me if I try to leave this room? Or if I need to go to another part of the station?"

The Brady smiled. "Sir, I will have a word with them. They were also a bit confused when the little prince and I first arrived. Once they understand who you are, I assure you everything will be fine."

"That's good. Could you see to that now, while I have a word with Pizlo?"

Druz waved one of the Pandas over to her as she walked to the other. Soon the three were conversing in hushed tones, and the occasional furtive glance back at Jorl.

Meanwhile, he set Pizlo on the ground and wrapped his trunk around the boy's ear, grinning. "Little prince?"

Pizlo blushed. "It's just something she calls me. I don't know why. It's stupid but . . . Jorl, she talks to me. There's a whole new person who talks to me!"

"I noticed that. I'm just sorry you had to go through all of this to find one. Are you ready to go home, too?"

"Yeah."

"Good. But I need your help with something. Remember that

place that wasn't on the map? Do you think you could help your new friend to find it and take us there?"

"I get to fly a space ship?!"

"No . . . you get to help with navigation. Which, um, is even better. Otherwise the ship would just be flying without a destination. Okay?"

"Okay."

Jorl stood up, and as he did the pair of guards rushed to flank him. He looked over at Druz. "You said it would all be fine. This doesn't look fine."

"If it please the senator, they would like to serve as your security detail until such time as you are ready to leave the station."

"Bother. Well, no, that's fine. I need a guide around here anyway."

~~~~~~

WITH what struck him as a fair degree of reluctance, Jorl's pair of Pandas led him to the suite of rooms that had been assigned to the Lutr telepath. They opened the room and, at his command, remained outside. He deliberately closed the door after entering and passed through the outer room. As he stepped into the bed chamber, gravity vanished and he flailed a moment before wrapping his trunk around a wall hook. He anchored himself, oriented his body so that his feet pointed at the floor, and at last surveyed the room. The Otter lay lightly belted and sprawled across a sleeping platform bolted to the floor at one end of the room.

"Are you still here? Still inside her?"

The Otter opened her eyes and showed him a weary smile. "I wondered if I would see you again. Prophecy only takes one so far, and even with the threat to his son I wasn't sure I could depend upon your friend to take the drug once he'd re-created it."

"He didn't. He left the decision to me, such as it was. That's all the choice you left him to pass on, Margda. Dead all these years and you're still controlling lives. This Lutr's for the past however many days, and mine . . . how many years now has my entire existence been dictated by your machinations?"

He shifted his grip on the wall hook from his trunk to his hand and back again. It wasn't even remotely like pacing, but it was the closet bit of rhythmic movement the room's null-gravity permitted. He fanned his left ear and glared at the recumbent figure inhabited by the centuries-dead woman who had shaped his life.

"Quit complaining, Boy. You've won, or you wouldn't be here. The drug worked. You defeated that Bos bastard who would have destroyed us all. And if I'm not mistaken, that's a senatorial sigil on your hand. Huh. I certainly hadn't foreseen that."

"You remember Bish?"

"Why wouldn't I?"

"Because he's gone. Stripped from the memory of every living person, except for a child who remembers him from visions, and me because I'm the one who destroyed him."

"Ah. Arlo described that possibility. I confess, I didn't believe him, but then his understanding of the science of nefshons had advanced far beyond my own work."

"He didn't tell me. Barely a hint. I'd never imagined something so wrong. I removed a man from the universe. His entire life is gone."

"You did what you had to do."

"I didn't. It wasn't a choice. It just . . . happened."

"And you're complaining? You saved our entire world."

He shook his head, both ears fanning as his anxiety climbed.

"I never asked for this. I'm not suited to it. Why didn't your visions tell you that? I'm a historian; I write about the people who shape events, I don't do the shaping!"

Margda laughed. She rose from her bed and flew toward him, more fluidly than any Fant might move, but with only half the innate grace that an Otter possessed. Jorl stood still as she reached out and ran the fingers of one hand over his cheek. "Poor dear, forced to take some responsibility for a change? Did I not say that prophecy only takes us so far? It's not foolproof, Boy. At best, it's porous. In my life I rarely saw closure. More typically I had glimpses of fine details and had to work out the connections between them. I saw a crisis, but not the precise nature of it. I saw the critical value of your friend's discovery, but not what it did or how. I saw a Lox with the potential to be in the right place at the right time."

"Is that what Bish's precognitivists saw, too?"

"In all likelihood. The real difference though was that I had a motivation they lacked. I gave destiny a push to make it happen. You study history, so stop your pathetic whining. You know better than most that destiny happens *to* us, it is never something we call forth."

"I used to think that. But you controlled others' fates. The choices you made have manipulated me, and Arlo, and the telepath whose mind and body you've stolen. How many others? By what right have you imposed your will on us?"

"By the most basic of rights, Jorl. Because I *can*. Prophecy is first and foremost a self-serving gift. I used mine to gain power, but not just for me. What I have done has preserved Barsk for generations. And with your help I have obtained a closure in death that I knew I would never possess in life. Can you truly find fault in that?"

"Yes, I can. You just admitted that your sight wasn't complete. You don't know what might have happened if you'd done nothing. How much of what you feared actually came about because you inadvertently set it in motion? You created the Speaker's Edict. You helped craft the Compact that Bish and others in the Alliance would come to resent. You created the aleph which empowered Arlo's drug. And you didn't do any of these things because they were necessarily good unto themselves, but because you saw them as means to shape events to serve your own ends. The entire legacy of the Matriarch is the exploitation of others like pieces in some great game."

She laughed in his face. "You can see it that way if you like. The weak usually do, if they see it at all. But you disappoint me. Despite your study of history, you fail to understand power. It's obvious you never will."

Margda turned from him then, her feet not quite touching the floor as she carefully crossed to the middle of the room and let a hand hover just above the surface of the large globule of water floating there.

"There's really only one choice you ever have to make in any act of creation. Will you be the instrument or the artist? If you're only now coming to realize that you've been a tool all your life, there's no one to blame for it but yourself. If you don't like that state of affairs, then act! Impose your will upon the world and walk your own path. If you don't, you'll just end up being a token in someone else's game; you'll continue to be used as they see fit. That's how the universe works. You don't have to like it, but you'd do well to get used to it."

He shoved himself from the wall, relying in part on old reflexes from emergency drills and mind-numbing training from his days in the Patrol. He rotated in mid-air and he struck the far wall feet first, bending at the knee to absorb the impact and launch himself along a new vector. Arms and trunk reaching out in front of him, he passed through the room's watery sphere. As he emerged through the far side, his momentum carried him into the Otter, tackling her, and eventually pinning her against the floor where he grabbed at an edge of the bedclothes to prevent any further rebounding.

"No, maybe that's the way the world looks once you've already decided to take your path. Or maybe it's just you're so jaded, or you've bought into your own delusions. I don't know which, and I don't care. Those aren't the only choices: use or be used. There is more than being tyrant or servant. I reject both options and I reject you. You've been dead for centuries, Margda, it's about time you accepted that."

Jorl closed his eyes, not bothering to invoke any ritual or to summon up a mindscape. He saw the concentration of Margda's nefshons that had embedded themselves throughout the golden fabric that were the living particles of the telepath Lirlowil. What he had done before, out of fear and without limit, he now did with careful and delicate control. Instead of calling the nefshons of the Matriarch to him as he might in an ordinary summoning, he drew them exclusively from the Otter. He began with those particles that she had originally summoned herself when she broke the first rule of the Edict, and then took away all the others that represented her memories of the experiences that had followed. And yet still they clung together, some after effect of the imprint Margda had forced, or possibly just some lingering effort she'd set in motion with the last of her usurped telepathy.

Jorl would have none of it. He imposed his will on the particles, giving each its own direction and push, and forced their diffusion. As simply as that, the Matriarch was gone.

"Pool of my birth, isn't it enough I'm being forced to study and summon you ugly people, do I have to wake up to find one in my bed as well?"

Jorl opened his eyes and found himself face to face with the Lutr. She bore an expression that was equal parts disgust and annoyance, but otherwise showed only exhaustion to indicate she had ever been possessed by the long-dead Matriarch.

He glanced over his shoulder to get his bearings, and then shoved himself in the direction of the entrance to the outer room.

"My apologies. This was just a, uh, professional visit. One Speaker to another."

"What is that supposed to mean?"

"It's not important. I came to tell you that your work here is done."

The look on her face brightened with an expression of hope. "I get to go home?"

Jorl smiled. "Unless you can think of a better place to be."

~~~~~

AFTER finishing with the Lutr, Jorl paid a visit on the Bos. Bish had exhausted himself shouting commands into a comm system that ignored him, issuing ineffective orders to the Ailuros guards that had brought him a meal, and in general ranting. When the Pandas had opened the door to allow Jorl to enter, Bish had pulled himself together and treated him to a haughty glare, but there was little strength to it.

"I hadn't intended to do it, but I'm not making any excuses. I can't even say I did it in self-defense. It's my fault, and it's something we'll both have to live with."

"What are you yammering about?" said the Yak.

"You've been forgotten. No one remembers you, or anything

you did, any connections you made, any interactions they had with you. Any relationships. You have all your own memories still, all your talent and skill, but any effect you had on any other person has been lost."

"Utter nonsense. Even if what you say is true, there are records. I've written legislation, struck down laws, the senate may not remember me, but I can point to what I've done and it will come back to them."

"Memory doesn't work that way. If you marched in with an annotated history of all your accomplishments it would only confuse the memories they're already trying to resolve. Which is why I'm not taking you back to Dawn."

"Why don't you just say it. You've come to kill me."

Jorl fanned his ears, embarrassment coloring his face. "I'm not a murderer, despite having killed your past. I'm taking you where you'll be no threat to Barsk but can have a chance to build a new future."

"Why would I want a new future when I'm not done with the one I've planned? Even if no one else remembers me, I still recall all of them. I know the strengths and weaknesses of powerful people on a hundred planets. It doesn't matter where in the Alliance you drop me, I'll maneuver myself into a position to come after you in time."

"I thought of that. If anything, armed with that kind of knowledge, you're more dangerous to those people because they won't have a clue. Which is why I'm not taking you to any world in the Alliance. On the other hand, there are independent colonies at the farthest edges of Alliance space where your spirit and strength might do some good. It's a long trip, and you'll be kept in this cabin as a prisoner until the ship arrives, but at least you'll have a chance to make a new start."

The Yak scowled. "And if I choose not to?"

Jorl shrugged. "As far as anyone remembers, you're no longer a citizen of the Alliance. No one cares what you do any more. Least of all me."

~~~~~

AFTER finishing with the former senator, Jorl left his Ailuros escort outside the door to the station's mess. He seated himself before the massive window wall and gazed out upon the planet below. He'd promised T'Minah and the rest of the committee to keep their secret, and he had one more chore ahead if he meant to be his word. He spun the surrounding setting in his mind and with a simple thought caused his new human friend's nefshons to gather again.

"Hello, Jorl. That was . . . interesting. This is a new summoning, yes? I can recognize the beginning of a new cycle. It's not quite instantaneous to me, but the sensation isn't one of time passing. I can't quite explain it."

"There's no need. It's actually well documented."

Dr. Castleman's smile lit up her face. "To your time, maybe. I'm still grappling with the implications of the science you've built based on nefshon particles."

"That's part of why I've summoned you again. I was only able to speak to you at all because a special gift allowed me to bring together your nefshons despite their vast dispersal. But because I've done that, any other Speaker who knew of you could summon you now."

"So I can expect more of these chats? With other raised mammals?"

"I'm afraid not. You heard the history of our shame. I think the committee is correct; there's nothing to be gained by that knowledge getting out. Which means other Speakers must *not* summon you."

"But you told Bish you had a failsafe. Won't the other Speakers you told about me make the attempt? Even if you follow up with each of them and assure them it's not necessary, surely some will try."

Jorl nodded. "You're right. Curiosity is a universal trait. There's no way I can prevent them from trying; I have to attack the problem from the other end and prevent them from succeeding."

"I don't understand, what will you—"

"This isn't 'goodbye,' Dr. Castleman. I've managed the trick once, I can do it again. But it's important to be sure no one else can."

Without another word, Jorl filled the mental space around him with a hundred versions of himself. Then, as he had done with the Matriarch's nefshons, the multitude of him focused on dispersing the particles that defined Chieko Castleman and scattered them farther and wider than any other Speaker could hope to summon back together, even with a lifetime of effort.

Jorl let his duplicates fade and brought his attention back to the real world. He took a final glance at his cloud-covered home before turning to leave. The pair of Ailuros snapped into position as he exited the mess. He'd only been on the job a short while, but he already knew he was not going to like his new role as a senator.

~~~~

UNLIKE the *Resolute Purpose*, Bish's ship had only a single hold that doubled as a bay. It had been turned into a pantry and stocked with sufficient cases of food and drink to allow the senator to travel for years if necessary. At Jorl's request, Druz had the Pandas move those goods into the warehouse where less than a day before they had stowed everything that had been removed from the polar base. Then, in turn, they moved some of that onto the senator's ship, including the boat borrowed from the Provost. When the swapping back and forth had been completed, the ship detached from the orbital station and dropped.

Druz operated the pilot's board on the tiny bridge of the ship. To her right, Pizlo sat at second, eyes fixed upon screens that should have been unintelligible to him. Jorl stood behind him, and the way the boy nodded and switched his gaze from one display to another unnerved Jorl more than he wanted to admit.

Under the terms of the Compact, only Lox and Eleph were permitted to set foot upon Barsk, nor could any other Alliance craft enter its atmosphere. Having inherited Bish's ship, Jorl considered himself within the spirit of the law so long as only he and Pizlo disembarked. The ship followed the beanstalk down into the atmosphere. It leveled off high above the island of Zlorka and sped east into a storm.

"Stop! You went past it!" Pizlo unstrapped from his seat and jumped down.

Jorl nodded to the Sloth. "Can you drop us here?"

"Here? I can, but there's nothing here." Druz studied her console and set her controls so that the ship began executing a low, wide circle. "The nearest land is far behind us, sir. Are you sure?"

"Give us a bit to reach the boat and open the hold. Take us as low as you can, and try to ease us into the water. Once we're underway, return to the station for your supplies. Then, as we discussed, take Lirlowil home. And when you're ready, set a course for the technologically weakest of the far colonies and drop off their newest member."

"I'll be back as soon as I can."

"Yes, well, no need to hurry. It's going to take a while for me to figure out my new role. I don't plan on leaving Barsk ever again, so I don't know what I'd do with a vessel like this."

"I do," said Pizlo. "There're are all kinds of places I could go. Think of all the insects that they have on other planets!"

Jorl smiled. "I don't think your mother would be happy with me if I let her six-year-old son go traipsing around the galaxy."

"I won't always be six. Plus, I have moons!" He slapped his bandaged hands against the designs on his chest.

"We'll talk about it. For now, let's get you and your moons to the boat." He turned back to Druz. "Thank you."

"You're quite welcome, Senator. I will see you when I return."

Jorl and Pizlo made their way to the hold and onto the boat that lay braced against a vast gate on the outer wall. Moments later, that gate opened and water began rushing into the hold. The boat slipped out and free, and the ship skipped along ahead of them before rising up again. Wind and rain struck at the Fant on the little boat, and as one they turned their faces up in pleasure and watched the ship rise. The ocean cascaded from the open hold like a waterfall and then stopped. Clouds swallowed the ship, and the man and boy were alone on the ocean.

Pizlo stood in the front of the boat. It was late afternoon. Rain poured down upon him and he pointed the direction they had to go. Jorl set the controls. They sailed until dusk and slept beneath clouded skies caressed by light rain. The following morning, as the cloudy sky brightened, they saw the shore of a nearby island that appeared on no map. They paused to have breakfast and then made landfall. Before leaving the station, Jorl had instructed the Pandas to lash two plastic drums to the boat's deck. He transferred them to the beach.

Pizlo sat at the water's edge, eyes closed as if communing with the waves that now and then knocked him over. He'd discarded his bandages and when the cool water wasn't washing them clean he kept burying his hands in the sand.

Further up shore, Jorl opened both drums, tilting them to pour out the coarse ash from inside. He rolled the empty containers back to the boat, already planning where he might keep them until Druz returned and could take them off Barsk for good. Then he went to sit with the boy, smiling as the water soaked his clothes that had only recently dried from the night before.

Pizlo continued to roll with the waves a while, then opened his eyes and asked, "Can I watch?"

Jorl hesitated. "We're only here at all because of you. It's not fair, but no. It would only upset them to see you, and they've been through so much. Honestly, many of them were never happy to see me, either. But this is something that has to be done. I won't be long."

He closed his eyes and, unbidden, the memory of the burning Dying came to him. Jorl shoved it aside. He'd had too many nightmares in his life already and hoped to exorcise this one before it took root. Instead, he imagined the familiar scent of spiralmint. He fanned himself with his left ear. In his mind, he re-created the shore where he sat, editing out the details of Pizlo and the boat. In their place, he began summoning the many Dying Fant that had shared the internment camp. He knew their names, and even though his personal knowledge of many of them was slight, no other nefshons had the feel of the recent days he'd shared with them. The handful he'd shared tales with took form closest to him. The rest materialized just beyond them, until they filled the space around him in a line along the water's edge.

"Your time in life has since ended; you are now as you were in life, but not alive. Your journey here did not take the traditional form, and your arrival is decidedly tardy, but you have at last achieved your destination. I bid you welcome."

"This is it," said Rüsul. "I've seen this beach in my dream."

"And those trees," said Kembü.

Phas turned to him, one hand reaching out. "Jorl? How is this possible? What you just said, it sounded like the words from a summoning . . . but we were all just in the camp. The Pandas, they were rounding us all up—"

"What matters is you're here, where you all intended to be. Let what happened at the camp go. None of that matters."

"I think we'll hold on to one piece of it," said Tarva, his trunk entwined with Abso's, who nodded in response.

"Thank you, Jorl. I'd compose a poem in your honor, but I've left that life behind."

"What happens next?" asked Jorl.

Almost as one, the two hundred sixteen summoned Fant looked at him with surprise.

"How can you not know?" said Rüsul. "It's part of the dream."

Jorl shrugged. "I never had the dream. I . . . found this place by other means. Beyond bringing you here, I haven't a clue."

"You oaf," said Kembü, though not unkindly. "We walk up the beach and into the trees."

"That's all?"

Phas nodded. Others were already moving toward the trees. "You're a good historian, Jorl, but this isn't something for you to record or witness. You can't go with us."

"I understand."

She turned away and took Rüsul's hand in hers. "Walk with me?" The carver nodded, glancing once over his shoulder at Jorl, and then together they joined the rest of the Fant walking up the beach and into the trees." As they reached the limits of the land-scape he'd crafted, he released the constructs of each of the Dying, laying them to rest at last.

Jorl let his awareness return to the real world where Pizlo still played at the ocean's edge. He glanced up the beach to the tree line where in the other world the Fant had vanished. A trick of the light or perhaps his own wishful imagination made him think he saw movement there, several Fant watching him from the shad-owy safety of the trees. He knew better.

"Ready to go home, Pizlo?"

EPILOGUE

PROPER GOODBYES

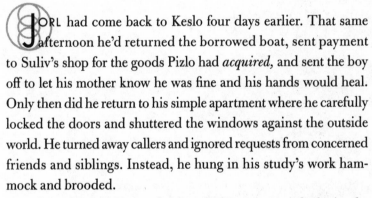

JORL had come back to Keslo four days earlier. That same afternoon he'd returned the borrowed boat, sent payment to Suliv's shop for the goods Pizlo had *acquired,* and sent the boy off to let his mother know he was fine and his hands would heal. Only then did he return to his simple apartment where he carefully locked the doors and shuttered the windows against the outside world. He turned away callers and ignored requests from concerned friends and siblings. Instead, he hung in his study's work hammock and brooded.

Now and then he moved about the house to satisfy the intake and output needs of his body, but he always returned to his study. He neither read nor wrote, and the idea of doing any sort of Speaking lay further from his mind than the outermost colonies.

On the morning of his fifth day back, he noticed a crumpled scrap of brown paper on the floor. He stared at it, knowing he was not so far gone that he could have failed to mark its appearance earlier; the paper had *not* been there all along. He checked his doors, both the main entrance and the seldom used back door that led down to a community compost bin. Both remained locked from the inside.

Returning to his study he discovered one of the windows' shutters had been dislodged and lay open a crack. Nodding to himself he at last examined the brown page. The paper had once wrapped a parcel of some sort before being repurposed. It was quite worn, variously stained, and had been folded so often it appeared fractured and had become as supple as cloth. As he scanned the tight circles of the glyphs Jorl recognized Pizlo's style. He found himself smiling, and in that simple act returned to himself from wherever he had been for the past days. The paper was an invitation.

The pleasure of your company is requested next year, on the seventeenth day of the season of dark, at the westernmost edge of the island of Phran, just before dawn, when Wella will appear to share his wisdom.

P.S. Bring lunch for us both.

Shrugging off his melancholy, Jorl opened the windows of his study. He seated himself in his hammock again, but this time went to work. By late afternoon he had completed an overdue monograph. He sealed it in a large envelope and set it on the edge of his desk to remind him to drop it off the next morning. Then he pinned Pizlo's invitation on the wall over his desk, and headed out the door toward Tolta's home.

As he walked through the dusk of the Civilized Wood, Jorl spun himself through the rituals of a summoning. He didn't need to do so, but the familiarity set him at ease. He'd never tried to Speak while walking before, but the trick lay well within the range of his talents now, just as it was simplicity itself to hold the nefshons of his conversant in his mind, all but fully formed, like a word waiting to be spoken.

Jorl let himself into the house and paused in the greeting room. It was one thing to presume to step over the threshold without an invitation, and quite another to breach the inner house unannounced.

"Tolta? Are you at home?" He already knew the answer. An alluring aroma came from the kitchen where someone had prepared a fragrant vegetable stew and set it aside to cool. The sound of running water and the clunk of a pot suggested the post-cooking cleaning had begun. He called her name again. The sound of water stopped, an instant later Tolta bolted into the room.

Jorl froze. Looking at her, he realized that she would surely have been among those who had come to his home in the days since his return and been turned away with silence. And he knew he must have hurt her.

"Oh, Jorl, Pizlo told me—"

"Tolta, I'm so sorry. I've not been myself these last few days. I'm . . . I'm sorry."

She rushed across the room and hugged him tighter than he'd ever been hugged. "Don't you try leaving again. You've no cause for it. You belong here, among the friends who love you."

She embraced him for a long while, but then, too, he had to admit that he held onto her as well. He'd seen so much, and been altered by it, but that contact assured him he would be all right. When she stepped back, he held onto her hands and gazed deeply into her eyes. He saw the same face, the same Tolta, that he had seen when he stood Second at her and Arlo's wedding. Nothing important had changed.

"I've brought you a gift," he whispered. "I hope you like it."

Jorl closed his eyes. He concentrated on the nefshons he'd already gathered and set to one side of his awareness, and then began anew with a second summoning. When he opened his eyes again it was to a mindscape of the same room in the house, and with barely a blink of effort he pulled enough of Tolta's nefshons together to create a construct of her there.

From her perspective, nothing would have changed. She stood in front of Jorl in the real world greeting room of her home, and her awareness occupied an identical place that existed only in his mind.

He shifted his focus for an instant, pulled the other construct into existence in another corner of his mind, little more than an empty plane of light. Arlo took shape and stood before him there.

"I didn't think I'd see you again. What happened—"

"This is the last time I'll call you, my friend. Everything worked out, but I thought you needed some closure. A chance to say a proper goodbye."

He gave a final push, and Arlo's construct slipped from one venue to the other, materializing in the illusion of Tolta's home in the very spot where he had been standing, his own construct fading away as his friend appeared. He heard Tolta gasp as she held her husband's hands again.

"Hello, Tol," Arlo breathed, "I love you, you know."

As the living Tolta construct threw herself around the Arlo summoning in an embrace that was long overdue, Jorl discretely closed off his awareness of the created space. He slipped into the kitchen and helped himself to a bowl of stew and a wooden spoon. A moment later, he was crossing through the greeting room again on his way out the front door. He paused for just a moment to see the smile and tears on Tolta's face, and went outside into the night.

APPENDIX ONE:
RACES OF THE ALLIANCE

The astute reader will have noticed that the characters portrayed in this novel appear to represent a variety of anthropomorphic animals. In fact, at this point in time, there are some eighty-seven different species or "races" existing in the Alliance, more than a hundred billion sapient beings occupying approximately four thousand planets.

These races are identified by the common names of the animals they resemble—rendered here as proper nouns—or by a clipped version of the applicable Latin genus. Of these races, all are mammals, and all but two are furred. This pair of exceptions, collectively known as "Fant," appears to bear a connection to the two species on Earth known as African and Asian elephants. Thus Jorl is identified as an Elephant or Fant, but also as a Lox, from *Loxodonta africana*.

The list below identifies the races of characters seen in this book, but is only a small portion of the raised mammals that comprise the Alliance.

- Ailuros, *Ailuropoda,* Giant Panda. Jorl's only friend during his time in the Patrol was an Ailuros named Dund. Krasnoi's security team aboard the orbital station are all Pandas.
- Aplodon, *Aplodontia,* Mountain Beaver. A lieutenant sitting at navigation on the bridge of the *Resolute Purpose* was a Beaver.
- Bos, *Bos,* Yak. Senator Bish, chairman of the Committee of Information is a Yak. Jorl once wrote the foreword to a book by a Bos historian named Fenna. The most well-known Bos is probably Thelos, a mass murderer said to have been possessed by a demon.
- Brady, *Bradypus,* Three-toed Sloth. Druz, the personal assistant to the chair of the Senate's Committee of Information is a Brady. So are Hrum and Morth, the captain and a lieutenant (respectively) of Jorl's Patrol ship.
- Cans, *Canis,* Domestic Dog. Most of the rank and file members of Major Krasnoi's crew are Cans.
- Cynomy, *Cynomys,* Prairie Dog. One of the "junior stature" races of the Alliance, the Cynomy include the civil parson who oversaw Lirlowil's reclassification from citizen to resource. Senator Welv of the Committee of Information is also a Prairie Dog, as are a third of Senator Bish's precognitivists (e.g., Tekki).
- Eleph, *Elephas,* Asian Elephant. Margda, the Matriarch of Barsk, was an Eleph, as was the legendary Pholo, the only Fant who could fly. Other Eleph include Emil, Phas, Grummel, Mickl, Rüsul, Shtev, and Yeft. Along with the Lox, Eleph make up the other half of the pair of races referred to as "Fant."
- Feln, *Felis,* Cat. Several Feln worked at Krasnoi's polar base, processing the Dying. There is also at least one Feln among the senators who comprise the Committee of Information.

- Geom, *Geomys,* Gopher. The secondary and tertiary navigation boards on the *Resolute Purpose* are manned by Geoms. Senator T'Minah of the Committee of Information is also a Geom. These are another of the "junior stature" races.
- Lep, *Lepus,* Hare. One of the senators on the Committee of Information is a Lep.
- Lox, *Loxodonta,* African Elephant. Jorl is a Lox, as was his friend Arlo, Arlo's mother Kembü, Arlo's wife Tolta, and their son, Pizlo (it should be noted that soulless children can also be born among the Eleph, the other race that together with the Lox comprise the "Fant"). Other Lox mentioned include Adri, Golub, Belti, Tral, and Yarva.
- Lutr, *Lutra,* Eurasian Otter. Lirlowil, the telepathic Speaker from Sharv, is a Lutr.
- Marmo, *Marmot,* Groundhog. This is another of the "junior stature" races. Two members of the Committee of Information are Marmos.
- Myrm, *Myrmecophaga,* Giant Anteater. Kengi, the communications officer on Jorl's vessel during his time in the Patrol, was a Myrm.
- Nonyx, *Acinonyx,* Cheetah. Selishta is the Nonyx-Captain of the vessel Krasnoi used to abduct Dying Fant (and Jorl) while on Barsk.
- Taxi, *Taxidea,* Badger. The squad of six interrogators that questioned the Dying Fant at Krasnoi's polar base were all Badgers.
- Theraonca, *Panthera onca,* Jaguar. Rismas, the ensign assigned to keep watch on Jorl while aboard the *Resolute Purpose,* is a Theraonca.

- Vulp, *Vulpes,* Fox. Another of the "junior stature" races of the Alliance. Shtev had a Vulp penpal on an Alliance medical station.
- Urs, *Ursus,* Bear. Krasnoi the Alliance Major is an Urs. As is a senator from the Committee of Information. Jorl recounts having met several Urs during his time in the Patrol.

APPENDIX TWO:
THE ISLANDS OF BARSK

Barsk is a watery world with only a single, uninhabitable continent located at its south pole and two chains of islands. These archipelagos lay just south of the equator and stretch east and west to span nearly a fifth of their hemisphere. The planet's ubiquitous cloud cover ensures none of this is visible from orbit.

Within the archipelagos the islands differ from one another in shape and size, the largest as much as eighteen times the size of the smallest. Some possess natural harbors, some do not. All are within a day of hard paddling from at least one other, and most have a neighbor close enough that ferries transit back and forth from dawn to dusk. Beyond minor patches of beach, all are covered with rain forests representing several dozen types of meta-trees that could easily be considered the dominant native life form. On every island, the Fant have built their homes high in these trees, in a section that is always referred to as the Civilized Wood.

Belp—a central island of the eastern archipelago, famous for having a shape like a Lox's left ear.

Emmt—a popular destination for young bachelors traveling from Keslo.

Gerd—a smallish, nearly circular island that is considered the central island of the western archipelago. Fant often refer to other islands in the chain with respect to their position relative to Gerd.

Kelpry—an island south and west of Gerd in the western archipelago.

Keslo—an island located near the northeastern portion of the western archipelago. It is home to Jorl ben Tral.

Phran—an island north of Gerd but still a good ways south and west of Keslo. On an eastern beach of Phran, Pizlo believes he will see his fifth moon in the near future.

Relfa—the westernmost island of the eastern archipelago, it is a popular destination for groups of young men crossing over from the other island chain.

Telba—an island to the north of Keslo. A Speaker there published a book of *imramha* after interviewing various adventurers.

Yargo—a tiny island in the southeastern section of the eastern archipelago, it is famous nowadays as the birthplace of Margda, the Matriarch of Barsk. Her childhood dwelling, once home to nearly a hundred children, mothers, aunts, and female cousins, is now a vast museum, complete with research library and gift shop. Tours are given twice daily.

Zlorka—a part of the western archipelago, it is considered the most cosmopolitan of islands. Zlorka is the only land mass on the planet to touch the equator. It is home to the premiere university on Barsk, as well as the anchor point for the space elevator that transports goods to an automated station in orbit.

APPENDIX THREE:
THE MOONS OF BARSK

Barsk has seven natural moons orbiting it (eight if you count the artificial station that serves as the planet's export facility and hovers at the top of the space elevator high above the only island situated on the equator). Every schoolchild knows that rain is the greatest constant on the planet, and regardless of the season the skies are always filled with clouds. That said, weather is by definition a dynamic system, and the only true constant is that now and then you have to expect inconstancy. So it is that at times a small patch of cloud will clear and a view of the sky occurs for anyone lucky enough to be there to enjoy it. On exceptionally rare and unpredictable occasions, that brief opening will align with a particular orbit and allow a glimpse of one of the moons. Of course, living within their islands' respective Civilized Woods, most Fant are not out and about with a view of the sky when such providence occurs. Most females go their entire lives without seeing a moon, and though males are more apt to be in the right time and place while traveling between islands, even so it is considered a moment of profound portents to see a moon.

Pemma—the second smallest of Barsk's seven moons. It was the third one Pizlo saw, and the moon which (he claims) instructed him to stowaway aboard a cargo pod and travel up to the orbiting space station.

Telko—the largest of the moons. This was Pizlo's fourth moon, seen from the viewport of the orbiting station.

Wella—the smallest of the moons, it has a more oblate shape, heavier in its bottom half than top. Pizlo believes he will see this moon during the season of dark in the next year. For reasons that are unknown to this author, Wella is always referred to as having a masculine aspect.